PRAISE

MW01193671

THE LAST LETTER OF RACHEL ELLSWORTH

"A compelling journey across the globe as two women search for a path from the darkness into the light. Barbara O'Neal's latest is an exploration of Parsi cuisine, learning to let go, and finding purpose in the most unexpected places."

—Mansi Shah, author of *A Good Indian Girl*

"A moving and engaging tale about an unlikely duo whose quest to find answers about a culinary project takes them through different countries, scattered Parsi cafés, and the hidden reservoirs of grief. As Veronica deals with the loss of a life she loved and Mariah grapples with lost dreams and the loss of a parent, the bond they develop with each other (and with beloved Henry!) is life affirming. A testament to the power of self-discovery and strong connection and how both can help us heal and recover."

—Marjan Kamali, bestselling author of *The Lion Women of Tehran*

"This journey from unspeakable pain to finding your place in the world is at once heart wrenching and hopeful. I traveled across the globe with these broken characters as they put themselves together one step, one meal, and one act of human connection at a time. Barbara O'Neal's books have an epic quality that makes me feel rage and healing in a way no one else can, and always expand my lens of empathy in surprising ways. A shatteringly honest yet deeply hopeful read!"

—Sonali Dev, bestselling author of *There's Something About Mira*

MEMORIES OF THE LOST

"Just when I thought Barbara O'Neal couldn't get any better . . . she does. *Memories of the Lost* is a study in pitch-perfect storytelling; an intriguing mystery and a tender love story, meticulously woven around a pair of protagonists who feel so wonderfully real I suspect I'll miss them for a very long time. I couldn't read this novel fast enough and yet the story never felt rushed, and ends just as beautifully as her characters—and her readers—deserve."

—Barbara Davis, bestselling author of *The Keeper of Happy Endings* and *The Echo of Old Books*

"*Memories of the Lost* is everything I love about Barbara O'Neal's novels—dreamy, artistic, hopeful, magical. Its dash of mysticism boldly explores the power of art, the power of love, and discovering who you really are. Barbara has a poet's touch, an artist's eye, a chef's palate, and a romantic soul. She truly makes the book world a better place."

—Sarah Addison Allen, *New York Times* bestselling author of *Other Birds*

THE STARFISH SISTERS

"Barbara O'Neal is at the top of her game. *The Starfish Sisters* is a gorgeous, heartfelt story about two lifelong friends who, now estranged, must battle their way back to each other after years of betrayals and jealousy and misunderstandings. Suze is a famous, world-traveling movie star who seems to have everything but love—while her former best friend, Phoebe, does art and nurtures the people around her. O'Neal has written a deeply harrowing, suspenseful, and ultimately loving book that explores the nature of women's friendships and the lengths to which we all will go to protect those we love from danger. I read it far into the night, and, yes, I wept a few tears along the way."

—Maddie Dawson, *Washington Post* bestselling author of *Matchmaking for Beginners*

THIS PLACE OF WONDER

"*This Place of Wonder* is a wonderfully moving tale about four women whose journeys are all connected by one shared love: some are romantic, some are familial, but all are deeply complicated. Dealing with loss, love, hidden secrets, and second chances, this stirring tale is utterly engaging and ultimately hopeful. Set along the rugged California coastline, *This Place of Wonder* will sweep you away with the intoxicating scents, bold flavors, and sweeping views of the region and transport you to a world you won't be in any hurry to leave."

—Colleen Hoover, #1 *New York Times* bestselling author

"Kristin Hannah readers will thoroughly enjoy the family dynamic, especially the mother-daughter relationships."

—*Booklist* (starred review)

"Barbara O'Neal's latest novel is simply delicious. Engrossing, empathetic, and profoundly moving, I savored every sentence of this story of several very different women who find solace and second chances in each other after tragedy (though not before facing some hard truths and, yes, a few rock bottoms). *This Place of Wonder* is one of the best books I've read in a long time."

—Camille Pagán, bestselling author of *Everything Must Go*

"I have never much moved in the elevated circles of California farm-to-table cuisine, but O'Neal makes me feel like I'm there. Rather than simply skewering the pretensions, *This Place of Wonder* pinpoints the passions. Some of these characters have been elevated to celebrity, some are newcomers to the scene, but all are drawn together by the sensuality, the excitement, and ultimately the care that food brings them. Elegiac but also forward-looking, this is a book about eating, but more than that, it's a book about hurt and healing and women finding their way together. I loved every moment of it."

—Julie Powell, author of *Julie & Julia* and *Cleaving*

WRITE MY NAME ACROSS THE SKY

"Barbara O'Neal weaves an irresistible tale of creativity, forgery, family, and the FBI in *Write My Name Across the Sky*. Willow and Sam are fascinating, and their aunt Gloria is my dream of an incorrigible, glamorous older woman."

—Nancy Thayer, bestselling author of *Family Reunion*

"*Write My Name Across the Sky* is an exquisitely crafted novel of three remarkable women from two generations grappling with decisions of the past and the consequences of where those young, impetuous choices have led. A heartfelt story of passion, devotion, and family told as only Barbara O'Neal can."

—Suzanne Redfearn, #1 Amazon bestselling author of *In an Instant*

"With its themes of creativity and art, *Write My Name Across the Sky* is itself like a masterfully executed painting. Using refined brushstrokes, O'Neal builds her vivid, complex characters: three independent women in one family who can't quite come to terms with their fierce feelings of love for one another. O'Neal deftly switches between three points of view, adding layers of family history into this intimate and satisfying study of how women make tough choices between love and creativity and family and freedom."

—Glendy Vanderah, *Washington Post* bestselling author of
Where the Forest Meets the Stars

THE LOST GIRLS OF DEVON

ONE OF *TRAVEL + LEISURE*'S MOST ANTICIPATED BOOKS OF SUMMER 2020

"A woman's strange disappearance brings together four strong women who struggle with their relationships, despite their need for one another. Fans of Sarah Addison Allen will appreciate the emphasis on nature and these women's unique gifts in this latest by the author of *When We Believed in Mermaids*."

—*Library Journal* (starred review)

"*The Lost Girls of Devon* draws us into the lives of four generations of women as they come to terms with their relationships and a mysterious tragedy that brings them together. Written in exquisite prose with the added bonus of the small Devon village as a setting, Barbara O'Neal's book will ensnare the reader from the first page, taking us on an emotional journey of love, loss, and betrayal."

—Rhys Bowen, *New York Times* and #1 Kindle bestselling author of
The Tuscan Child, *In Farleigh Field*, and the Royal Spyness series

"*The Lost Girls of Devon* is one of those novels that grabs you at the beginning with its imagery and rich language and won't let you go. Four generations of women deal with the pain and betrayal of the past, and Barbara O'Neal skillfully leads us to understand all of their deepest needs and fears. To read a Barbara O'Neal novel is to fall into a different world—a world of beauty and suspense, of tragedy and redemption. This one, like her others, is spellbinding."

—Maddie Dawson, bestselling author of *A Happy Catastrophe*

WHEN WE BELIEVED IN MERMAIDS

"An emotional story about the relationship between two sisters and the difficulty of facing the truth head-on."

—*Today*

"There's a reason Barbara O'Neal is one of the most decorated authors in fiction. With her trademark lyrical style, she's written a page-turner of the first order. From the very first page, I was drawn into the drama and irresistibly teased along as layers of a family's complicated past were artfully peeled away. Don't miss this masterfully told story of sisters and secrets, damage and redemption, hope and healing."

—Susan Wiggs, #1 *New York Times* bestselling author

"More than a mystery, Barbara O'Neal's *When We Believed in Mermaids* is a story of childhood—and innocence—lost, and the long-hidden secrets, lies, and betrayals two sisters must face in order to make themselves whole as adults. Plunge in and enjoy the intriguing depths of this passionate, lustrous novel, and you just might find yourself believing in mermaids."

—Juliet Blackwell, *New York Times* bestselling author of *The Lost Carousel of Provence*, *Letters from Paris*, and *The Paris Key*

"In *When We Believed in Mermaids*, Barbara O'Neal draws us into the story with her crisp prose, well-drawn settings, and compelling characters, in whom we invest our hearts as we experience the full range of human emotion and, ultimately, celebrate their triumph over the past."

—Grace Greene, author of *The Memory of Butterflies* and The Wildflower House series

"*When We Believed in Mermaids* is a deftly woven tale of two sisters, separated by tragedy and reunited by fate, discovering that the past isn't always what it seems. By turns shattering and life-affirming, as luminous and mesmerizing as the sea by which it unfolds, this is a book club essential—definitely one for the shelf!"

—Kerry Anne King, bestselling author of *Whisper Me This*

THE ART OF INHERITING SECRETS

"Great writing, terrific characters, food elements, romance, a touch of intrigue, and more than a few surprises to keep readers guessing."

—*Kirkus Reviews*

"Settle in with tea and biscuits for a charming adventure about inheriting an English manor and the means to restore it. Vivid descriptions and characters that read like best friends will stay with you long after this delightful story has ended."

—Cynthia Ellingsen, bestselling author of *The Lighthouse Keeper*

"*The Art of Inheriting Secrets* is the story of one woman's journey to uncovering her family's hidden past. Set against the backdrop of a sprawling English manor, this book is ripe with mystery. It will have you guessing until the end!"

—Nicole Meier, author of *The House of Bradbury* and *The Girl Made of Clay*

"O'Neal's clever title begins an intriguing journey for readers that unfolds layer by surprising layer. Her respected masterful storytelling blends mystery, art, romance, and mayhem in a quaint English village and breathtaking countryside. Brilliant!"

—Patricia Sands, bestselling author of the Love in Provence series

THE LAST
LETTER
of
RACHEL
ELLSWORTH

OTHER TITLES BY BARBARA O'NEAL

THE LAST LETTER

of

RACHEL ELLSWORTH

A NOVEL

BARBARA O'NEAL

Published by Lake Union Publishing, Seattle

www.apub.com

Amazon, the Amazon logo, and Lake Union Publishing are trademarks of Amazon.com, Inc., or its affiliates.

EU product safety contact:
Amazon Media EU S. à r.l.
38, avenue John F. Kennedy, L-1855 Luxembourg
amazonpublishing-gpsr@amazon.com

ISBN-13: 9781662514944 (hardcover)
ISBN-13: 9781662514937 (paperback)
ISBN-13: 9781662514951 (digital)

Cover design by Faceout Studio, Jeff Miller
Cover image: © Olena Malik / Getty; © Pixel-Shot, © Preto Perola / Shutterstock

Printed in the United States of America

First edition

For my good friend Janet Mohler, who loves London. I am grateful for the endless hours you've spent listening to me talk out my books, and for years and years of good discussions on art, books, our lives and times and histories. Oh, and that endless, endless trip when I was stranded by COVID in England and you saved the day with Neko, Rafe, Gabi, Tucker, and Peaches. Meow, meow, meow. My world is so much richer with you in it.

PROLOGUE

Everybody in the neighborhood came out to see who was being arrested. Huddling in knots of two and three, they watched Veronica take an actual walk of shame down the sidewalk, escorted by two police officers who looked like they were barely out of high school. The woman apologized for handcuffing her, but it was protocol in these situations.

Veronica didn't look at them or at Spence. Her face was a mess of snot and tears. She felt her hair sticking to her cheeks, and she was cold because her jacket was on the floor where she'd thrown it.

She didn't look at her gawking neighbors. She didn't want to see the pity or the horror masking their bald curiosity. She shuffled down the old concrete between the perennial beds she'd planted, every single inch, flowers that once bloomed in such extravagance that people slowed down to stare, even stop to take a photo. The newspaper had once done an article on it.

Gone. Lost beneath the most ordinary bark mulch a person could imagine, the entire side garden lost to a swimming pool. A pool that could be used maybe three months out of every twelve.

That brought a fresh wave of tears. All her flowers! How many hours had she spent on her knees, nestling gaillardia next to tiny dianthus, the pink and orange echoed in the beds by the house with gladioli and roses? It underlined the end of her marriage more forcefully than anything else could have.

The female cop put her hand on Veronica's head as she helped her into the back seat. She looked back to Spence. "Are you sure, Mr. Barrington?"

"Doctor," he corrected. His jaw was WASPy stone. "Quite sure."

The car pulled out, driving past the thin row of neighbors watching her banishment. She didn't look at any of them.

PART ONE

COLORADO

CHAPTER ONE

Eighteen Months Later

Thanksgiving was Veronica's favorite holiday. She loved the pure extravagance of food, the little family traditions built over the years— like the fresh strawberry- and blueberry-infused sparkling water that her youngest, Ben, had invented when he was six, and the banoffee pie Spence had discovered on an academic trip to England. Veronica practiced it until he swooned. Her own favorite dish was a yam casserole baked with mini marshmallows, the only recipe she really had from her mother. When her kids were small, they'd loved that dish more than anything.

Today, it sat forlornly on the table with only one serving removed. Hers.

The orange casserole was served in a glass dish she'd rescued from an antique shop, and the dishes were a set of china she'd collected over time. It was an antique pattern with lacy edges and delicate roses, called Chateau Dresden. She'd found a saucer, bowl, and teacup at a thrift store when she was an undergrad, one of the most beautiful things she'd ever owned, and made a vow to herself then to have a life that included a full set.

And so she had. *Had* being the operative word.

She *had* especially loved her dining room, a broad space with wide pine-plank floors and a row of leaded-glass windows looking out toward her side garden. It had been beautiful even in deep autumn in Boulder because she'd planted things that had interesting dry leaves and colored stems to duplicate themselves in the edges of the leaded glass.

The walls of the dining room were painted light green, with William Morris wallpaper in a wide border above the wainscoting. Below a 1920s chandelier with rare green carnival glass sat a big table they'd found at auction long before "farmhouse" became a named decorating style. The china she had collected one piece at a time looked splendid on that table.

The most beautiful room in the world, she thought, when her family and friends were arranged around the bountiful food she'd prepared for them. It could be a Dutch painting, with bowls of steaming carrots and the gleaming bird and bread in a basket, everyone lit just so by that bank of north-facing windows.

It was even more delectable when everyone went home or into their own spaces, leaving her to her beautiful home, each room a creation from her very soul. Home.

Her space no longer.

Today, in her much smaller apartment kitchen, she'd prepared the turkey—which was not an easy bird to make delicious—and fresh cranberry sauce with orange zest and walnuts. She'd made her daughter's beloved stuffed celery and the apple upside-down cake her youngest son loved. Now that he'd gone vegan, she had to alter the recipe, but she was quite proud of the adaptation. It had turned out so perfectly that she took a photo.

She'd set the much smaller table in her apartment and had created a playlist of favorites to cast a background to their meal and, frankly, offset the quiet. Even with all the effort, it felt a little hollow, an imitation Thanksgiving.

They did their best. They ate and laughed and joked. It was as she stood up to clear and picked up the sweet potatoes that Jenna said, "Mom, maybe it's time to let the old-school sweet potatoes go."

"I can see none of you like it now," she said. Some small, barely audible voice said, *But I do!*

Tim snickered. "That's because it was popular in 1959, boomer."

"I'm not a boomer!"

"Close enough," he said.

For some reason, it stung, the teasing that made her feel outdated. "I'm Gen X, and you know it."

She began to clear the rest of the table, Jenna and Ben standing up to help.

Balance had only very recently been restored to the family. She let it go, piling dishes on the minuscule strip of counter.

Jenna paused by an enormous Boston fern thriving next to a window. It was a thirty-year-old plant, one of the few things she'd dragged with her from her old home.

"I don't get how to make ferns thrive like this," Jenna said. "I've watched a million things on TikTok, but nothing seems to work."

"Maybe try watering it less," Veronica suggested. "People tend to overwater more than underwater."

"Okay, boomer," Tim said. It was clear he was joking, but it landed wrong.

"Quit that! I just told you I'm not a boomer."

He grinned, looking so much like his father at the same age that he could have skied right off the slopes into her apartment. "Close enough."

She shook her head. "Never mind. Who wants dessert and coffee?"

They all glanced at each other, then Jenna spoke for all of them. "Um . . . we're going to go to Dad's for dessert. It seemed only fair."

"Fair." Tears stung her eyes, but she refused to let them see. "Ah." She crossed her arms, feeling the familiar pinch—the unfairness of having lost everything to—

"Mom, don't be mad," Tim said. "We ate the meal here, with you."

"I'm not mad," she said, sliding silverware into a pot of water, but a pulse at the base of her throat felt as if it would tear open her skin. For a moment, it was a satisfying image, the artery exploding from her neck, spilling the blood of her wound down the front of her well-tended—though now-ancient—cashmere sweater.

Three sets of blue eyes watched her, filled with worry and, if she were honest, the need to escape the discomfort.

All at once she was sick to death of feeling like a victim, of everyone feeling sorry for her, looking at her with pity or slight embarrassment. A wild impulse swelled through her. "Don't worry about it." She blurted out a lie: "I'm going to India, so I have some things to plan."

"India!" Jenna cried. "When?"

"I haven't nailed down the dates."

"You can't go to India. By yourself?" Ben said. Her baby, the one for whom she'd made a vegan apple upside-down cake that would now go uneaten. It seemed ridiculous that she'd thought it such an important task. A cake!

"Of course I can," she said. "I'm not feeble."

"You're kind of old, though."

"Well, hardly. I'm fifty, which is not as young as Fiona," she retorted, and instantly regretted it. Fiona was her ex-husband's new wife, ripely pregnant and juicy at the age of thirty-two, the cliché of all time, and Veronica burned with the agony of it.

At least Fiona, unlike Veronica, had completed her master's degree before embarking on the affair that had led to marrying her professor husband.

Today, Fiona would be serving dessert in that beloved now-lost dining room, cleaning up in that oceanic kitchen.

The thoughts were arrows, sticking in various organs—lungs, liver, kidneys. Her children looked at her with pity, all three pairs of eyes the same clear blue as her own, their mouths and cheekbones belonging to their father. "Sorry," she said, shaking her head. "Go. Enjoy dessert."

She ripped a piece of foil from the roll and covered the cake. "Might as well take this. You know she only cooks Sara Lee."

Jenna snorted in appreciation. Ben grabbed the cake. "Love you," he said before kissing her cheek.

Tim, too, bent to give her a hug. "I didn't mean to hurt your feelings," he said. "You're just so easy to tease."

"I know," she said.

It wasn't until they left and she was standing in the middle of her kitchen, emptiness below the Louis Armstrong playing, that she realized what she'd said.

India? Where had that come from? Obviously, it was ridiculous—she was struggling to make rent, much less afford a trip to the other side of the world. Eventually she'd have to admit her lie. It humiliated her that they'd know she'd made it up.

But not today.

～

That evening, she sat in the cold, tiny second bedroom at her desk and watched the snow falling. It was a magical scene, flakes sparkling through the bar of someone's porch light. A girlhood in northern New Mexico had given snow almost mystical properties, and she loved it every single time.

It was quiet. *So* quiet. That was the thing about the apartment that bugged her the most. She'd prepared for an empty nest—as much as was possible, anyway—by taking on a new volunteer position at the tiny gold rush history museum. She'd already had her garden club and the part-time position at the nonprofit.

But just as the kids launched—Tim off to graduate school in Chicago; Jenna starting her junior year at the University of Colorado, where her dad taught philosophy; and Ben starting his freshman year at Stanford—the world closed down for COVID. Lacking resources on their various campuses, the kids all drove home, and the family sheltered together.

Veronica loved it. It was an unexpected reprieve, having everyone under the same roof for over a year, the kids enrolled remotely in classes. She'd hear one professor lecturing on Shakespeare, another on some math formula that was over her head. In his own den/office, Spence held forth on Socrates and Marcus Aurelius and the reliability of logic. Ruler of the house again, Veronica happily made vats of soup, baked sourdough bread, and served meals every night in their cozy dining room.

Then, over the course of eight months, her world shattered. The kids went back to their various apartments and dorms.

But then her marriage abruptly—or it seemed like it at the time— fell apart. Her husky mutt, Sophie, had died at fifteen. She had to move out of the house she adored.

Veronica had not been the slightest bit silent or docile or dignified about that, much to her embarrassment now. Among other things, there had been one memorable night she had called him twenty-seven times after drinking a bottle of rosé.

She had prepared for the loss of her beloved dog, as much as a person could. She had prepared for her children to leave home. She had even been looking forward to the next chapter of her life with a certain amount of anticipation.

The loss of her marriage had blindsided her. Everyone said that wasn't possible, that she must have known on some level, but she hadn't. One day she'd thought she was happily married, and the next, she was the unwanted wife. He sobbed when he told her that he'd fallen in love with a visiting professor. An Irish poet as ethereal as a Maxfield Parrish painting.

Spence was so sorry, but he had to end the marriage. Immediately. Not that Veronica gave in, just like that. Oh, no.

She *believed* in their marriage, the union other people envied. How could they have such great sex (twice a week!) if they weren't still very attracted to each other?

But in the end, she lost him. He was in love with someone else. Because the house had been handed down through his family like some medieval manor, not to mention she couldn't afford the upkeep of a hundred-year-old house, she'd had to give up her beloved house and garden to move to this apartment, where the only voice was her own.

Now she didn't just have an *empty* nest; she had *no* nest. It was just an apartment in an old house without even a pet to keep her company. The only noises were noises she made—clattering dishes or singing against the dark. Sitting here in the cold of a Thanksgiving night that should have been spent around the raucous noise of board games with her family, it was so quiet she could hear the creaks of the old floorboards.

The all-too-familiar waves of fury and grief rose like magma through her body, but she had cried and screamed enough for twenty women. Irritated, she stood up, snapped on the Bluetooth speaker, and played an upbeat list of favorites.

Do something productive, her therapist's voice said in her mind. She'd had to quit the expensive sessions a couple of months ago, but that didn't nullify the help she'd discovered.

Instead of scrolling through Facebook, she clicked on LinkedIn to look for a job. Her alimony was meager because even a full professor didn't make a huge sum of money, and he did have a second family on the way, along with three kids still in college. She had to find something soon, and preferably not secretarial. Not that there was anything wrong with the work, but it had never been something she could bear. It literally made her fall asleep.

She liked being active. Maybe something outside.

It wasn't like she had many credentials in any field. Good education, but no experience in anything except raising children and grant writing. She'd done a lot of grant writing for various nonprofits over the years and was good at it. She hoped there might be a position for her somewhere in one of the many nonprofits in town, but she had not had much luck so far.

A person could find work, she told herself. She would. She scrolled down and stopped, electrified.

> Seeking female companion to assist with travel and research. History major preferred, must be able to lift 40 lbs., walk for several hours in any weather and climb steps. Three to four weeks, itinerary including London, Paris, Morocco, India. Fluent French preferred, other language experience a plus. Salary dependent upon experience. Contact mariahwind@ usaathletes.com.

For a minute, she stared at the entry as if she might have imagined it. How could this even be a real job offer? The cadence of the destinations sang through her—London, Paris, Morocco, India.

India. As if she'd conjured it.

Fierce, hot *want* suddenly awakened in her chest. It was such a strange sensation that she had to press a hand to her sternum. Her heart thudded beneath her palm, and the music of place-names sang through her body. *London, Paris, Morocco, India!*

Her heart raced, and she told herself to calm down. It was probably some weird scam. And even if it was real, she probably wouldn't qualify. But she was fluent in French, though it was rusty, and she'd graduated with degrees in history and women's studies, and she could certainly walk several hours and lift forty pounds. It couldn't hurt to try.

If bad luck could fall on a person all at once, maybe good luck could, too.

Without a second's hesitation, she sent an email.

CHAPTER TWO

On Thanksgiving night, Mariah Ellsworth ate chicken noodle soup and a grilled cheese sandwich. Her mother, a gourmet before the word *foodie* was invented, had hated the holiday. She'd said it was filled with overcooked meat, oversweetened everything, badly cooked vegetables, and sloppy potatoes. She liked to skip it in protest, and whenever Mariah happened to be home, they'd spent it watching the rich historical dramas her mother loved.

She was making tea in her mother's cavernous kitchen when her phone dinged with an email notification. It was on the table in the dining room, approximately fifty million steps away, so she'd just pick it up on her way through.

The house was freezing. It was always freezing, a fact she'd complained about before, and now was even worse. Her mother used to tell her to put on more clothes and stop complaining. *For a snowboarder, you're awfully sensitive to cold.*

Her retort had always been that she had the right gear to stay warm on the slopes. A person shouldn't have to wear insulated pants inside a house.

To counter the cold and the emptiness of the day, she'd built a fire in the sitting room. Now she hobbled through the hallway, leaning on her cane, tea in the other hand. All the lights downstairs still burned, but she couldn't be bothered to turn them off.

Actually, the truth was, she never turned off most of the lights. Being alone in the house scared her. The noises; the dark rooms upstairs; her mother's bedroom, barely touched since her death. A lamp burned beside the bed all the time, as if awaiting Rachel's imminent return.

Now settled by the crackling fire, her bad leg facing the nourishing flames, she opened the email app. Her interest perked up when she saw that the subject line said LinkedIn.

From: VeronicaBarrington@timelink.com
To: mariahwind@usaathletes.com
Re: LinkedIn Travel Companion

I saw your job opening on LinkedIn, and I would be very interested in the position. I haven't traveled extensively, but I am fluent in French, and I have degrees in history and women's studies from CU, and I love research. As for the physical requirements, while I'm not going to be running the Leadville 100 anytime soon (or ever), I keep up a regular walking and hiking habit. Stairs are not a problem, and I'm well versed in the organizational challenges of packing. I'm currently at a bit of a crossroads and would especially love to be out of the country at Christmas. You can reach me at 303-555-7412 anytime.

Veronica

A little whip of excitement jolted her. She'd been sure she'd have to cancel the trip, that it would be impossible to find anyone on such short notice.

Originally, her aunt Jill had been planning to accompany Mariah, but three days ago, her husband had suffered a serious heart attack. Understandably, Jill could not go. But understanding didn't dampen

Mariah's devastation. There was no way she could manage the trip herself. Jill had been the one to suggest advertising on LinkedIn.

She texted immediately:

Hi, Veronica. Mariah here. I got your email. The trip starts soon, so I'd like to meet with you tomorrow, if you can. I don't drive, so you'd have to come to me in Cherry Creek. Is that possible?

Yes! Name the time, and I'll be there. I'm in Boulder, so I would rather set out after rush hour.

Mariah typed in the address, then: Awesome. I'll see you around 11? You have a current passport?

Yep, already checked the expiration. See you then, thanks.

Mariah dropped the phone on the table, then picked it up and texted her aunt. I have a lead on a person to go with me. How do I make sure she's right?

And then: How is uncle mike?

No response. Mariah sipped her mint tea, remembering when she and her mother had visited Morocco the first time. They'd drunk from small, beautiful glasses, in a *riad* that was covered ceiling to floor with blue tiles.

Mint tea in Marrakech, she thought. Maybe that would be a good title for the book.

Or not. Jill still hadn't responded, so she would have to ask herself how she could feel comfortable with a stranger for more than a month of travel. Was that even possible? As Jill had pointed out, she'd traveled plenty with people she didn't know, sharing dorm space and rooms with other snowboarders at competitions and training camps since her earliest days.

But that was different. They were all similar ages, with a built-in language for life—snow, boards, times, training, diet. Sometimes girls or boys they liked, but who really had time for that? There was only the sport.

She rubbed her thigh, adrift for a moment in her longing for the taste of dry snow and sharp cold and fierce competition. Would she ever get that back?

This Veronica person didn't sound anything like an athlete. What would she have in common with a history geek? Mariah imagined a skinny woman with big glasses and bad jeans, but that was a caricature of her mother, and not fair.

All she really had to be was not completely annoying, reasonably fit, and able to really help with the research bits Mariah didn't know. If they got along too badly, she could just send her home.

A little pressure flowed out of her at that.

Her phone dinged. Jill. Trust your gut, kiddo. You have good instincts. What do you know about her?

> Not a lot. Maybe a student? She
> lives in Boulder.

Get references, obviously.

> Right. Like what counts as
> reliable?

People with verifiable contact info
that you can look up and then call
independently of her references

K

I'm so so so so sorry I can't go after
everything.

A well of emotion threatened to spill out. Blinking hard, Mariah typed, Don't be. I get it 100%. How's he doing today?

A little setback, but I think they'll
let him out in a few days. Just
worry about your happiness. He's
gonna be fine.

Good. Take care of yourself, too, k?
I need my auntie.

♥

After she ended the conversation, she paused and texted the applicant.

Pls bring character references.

CHAPTER THREE

It was snowing again the next afternoon when Veronica pulled up in front of a Victorian house in a well-tended Denver neighborhood. As she got out of the car, she peered upward at three stories, painted in a subdued but very pretty palette of plum, pink, and gray. As a history buff, she knew the mansions had almost all been built by gold and silver barons, and no expense had been spared on this beauty.

She climbed the worn concrete steps, feeling as if she were in a Christmas snow globe. She thought of her Christmas tree, stashed in the storage unit below the apartment, and it made her heart ache. If Thanksgiving had been bad, Christmas would be even worse. The kids and Spence were all going to his folks' place in Breckenridge, a ski-in, ski-out lodge on Peak 7, and she wouldn't see them until after New Year's.

The thought of those vast, empty days made her skin shrivel.

On the wide wooden porch, she stomped her feet lightly to clear the snow and rang the bell. Through the frosted glass of the door, she saw a figure with an uneven gait coming forward. She'd imagined a slightly elderly woman, possibly a bit frail.

Instead, the woman who opened the door was in her mid-twenties, with long, blond hair and a pale face. She leaned on a carved-teak cane with a lion's head at the top. "I thought you'd be younger."

"And I thought you'd be older."

For one more moment, Mariah stared at her, then stepped back. "Come in." She pointed to a doorway to the left. "We'll be in there."

The foyer was a circle with stairs rising at one end, and it must have gone to the top of the house, because light fell into the area. A fern bloomed on a stand. Wide doors faced each other, east and west, and a hallway opened at the side of the stairs, likely leading to the kitchen. In the dark day, lamps burned in various spots.

Veronica followed Mariah's limping gait into a room that would once have been called a parlor. The walls were papered in a tasteful violet stripe, and the furniture was wine-colored velvet, modern but appropriately oversize, settled around a vintage Moroccan rug in pinks and blues. Veronica, a house-design devotee, mentally clocked the cost of the room, and her eyebrows rose slightly.

Mariah perched on a wingback chair. Veronica sat kitty-corner on the velvet couch. Between them was a table set with tea, clearly too low for Mariah to reach without another adjustment. "Shall I pour?" Veronica asked.

With some relief, Mariah nodded. "Thanks. Three sugars for me," she said, and then, as so many people did these days, explained her choice. "I'm—or I *was*—a full-time athlete. Can't quite break the habit."

The tea was fragrant, deep caramel in color. "I am no athlete, but I still like three sugars," she said with a smile, carefully handing the tea over. As Veronica poured her own, she asked, "What sport?"

"Snowboarding," Mariah said, glancing toward the windows, where snow floated by. "Not anymore." She pointed to her leg. "Messed it up pretty bad this time."

Veronica nodded. "Sorry to hear that."

"That's actually why I need help for this trip. I thought I could do it on my own, but . . ." She looked down, paused. "I can't carry or drag a suitcase. My aunt has talked me into hiring someone to help." She frowned and blurted out, "I really thought you'd be a grad student or something. It's not really a job for a—"

"A woman who should be further along in life?" Veronica said.

"No, that's not what I meant. Sorry. It's just . . . this is all weird and new to me."

Taking pity on her, Veronica said, "I'm newly divorced, and the alimony isn't enough to support me." She shrugged. "So."

"Okay. I get that. What have you done for work during your marriage?"

"Managed the life of a busy professor and our children. I've done some nonprofit work, grant writing and that kind of thing, but mainly that was my job."

Mariah frowned. "I need research help, not just the . . . physical help."

"As I said in my email, I have undergrad degrees in women's studies and history. Most of a master's thesis on one of the outliers of the Bloomsbury Group."

"You didn't finish?"

Veronica shook her head. "No. Got married, started having children. Always said I'd go back to it." Suddenly, it sounded so conventional, especially to a woman who'd lived as a snowboarder, taking chances.

Mariah seemed to pick up on her insecurity. "Are you sure this is the right job for you? I mean, it's not like being a nurse or anything, but you'll be kind of . . . a servant."

"Oh, trust me, I've got the servant thing down pat." She made a wry face. "My whole job was making his life easier and my kids' lives easier, and maybe that's cliché—I get that it is, kind of, but to tell you the truth, I really need a job, and I really love the sound of this. I do speak French."

The torrent came out without her permission, but sitting there in that well-appointed room, Veronica just wanted something for herself. The manual parts of the job would be annoying—hauling and whatever—but it wasn't like she hadn't been doing that for her family for twenty-five years.

Mariah just looked at her, and for the first time, Veronica saw that her mouth turned down on the right side. A thin white scar led to her temple under her hair.

That must have been some accident, which was exactly why Veronica didn't ski or snowboard. Her whole family thought it was a waste—living in Colorado and not partaking—and they'd spend days on skis or boards, depending on the generation. All their vacations were taken in the mountains over winter breaks. Veronica happily packed up, cooked for them, made sure everyone had what they needed, but she had no desire to hurtle at high speeds down a mountain. Every single one of them had been rushed to the ER with injuries of greater and lesser degrees, ranging from a broken ankle to a torn rotator cuff and two knee surgeries, to a concussion and twenty-seven stitches across the back of the skull.

She'd never tried it, so she'd never gotten hurt.

Instead, she spent her ski days curled up in some warm spot by a fire, drinking cider in a cozy sweater and reading a book. So many books. Such good memories.

"It doesn't pay a ton," Mariah said. This must have been a sticking point with other applicants, Veronica thought, and braced herself. "I'll cover your travel expenses, of course, all the meals and everything that goes with it, but the pay is minimum wage, calculated on a forty-hour week. It might end up being more than forty hours, but that's what I can pay."

For a minute, Veronica felt an acute sense of disappointment. The sum would barely cover her rent, although that was technically being paid by alimony. A buzzy sense of panic sent her nerves into high alert. What if something went wrong? She had zero cushion.

She found herself biting her thumbnail and forced her hand into her lap. "How often will you pay me?"

This had not crossed Mariah's mind, obviously. "Oh, I don't know. What works for you? Every week? The first payment on the second Friday after we leave?"

"I can live with that. What is the job, exactly?"

Mariah picked up a sheaf of papers and handed it over. "I'm finishing some work my mom had assembled for her next book on cafés around the world. She'd already done a lot of writing, but there are big gaps where she needed on-the-ground research to fill in the details."

Veronica looked at the notes, and a little bubble of excitement pushed itself into her anxiety. The sheaf of papers held a list of cafés, each with low-grade printout photos, bare facts, and addresses. Veronica had never heard of any of them except one, Angelina in Paris. Long, long ago, on one of her two trips abroad, she'd drunk hot chocolate there with Spence on their honeymoon. A wash of memory—gilt and mirrors and the musical sound of French—lit up her heart.

The other cafés were in London and Morocco, and a handful was in India.

"It's a lot of ground to cover," Veronica said, tucking her gnawed thumbnail out of reach into her palm. "How long are you planning to be on the road?"

"About three or four weeks. Through the holidays, just so you know."

"That makes me want it more," Veronica said.

"A photographer will meet us in London," Mariah continued. "A family friend who wants to help finish this book in memory of my mom."

Veronica nodded.

"Mainly I need help with the research and how to organize it—and I need you to sign a release assuring me that you won't try to write the book yourself."

"Of course! I'm happy to sign anything."

"Good."

"Related to that," Veronica said, "there are a couple of sites in both London and Mumbai that I might want to visit. Will there be any downtime for my own research?"

Mariah's mouth turned down in consideration. "I don't see why not. We can make that happen as long as you make the cafés your first priority."

"Great."

A small silence fell into the room. Mariah drank her tea and eyed the snow outside. Veronica pretended to read the notes, but her brain was buzzing too much to take it in. She noticed her hands were shaking a little, and to bring down the level of pure *want*, she asked, "When would we need to leave?"

"Two weeks from today. You'll need some immunizations. Can you get those done next week?"

Veronica straightened. "I have a few. We'd been planning a trip to Africa when COVID hit." And then Spence fell in love with a visiting professor, and Veronica lost her mind. "But I'll need to check to see what's recommended."

"Cool. I'll send you the list, and you can make sure you have what you need."

"What about visas?"

"Won't need it for Morocco, but you do need one for India. You should apply right away so we have some time, though mine only took a couple of days."

A swell of possibility rose through Veronica's body. "Does that mean the job is mine?"

"After I check your references . . . if you want it, it's yours. Please say yes."

Veronica touched her heart. "Yes, please."

CHAPTER FOUR

Mariah had been struggling to make sense of a life that had been completely emptied of everything she loved when she stumbled on her mother's notes.

Trapped by the snowstorm a month ago, she knocked around the empty house with her cane, maybe subconsciously seeking the closet where she'd finally find where her mother was hiding.

It was a relief to be home, in some ways. Her recovery had been long and institutional—hospitals, then rehab centers—and sleeping in her own bedroom was heaven. She liked eating cereal at the table in the kitchen, as she'd done a million times before. Her athletic life had begun when she was quite young, so she'd always spent more time away from home than there. She and her mom traveled all over, Rachel working on whatever writing or research project she had going, Mariah working with a trainer or a coach or a team.

Daytime in the house was fine. At night, she liked it less. For one thing, it was cold and hard to heat. It was an old Victorian, built in the 1880s by a silver baron on one of the toniest streets in Denver. Understandably, there were pockets of cold everywhere.

But it was hard to convince herself that those chilly areas were probably not ghosts. She knew that it was completely idiotic for her to believe in them. She was direct and down-to-earth to a fault, ask anyone.

Nonetheless, she felt them. Something in the downstairs bathroom that was sad and weepy, not threatening. And not always there, either.

Her mother scoffed, said it was her imagination, but that didn't change the prickles that ran up Mariah's arms when she sat down to pee sometimes.

There were other spots, too—an empty bedroom, a cold spot by the fireplace in the living room they also never used, preferring the smaller, cozier parlor.

The one place she wouldn't go was the basement. Not ever, not for anything. She'd gone down there with her mother as a six-year-old and had to be carried out screaming. Never again.

Her mother, for the record, thought Mariah was letting her imagination get the better of her.

Now that she was back after her mother's death, Mariah often felt lost in the eleven-room mansion. Much too large for one person. It had been too big for two, but her mother had a lot of personality and presence, and she had loved the old-fashioned rooms, the parquet floors, the sense of time and history sitting in the rooms like wallpaper. It wasn't really Mariah's taste, but she hadn't figured out what to do, how to change it or maybe sell it. Her aunt Jill, her mom's sister, had said not to do anything for a while.

So she didn't. She focused on her PT, taking a Lyft down to the hospital three times a week, and focused on healing. Everyone said she'd never snowboard again, but they didn't know how hard Mariah could work. They hadn't even been sure she'd walk again, and here she was, walking just fine. Well, with a limp, but not a very big one.

The rest of the time, she didn't have a lot to do. She'd gone from going 150 miles an hour all the time to . . . nothing.

Now what? Now what? Now what?

That night, a month before, restless and grieving, she'd decided to do something useful. She visited her mother's office. The air still smelled of her mother, faint soap and coffee and a particular hair product Mariah wanted to track down, and mainly the incense her mother loved that, to Mariah, smelled like something had gone bad in the trash. Rachel laughed and laughed when Mariah had said that, and kept the sticks in her office.

The combination of scents had filled her with vast loneliness. She looked for the package to light a stick, which she placed in the ceramic holder near the computer. The scents of cedar and patchouli fused like a body.

Rachel's desk was an antique made of walnut, the golden wood polished to a muted shine. The surface was tidy, file folders lined up in an elegant holder, pens and pencils in a carved-pottery cup. The silent monitor and a keyboard. A desk pad covered the surface. Only a few notes there, all written in Rachel's trademark turquoise fountain-pen ink. The letters and numbers were more rounded than elegant, the handwriting of a teenager, but they were notes her mother had written with a still-living hand. She ran her finger over each one: *Collect book numbers for 2023. Send Berta a thank-you card. Pick up cleaning. Call Henry.*

So prosaic. As if life would just keep going forever.

Drawers lined both sides, each with a crystal knob. Mariah pulled out the central one, long and shallow. It held pens, pencils, erasers, paper clips, and two bottles of peacock-colored ink. The inlaid Monteverde pen she liked was already in Mariah's possession, along with the rest of the contents of her purse.

She closed the drawer, opened each of the others in turn. The usual desk things: paper for the printer on a stand nearby, extra ink cartridges, extra files in multiple colors.

Jill had tried to open the computer, but it remained locked tight, secrets (if there were any) trapped behind a password. Mariah didn't bother to turn it on. Instead, she plucked a file from the stand. It was labeled "History." She leafed through the contents curiously, finding articles about cafés in London and Mumbai, all with a particular sort of art deco spirit. There was a photo of a man and woman, Indian, dressed in the styles of the 1930s; another of an art deco teapot made of green glass. It looked like the start of a project.

The trouble was, now her mother had gone and died, and Mariah couldn't ask her.

She grabbed the other files and opened them one by one. A single page of contact information—maybe fifteen names, more than half in Mumbai, the rest in London, Paris, and one in Marrakech. Another list of names, which looked to be restaurants or cafés. A chronology of dates labeled "Parsi History" and a printed flyer from a restaurant called Dishoom in London with more of the same art deco detailing.

Intriguing. She wondered what her mother was doing with it. "Too bad," Mariah said aloud. She wanted, suddenly, to know what her mom had been thinking. What had been her last book project? Rachel had written seven highly popular food books—not cookbooks, although they had recipes, but stories told around food of various kinds. Her most popular had been one grouped around the stories of spices in various cuisines, *Spice Roads*.

Was this the project she'd been planning to undertake next? Mariah had called Jill to ask more about it, and that was how the whole project came to be.

Mariah would trace the steps of her mother's last project, and Jill would go with her. It would be a chance for both of them to heal and honor the woman they missed so much.

CHAPTER FIVE

Veronica texted her daughter on Sunday afternoon.

Got a minute?

Yes

Her phone rang, and there was Jenna on FaceTime, her hair yanked into a tight, high ponytail, her nose ring catching the light. "Hi. I stopped by Friday, but you weren't there."

"I had a job interview, actually."

Jenna carried the phone somewhere into the kitchen she shared with three roommates. "That's awesome. I know you've been looking. Did you get it?"

"I did. That's why I'm calling. I'm going to be a research assistant for a woman who is digging into café culture."

Jenna propped her phone up on a windowsill as she took down a cup and poured coffee from a pitcher of cold brew in the fridge. "That sounds great. Right up your alley, for sure."

"The thing is," Veronica interjected before Jenna could move on to the more exciting things in the world, like her own interests, "I'm leaving for three or four weeks, and I need you to water my plants once a week."

"Wait. Where are you going?" She paused. "You're not actually going to India? I thought you were just trying to save face."

"Wow, thanks," Veronica said. Although it was true, she still wanted to save face. "Not only India. London, Paris, Morocco."

"Someone's *paying* you to do that?"

"I know. I'm so thrilled."

"Mom. Are you sure it's not a scam?"

Veronica rolled her eyes. "It's not a scam." But suddenly, she worried that it was. Could this just be some elaborate setup to, what? Give her minimum wage? She was a bit long in the tooth to be trafficked, although she supposed it happened. Maybe she should—

Stop it. Just in case, she'd go over the paperwork carefully. And honestly, if she got stranded somewhere, she'd just use her credit card to get home.

In the meantime, she said to her daughter, "She has some mobility problems and needs help with bags and that kind of thing."

"Oh, I get it." She nodded. "Like a companion?"

"I think that's the main part of the job, honestly. Will you water the plants?"

"Of course."

"Once a week. Put it on your calendar. I've had some of these since you were a baby."

"I promise." The information seemed to settle. "Do you think you're up to such a big trip?"

As if she were a hundred, not fifty. "I'll be fine."

"What if I need you?"

"I still have a phone, and your dad lives here, too."

Jenna rolled her eyes. "That helps."

"You'll be fine. You'll be in Breck for the holidays, and I'll be home in early January."

"Oh," Jenna said, a light bulb going off. "Are you doing this as a change of scenery for Christmas?"

"Maybe," she admitted. Last year had been terrible. "But I also do need a job, and this will be better than being a clerk somewhere."

"True." A voice called from off-screen. Jenna glanced over her shoulder. "I'm happy for you, Mom. Gotta go." She blew a kiss and ended the connection.

Unlike Jenna, her sons never liked phone calls. She texted them both at the same time. Hey, I got a job, and I'm going to be on the road for a few weeks, leaving next Wednesday. If you need anything, you'll have to go to your dad. Do you want to come over for dinner Tuesday?

The only other person who'd care was Amber, a friend she'd met in forced group therapy after her arrest. Everyone else had either decided to take Spence's side or had been horrified by her arrest. Understandably.

Eventually, she'd have to tell Spence about the trip, but there was time. She didn't have to do it now.

She managed to get in to see her doctor on Thursday, was dosed up with vaccines and malaria pills. "I'm also giving you a prescription for antibiotics and an antidiarrheal," Dr. Romero said. "Take IMODIUM with you, lots of it. And a really good mosquito repellent with DEET."

Veronica typed notes into her phone. "Isn't DEET bad for you?"

"Not as bad as malaria or dengue fever."

"Point taken."

"Also, you'll want Benadryl, and the usual NSAIDs. Do you have a water bottle with a filter?"

"No."

"You can buy a good one at REI." She dropped her readers on the table. "Saves a lot on discarded single-use plastic, and you'll always know you have it. Don't drink the water in Morocco or India, even to brush your teeth."

"Got it."

"Also," she said with a smile, "don't let the warnings scare you. It's going to be an amazing trip. Happy for you."

Dr. Romero had been the one to see Veronica after she broke her wrist one winter night, and when she'd been arrested, she prescribed

Xanax to help get her through the worst of the madness. Thinking about it now, she felt deep shame. A normal person would not have lost her mind over the loss of a marriage.

"Thanks. I'm really excited."

Both arms vaguely tender from the vaccinations, she drove to the giant REI near campus and found the filtering water bottle, then wandered the aisles looking for other things that might make travel easier without loading herself down. In light of Mariah's needs, Veronica had already mentally limited herself to one medium bag. She picked up a stretchy clothesline that could be hung up in a shower, individual packets of laundry soap, a cube that adapted electronics to various power sources, including direct plugs for USB and C cords. She eyed the first-aid kits but decided she could make one herself. Although she browsed through the hiking pants and wicking shirts, she didn't see anything she didn't already own. Before the divorce, she'd hiked most weeks with a group of women from the neighborhood. Those outings had ceased with her arrest, but she still had the clothes. They were sturdy and drip-dry—perfect for this. She did add some drip-dry underwear, and then, wary of putting too much on her credit card, checked out.

She was loading it all into the back of her Subaru when her phone buzzed and Spence's face showed on the screen. She almost ignored it, but as they were coparents, he did have a right to know that she'd be out of the country.

"I guess you heard the news," she said.

"Uh . . . what news?"

She took a breath, unwilling to do this in a parking lot. "Nothing big; I'll call you later. What's up?"

"Did you sign the papers my lawyer sent over?"

She scoffed. "The reduction in alimony, you mean? No. I'm barely making it as it is."

"Ronny, come on. I'm going to have a new baby! And we have three kids in college. I'm not a wealthy man. Give me a break."

"Don't call me Ronny," she said for the millionth time. "You're the one who wanted a divorce. These are the consequences." A fit young man with messy hair carried a sleeping bag to his car. Veronica realized she was appreciatively watching only when he gave her a sunny smile and lift of the chin. She smiled back. "If it's that dire, sell your precious house."

"It's been in my family since 1925!"

Across the screen of imagination flashed a memory of her dining room, the windows looking out onto the garden of rare irises—now gone—she'd hunted down over decades, the glow of that table she'd polished so earnestly. She had to take a breath to ease the pinch in her chest. "I don't know what to tell you," she said. "I'm on minimal alimony as it is."

"It's only you!"

"And whose fault is that?"

"Maybe if you hadn't been so out of control, we could have worked things out ourselves and saved all the lawyer fees."

She pressed her lips together, feeling the ache of those memories rising, too, tangling in all the losses of that year. With effort, she looked up at the blue, blue sky, repeated the mantra she'd found in therapy. *Not worth it, not worth it, not worth it.* She opened the door and settled behind the wheel. "I can't really talk right now, Spence."

"Ronny! Don't hang up!"

"What?" she said sharply.

"Have a heart. Please, just think about it."

"No," she said cleanly and firmly and without heat. It was a trick she'd worked hard to learn. How to set boundaries without losing her temper.

She hung up. She would have to tell him she was leaving, but choosing when to do it gave her a sense of calm.

Less alimony. As if.

~

At home, she laid everything out on the bed. She had not packed for such a long trip for herself before, but she'd done it plenty for Spence. Ten years ago, he'd published a pop-philosophy self-help book that had been translated into quite a few languages. He was on the circuit, speaking in various places as the author of the book, always imagining he'd hit the big time any minute. He hadn't yet. The royalties for the book were thin these days, and the pressure to write something new was mounting, but he had not written in years.

But she had learned to pack for him. What you needed was a week's worth of clothing that could be recycled, with maybe a few extra bits. It saved mental energy to think that way.

She packed eight pairs of underwear, two pairs of pants (khaki and dark blue), two skirts that would shake out easily, four short-sleeve and two long-sleeve T-shirts, a swimsuit (one piece), a dress that could be worn with tennis shoes or sandals, a scarf that could be worn with anything, and three bras in various thicknesses and colors. Everything went into compression cubes.

As she was deciding how to pack the first aid, pharmaceuticals, and her cosmetics, the doorbell rang. She practically skipped toward the door, so buoyed by her excitement, to find all three kids standing in the hallway. "Hey!" she said, touching the screen of her watch. "I thought you were coming for dinner tomorrow."

"That's not why we're here, Mom," Tim said.

"What, then?" It was either the trip, or Spence had sent emissaries to plead his case, but she didn't think he'd stoop to using the kids.

"Can we just come in?" Tim asked.

She sighed and stepped back to let them in. "Of course."

They made themselves at home around the dining room table. All big discussions—which colleges to choose, what to do about the car Jenna had wrecked, boyfriend or girlfriend troubles, the announcement of Spence and Veronica's divorce—took place around dining room tables. "Must be serious," she said, trying to lighten the mood. "What's up?"

"We're worried about you taking this trip, Mom," Jenna said. "It's too long and too far, and you'll be gone at Christmas!"

"What do you even know about this person?" Tim interjected.

Veronica frowned and started to speak, but—

"You've hardly traveled at all, and now you're going off with somebody you don't even know?" Jenna said, eyebrows raising in total horror.

"If this is a reaction to the boomer comment on turkey day, I'm sorry," Tim said.

Only Ben was quiet. He was always the quiet one in the family, a graphic artist who had stuttered as a boy and even now had to focus to speak. She looked at him. "And you?"

He shrugged. "It doesn't seem that safe."

"Hmm." She folded her hands, feeling a dual sense of gratitude and annoyance. "Let me ask you all a question."

"Okay."

"If one of your friends was going to make this trip, would you be worried?" She looked at Tim, who was a carbon copy of his father, tall and blessed with thick blond hair, with cheekbones born of centuries of great genes.

"No," he said, "but you're not really . . ."

"What?"

He glanced at Jenna. "Well traveled."

"Oh, so I shouldn't travel because I haven't traveled?"

"Mom, you're also a lot older than our friends."

"True."

"And there are the . . . uh . . . mental health things," Jenna blurted out.

"Fair," Veronica said, even if it wasn't, not really. She was referring to the arrest and everything around it. Her—very temporary—madness. "Well, you and I both know there were extenuating circumstances, and I am as sane as anyone. It's been over a year, and I'm fine."

"But what if it gets stressful? What if . . ." Jenna looked slightly teary, which softened Veronica's stance. She covered Jenna's hand with her own.

She tried never to cast blame, even indirectly, but she'd been suffering a desperately broken heart at the time. "I'm fine, as I think you know. And I really need this job."

"Can't you get something nearby?" Jenna asked.

Tim said, "It will be weird with you gone at the holidays."

"I know, but I wouldn't be with you guys in Breck anyway."

"Come on, Mom," Jenna pleaded. "Can't you just stay here and find something after Christmas?"

The buoyant excitement she'd been feeling as she packed started to drain away. The clear, bright path ahead suddenly looked as gray and winter-dull as it had for months.

The plunge reminded her of the winter of her senior year, waiting for replies from colleges—the joy of being accepted, the potential inherent in each opening, followed by the reality of the enormous cost. They all offered aid packages, but nowhere near enough, and each time, her heart sank into the gray landscape of her future like a deflated balloon. Only CU had finally offered enough aid to allow her to say yes.

But this time, she had some autonomy, some control over her situation. "I won't even see you for a week." She spoke honestly, clearly. "Last year was pretty awful for me."

"I guess I get that," Tim said.

"I don't want to look for anything else." She glanced at Jenna. "You said yourself it was right up my alley."

Ben spoke. "Dad isn't even talking to us all that much. The only thing he cares about right now is the b-baby."

"I'm sorry." She looked at each of them, cupped a hand around Ben's face, which was starting to fur at the jawline as he grew a scraggly beard. She understood the pain and confusion they felt, but she couldn't do their grief work for them. They had to work out their relationship with their dad on individual terms. "You guys know I love you so much, right?"

Nods.

"There's nothing I can do about your dad, but your grandparents will be there at Christmas, and probably Aunt Ellen and Uncle Clint and your cousins. You won't feel lonely." She lifted a shoulder. "It's not like I ever got on the slopes with you."

"That's true," Ben said.

"On the rest of your concerns: First of all, it's research. I'm traveling with a twenty-five-year-old, so she's still got all her faculties, and I won't be hoodwinked at a train station."

Tim grinned in appreciation.

"I got all my shots and a prescription for antibiotics, so all of that is covered." She took a breath and spread her hands. "Most of all, I'm *really* excited about it. Can you just be happy for me?"

"It's almost too good to be true," Ben said.

"Yeah," Veronica said. "Maybe it's just my turn for something good."

"Will you at least let me check the credentials and history of this person you're traveling with?" Tim asked.

For a moment, Veronica considered it, but then she imagined how they'd react if she asked to google their friends. "No. I'm an adult and perfectly capable of taking care of myself." She stood, hands on the table. "Now, if you want to discuss actual logistics of staying in touch and all that, I'm happy to do so, but otherwise, I need to get back to packing."

⁓

Veronica had just made her second cup of coffee the next morning when a knock sounded at her door. She glanced around automatically to see if one of the kids had forgotten something, but she didn't see anything out of place. It was too early for solicitors. *Maybe a neighbor,* she thought.

She opened the door a crack. It was Spence standing there, looking as smooth and handsome as always; honestly, he was almost a caricature of a handsome professor—his blond hair going gray but still wavy, the high cheekbones her children had inherited, the full-cut mouth. He wore a tweed jacket over jeans without an ounce of irony.

He turned when she swung the door wide. "Veronica! Good morning!"

She kept her hand on the doorknob. "What's up, Spence?" But she knew. It wasn't the first time.

"Can we chat for a few minutes?"

She folded her arms. "About?"

"The kids told me you're going on a long trip."

"Mmm. I was going to text you today."

"Can't we just sit down for a few minutes? Talk?"

"I'm not changing my mind about the alimony," she said.

He raised his hands, palms facing her. "I know. The kids wanted me to talk to you about India."

She narrowed her eyes. "Seriously?"

"I just have to say I did," he said with a half grin. That disarming boyish expression that had always worked.

Nor did it fail now. She knew what she should do—send him away and get back to her morning. "I'd rather not," she said. "There's not really anything to talk about."

"We are still coparents," he said. "We should discuss anything that impacts the kids."

He ran a hand through his hair, touched his chin. An answering rustle of awareness moved over her shoulders. "Fine, come in." She left the door open and walked into the kitchen, reaching to get a cup out of the cupboard, automatically pouring coffee for him. Black coffee, stringent and bitter.

Before she could turn, he came up behind her. Veronica did not move as he swept the hair off her neck and bent in to press a kiss to her nape, his lips brushing the small hair there in a way he knew aroused her.

"Spence," she protested. But weakly. She missed sex. Missed his body, even if the man himself had lost appeal.

That body pressed against her lightly, invitation rather than aggression. His mouth moved to her ear, and she softened backward, opening to his hands pushing under her top.

It had started only a couple of months into the separation, not long after she moved out. He came to her in the dark cold one night, weeping and sorrowful, and she'd been moved to open her arms. Her legs.

And then he came back, sporadically. Not every week, but often—sometimes during the day, sometimes late.

She thought the episodes meant that they would get back together.

And then there'd been the mess of Veronica's arrest. The sex stopped. For a while.

Now Spence moved against her, sparking desire, his hands familiar with every inch of her. When he lifted his hands to her breasts, she knew she should stop him, a married man with a pregnant wife.

But she didn't. In some way, it felt like he still belonged to her. When he tugged the hem of her top, she lifted her arms and let him take it off. He unbuttoned his jeans, and she shimmied out of her pj bottoms, and they had sex right there on the counter, the same sudden, intense sex that had overtaken them thousands of times since the first night of their meeting, when they'd had sex in a rose garden off-campus beneath a full moon.

When they were clinging to each other, sweaty, she said quietly, "I'm still not going to sign anything."

"That's not what this is," he said in his coaxing voice, low and persuasive. "I just thought about you leaving, and it made me . . . hot."

"Mmm." She lingered a few more seconds, then decoupled and picked up her pajamas from the floor, aware that the sun was striking her still-naked body in ways that were probably unflattering. "I have a lot to do. You need to go."

"Just like that?"

She met his eyes. "Why not? You got your fuck. That's what you came here for, right?"

He winced at the profanity, yanking up his pants. "You can't go traipsing all over the world, Ronny."

"Veronica," she said. "And it's not 'traipsing.' It's a job." She kept heading for her room. "A job I desperately need."

He followed her, standing in the doorway as if they were still married, his hands on the doorjamb on either side. "And I've got a new baby on the way."

"Not my problem." She tugged a T-shirt dress over her nakedness. "You need to go."

He came into the room, all six foot one of him, and stood over her. "I miss you," he said in a raw voice. "The sex between us has always been—"

"Hot," she agreed. "But that's the last time."

"Is it?" He started to press himself into her. "You say that every time."

"I mean it this time," she said, pushing him away. "Now go."

As soon as he left, she collapsed onto the edge of the bed, flooded with shame. She did keep saying it was the last time, and she kept letting him in. Her therapist called it *grief sex*. *Storm sex*, she called it, like storm eating. Her friend Amber said she was just horny and should find another guy to have sex with—but how did you do that when you were in your fifties?

She thought of Fiona with remorse and not a little anger. Her mind flashed images of herself, exaggerating her leering at the door, flinging off her shirt, crying out so noisily.

Never again. Never again. Never again.

CHAPTER SIX

On the day of departure, Mariah awakened to the particular pale-blue light of a snowy day. For one second before she remembered, a swell of anticipation swept through her body, lighting all the cells that loved the taste of sharp, high-altitude air, the bite of cold. Happiness spread through her veins.

And then she tried to move, and her shattered leg reminded her that it would be a long time before she could ever hit the slopes again. The leg had no strength. All the metal holding her femur together would get freezing cold as soon as she exposed it to the air. She wouldn't be able to even get off a lift.

But she didn't move right away. For a minute longer, she could lie here, in her childhood bedroom hung with posters of Hannah Teter and Shaun White. She'd torn down her medals in a fit of fury not long after she'd come home from the hospital. No one had to tell her she'd never compete again. Her femur had not just been shattered—three inches had been basically pulverized, and so little had been left that the surgeons needed a lot of nails and screws and other metal to create a facsimile of her original leg. That she'd not bled to death on the spot was still considered a miracle.

Which depended on your point of view, she thought with some bitterness, an emotion she'd learned not to express aloud. She *was* grateful she was alive, more or less.

But what would she do with the vastness of years that—presumably—stretched ahead? She couldn't see anything on the path, just a dull, empty road filled with nothing.

Her phone started playing a wake-up ringtone, and she rolled over to turn it off. At least this one thing was a goal, a way to get moving, focus on something besides her ruined life. As she swung her legs over the side of the bed, gearing up for the discomfort that came from standing, she breathed deeply, offered one moment of gratitude. Her mom's sister, Jill, had suggested the practice, and it had been immeasurably helpful.

"Thank you for something to do today," she said to the emptiness.

Veronica arrived fifteen minutes early. Mariah was relieved. They'd only settled details of employment, as well as the visa, two days ago, texting back and forth.

It was still kind of a shock to open the door to her a couple of hours later. Mariah had been so sure she'd be traveling with a grad student, someone close to her own age.

Veronica was totally a mom person, with her inoffensive bob, her cheery expression, her predictable hiking pants and boots that admittedly did look as if they'd been used a lot, and an olive-green fleece. Mariah had been afraid that she'd be an overpacker, but she had only a backpack and a small suitcase.

The mom-ness gave her an unexpected pain. Unwelcome tears welled up. She wanted her *own* mother, not someone else's. She'd hoped for a friend, not a . . . companion, like somebody from an old novel. It embarrassed her that she even needed it. It was ridiculous that this was her life—Mariah Ellsworth, Olympic snowboarder and generally considered the strongest person almost anyone in her life knew.

"Hi," Veronica said breathlessly after hauling the suitcase up the stairs. "I assume the Uber will be here soon, so I'll just leave this on the porch, right?"

"Sure."

"Do you need me to bring out your bags?"

Mariah blinked, heat and pain mixing in her throat. "Yes," she said shortly, limping backward to reveal the suitcases behind her. "It's more than you have."

Understatement. Veronica stood just inside the door for a minute, eyeing the pile of luggage. Backpack, large suitcase, small suitcase. Mariah winced, suddenly embarrassed, an emotion that increased dramatically when Veronica asked calmly, "This is a lot. Do you need *all* of it?"

"I don't know!" she cried. "It's three different climates, right? Hot in India, less hot in Morocco, wet and rainy in England. I don't even know what I need for Paris. I just couldn't figure out how to pack for all of them."

Veronica nodded, sucking on her lip. "This is going to be a lot for the two of us to manage. It would be better if you could condense it to the small bag and the backpack. Is there medical equipment you need?"

"No. It's not like that." Heat crept over her jaw. "It's mostly healed."

"Okay," Veronica said reasonably. Which irked Mariah even more, and yet, this was what she'd needed, right? Someone calm. Someone who could help her. "That's good, then. Do you trust me to repack for you?"

"We don't have time!"

Veronica looked at her watch. "We do. It won't be tidy, but it will get done."

Mariah shrugged sullenly. "Okay."

Efficiently, Veronica knelt and swung the first suitcase to its side and snapped the clips open, then set the other suitcase beside it and did the same. "I love the packing cubes. That makes it easier. What's in the backpack?"

"Stuff for the planes, mainly. Tablet, extra chargers and headphones, socks, meds."

"Perfect."

"It's not like I haven't traveled at all," Mariah snapped. "I was an Olympic snowboarder. I traveled all the time."

Veronica looked over her shoulder, measuring. "Got it. So let's winnow things down. Socks and underwear?"

Mariah pointed to the cubes. "I think. You should double-check. I've been on some meds."

"No worries." She zipped the cubes open. "Check and check." Without asking permission, she took everything out of the small suitcase and opened each of the other cubes, one at a time. "You need a raincoat, warm sweater, jeans, leggings, T-shirts, and something pretty. This dress?"

She held up a light cotton dress enhanced with embroidery. Mariah nodded tightly as the phone in her hand buzzed. "The Uber is here."

"He's early," Veronica said. "Text him that we're on our way out in a minute."

"He won't wait!" Mariah cried.

"Of course he will." She scrambled to her feet, went out on the porch and waved. "Tell him we'll tip extra if he helps carry it down the stairs."

Tension swirled up Mariah's body, tension that had always lived with her, anxiety that sprung to life at the slightest trigger, but she'd always been able to burn it off—running, snowboarding, lifting weights, whatever. "But that's not how this works!"

Veronica ignored her. At least it kind of seemed that way, and wasn't *she* the boss of this whole thing? But how did you boss somebody older than you? And maybe Veronica was doing what needed doing, too, efficiently emptying cubes and placing other things in them. "Wear your warm coat," she said, tossing it at Mariah, who automatically reached out to grab the puffy jacket, forgetting she couldn't always move the way she thought. A wrenching pain burned through her leg and hip, and she yelped, but she caught the fabric of the coat in her hand. It was quite satisfying.

"You okay?"

"Yep."

The Uber driver appeared at the door, a small, lean man in his fifties with black hair neatly combed away from his face. Veronica said, "Hi, what's your name?"

He smiled, apparently undaunted by the mess in front of him. "Jorge."

"Jorge, glad to meet you. I'm Veronica and this is Mariah, and I'm almost done here even though it doesn't look like it. You can start with the bag on the porch. I'll be finished with this in a minute."

"No hurry," Jorge said.

Veronica had opened and emptied the packing cubes and now repacked them and tucked them into the small case. "Cosmetics and things like that?"

Mariah shrugged. "I don't really wear makeup, and I figure the hotels will all have soap and shampoo."

"Ah, youth," Veronica said, and closed the big suitcase. "That should be fine until you get back, right?"

"Yes."

"All right, then." She closed the small case, click-click, tugged it upright. She brushed off the knees of her pants as she stood up, and Mariah had a moment of extreme longing to be able to move like that, with such easy grace. "Let's get out of here."

CHAPTER SEVEN

When they boarded the plane, Veronica realized they were seated in first class. First class! She sat in the little pod with its bedding package and just absorbed it for a minute.

She took a photo and sent it to Jenna, then settled in, backpack at her feet so she could reach her stash of gum and lotion and the mints she liked when she flew, not that it had been all that often in her life, honestly. Her honeymoon to Paris, short and sweet. A couple of times with Spence to conferences. He had presented academic talks around the world, but she'd only gone with him to Vancouver, Canada, which was why she had applied for a new passport in the first place, and then a thrilling one to Italy when they celebrated their twenty-year anniversary. That trip had kindled something deep in her, a longing she'd almost been unable to admit to herself: What if she could see the world, be one of those people who'd been to sixty countries?

How many countries were there in the world, anyway? She googled for the answer as the plane filled around her.

There were 195. So many!

A text popped up on her screen, from Spence. Do you have a minute to talk?

Sorry. On the plane, about to turn off the phone.

Now? You're really doing this?

She scowled at the screen. She'd told him her itinerary the day before yesterday. Yes, she typed with more than a little satisfaction. I'm really doing it.

You don't know anything about
this woman.

> I know enough. She's paying me
> to be her companion for a month
> of international travel. I'll try to
> suffer through.

Can you just talk for a minute?

Veronica felt a sting of obligation. They were coparents, after all, and she'd resolved to avoid as much of the nastiness of divorce as possible, even if she was the wronged party.

But the aisles were full of people, and her heart was filled with a sense of anticipation, and she wanted to enjoy it. Sorry. I'll try you from London.

It's just the settlement. I *really* need
you to sign that amendment. I'm
feeling the pressure.

Veronica felt a thud of embarrassment. Why did she keep thinking he was somebody better than he was? Whatever happened right now was him getting her to sign the paper—including the sex, she was sure.

The alimony award had been substantial, more than she'd expected by twice, but when she protested, her lawyer, a hard-eyed woman of seventy who'd been a divorce attorney for more than forty years, said, "It's never going to be enough to make up for the financial comfort you've lost. Take the money and run."

Sorry, she texted. No time. Gotta go.

She turned off the phone and watched bags being loaded on another plane through a window across the aisle. Mindlessly, she found herself about to gnaw on her left thumbnail and stopped in time, tucking it into her palm for safety.

What are you feeling?

So many things. It might not be the easiest job of all time. Mariah seemed both prickly and vulnerable. Clearly, she had been badly injured. Snowboarding was a dangerous sport, even for the young.

Mariah made her think of her own kids, but there was something more to Mariah, an aura of weariness that went beyond sorrow. She was grieving the loss of her mother, obviously, because the trip was all about finishing a project her mother had left behind.

What else was going on there?

~

As the plane found its altitude, Veronica opened her tablet and pulled up the materials Mariah had sent to her about her mom's project. Rachel Ellsworth, Mariah's mother, had assembled a loose set of notes for a book about cafés. There wasn't a huge amount of information, but Veronica could sense a shape to it, in keeping with the woman's previous work, most of it set in the intersection between travel and food. She had downloaded a couple of the previous books to get a feel for what Rachel had done, and planned to read them on the plane. They both seemed written with an eye toward popularity and delving deeply into the culture and background of her subject. The one she planned to read on the plane explored Mexican food across the southwest, comparing

Tex-Mex, Californian, and New Mexico versions of the same foods, with stories and lore and particular restaurants highlighted.

After a little while, she switched to her own project, a thesis on Elsie Turner, a little-known Bloomsbury artist Veronica had abandoned when she got married. She'd been so eager to create her family that she had turned her back on her academic work without a blink. Spence was happy enough to have her focus on their family, on him.

Never a great idea, she thought now. *Never, ever put all your eggs in one basket.*

She'd been thinking of her thesis quite a lot lately. It was exciting to imagine they'd be in London, that she might have a chance to explore Bloomsbury, where the subject of her thesis, Elsie, had lived.

Elsie had been connected to the infamous Bloomsbury group, a network of writers and artists in the early twentieth century. Elsie had grown up in India until her father had inherited his title from an older brother who died of typhus. Her life had changed utterly, from the mysteries and heat of the British Raj to the misty, damp world of privilege she entered at the age of fifteen.

Veronica had stumbled over a handful of Elsie's paintings when she'd been casting about for a subject for her thesis. Elsie had struggled to make her art in a patriarchal world, trying (and failing) to avoid marriage so she could live on her own terms.

Leafing through her original notes, Veronica remembered how moved she'd been by Elsie's struggle to avoid marriage.

Had her younger self really not noticed the parallel? Veronica had thrown her studies aside to marry, and her spouse really had controlled her life in many ways.

She shook her head.

It was surprising, really, that no one had written about her before, but aside from a handful of footnotes in various other biographies, there wasn't much. Veronica's advisor had discouraged the project, citing the challenges, but she had been insistent. She'd spent six months in dusty archives, both in Boulder and at Yale, before being swept into Spence's fantasy of their lives together.

She found herself sighing. It would be impossible to call the choice a mistake, since she'd had three kids she adored, and that graceful home, her beautiful garden.

But now she had a chance to redeem herself as a scholar. Before leaving home, she'd scanned the research and the bits of writing she'd done on Elsie all those years ago. Veronica pulled up the file of photographs, showing a dark-haired woman with enormous luminous eyes and the sober mouth of old photos.

I haven't forgotten you.

The promise was as much to herself as to Elsie.

CHAPTER EIGHT

Mariah curled into her window seat, pulling a blanket she'd carried on around her. It was extra soft, the kind of blanket her mother loved to drape over the side of couches and armchairs. Buckled in, complimentary mimosa at her elbow, she scrolled through the downloaded podcasts on her phone, and double-checked the TV and movies on her tablet. In her ears, Taylor Swift sang about a broken heart.

Weirdly, Taylor had been her mother's favorite, not Mariah's, but the young pop star had grown on her. Mariah had made sure the funeral music was Taylor heavy.

Not that she'd been able to attend. She'd been far too badly injured to leave the hospital at that point. Aunt Jill had taped every minute of it for her, the packed church, the speeches, the procession out through the front doors. Mariah had been unable to watch it, but she had it. Eventually, she would get to it.

The flight attendant paused beside her. Mariah had taken a pain killer just before they boarded, and it was kicking in nicely now, blurring the edges of her emotions as well as the ever-present ache in her thigh and hip. She watched Veronica setting up her space, creating a little room.

She saw Mariah watching her. "I've never had such a great seat before," she said quietly. "So cool!"

So cool. It was exactly what her mother would have said. The drugs in her system blunted the sting of the echo, said in almost the same tone of voice. She was able to smile, at least halfway. "Makes it a lot easier to sleep."

"I'm sure." She waved a paperback book, a thick one, with worn pages. "But I'm also looking forward to a serious reading session."

"Who reads paper books anymore?" Mariah said without thinking. The drugs also lowered her social inhibitions, and she wasn't exactly known for biting her tongue. A woman in a man's sport couldn't afford to play nice.

To her credit, Veronica chuckled and picked up a small, leather-covered e-reader. "I read both ways, but sometimes there's just something comforting about paper." She held it to her nose and sniffed, nodding. "Do you like to read?"

"Sometimes. I haven't had the best concentration since—" She gestured at her leg. "A year of surgeries, basically."

"I can't imagine," Veronica said, and Mariah liked her for saying it that way, that she couldn't imagine, rather than she *could* imagine. "What did you like before that?"

"Um. Lots of things, really. Stories about adventure, you know, like the Iditarod and stuff like that." She sought more detail, and the titles floated around her mind like they were cushioned in clouds. "My favorite book as a kid was *The Call of the Wild*. I still like novels, sometimes, but they have to move fast."

"That tracks," she said. "I read a couple of things recently I can recommend, if you like."

"Thanks. I'm going to be pretty doped up within an hour, so maybe not today."

"Okay. Is there anything you need from me?"

"No. I'll just sleep, probably."

"Well, I'm right here."

The flight attendant brought the water, and Veronica worked her eyebrows, whispering dramatically, "It's real glass."

She didn't laugh, but she could feel the sides of her mouth lift.

Mariah waited until the lights were all the way down and pulled out her flask, a carved silver beauty she'd stolen from a boyfriend who'd dumped her after she won a race and he lost. Petty bastard. She showed him. The flask was loaded with cinnamon vodka, and a few sips killed the pain in her leg and back a lot faster than oxy. Still, a person had to be sure not to OD or something stupid like that, and she paced herself.

It wasn't her first major injury. Three times before, she'd faced a stretch of injury, pain, and recovery, starting with a torn ACL at the age of thirteen. The others had all been repairable with surgery and physical therapy, but there was no coming back from this one. Not with a three-inch rod in her thigh.

Still, the process was the same, the mental process and the physical process. Her team, her former team now that she'd fired them officially, poor saps, had tried to get her to go to trauma counseling, but she didn't need any of that shit. She was an athlete with plenty of time in the trenches. It would take longer this time, but it had really only been sixteen months. By the time she hit the two-year mark next August, she'd be over it.

Physically, probably not. She hated that, but you didn't get anywhere making up stories. Her body would never again be up to the feats of athleticism that had marked her life before.

Mentally, she had more to do. She saw that. This trip was part of the process. It was her aunt Jill's idea to complete the research her mom had been doing on cafés and then maybe pull the research together into what? A book? That was what her mom had planned, but that wasn't really Mariah's forte. Maybe she'd hire someone to ghostwrite it.

She glanced across the aisle at her companion, tidy even at rest, her blanket pulled up to her neck as she leafed through the book in her lap. Maybe she'd be good enough at writing to want the job.

But Mariah didn't have to decide that part right now. As the warmth of the vodka and oxy spread through her body, she opened the file with her mother's notes. Several cafés had been documented by Rachel already, the iconic Russian Tea Room in NYC, and in Mariah's opinion, the overly touristy Sally Lunn's in Bath. She'd visited with her mother on a trip when she'd graduated high school on time, a bribe because Mariah wanted to quit school and hit the circuit. Her mother had adamantly refused—citing the stats on injuries and washed-up athletes until Mariah finally gave in.

And look who'd turned out to be right.

She refocused on the list of cafés, but the pills and booze had done their work, and she fell asleep, to dream of a trip when nothing had yet gone wrong, and her mother was still alive, and the whole world spread in front of her like a yellow-brick road.

CHAPTER NINE

The plane grew quiet and dark as they flew. Veronica tracked the flight on the screen in front of her, delighted to see Hudson Bay, then the Atlantic. She'd tucked herself in after dinner, legs up and pillow propped under her neck, and had been happily reading ever since, carted away to the world of the novel she was reading. Mariah was out cold, curled up beneath the velour blanket she'd carried on. She hadn't stirred for dinner, which was maybe a mistake, especially as she'd taken something. For sleep? For pain?

It was as they crossed below the tip of Greenland that Mariah began to whimper. It was slight at first, and Veronica just glanced across the aisle. But in a few minutes, the whimpers grew louder, and she started moving restlessly, talking incoherently. Her hand rubbed her thigh, and she gave a single, sharp cry.

The flight attendant appeared at the doorway, but Veronica waved her back, unbuckling and standing to bend into Mariah's pod. "Mariah," she called quietly, then put her hand on her arm. "Wake up, honey, it's only a dream." She winced when she heard the *honey* land—she didn't want to create that dynamic here, although she could feel the need to mother this lost girl. "Wake up."

Mariah bolted up, slammed into her seat belt, and made a soft cry. "Shit!" She grabbed her leg. "Why are you waking me up? Oh my God, my leg is on fire."

"You were crying out in your sleep. I thought you might need more meds."

Mariah blinked up at her blearily. "In my sleep?"

"Yes. Can you get the pills easily?"

"Um. I don't know. They're in that little bag." She pointed to a small purse hung on a hook.

Veronica handed her the bag. "Do you think you might need some food and something to drink? You don't want to land all dehydrated." She glanced toward the galley where the flight attendant stood at the ready and headed up the aisle. "Is there anything she can eat, bananas or some yogurt, maybe both?"

"Yes. I'll bring it right now."

"Maybe some fresh water, too."

"Of course."

Mariah was rubbing her leg when Veronica returned, and her face was the color of lime juice, entirely too pale and faintly green. She rubbed her leg up and down, up and down. "Will you help me? I need to walk it off."

Veronica offered her hand, and Mariah limped down the aisle by herself, turned in the narrow space by the bathrooms, came back, and repeated the circle several times. The flight attendant offered Veronica the yogurt and fruit. "Anything else you need?"

"Not right now."

On the third rotation, Mariah's face was less pinched, and some of the color had come back to her cheeks. She paused at the chair and let go of a big breath. "Thanks. I'll be okay now."

Veronica stepped back to give her space to get back into her pod, then when she was settled, offered the food. Mariah shook her head. "I can't right now."

It took a lot for the mothering part of her not to insist she eat something with the meds, have something to drink, make sure she didn't mess up her system with whatever she was taking. She had noticed that Mariah hadn't eaten any dinner, only drank two mini bottles of wine and went to sleep. "Maybe try in a little while? It won't hurt anything to have them handy."

For a moment, the food hung between them in Veronica's outstretched hands. Annoyance and something darker snapped over Mariah's face. She snatched the food. "Fine. Now I'm good, okay?"

Veronica settled back into her own space and picked up her book, glancing over at Mariah periodically. This could be more challenging than she'd thought.

PART TWO

LONDON

Travel brings power and love back into your life.

—*Rumi Jalalud-Din*

CHAPTER TEN

Veronica realized within five minutes of landing that her employer was more than a little drunk. Or drugged. It was hard to wake her, and then she was groggy—and cranky—as they made their way through the long snaking customs lines. Veronica had raised three teenagers and knew to simply refuse to engage, though she made a mental note to have a little chat about it before their next flight.

Once they got through the line, they had to wait for another half hour for their bags. The whole time, Mariah was bleary eyed and bad tempered, snapping at a woman who bumped them as she passed with a big suitcase.

"She's just cranky," Veronica said to the woman, who looked alarmed and hurried by. "Maybe don't spit on the passersby," she said mildly.

"She ran over my foot! The sore leg."

"It's crowded. She didn't do it on purpose."

"Don't," Mariah said with venom. "You're not my mom."

"That's true. But I am your companion and deserve not to be embarrassed."

She glared through red-rimmed eyes. "Fine."

Veronica rescued the bags, and they made their way into the main terminal. "I think it might be a good idea to get a quick meal," she said. "Some tomato juice for the . . . grogginess?"

"Henry is meeting us."

"Henry?"

"The photographer my mom wanted for the book. They're old friends."

Veronica blinked, scanning faces for anyone who looked like a photographer. "Okay. Is he traveling with us?"

"He's not staying with us, but he'll do some driving and that kind of thing."

"Do you know what he looks like?"

"Yeah, they were friends from, like, college days."

Veronica stood by as Mariah scanned the waiting people. Even this gave her a thrill, seeing so many faces and modes of dress. A swell of excitement penetrated the slight anxiety of arrival and not having a clear plan. She liked a plan.

"I don't see him." Mariah exhaled heavily. "There's a café. Let's get something." She set off limping. Veronica pulled the bags, reminding herself that this was not her child, but her employer, and this was what she'd signed on for.

And her own need for caffeine had hardly been touched. They ordered lattes and tomato juice. Veronica lingered over the pastries, not wanting to overindulge but aware that she was very, very hungry. She finally chose a flaky-looking Danish with apricot filling and a sugar glaze. Mariah took her time, too, and finally chose a croissant and an enormous cookie. She carried the bags and cups while Veronica wheeled the suitcases, and they settled where they could see the open area outside arrivals.

"What does Henry look like?" Veronica asked, taking her pastry out of the white paper bag, leaning in to take a grounding whiff of butter and yeast and the reassuring sweetness of apricot.

Mariah gulped tomato juice, all of it at once like she was chugging a beer, one finger raised. She slammed it down and took a breath, wiping her face with a paper napkin. "That was great." In seconds, her color was better. It was like watching a video-game character revive. "Henry's tall and skinny and kind of eccentric looking. Not like a war photographer, actually. More like a . . . I don't know. You'll see."

Veronica squinted into the distance, trying to imagine what an eccentric war photographer would look like. "He's a war photographer, and he's going to shoot pictures of cafés?"

"He'll do a great job."

Veronica took a delicate bite from the edge of the pastry, trying to catch a bit of sugar with the dough. It crumbled exactly right, dough layered with butter, baked to a perfect crispy brown. "Mmm," she said with approval, and took another, bigger bite. Pretty dry, but decent. Licking sugar off her fingers, she asked, "What is this book, exactly? Do you have an outline, or a prototype or anything? I'm not sure what we're going to be looking for when we visit the spots on this list."

"I don't really know a lot, honestly. I brought all her notes, but I'm not a writer, so . . ." She shrugged. "I think Henry knows more."

Unease settled with prickly edges against her solar plexus. This was the opposite of having a plan. She pinched off a teeny tiny piece of the pastry and settled it in her mouth. It was too small to taste, and she took another one, bigger. "Can you make me copies of all that material?"

"That's the stuff I already sent you." She wolfed down bites of her pastry like she might lose the chance if she didn't hurry up. Brushing her chin and the front of her T-shirt, she said, "Is there, like, a special way to do research?"

"Not necessarily, but it would be good to have some background. History of the place, who owned it first, how it started, why she chose the particular places she wanted to write about."

"And you downloaded some of her other books, right?"

"Yes." Veronica picked up the pastry and took another bite, which technically took her over the halfway mark. Fruit spilled into her mouth, slightly spiced with something, and she closed her eyes to see if she could figure out what it was. Nutmeg? No, maybe allspice.

So good.

Spying someone in the crowd, Mariah waved vigorously. "There's Henry."

The man was well over six feet tall, with darkly tanned skin and salt-and-pepper hair grown a bit too long. Veronica would not have called him skinny, though. Rangy, long limbed.

Mariah leaped up and greeted him with a little cry. He wrapped her in a bear hug. They clung to each other for a long moment, and Veronica noted the tears on Mariah's face. This was someone important.

In a gravelly voice, Henry said, "How're you holding up?"

"It's only been three weeks since you've seen me," Mariah said wryly. She gestured toward Veronica. "This is my assistant. She was asking me about the background of the places we're shooting."

His attention shifted. Without expression he held out a big hand. No jewelry, no watch. "Henry Spinuzza," he said. His voice was intensely deep, resonant, and his face showed the years he'd spent in the elements—creases around his eyes, cheeks weathered.

"Veronica Barrington. Nice to meet you."

"You're not what I was expecting in a companion," he said, gaze direct.

"Yeah. I get that." But she didn't know what else to add.

"Are you ready?" His accent was New Jersey, softened but still distinct. "We should have a window after the morning traffic."

Mariah allowed herself to be helped up, but she swayed a little unsteadily. He grasped her elbow and glanced toward Veronica, eyebrows up in a question. Veronica nodded.

Mariah reached back and grabbed the rest of the Danish. "You're not going to eat this, right?"

"No. Go ahead."

She did, wiping her fingers quickly on the last of the napkins.

In addition to having Mariah lean on him, Henry dragged one of the bags, which freed Veronica to look around. She took in the various languages and accents, so many different kinds of people. A young woman in a bright-pink hijab spoke a quick lyrical language into her phone. A straw-thin businessman in a blue suit and pointed shoes huffed around her. Men with placards, looking as serious as bodyguards, stood near the exit doors. She peered into kiosks and saw candy she'd never heard of lined up in rows, and made a mental note to try them, and an advertisement for a biscuit she wasn't sure was sweet or savory.

Outside, the air was wet and cold. Veronica was glad of her lightweight, very warm ski jacket, a piece of clothing that had cost half of her now-rent. It was totally worth it as they moved slowly for the sake of Mariah, who was also cloaked in a high-end puffer coat. At last they arrived at a midsize SUV-style car, black and ordinary. Or so she thought until she saw the Range Rover name on the tailgate.

Interesting. Her life did not usually include first-class flights or luxury vehicles.

Henry loaded the back with their bags. Veronica started to get into the back seat, but Mariah stopped her. "I need to lie down."

"Of course." She opened the front door, but of course the steering wheel was on the opposite side, and with an embarrassed chuckle, she rounded the car and got in. Mariah was already spread out in the back, her coat over her face. Veronica half grinned, thinking she'd be snoring any second.

Henry glanced over the seat and shook his head. "Pills?" he asked.

"Maybe? I think she has a flask, too."

"I can hear you," Mariah said. "Yes, to both."

"Can you not kill yourself, please?" Henry said into the rearview mirror.

"I'm careful," Mariah mumbled.

"That's what they all say. And they're just as dead."

"Fine," she said with a growl. "I'm not dead, though, so can you let me sleep off this hangover?"

Henry gave a curt nod, adjusted the mirror, and pulled out. "Do you mind if I play music?"

It surprised her that he'd even ask. "Of course not. It's your car."

He plugged in his phone and a mellow brand of jazz emerged. Of course it would be cool. She smiled.

"What?" he asked. "Does this bring back memories?"

"Not at all." She tried to think of a way to say what she thought without sounding like an idiot. "Just"—she spread a hand toward the radio—"I'm so not surprised that you'd like something hip like jazz."

He slowed at the entrance to the parking structure, waiting for traffic, glancing over. His eyes were a clear hazel-y green. "Am I hip?"

"Maybe," she ventured. "You're a photographer in London. You're driving a pretty fancy car. That's seems kind of hip."

He shifted, pulling into traffic. "I guess. I don't live in London, though. I'm just here for this."

"The book, you mean?"

"Partly. It's really for Rachel."

"Mariah's mother?"

He nodded. "She'd want somebody to be in Mariah's corner."

"Are you familiar with the project?"

"A little. She'd been working on it in the background for a while. We were in Morocco a few years ago, and she got into it. We did some planning, but nothing all that detailed. I'm not sure what Mariah has now."

"I can still hear you," Mariah said from the back.

"We don't care," Henry called back. "Jump in any time."

Henry continued, "I think her main fascination is—was—with Parsi cafés. Are you familiar?"

His voice was resonant enough that she wondered if he'd done on-screen reporting himself. "I'm not," she said.

"The Parsis arrived in India a long time ago, around the seventh century. They were fleeing persecution, and they needed to find a new place to live, so they went to northern India."

"Say more?"

"I don't know a huge amount about the history, but the cafés were big in the 1920s and '30s." He changed lanes. "The food is a mix between Persian and Indian. The cafés are known for a kind of art deco look, and the buns they make. It was my idea to start with Dishoom in

London because it's a modern take, but they're based on the old cafés in Mumbai."

All the talk of food made her stomach growl. Loudly. She clapped a hand over it, appalled. "Sorry."

"I'm always starving when I land. They have good room service at this hotel."

"Thanks." She glanced at her phone, wondered if there were messages. She hadn't turned it back on in order to avoid charges.

Henry said, "There's Wi-Fi in the car."

"Cool." She powered it on, pleased when she was prompted to connect to Wi-Fi. A long line of texts scrolled over her screen, some from her kids, and her friend Amber, and also Spence. Several from him, which twisted a rope of anxiety in her gut.

Or maybe she was just hungry.

She didn't want to hear from Spence and maybe could pretend she didn't get his messages. Instead, she started with Jenna, who'd texted eleven times over the course of the previous day, which wasn't even slightly unusual. Most of it was just chat, staying in touch. The last was Text me when you get there or I'll be worried. G'night!

She texted back, Here, safe. On the way to my hotel. ttys

She answered the others, then opened Spence's. Call me when you can. Trouble with Tim.

Rolling her eyes, she put the phone in her bag. Nope. Maybe she wouldn't answer him at all for the entire trip. How freeing would that be?

Very. But she knew she wouldn't stick to it. He deserved her attention when it came to the kids.

"Bad news?"

"Did I sigh? Just an annoying ex."

He smoothly joined traffic on a busy throughway. "Block him. Or her."

"My ex-husband. He's in charge of my kids while I'm gone, so that's not all that workable."

"There's always email," he said mildly.

Veronica nodded, but she knew she wouldn't tell him to email her. What if there was an emergency?

Watching traffic whiz by, she realized she felt ever so slightly nauseated at the way the cars moved on the opposite side of the road than she was used to, and took a breath, and looked away, focusing on his hands on the steering wheel. A thick scar ribboned from his little finger around his wrist.

"I almost lost my hand," he said, noticing. He lifted his pinky.

"Let me guess. You were lost in the jungle and ran into a bandit with a machete?"

He let go of a small, low chuckle. "No."

"Axe?"

"Fell out of the back of a truck."

Veronica tsked. "That is *not* a very good story."

He glanced at her. "Maybe you could help me make one up."

She looked back. Was he flirting a little bit? She'd been so lost in her head that she'd kind of forgotten what that might be like.

Maybe she'd been flirting first. "I bet I could come up with something good."

"Writer?"

"No. A reader."

"Yeah? Me, too. What do you like?"

"Everything, honestly," she said. "Nothing too gruesome in mysteries or horror, but most of the rest. Fiction, though, almost completely. Do you read novels?"

"Sure. I also read a lot of history." He pointed to a thick paperback in the well between the seats. "That's my current."

She pulled it out curiously. The pages were worn, and a rubber band held it together. *A History of the Mughal Empire.* "Not sure I know who the Mughals are," she said. "I'm thinking . . . Genghis Khan?"

He glanced at her. "Not bad. He was one of the originals, though they don't really like to claim him. He was a bit of a monster."

"I'll have to check this out," she said.

"Especially for the India leg of the trip."

"Thanks."

They left the highway and wound through busy streets, past a long park and rows of tall apartments, and slowed on a street full of shops that served quick food and offered phones, other minor tech products, and cheap clothes. It reminded her of the area near the main campus in Boulder. "Is there a university nearby?"

"Not sure. The British Museum is around the corner, but I don't really know the neighborhood otherwise."

Mariah came to life in the back seat, rising like a zombie and with about that much grooming. Her hair was wild, and mascara had smeared under her eyes. "There's something over there somewhere." She caught sight of herself in the rearview mirror and used a licked finger to try and rub some of the mascara away. It wasn't successful.

"Here we are, guys."

"Guys?" Mariah echoed.

"I didn't say *ladies*." He turned on the hazard lights and jumped out, waving at an annoyed driver behind him. Veronica hurried around to the back to take the bags, while Mariah tumbled out, pulling her hoodie over her hair. She cried out when she landed and Veronica left the bags to steady her. "You good?"

"Yeah." She accepted an embrace from Henry, who wrapped her up in a bear hug, kissing her head. The big, ready affection made Veronica like him more.

As she started toward the door with the bags, one in each hand, he said, "At least let me get one of them to the door."

"We'll see you for dinner tonight?" Mariah asked.

"Tomorrow. I've got some work to do."

"You're working for me, aren't you?"

"Something else came up. Lucrative."

"Huh. Must be a woman."

He shrugged, leaving the bag in the doorway and waving himself away.

Veronica looked across the street to the ornate hotel, which her brain suddenly told her was the Fitzroy, some tidbit of knowledge squirreled away in her research. "Are we in the Bloomsbury neighborhood?"

"Um . . ." Mariah looked around. "Maybe?"

A shiver moved down her arms at the coincidence. Or synchronicity, as her friend Amber would have said. Veronica had never been one much for woo-woo things, but this was hard to ignore.

Somewhere in this stretch of city blocks, Elsie Turner had lived and loved. Veronica could hardly wait to walk in her footsteps.

CHAPTER ELEVEN

Mariah had not expected it to be so hard to come back to the hotel where she'd stayed with her mom several years before, way before the pandemic. The place smelled the same, both fresh and softly mildewy. They took the elevator down to the check-in desk and a very elegant young woman greeted them. "Veronica, will you?" Mariah said, handing over her phone with the reservation and a credit card.

"Of course."

Mariah sat down on the velvet couch, trying to ignore the little cold spot just to her left. She didn't have the energy to deal with a presence at the moment. There were probably a lot in such an old building.

The drag of her hangover clouded everything, and her very blood ached with the weight of the trip and the sitting in one position and cinnamon vodka. She wanted to pop a painkiller, but until she'd had a shower and something to eat, that seemed like a bad idea.

Veronica looked a little worse for wear, too, her clothes wrinkled, her hair losing the smoothness of her blowout, but she handled everything like a mom. Mariah was glad. The two of them rode the elevator up to the fourth floor and opened the doors to a corner suite with two bedrooms, a tiny kitchen, and a small living area overlooking Russell Square. Outside, rain had started to fall, blurring the scene.

"Oh, look," Veronica said from the window. "A red phone booth!"

"I think they left them there for tourists. There are a few around the city so people can take pictures."

"I'll have to do that." She turned. "Let's get you settled. Do you need to eat? I can run out to the café across the street, or look for a grocery store."

"Ugh, no." Mariah felt her irritability rising, a thin red buzz just beneath her skin, and took a breath. "I need food faster than that. Let's just order room service for now, and then you can go to the store. I think there's a Waitrose a few blocks away. Or there was." She sank down into the chair by the window, feeling depression creep in.

The Waitrose was there when Mariah and her mom had stayed here in 2018. Mariah had done well in the PyeongChang Olympics, but had injured her shoulder badly enough that she'd needed to give it a full-on rest.

Rachel whisked her off to Europe. They'd explored London, eating everywhere because that was what you did with Rachel, and they met Henry in Morocco. Mariah had hoped their romance would reignite there—she always wanted them to get back together—but it didn't happen. They were friends. Would stay friends.

Rachel had slipped into a new relationship with a food editor, but Henry stuck around in Mariah's life. He showed up at competitions sometimes, and she had a zillion great action shots of her career that he'd taken. He was the only man in her life who could even remotely have been called a father figure, and she was glad he was on this trip.

"What do you want from room service?" Veronica asked. She'd already pulled up a menu on her tablet.

"Uh." Her stomach growled and protested in two different directions. "Oatmeal with bananas, if they have them. Whole-grain toast with butter and jam. A good-size pot of tea with lots of sugar and milk." She paused, feeling into her body for anything else. "And Marmite." Rubbing her thigh in a circular motion, she added, "And whatever you want."

"I'm not that hungry," Veronica said. "I'll just have some tea and toast."

"Dude, we haven't had a meal in twelve hours. Don't be shy. Eat." She pulled an ottoman over to prop up her leg. "Your meals are covered, and you can't be weird about it."

"I'm not being weird," Veronica said, and frowned. She looked over the menu. "Just feels like a lot."

"What looks really good?"

"Brioche french toast, honestly."

"Order that."

"No, that's too much food. We've been sitting for two days. I'll feel bloated."

Mariah shrugged and opened her phone, trying to distract herself from the ache in her leg and hip. The hip hadn't been damaged in the original incident, but it had been really touchy with all the unevenness in her walk. She tried to walk steadily, but there was nearly an inch difference in the lengths of her legs, so it wasn't easy. It seemed like a lot, and at first she'd been horrified, but then a plainspoken nurse said, "They saved your leg, sweetheart. That wasn't a given."

Veronica picked up the phone and ordered oatmeal for two, and toast, and tea, and bananas. Mariah called out, "And bacon! Two orders!" After Veronica gave the order, Mariah said, "They have the best bacon in England. Just wait."

"While we wait, I'll get unpacked. I mean, if we're going to be in this hotel for a bit."

She was way more type A than people Mariah knew. Irritation slithered through her veins, snapped against her forehead, and she carefully didn't look at Veronica. "A week at least, I think. Maybe two. You can check the schedule I gave you."

"Right." Veronica gestured between the two rooms. "Should I choose, or do you want to look?"

Mariah had been about to click a TikTok with a cake pour, and the interruption tweaked another thread of irritation. "Fuck, man. I don't care. Just pick one."

Veronica stood where she was, her cheeks going red. She looked so suburban with that little swingy haircut and her tidy cargo pants and tucked-in blouse. She was a cliché of a soccer mom. How would Mariah spend *three or four weeks* with this person?

But instead of saying anything, Veronica grabbed her suitcase and opened the door on the left side of the room. Mariah ignored her, hearing drawers open and close. Zippers shutting. The noises themselves aggravated her and she—

Took a breath. She really would not be able to do this without help, and if she pissed off Veronica first thing, it would be a problem.

Mariah's worst character trait was her impatience and abruptness. A lot of people on the circuit and in the media disliked her because of it. She'd been working on it for years without showing a lot of progress. They called her Snape on the slopes for her irritability.

But it could be a long trip if they didn't get along. She struggled to her feet and limped to the doorway. "Look," she said, "I'm kind of known for being a dick, and I'm sorry. I'm not feeling great, and I'm starving, and I'm meaner than hell when I'm hungry, so it's nothing personal." She took in the room. "Wow, this is nice."

"It is," Veronica agreed. "But it is personal when you swear at me. Please don't do that."

A blister of annoyance broke over the top of Mariah's eyebrows. She wanted to snap, *Get a fucking life, lady,* but forced herself to nod. "Sorry."

"When I'm finished here, I'll get your stuff in your room."

"Cool. I mean, thank you. That would be great."

Veronica gave her a half smile that looked forced. Mariah turned away to avoid snapping again.

What had she gotten herself into? Maybe they should just forget the whole thing and go home.

But first she had to get some rest.

CHAPTER TWELVE

After they ate, Veronica called up a map on her phone using the Wi-Fi, saved it, and turned off her phone, which was well into the yellow on battery power. She'd charge it up when she got back, but the errand wouldn't take long. The grocery store was only a few blocks away.

Mariah warned her that it was going to get dark early, but the rain had slowed, and it was only midafternoon. Veronica desperately wanted to stay awake a little longer. Mariah wasn't even attempting it. She ate everything she'd ordered, poured down most of the pot of tea, and limped into her bedroom.

She didn't even comment on the fact that she had the lesser of the two rooms and when Veronica would have helped her get situated, she waved her away. "I don't really unpack," she said.

Like a man, Veronica thought, and was embarrassed by the sexism in the observation, but it came to her twice—also while Mariah wolfed down everything on the tray as Veronica nibbled her toast. In fact, her stomach was still growly, and she wished she'd eaten more, but she didn't want to go home busting out of her clothes, and she'd had zero exercise the past few days.

The walk would help, and maybe she could pick up some food that wouldn't feel so extravagant. Bacon! She couldn't even remember the last time she'd eaten it, though she'd taken one piece and found it ridiculously delicious. She'd have to watch herself.

Pulling up her hood against the drizzle, she tried to glance at the map on her phone as little as possible. The street was not exactly thick with humans, but there were more than she would have expected on such a rainy day. They clambered out of a bus, and ducked in and out of shops and pubs. They carried umbrellas and huddled under them without looking around, feet sloshing through puddles on the pavement. At the corner, a car splashed her ankles with water, which muddied her pants.

She shrugged it off, determined to show up for this. All of it. Rain pelting down, streaking the face of her phone. Mud splashing her. She thought of Elsie and wondered if it looked the same as it had a hundred years ago. Many of the buildings had probably been the same. She looked around curiously at the slim pharmacy tucked between a bakery and launderette. A tiny café smelled of roasting meat, its doorway and windows adorned with plastic flowers.

Two blocks up, turn right. The secondary street was more of a lane, with rows of brick buildings that were clearly apartments and less grand hotels. She looked across the uneven street to see a calico cat looking out of an upper story window. In another was a tangle of plants. In a third, a woman talked on the phone, staring out the window, her chin up in what looked like defiance.

The road dead-ended in a shopping center. Whew. *That was easy,* Veronica thought, and tucked her phone in her pocket. She had a credit card Mariah had given her, so she didn't have to worry about keeping track of her budget. Such luxury! Her means had been quite thin the past year.

Taking a shopping cart that was much smaller than any she'd encountered before, she made her way around the aisles, promising herself she could come back when she had more time.

But within moments, she was delighting in the offerings she'd never seen. Quail eggs right next to the chicken eggs, all of them on the shelf, not in the fridge. Goat cheese and beetroot pasta, "seriously extra strong" cheddar cheese, frozen fish pie, Thai curry soup, and dozens of packaged Indian and Chinese ready meals. It was hard not to want to put everything in the cart, just to taste them, but she had to carry whatever she bought. She could always come back. In the produce aisle, she gathered bananas and grapes and baby carrots; some pots of yogurt and a quart of milk, cheese and crackers. In time, she'd find out what Mariah liked eating, but for now, this would be enough.

Her mood was light as she stepped outside. The gloaming had started to gather on the edges of the sky. Cold rose from the ground. For a moment she stood just outside the door, trying to get her bearings.

It didn't look the same. The street she'd walked to get here wasn't there.

Maybe she'd just come out the wrong door, she thought, and pulled out her phone. It was on red power, but showed her the map she'd downloaded before leaving. Of course, she wasn't connected, so it didn't reorient her to where she was now, but she could read a map, and she remembered a couple of things about the hotel. It was diagonally across the street from a park, the one with red phone booths. She found the green space on the map, and traced her way to the grocery store, and realized she'd just got turned around. No big deal.

Centering herself, she strode out, following the street that ran alongside the one she'd followed down here. She passed a few shops she thought she recognized. The rain had lifted to a mild drizzle, and she had plenty of time.

And then she came across a tube station, belching passengers out onto the wet pavement, all of them hurrying home. She imagined them going to the apartments where lights were coming on, friendly.

She began to realize she must have taken a wrong turn.

Veronica turned on her phone. A flurry of messages filled her screen, but she ignored them and opened her map. It took an agonizingly long time to refresh, and she felt power spilling out of her nearly dead phone like sugar from a bag. The marker opened—

And the phone died. "Shit."

She lifted her head. It was definitely getting dark, and colder, but somebody would know where she'd made her wrong turn. At the first shop, she went inside.

It was a grocery store, with narrow aisles and a short produce section. People lined up for the cash registers looking miserable, tired.

For a moment, she was struck again by the diversity of the space. Boulder was a student town, but it was still heavily Caucasian. This was the opposite of homogenous—people of many ages and colors and backgrounds stood in line, heads covered with hats and turbans and scarves, arms covered with brownish tweed and silky red and pattered shawls. Her heart lifted—she wasn't in Kansas anymore.

But this wasn't the venue to ask for directions. She headed back out, where the rain had picked up, slanting sideways into her face. She blinked against it, looking for a friendlier shop. A bakery was already closed. A little dark shop seemed a bit intimidating, and then she came across a café that didn't look too busy. She ducked inside and couldn't help shaking off a little, like a dog. "Hello," said a man behind the counter. It smelled wonderful, and her still-yearning stomach pulled her up to the glass, where skewers of meat and vegetables lay in steaming hues. In the back of her mind, Spence dismissed the food as too fatty, too spicy, too whatever.

But *her* mouth watered. "Is that lamb?"

"It is, madam. Would you like a plate?"

"Do you take cards?"

"Of course." He was already dishing up a hefty helping of meat and roasted onions and peppers, adding perfect rice, and a creamy dressing, and tomato cucumber salad, and a pita or naan bread, she wasn't sure which. Her stomach growled again.

She gave him the card, accepted a bag with the box of food, napkins, and plasticware, and bent down to inhale the spices. "Thank you," she breathed, and tucked the card back into her wallet.

It wasn't until she was on her way out the door that she even remembered that she wanted directions. "Can you tell me where the Morton Hotel is?"

"One block," he said, smiling. He pointed in the direction she'd been going.

She smiled and gave a lift of her chin, an old New Mexico gesture she'd never lost. Carrying her multiple bags, the food sending up a mouthwatering aroma, she entered the human flow, humming under her breath, and came across the hotel just where he'd said it would be. She must have looped back up another street. A man was coming out as she came up the steps, and he held the door. "Thank you," she said, and he tipped his hat.

The smell of the food enveloped her in the elevator, and she floated toward the room, letting herself in. Mariah had gone to bed. The rooms were dark. She turned on a lamp, put away the groceries in the little kitchen, took out a plain white glass plate and some heavy flatware, and put the kettle on to boil. She arranged the meat and vegetables and bread on the plate, carried it to the table, and sat down with it by the window overlooking the little square.

It was the kind of meal her family never liked—Spence abhorred red meat, and her children wouldn't eat lamb or veal and would have lectured her about it. But she didn't have to answer to them, or to anyone.

Breathing in the scents of spice and roasted meat, she gave herself the time to anticipate as she admired the rain on the window, the lights flashing across the street, the sense of peace she felt. Finally, she lifted her fork and began to eat.

The lamb was tender, falling off the bone, the spices exactly perfect. The tomato salad could have been mushy, but it was fresh and flecked with fresh parsley.

She didn't inhale food, ever, but she ate every single bite. Every last shred of meat. Every tiny cucumber, every corner of the pita, because it had turned out to be a pita. She thought of the people in the airport and the people in the shops, and her heart was lighter than it had been in years. Maybe decades.

It came to her softly, a question: *What do you want your life to be?*

CHAPTER THIRTEEN

Mariah slept hard.

Until she didn't, and awakened from a dream about blue boxes of macaroni and cheese tumbling across a white floor, piling up in giant mountains, burying her.

She woke up gasping for breath, panicking, and for a long moment she had no idea where she was. Hospital? Nursing facility? Home? A crack of light between the curtains showed a streetlight, and she remembered.

London.

Forcing herself upright, she hung her knees over the bed and inhaled deeply. Slowly. In. Out. She focused on the streetlight, the patters of rain against the window. Better. In a moment, she was fine. Wide awake, but fine. Her performance watch, which she couldn't help wearing even though she wasn't performing anything, said it was just after midnight.

Grabbing her cane, she hobbled into the living room area. Veronica's door was closed. It was safe to make a hot drink of some kind. On the counter were two boxes of tea, demerara sugar, hot chocolate, and a jar of instant coffee. Mariah thought wistfully of the apple-cider packets she kept at home, but she hadn't asked Veronica to get any, so it served her right.

She was used to her mom knowing what she'd want, and when. Now she had to train someone to know.

Or maybe you could do it yourself, said a reasonable part of her brain. A part that sounded very much like her mother, who threatened to stop cooking for Mariah if she didn't learn to cook. Mariah had insisted that she knew how to cook—pour the macaroni in the water and add the packet of cheese, or ask Marie Callender to do it for her. It made her mom laugh every time.

Despite not knowing her tastes, Veronica had brought back a decent variety of stuff. Mariah grabbed some yogurt and a couple of bananas, and made a cup of hot chocolate. She took it to the table by the window overlooking the dark square. Not terrible, the snack, but it left her restless. Below, a straggle of young people headed for the subway stop down the block, three or four knots of them, mostly together, it seemed. Partying, probably. One girl shouted out a laugh, and two of them ran in front.

God, how long since she'd been out for a beer with her friends? Centuries. A heat of longing pushed through her. Man. That was what she wanted. Out. Impulsively, she checked her phone to see if there were any bars or pubs close by, and she was rewarded with a long list. One was in the basement of the hotel, another across the street in the hotel facing, and a pub was just down the street. She looked down at her clothes, still rumpled from the trip. She changed into a sweater and some jeans, washed her pits and her face, and headed for the door. Her cane leaned there, and she hesitated. She'd stick out like an idiot if she had it, but she was kind of afraid to go without it.

Fuck it. She'd stand out, anyway, and she wasn't going down to make friends. Just find a beer. A big cold English pint.

The first bar, in the hotel basement, was dead. A single middle-aged man sat nursing a whiskey, scrolling through his phone.

Nope.

Outside, a crisp breeze was blowing, and she shook her upper body slightly to stay warm, waiting for the light to turn even though there were barely any cars. Pedestrians brushed by her, most of them reassuringly young, probably younger than Mariah, if she were honest.

Once the light changed, ticking loudly to count down the time, she joined the little stream. The bar in the posh hotel was too stuffy, and she didn't even climb the steps.

Her phone took her to the Oat and Hand pub. The tables in front were empty, but people stood holding pints and smoking cigarettes outside, and her neck muscles relaxed. Yes. This was more like it.

It was not packed, but fairly busy. She found a place at the bar, and struggled to get up on the high chair, which gave her a moment of extreme embarrassment until the bartender said, "Bit of a jump, init?"

"Totally."

"American," he said happily. "What can I get you, love?"

"A pint," she said, and looked for the taps. "Ale, something not too dark."

He winked and tossed down a cardboard coaster. He was fit, his lats working beneath his T-shirt, arms nicely defined. Not too tall, hair dark and a little unruly. He carried back the beer with bright eyes. "Tab?"

She shook her head and pushed a ten-pound note toward him. Mariah took a sip of beer.

"Holy fuck," she said aloud. It was cold and rich, ever so slightly bitter, but not hoppy, and it was one of the best five things she'd tasted in a year. She took another deep swallow.

The bartender grinned, dropping her change. "What brings you across the pond?"

It had been a while, but she recognized the glimmer in his eye. It stirred an almost forgotten response, across the back of her neck, down the sides of her belly. "It's complicated," she answered, "but mainly, I'm doing some research."

He leaned on the bar, his arms taut, his hands clean. "Tell me about it."

～

Two hours later, being of slightly less sound mind but only two pints in, she took him back to the hotel. Rain had started up again, but she couldn't run, could she, and he was sweet about it, holding a giant black umbrella over her head. In the elevator, he kissed her, and he knew what he was doing. She remembered all kinds of sensations that had been buried for eighteen months. She ran her hands up his strong back and opened her mouth, and they kissed until the elevator door opened, which took longer than she would have expected.

At the room, she shushed him. "I have a friend traveling with me."

He touched his finger to his lips and followed her in, through the little sitting room and into her room, where she closed the door and shed her sweater all in one gesture. He came forward and ran his hands over her bare skin, and she practically came right there, just from being in contact with other skin. There was one bad moment when she had to have help getting her jeans off and then one more when she had to stop and let a cramp in her calf pass, but he just kissed her through it, and it was good. Good enough that when she reached for him a second time a little while later, he was quite willing to engage again.

"Do you want me to go?" he asked, afterward.

She purred a little, feeling at ease in the way only sex could deliver. It was cold and wet outside, the bed warm. "You can stay, as long as you know this is it."

He grinned. "Understood."

They slept.

CHAPTER FOURTEEN

The rooms were quiet when Veronica got up. It was still dark outside, but her phone told her it was seven a.m. She made some oatmeal out of the packets she'd picked up, and some instant coffee and settled in to read her texts and emails.

Such as they were. Jenna had texted a handful of ordinary things, about her exam and a new shirt she bought, and a wish for a good time. Her friend Amber had sent a flurry, too, which was unusual.

hope ur having a good time, so
jealous ☻

court today

bad news

assfuck judge threw the book at
me

full damages

have no idea what Ima do

know ur prolly asleep. sorry. hope u dont have notifications on (better not, u idiot). really thought I might get some kind of leniency given the extenuating circumstances, and family court is usually pretty good to moms, but the bitch thinks I'm a lowlife and I knew that but still

glad one of us caught a break.

DO NOT CALL ME

just wanted to vent xoxoxoxoxo

eat a scone for me

Sipping coffee in the dark coziness of the sitting room in a ritzy hotel in London, Veronica felt a wash of guilt. She'd met Amber at a court-ordered support group. Every single step of the way, Veronica had always had a better result than Amber. She landed substantial alimony while Amber struggled to even get child support from her deadbeat ex. Veronica only had to attend three months of support group, while Amber wore an ankle bracelet. Veronica found an apartment in a nice building for a ridiculous amount of rent, and Amber had finally qualified for a rent-assisted apartment, but because of the bracelet, Amber couldn't leave Boulder. That made finding a job and a place to live doubly difficult.

Taking a breath, Veronica typed, Oh, I HATE THIS FOR YOU! To hell with that judge and loser ex and the whole stupid system—I wish I was there so you could cry on my shoulder

She smiled and continued typing. No, that's a lie and you know it. I'm glad I'm here. I have 1000 texts from Spence, but I decided I'm not going to read them today.

I will you call you when the times
match, you idiot.

She shut the phone down. Ate her oatmeal and finished her coffee. Only then did she look at Spence's texts. There were seven. They all said the same thing: I can't pay this much alimony. I'm drowning.

Seven times in a row.

Sorry, she texted. The court decided, not me.

He did not reply, because it was the middle of the night in Colorado. What a relief! She headed for the shower, feeling bold and smart. And then feeling like hell because Amber's situation was so different. She'd paid so much more than Veronica had.

It wasn't fair.

And yet, she had no idea what she could do about it.

It was heaven to be able to blow out her hair, get her modest makeup on, and look presentable in her jeans and sweater. She wanted to spend some time with the book Mariah's mother had planned. Flipping pages in a yellow notepad until she found a clean sheet, she started listing the important points from the file Mariah had sent.

Here in London, the itinerary was fairly thin—a stop in a café called Café Guli and an address in Brick Lane, which of course Veronica had heard of. A little wisp of curious excitement lifted her spirits. Maybe they could wander around a little, although that might be hard with Mariah's mobility issues.

She frowned. What were Mariah's limitations, anyway? It was hard to tell, and as a companion, Veronica needed to understand what the issues were.

Back to the notes. After London was a short jaunt to Paris, with directions. *Russell Square—>Kings Cross—>Eurostar—>Gare du Nord, Paris.*

A lot of time was allotted for London. Had the time been built in to allow for Mariah's injuries? And who had planned the route? Maybe it had been the aunt.

It would be helpful to have this information.

In the meantime, she pulled up her own research on Elsie Turner. She'd lived somewhere nearby, as had Virginia Woolf and her sister Vanessa Bell, a painter.

Of course, there might be nothing left, although even on her little walk yesterday, it felt like there were identifiable buildings from other centuries. Using the hotel Wi-Fi, she looked up maps of the area and sent them to her phone, feeling a strange new hum in her brain. It took a minute to recognize what it was—the scholarly part of her brain, buzzing with sustenance.

How long had it been? Decades and decades.

Just as the sky was lightening to show another dark day, Mariah came out of her room—with a guy. He was a tousled sort, a haze of beard on his jaw. He gave Veronica a wave as he made his way to the door and let himself out.

Veronica blinked. "Where did you find him?"

She stretched, leaning on the threshold for support. "Cute, right? At the pub down the street."

Veronica struggled with what to say. "You just went down to the pub and found a guy and brought him back? Is that like, Tinder or something?"

"Wow." Mariah grinned, showing a dimple in her left cheek. "I mean, it could have been." She rubbed her back against the doorjamb, scratching. "But he was the bartender."

"Oh." It seemed so . . . shocking. Or maybe bold. Mariah wanted what she wanted, without apology. Veronica found her voice. "He was cute."

Mariah wiggled her shoulders. "Henry will be here around ten so we can head out, if that's okay."

"Sure."

"I'm going to take a shower."

Without even thinking, Veronica asked, "Do you want breakfast?"

Mariah didn't answer immediately. She stood by the door, unmoving, and looked out the window.

Veronica felt suddenly embarrassed. "Sorry, was that wrong? I have a daughter your age, and I find myself falling into the role I'd play with her."

Mariah tucked her long hair behind her ears. Her eyes when she looked at Veronica were the clear pale blue of a winter sky. "I don't need a mom," she said, "but I would like breakfast. Scrambled eggs and oatmeal and some kind of fruit, and a big pot of coffee. Get something for yourself, too. We have a lot to do today."

"Oh, I had a big meal last night when I got back. I'm okay."

"I'm gonna need you to eat something, V."

Not Ronny, which she hated. V. She liked it. "Okay. I'll eat."

~

During the room service meal—Veronica had ordered a slice of toast and one egg, scrambled—Mariah ate heartily and gulped down copious amounts of coffee with cream and sugar. Her skin had that youthful luminosity that faded with time, and the vigorous outdoorsy good looks that would sell a million copies of *Outside* magazine. "What's the agenda today?" Veronica asked.

"I'm not a hundred percent sure, but I think we're starting with a Parsi café in Southall."

"So, how did you even get started on this project?" Veronica asked.

She twisted her mouth wryly. "I have been a pretty obnoxious patient, frankly. My mom's sister, Jill, thought it would be a good thing for me to get away from home around Christmas to do something kind of productive." She buttered her toast generously. "And one night I found this weird file in my mom's office." She took a bite of toast, raised her eyebrows. "It's like a Nancy Drew setup, right? *The Case of the Parsi Cafés.*"

"I'm surprised you know about Nancy Drew."

She gave a dismissive shrug. "My mom had a whole set. They're probably still in the basement, actually."

Veronica nodded. She'd had a set, too, but Jenna had never cared about reading them. She'd keep that to herself, trying to keep the employee-employer balance rather than mother-daughter. "What was her connection to India?"

"I don't know a lot. She lived there when she was young, a study-abroad thing. She was pretty heavily influenced by Indian styles of cooking after that, particularly north Indian and Parsi."

"I'm not familiar with Parsi cooking."

"I'm not, either, honestly, so we can figure it out together."

"Do you like to cook, Mariah?"

She snorted. "Nope. I like to eat, though."

Someone knocked on the door and Veronica got up. It was Henry, freshly shaved and casual in a chambray shirt and a photographer's vest with a million pockets, and a camera backpack over his shoulder. "Hello, again," he said in that velvety voice.

"Hello." Veronica tugged up her sleeves as he passed, smelling oak and sandalwood. "We're just finishing up. Do you want a cup for some coffee?" She paused in the kitchen, awaiting his answer.

"Sure," he said, taking the empty chair with his back to the window. He took up a lot of space with long legs and elbows and shoulders.

"How was your 'assignment'?" Mariah asked, putting the quotes in the air.

"It was fine," Henry said, shrugging.

Veronica handed him a cup, and forced herself not to ask if he wanted cream and sugar. It wasn't her job to wait on him. But maybe it would have just been nice?

Stop. She sat down and eyed the rest of her toast.

"What's the first stop today, Henry?" Mariah asked, brushing crumbs from her palms.

"Café Guli. We can wander around in the area, if you like. Your mom liked it there."

"I remember," Mariah snapped. She shoved away from the table. "I have to braid my hair."

Veronica watched her go. "How long since her mom died?"

"You don't know?"

"No. What?"

He shook his head. "It's her story to tell. But it's been about sixteen months, maybe a bit more."

"Young," she said.

"Yes," he said gruffly.

She stood and placed the plates on the tray. "I'll get a coat."

"I don't mean to be curt," he said. "It's just . . . sensitive."

His apology surprised her. "I'm sure she'll tell me when she trusts me enough."

"Maybe."

A loud bang sounded from outside, followed by a flurry of shouting. Henry jumped up to look through the window. "Nasty crash in the intersection," he said.

"Do you call 911 here?"

"It's 999, but I see a bunch of people with their phones out."

She joined him at the window. A small car had tried to dart by a truck and hit another car head-on. All three vehicles occupied the intersection. A pain ran through Veronica's midsection. "That doesn't look good for the little car."

"No," he agreed, and turned away from the window. "I don't think we'll be driving today. We'll have to take the tube." He pulled out his phone and punched some buttons.

"You think Mariah can manage?"

"Yes," he said emphatically. "She needs to get back to her life."

Mariah appeared, combed, washed, presentable. "What do I need to do?"

He stood. "We're taking the trains today. Give you some exercise. Grab the cane."

She frowned darkly. "And pain pills. Are the tube stations filled with stairs?"

"Some of them. But you'll do all right."

"Will I?" She looked mulish.

"You will," he said. "Let's go."

CHAPTER FIFTEEN

As the trio headed out into the slightly drizzly day, Mariah realized she felt okay. Better than okay, honestly. Her body was rested, and the sex had given her a sense of normality and ease. As they exited the hotel, sirens whooped toward them, pushing through the traffic backing up thanks to the accident. Sometimes sirens could set off her PTSD, but the pattern of the English sirens was not the same as the ones in the US. The only reaction was a slight prickle down her arms.

It buoyed her. Maybe she was getting better.

The crowds were thick, rubberneckers slowing the usual foot traffic. Mariah used her cane mainly as a steadying tool, weaving along with Henry and Veronica to the tube station down the block. As she passed the pub, she looked in the window and smiled to herself, thinking of hands sliding over her body, the solid deliciousness of an actual human man.

In the station, she tripped a bit over a threshold, but they boarded the tube without incident. They sat side by side, Mariah at the end, Veronica between her and Henry. She wore an emerald-green sweater that made her look brighter and younger, but the hair was just so staid—smoothed to her shoulders, the bangs brushed sideways over her sunglasses. The lip color was understated, but Mariah thought she had put something on. Her mother had always worn full makeup out of the house, and Veronica was somewhere less than that.

Smugly, she was glad that she didn't need makeup.

At Southall station, they emerged into a bustling street. Mariah blinked happily. A woman in a blue tunic and pants bustled by, her black hair braided away from her face. Teenagers spilled out of a bus, laughing and jostling each other. A sign across the street was in Hindi. An older man in a pressed muslin tunic and a kufi regally moved by them.

Quietly, Veronica asked, "Is this Brick Lane?"

Mariah just avoided snorting. Luckily, Henry said, "Good guess. But no. This is Southall." He directed them to turn left, and they joined the people on the sidewalk. Mariah peered in the windows of the shops they passed.

Henry had his camera in his hand, and they wandered awhile. He took shots of various things, as he always did, his camera an extension of his hand. Veronica came alive, exchanging pleasantries with vendors offering fruit and trinkets, making one man with an enormous mustache laugh outright and offer her a free slice of watermelon, which she accepted with a smile. Mariah watched Henry shoot photos of the exchange and wondered what he was seeing. In the damp day, Veronica's hair had lost its smooth finish and started to frizz a bit, and her expression was open, curious, and for lack of a better word, bright. Mariah liked this side of her more.

"I think the café is down this close," Henry said, and they ducked into a narrow alleyway, where the footing was slippery enough that Mariah reached for his elbow. "You okay?" he asked.

"Good," she answered, holding on to the crook of his elbow. In the cold damp, her knee and all the bits of metal holding her femur together ached. She wished she'd brought a puffer jacket that reached her knees.

But she wasn't into regret. It was what it was. They passed a shop crowded with fabric, and flowerpots empty with the season. Overhead, someone spoke in a dizzying tumble of syllables Mariah didn't recognize, and someone else answered in English, "Ma, leave me alone! I'm *doing* it."

She laughed and Veronica glanced over, grinning in agreement. "Some things are always the same."

"So you have kids?" Mariah asked.

"Yes. Three. A twenty-six-year-old son, a twenty-five-year-old daughter, and a twenty-year-old son."

"Your daughter is the same age as me. Where is she?"

"In Boulder. She's finishing a master's in ecology and environmental biology."

"Whoa. Smart. Does she live with you?"

Veronica shook her head slowly, looking distant or maybe sad. "She has an apartment with a friend."

"That's cool."

Veronica nodded. "They all came home during COVID. I miss them now."

"Well, but if they still lived with you," Mariah said, "you wouldn't be doing this, right?"

"True."

Henry said, "Are the boys in school, too?"

"Ben is. Tim's applying for doctoral programs."

"Another smarty," Mariah said.

"They didn't get it from me," she said wryly. "Their dad is a philosophy professor."

"Wow, that sounds like a blast," Mariah said with a roll of her eyes. "Debating philosophy at every meal."

Veronica laughed. "Yeah, *just* that much fun." She shook her head. "They outtalked me all the time. I'm the person who thinks of the comeback three hours later."

"Not everybody likes verbal sparring," Henry said. "My family liked that, too, and I didn't."

The talk of families didn't make her sad, Mariah realized. She just wanted to be part of the conversation. "My mom's thing was *appreciation*," she said. "We should appreciate this apple! We should appreciate our shoes! We should appreciate buttons!"

Henry patted her hand on his arm, smiling, then looked up. "This is it."

The café was not what she'd expected, a simple small storefront with big windows on either side of the door. A sign overhead said "Café Guli" in English, and presumably the same thing in Hindi. The window said, "Authentic Parsi cuisine."

"Let's check it out," Veronica said, already opening the door.

But Mariah suddenly hesitated, swamped by a sense of foreboding as she spied a big chalkboard and tables filled with customers. A scent of bread escaped into the day. It was like some weird force was holding her back. "Wait. What are we looking for here?"

Veronica stepped back, letting a man and a woman in jeans enter in front of her. "You tell me."

Henry said, "This is the first café on the list. One of the only Parsi cafés in England." He pulled up his phone and held it out, squinting, then handed it to Veronica. "I forgot my glasses. Can you read that?"

"Established in 1997 by a family from Mumbai who carried the tradition from India. Enjoy the house specialties of *bun maska* and *keema pattice*."

Mariah stood in the narrow alley, feeling her leg start to ache loudly, and couldn't quite pinpoint her worry. "Did you contact them ahead of time?"

"Nope. That's up to you." Patiently, he added, "We don't have to do any of this. It's an adventure. Your mom wouldn't care one way or another."

Except Mariah thought she would. She thought her mom would want her to do this, finish her last project.

Standing there, eyeing the café, Mariah wondered how she'd missed her mother's love of India. Had she talked about it, and Mariah, as self-centered as every athlete in training, had just missed it?

In some ways, the threading of Indian motifs—bright colors and patterned cotton dresses and a love of well-spiced food—made up a core part of Rachel's style, but it wasn't unusual. Lots of people had Lakshmi and Ganesha statues in their gardens.

Suddenly, she was irritated with herself. It was unlike her to be so nervous. "Let's go in."

Henry and Veronica led the way. Mariah hung back, trying to be invisible with her limp and her very visible Americanness, which felt awkward in some way she couldn't identify. Nobody looked at them at all, so she was just being a jerk, and yet, she still felt stupidly self-conscious, leaning on her cane. She hardly knew where to look in case people were staring at her.

"Welcome," said a man in his thirties, taking menus from the counter. "Three of you for lunch?" His accent was pure London, with swallowed vowels.

"Please," Henry said.

He led them to a table right in the middle of the room. Mariah hesitated, but a voice in her head said, *What the hell are you so worked up about?* so she sat down, facing the open window into the kitchen, where a crew of three worked at a counter. She pulled her braid over her shoulder as a shield.

The photos she'd seen of Parsi cafés always looked slightly worn and grimy, but this was not. The walls were painted white, the tables covered with blue gingham and fitted with glass. On the walls were black-and-white photos of what she assumed were Indian scenes, family shots in front of another café, and vintage signs advertising NESCAFÉ and Brahmi Oil and Campa Cola, some in English, some in Hindi. A graphic of a man with bird wings around him hung over the door to the kitchen. She recognized it and suddenly remembered a yellowed notebook in her mother's things with this on the cover.

Her ears burned a little. What was she missing? And what if it was something bad? Maybe sometimes it was better to leave things alone. "Wow, maybe this isn't a great idea. I mean, if my mom had wanted me to know everything about her life, she would have told me."

Henry looked up. "Again, we don't have to do anything you are uncomfortable with. We can pull the plug anytime."

Veronica said calmly, "The worst that happens today is that we have a good meal."

"Right." The words took the heat out of her sudden weird worry. Mariah rubbed her palms down her thighs, wincing when she caught the knob of scar tissue that always bugged her. "I guess I just want to get it right. For my mom, you know."

"You won't get it wrong," Veronica said. Her certainty was reassuring. "Let's just have some drinks to start." She pointed to the menu. "Fresh lime soda sounds delicious, but maybe on such a cold day some chai?"

"Okay." Mariah was annoyed with herself. When had she become this shrinking-violet weirdo? It was like she and Veronica had traded personalities for the day. "My mom always ordered a bunch of dishes when we tried a new restaurant."

"Let's do that, then," Henry said. "I'm as hungry as a wolverine."

Veronica laughed. "Haven't heard that one."

Mariah scowled. The two of them were like old friends already, all cozy and comfortable. Which made sense, because they were of a similar age and all, but she couldn't quite shake the old kid-longing of wishing for Henry to be her dad.

She liked him so much better than any of her mother's other boyfriends.

But none of her mother's boyfriends lasted. She didn't want anything to do with marriage or settling down or any of those things.

But Henry had remained Rachel's lifelong friend, and so he was part of Mariah's life, too. "Henry," she said, "why did you and my mom break up?" Until the words landed, she didn't realize how out-of-the-blue they would be.

He raised his head, holding the menu lightly, and met her gaze. He didn't say anything for a minute, just measured her, as if trying to decide what she was really asking.

Finally, he touched his jaw. "I don't know, really. It just got to be pretty hard to get around the work problems—I was always somewhere;

she was always somewhere. I guess we didn't spend enough time together." He tilted his head. "We were better as friends. Why?"

She shrugged, and honestly didn't have the answer. "I was bummed, really. I think you were her best boyfriend."

He grinned and leaned back, touching his chest with his open palm. "Well, you know I agree with you."

Veronica didn't engage, keeping her eyes on the menu.

Mollified over something she couldn't identify, Mariah tried to settle and examine the menu, but she still felt something off, something odd. A warning, maybe. She looked around the room, but there was nothing.

Jeez. Get yourself together. "I would like some chai," she said to focus herself. "And whatever is making the room smell so good."

CHAPTER SIXTEEN

Sitting in the café with Henry and Mariah, Veronica was again filled with an acute sense of gratitude. She was here, not at home in her apartment. This morning, she'd ridden the tube for the first time. She was visiting a neighborhood in London she'd never seen, and eating in a place she'd never heard of. If she hadn't divorced, this would never have happened.

Mindful of her responsibilities, she took photos on her phone, and notes in an app. The menu gave the story of the cafe. *"Parsi cafés are rare in England. In 1996, Hufriya Mistry left India with her husband and settled in London, where he became a surgeon and Hufriya established a version of her family's restaurant, Café Guli, in Mumbai."*

They ordered a great quantity of food, so much it made Veronica feel strangely nervous. The table was filled with fluffy white rolls with butter and cream called *bun maska*; eggs two ways, in omelets and in a tomato sauce; a chicken rice dish studded with spices; spiced chai; and lime soda.

"This smells fantastic," Veronica said, bending in to inhale the steam coming off the dishes.

They all filled their plates, Henry and Mariah with copious helpings of everything, Veronica with bits and dabs, half a bun, a spoonful of eggs.

"Oh, come on," Mariah said. "How can you write about food if you don't *dig* in?"

"I'm not the writer here. I'm the companion." She tore a piece of the bun away and tasted it. It was fluffy, fresh white bread, the raisins making it slightly sweet, with fat slathered between the layers. She took her time savoring it, looking at the light crumb. "You don't need a lot of food to get the feeling of it. A little goes a long way."

"Does it, though?" Mariah countered. She dove into the chicken and rice—was that a *pulao*?—and big bites of the bun. She wiped her fingers, then her lips, and shot Veronica a glance that was just this side of flirtatious. "And I would love to have you do some writing if you wanted to. I mean, I can't write it. That's just not my skill set."

It took a beat for Veronica to understand her meaning. Once she did, her heart squeezed—oh, yes! That would be so much fun!—but there was worry in it, too. Could she pull it off? It was a big project, and she hadn't ever written anything like it.

But her thin finances were always at the top of her mind, and it would definitely be worth a try. "You'd have to pay me more."

She shrugged. "I get that. We can figure it out."

Veronica focused on taking a small bite of omelet, trying to hide the fire that suddenly burned in her chest. Excitement, possibility, but also pride in asking for more. "I still want to do the research I want to do, too."

"Maybe we could trade that out somehow."

Veronica raised her brows. "We can definitely talk about it. In the meantime, I'm taking the notes you wanted anyway." Which reminded her to type notes into her phone about the bun, about the dishes, all their names. "What is that called again?" she asked, pointing to the eggs and tomatoes. She looked at the menu she'd kept at her elbow, and typed *tomato per eedu*.

Henry said, "So good. All of it." He looked around, assessing the room. "I need to get permission to shoot photos, maybe make an appointment to come back at some other time."

Mariah nodded. "Whatever you need to do."

"You're supposed to be spearheading this," he said, cocking an eyebrow. "It's your project."

She'd just taken a massive bite of the *bun maska* and covered her mouth with her napkin, using a thumbs-up to show him she heard. "God," she said around the food to Veronica. "You've gotta try it."

Veronica nodded, but now she was assessing the room, too. If she wrote about it, what would bring it alive? She'd talk about the people, the young couple by the window, he in a turban, she in a bright-yellow outfit, a long tunic over loose pants—what was that called? She needed to find out. Several men sat by themselves, obviously businessmen out for lunch, some in short sleeves, others slightly more formal, with polished shoes. A woman in a rose-printed hijab sat with a child who ate a sandwich almost bigger than his face. She laughed when food fell out the other side.

"Is this connected to the places we'll see in India?" she asked.

"I don't know," Mariah answered. "I'm guessing maybe. I wish my mom had talked about this part of her life, but I only found out she'd been to India after she died, when my aunt gave me some stuff she bought."

"I wonder why she didn't talk about it. Was she private?"

"God, no." Mariah rolled her eyes. "Not private enough, if you ask me."

It seemed like a clue. She'd only hidden her time in India. Maybe Rachel had been planning to excavate something from her past. "What did your aunt give you?"

"Just some clothes and jewelry. I think she wrote letters, but I didn't want them."

"Hmm." Veronica perked up, but kept her external reaction small. "Letters might be helpful."

Mariah closed her eyes. "I can't look at her handwriting." She pressed two fingers into her solar plexus. "It just . . . I can't."

"Okay." Veronica touched her arm, and Mariah allowed it. In a moment, she was steadier.

"I'm going to go ahead and shoot a few things now, and he said I can come back in the morning before they open, too. Better light. His mom is the owner, and he thinks she'd love to talk about the café for a book. She's really proud of it."

"Can we interview her?" Veronica asked, a fluttery mix of nerves and anticipation mingling in her body.

"That would be the idea. He said she's just run an errand and will be back shortly."

Mariah excused herself to go to the ladies' room, limping dramatically enough that Veronica frowned. "Maybe the stairs to the train are too hard for her."

"Agreed. We'll head back."

A woman in her fifties came out of the kitchen, tying a red apron around her short, curvy body. She had thick, dark hair cut short and wore a single gold bracelet. "Hello," she said, standing beside Henry's chair. "I'm Hufriya Mistry. You wanted to talk to me?" Unlike her son, her accent rolled with the cadence of India.

Henry spread a hand toward Veronica, who gulped and said, "We're working on a book about café culture, and one aspect is Parsi cafés. It's fascinating that you opened your business here. There are not very many Parsi establishments outside of India, are there?"

"Not many at all! I'm surprised Americans even know about them. What brought you here?"

"It's kind of a treasure hunt," Veronica said, improvising. "I think Mariah might be able to say more. Here she is."

The woman watched Mariah limp toward them. Her brows pulled down in a frown as Mariah sat down.

Veronica saw the thunderous expression and felt suddenly protective of Mariah, wondering if she should stand between them or—

The woman spat out, "Is your mother Rachel Ellsworth?"

Stunned, Mariah stared. "Yes. How did you know that? Do you know her?"

103

The woman tsked loudly and stepped back, waving her hand. "Get out of my restaurant."

"But we—"

"I will never speak to you. Leave now."

Veronica stood up instinctively, using her body to shield Mariah. "We'll go. Don't worry. We just have to—"

"Go, now!" the woman shouted. Her hands were trembling as she pointed, and it seemed like fury, but also pain.

They gathered up their things and got out, everyone staring. Veronica's hands shook with an emotion she couldn't quite identify— the heat of protectiveness, the tangle of embarrassment, the wish to strike back.

In the alley outside, Veronica said, "Wow, what was *that* about?"

Mariah's face had drained of all color. She dropped her cane to limp hurriedly over to vomit in a nearby trash bin. Henry rushed toward her, taking her coat, which he threw over his shoulder as he held her shoulders. "Get her cane," he barked to Veronica.

Veronica picked up the cane, holding the round of the carved lion's head in her palm. She reached into her backpack and pulled out a bottle of water, holding it out when Mariah straightened, the back of her hand to her mouth. Strands of pale hair came loose from her braid and stuck to her cheek, illuminating the faint scar that pulled her mouth up so very slightly. She trembled visibly. Henry helped her into her jacket, and she leaned on him to drink the water.

What was going on here? Veronica thought. What had happened when Rachel went to India? "We're going to need some more information, I think."

Henry nodded grimly.

A man of about fifty, tidy, with short hair, had followed them out. "Is she all right, ma'am?"

Veronica frowned. "She'll be all right, I think."

"I'm sorry about that. My wife has strong opinions."

"Why is she so furious?"

"That I do not know." He clasped his hands in front of him. "I thought you might."

Henry said, "She must have known Rachel Ellsworth. Is that name familiar to you?"

"The food writer, yes? Her book on vegetables is a classic."

Mariah shivered. "I need to go home."

Henry pulled a card from his front pocket. "If you think she might come around, give me a call. We'll be in London for a week or so."

Accepting the card, the man tilted his head side to side. "I doubt that will happen, sir, but I will remember."

Mariah pressed her hand over her mouth.

"Let's take a cab," Veronica said.

~

Back at the hotel, Veronica walked Mariah to bed, helping her undress to her panties and a T-shirt. It was the first time she'd seen the scarred leg. The flesh held divots and lines and irregular fat pockets. "Ugly, isn't it?" Mariah said, pulling her bra off through the sleeves of her T-shirt.

"Looks painful. It must have been quite a crash."

Mariah was quiet for a moment, as if remembering. "You don't know," she said. "I just thought you were being nice, not talking about it."

Veronica pulled the covers back, smoothed the pillows, and helped the young woman settle. Her color was still pale green. "We don't have to go through it right now."

"I don't want to talk about it, ever," she said, closing her eyes. "Google me. It'll come up. Honestly, dude, it's weird that you didn't. What if I'd been lying about who I was?"

"My kids wanted to run a background check," she said with a smile, and ran a smoothing palm over the duvet. "Curtains open or closed?"

"Open, please. I want to see the sky." Her voice was thin. "And will you get my meds and bring them over? The pain meds."

Veronica looked through the bottles and found a tranquilizer and a pain reliever. "These?"

"Yep." Mariah popped two into her mouth and drank a long swallow of water. "Google," she said again. "But I don't want to talk about it."

"Okay." Veronica paused. "I also think I'd like to ask your aunt about the letters. You don't have to read them, but if I'm going to write about this journey, I need to know more about what happened."

"Makes sense." She picked up her phone, scrolled. "I sent you her contact info. Will you turn off the lights on your way out?"

Veronica did as she was asked, her mind whirling. She had some serious digging to do on Rachel's past.

CHAPTER SEVENTEEN

Henry had settled on the couch. "Is it all right if I stay for a while?" He held up the book from the car. "It's a lot more comfortable here than my hotel."

"Of course. Feel free." She filled the kettle. "Want tea or coffee or anything?"

"No, thanks." One long leg was propped on the other, ankle to knee, and he'd donned a thick sweater the color of sand. It set off the darkness of his tan, making him look like a rugged outdoorsy gentleman.

Veronica measured coffee into the cup, and sugar, and waited for the water to boil. "Mariah told me to google her accident." A rustle of warning stirred in her gut. "And to never talk to her about it. She thought I knew already."

"Mmm." He closed the book, swung his foot onto the floor. "You don't know what happened?"

"I assumed it was a snowboarding accident. Then, when I realized her mom was dead, maybe a car accident."

Henry said, "I'll sit with you while you do it."

She raised her eyebrows. "Will I need support?"

He lifted a shoulder.

Veronica made the coffee and carried it to the sofa. It surprised her again how large he was, lean muscle draped over a large frame—the long limbs and broad shoulders. His warmth was a comfort as she picked up her laptop and typed *Mariah Ellsworth* into the search bar.

Hundreds and hundreds of results popped up—and they were not the Olympic angle Veronica expected. "Oh my God," she whispered. She clicked on one from *The Denver Post*.

> Among the 11 victims of Tuesday's mass shooting at a local grocery store was celebrated snowboarder Mariah Ellsworth, a multiple Olympic medalist. She has undergone three surgeries to save her left leg. According to a hospital spokesman, physicians were unsure whether the operations would be successful. "We did everything we could, but the bone was massively shattered. It's a miracle she didn't bleed to death."

> Ellsworth's mother, cookbook author Rachel Ellsworth, was killed instantly, one of six deaths.

A weight pressed the air out of Veronica's lungs. "I remember this," she said hoarsely. It had taken place at the same brand-name grocery store that she shopped at, so she knew the layout and the angles, everything, making it devastatingly easy to imagine how it happened. It had been deeply unsettling. "Such a mundane place for so much horror."

"Aren't they all?" he said gruffly.

Veronica felt tears rise, and pressed her mouth together. Tears were so easy, such a surface-level response. And yet—she thought of mother and daughter in the store, picking up dinner, trading easy conversation, and then . . . "You don't think about the people who are *just* injured, do you?"

"It's hard to think about any of it. We're not equipped to cope with this level of horror."

She gave a short, humorless laugh. "Aren't you a war photographer?"

"Not anymore," he said gruffly. "But that's how I know."

She took in his stoic expression and wondered what hid beneath it. It felt schoolgirlish to react with tears when he'd faced so much, when shootings were so common now that it was hard to even remember them all.

And yet, all of them were not the one. All violence did not cancel the particular and piercing horror of this *one*.

"So her mom was killed," Veronica said, "and now Mariah wants to finish this book for her."

"It was Jill's idea, Rachel's sister. Mariah was struggling with a pretty substantial depression—her mom dead, her career on hold—and Jill came up with the quest."

Quest. Such a good word. A sense of purpose filled her. This was something she could do, right now. "I have Jill's number," she said, checking her watch to calculate the time difference. "We need those letters."

Henry covered her hand. "Take a minute."

It was a simple, quiet comment, one that tore a hole through her careful facade. Focusing on the bend of his brown thumb, she let the devastation of the shooting fill her up, then spill out in pity and compassion for her prickly boss. She remembered reading about it, obviously, a shooting so close to her own city. Another one. There'd been so many, which was part of the problem now. How could you find empathy for the enormity of endless, random violence?

No one could. But now this one was personal. Her empathy would not be wasted, flung into the red river of shattering news stories.

She opened the door to a picture of the mother and daughter being herself and Jenna, and it was almost more than she could bear. *Stay with it,* she told herself. *Stay with it.* It was terrifying and sad and impossibly horrific, to die violently while checking tomatoes for ripeness.

She wanted to text her daughter, but forced herself to stay with the intensity of feeling, the juxtaposition of clean white grocery store tiles, and—

Ugh.

After a minute, she blew her nose. Wiped her face. "Will she snowboard again?"

"Doubtful, but she's got a lot of grit."

Veronica nodded, took a long swallow of her cooling coffee, and looked up. "I'm glad she has a quest."

"Me, too."

Her phone buzzed a text alert, and it gave her an out to stop thinking about—all of this.

"Go ahead," Henry said, turning his book back to the pages he'd been reading.

She picked up the phone and carried it toward the window. The message center had eleven new messages, and she frowned. Why so many? Was there some kind of trouble?

Okay, three from Spence, five from Jenna, one from each of the boys, and one from Mariah with Jill's contact info. She opened the Jenna texts first, a series sent over the course of the morning about a section she'd figured out on her thesis, and a struggle she was having with her roommate over how to divide chores.

Their sweet ordinariness pierced her. Grounded her. Her daughter was alive and well and consumed with the mundane matters of life.

The final text was a long one.

Dad is being really weird about everything. He wants me to pay my rent starting next month!! And I get that he's under pressure with a new baby, but he should have thought of that? And I can get a better job, but I might need to get some more roommates, and that's fine, too, but I need a little time.

Veronica scowled, then texted: First of all, that is weird. A month isn't long enough to spring something like that. You can make it work, though. I have faith in you.

A text came right back: MOM!! don't take his side!!!!! this isn't fair

It isn't fair, but until I talk to your
dad, which I don't really want to do
from here, I can't figure it out.

Which wasn't at all what she thought she would say, but she realized she meant it. I love you, though. I'll send some pics from today.

Wow, thanks. Not. 🙄

For a moment, she looked at the text, her thumb hovering over the keypad. What if her daughter had been shot at a grocery store?

But the same could be said about almost anything. What if she was in a car accident? What if she was in a building that collapsed? What if she was kidnapped by a stranger? What if . . . what if . . . what if? A million things could happen at any moment.

What ifs had held her hostage as a young mom. She had exhausted herself trying to imagine all the disasters that could befall her babies, and scanned the horizon constantly trying to hold them off. Spence thought it ridiculous, but then he wasn't a mother, was he? She covered wall sockets and hid sharp things and installed carbon monoxide detectors and never traveled in a car with them during a threatened blizzard in case of getting stranded.

And then a three-year-old at Jenna's day care had tripped on an uneven sidewalk on the way home, cracked his head on a metal stake buried in the grass, and *died*. It panicked her for a time. How could you possibly prevent that?

But then, the very randomness of the event finally came home. She couldn't prevent everything. She settled into being a mother who could only do her best. Now she had to employ the same sense of reason. Jenna had plenty of coping skills, at least for a couple of months. Veronica really did not want to deal with Spence, and would do what she could to avoid him.

Right now, Veronica was on a quest. The word filled her with resolve.

She opened the text from Mariah that contained her aunt Jill's contact info. She clicked on Jill's number to open a new text. Hi, this is Veronica Barrington, she wrote. I'm traveling with Mariah. She said there are some letters Rachel wrote while she was in India, and I was hoping you might be willing to scan them into an email for me. She doesn't want to see her mom's handwriting, which is why they'd come to me. Are you comfortable with that? You can email me at VeronicaBarrington@ timelink.com.

"Jill contact, made," she said aloud, but Henry had gone back to his book.

Neither of the boys said anything about finances or their father. Ben said, sweetly, that he hoped she was having a good time. Tim, terse as always, said, I passed my final. Onward!

When she couldn't put it off anymore, she took a breath and opened Spence's texts. The heater went out completely, and I have to replace it right now. I can't afford it. You've got to sign those alimony adjustments. I can't do all of this on my own.

Veronica frowned. Did he really have to replace the furnace? Or was that another ploy? It had been on its last legs for a while, so it wasn't out of the question.

But how was that her problem? She didn't actually own the house anymore. It was his.

The next two texts detailed what he would do if she didn't sign the agreement—cut Jenna's rent, and go back to court.

She closed her eyes. What was the right thing here? She really didn't know. In light of what she'd learned about Mariah, alimony squabbles seemed ridiculous.

And yet—she had to live in the world, which required money. Her biggest bill was a repayment for damages she'd invoked in the incident that led to her arrest, and it came out before anything else, a substantial sum. If she signed the agreement, she wouldn't have enough to pay rent, even with the current income from this gig with Mariah.

For a moment, she stared out the window where the rain fell harder. The early dark was already creeping in. Henry had turned on the gas fire against the wall, and the warmth made the room cozy and snug.

Part of her conflict was her love of the house itself. She wanted it to be well tended. After a childhood spent in a single-wide trailer in northern New Mexico, she'd fallen hard for the space, the windows, the expansive kitchen. It was something out of a fantasy she'd spun, night after night, reading design magazines in her tiny room, earphones connected to her Walkman playing Sinéad O'Connor and Depeche Mode while her little brothers played Nintendo in the living room, her stepdad resolutely zoning out in his shed with a portable TV.

"I lost my mother when I was young," she said aloud to Henry, surprised to hear it come out of her mouth.

"I'm sorry."

She nodded. "I was younger, sixteen, and it wasn't violent, just run-of-the-mill cancer, but I was furious, for so long. She didn't really get the treatment she needed because she didn't have health insurance, and as much as we tried, it was pretty much too late by the time they found it."

Henry put his book down. He had such a calm way about him, not the tortured thing she'd expect from a man who'd spent his time shooting images of people in pain. He held his hands in his lap, his eyes on her face. He waited.

"Sorry, I didn't mean to bother you. You can keep reading."

"Or you can keep talking. I don't mind listening."

She closed her eyes, shaking her head. "She was so full of life. She taught me to cook, and sew. My stepdad thought she hung the moon, and he was just wrecked when she died. He only lasted a few years." She let go of a breath. "So sad, and yet, not as sad as—"

He nodded, still calm, still focused on her. Waiting.

"Life is really not fair."

"That is a true statement. Maybe the truest of all."

She put the phone down on its face. "Do you have family?"

"Lots." He half smiled. "Parents, a bunch of siblings, cousins, aunties, uncles. Even a grandmother who is still living."

A thread of envy wound through her. "That's unusual. Do you see them a lot?"

A single lift of his shoulder. "Not really. We don't have a lot in common. I get back a couple of times a year, kiss and hug everybody, and we're all happiest like that."

Her phone buzzed, and she looked at the screen, prepared to ignore it if it was Spence. Instead, it was Jill. Hi, Veronica. Good to meet you. There are quite a few letters. I have a lot going on, so I'm not sure how many I can do at once, but I'll get started tonight when I get home. How is Mariah?

She's okay. Sleeping right now.

Well, now that you have my number, feel free to call me anytime. And you can ask me anything.

Got it. Thanks.

Veronica looked at Henry. "Jill is going to scan the letters Rachel wrote when she was in India. Maybe there will be some clues in them."

CHAPTER EIGHTEEN

Mariah holed up in her room for three days. For the first two, Veronica hung around in case she was needed, reading a worn paperback copy of *Sarum* she'd found on a bookshelf. It was thicker than any book she'd ever picked up, but that was part of the pleasure. She felt like a teenager again, reading in a chair, then draping herself over the couch, then propping herself up in the bedroom, her windows looking out to the hotel across the street and endless sheets of rain.

She also forced herself to do some research on her Bloomsbury thesis when she got bored. It had been so long that her brain felt it was creaking with disuse, and she never lasted long. Each day, she walked around Russell Square seven times to give herself some exercise and limited herself to an egg in the morning, a slice of toast at lunch, and one of the packaged meals from Waitrose for dinner.

It was depressing. This was not what she'd had in mind.

On the third morning, she couldn't face being cooped up all day any longer. She checked with Mariah, who was still hidden under her covers, watching videos on her tablet. She made sure she had water, and some food, and her phone number.

Then, armed with a downloaded map and a list of places to visit in Bloomsbury and around the neighborhoods Elsie had lived, she set out. It seemed like a gift that this hotel was so close to the places she wanted to see: Virginia Woolf's house and some of the more notable spots in the history of the Bloomsbury circle.

And one of the places Elsie had lived was nearby, close to the British Museum. She had shared it with her husband, a man she'd never really wanted to marry, and one who'd caused her a great deal of hardship.

A hard life, Veronica thought as she set out, her phone map in hand. It was a cold, drizzling day, but she had a raincoat and an umbrella, a bottle of water and snacks in her bag, and her fully charged phone. Bloomsbury was only a short walk away.

The map took her exactly where she expected in just under fifteen minutes. Walking the outside of the square, she located Woolf's house and happened upon a tour group. A guide in sensible shoes and a rain hat gave details of the place when Virginia and her husband had lived there. The guide pointed out a building nearby and said an electrifying name, Elsie Turner.

Usually she would have been too shy to ask, but this might be the only chance she had to explore this territory. When the group pressed forward to look at the plaque, Veronica approached the tour leader. "Is it possible to join in?"

"Not for this one," she said, "but I'd be happy to take you around another day." She produced a card from her pocket.

"Thanks." As the group moved on, Veronica went back to Elsie's house. It was the same as the others around it, a four-story town house Elsie's husband bought for them upon their marriage. He'd been pursuing her for years, before the Great War and after. She'd resolutely ignored him and attended the Slade School of Art, one of the only schools that allowed women to study. Her work was bright and detailed, heavily influenced by her childhood in the tropics. She believed that marriage interfered with an artist's pursuit of her work and resisted all attempts from suitors.

And then her father died, and although she'd held an expectation of inheritance, it turned out his gambling debts and speculative projects had entirely depleted the family fortune. Peter swooped in to rescue her, and seeing that she had no choice, she married him.

Why am I so drawn to this woman? Veronica stood in front of the house, imagining Elsie bustling behind the windows, painting on the top floor with a view of the treetops and the square, although from all accounts, she'd only painted India, the place to which she longed to return the entirety of her life.

Veronica felt the familiar ache. Elsie's life had been hard, directed by others. And for all that Veronica had struggled to climb from her working-class world into a more privileged one, she had not struggled with people telling her when to get married or to whom.

Rain started to sprinkle down on her head, and pulling up her hood, she headed for her next stop, the British Museum. Because it was there. Because she could. First she texted Mariah. Anything you need?

I'm good, thanks

It started to rain harder, and Veronica pulled out her umbrella, determined not to be chased indoors by a little weather. Following the map she'd taken a photo of, she turned away from the square, then left, then right. A squall slammed down, and she laughed, ducking into a doorway to wait it out, feeling her feet get wet in her walking shoes. It didn't matter. After a moment, the squall subsided, and she set out again.

But within a few more blocks, it was plain she'd taken a wrong turn. Where the museum should have been was yet another street filled with shops on the lower level, hotels or apartments above. Damn. Where had she gone wrong?

A bubble of anxiety swelled in her chest. What if she couldn't find her way back?

So what? a little voice said. *You know the name of the hotel, and you have your boss's phone number. Can't get that far offtrack.*

Right. *Take a breath, open the Maps app, and reorient.* Nothing lost. The pin for the hotel was on the other side of where she thought she was, but she could walk there in no time. The British Museum was in the other direction. Maybe she'd save that for another day. The rain had settled into a steady, relentless presence. Even with her umbrella and raincoat, she was getting chilled and damp.

She headed for home.

Fewer people were out, likely because of the weather. Everyone hurried along, hunched into their coats. Veronica resolutely ignored the Christmas merchandise in the window, the tinsel and ornaments and flashing lights. She wouldn't have to celebrate this year at all if she didn't want to.

A pang caught her unexpectedly over that. No roasting turkey, no early coffee made before everyone else got up. No gathering around the Christmas tree in pj's to see what they'd all given each other.

She was deep in her thoughts, striding hard, when her heel slipped on something oily on the sidewalk. It felt like it happened in slow motion, her feet flying up, her umbrella flung to one side, and her butt and left elbow landing hard on the sidewalk. For a moment, she sat there, stunned, her tailbone bursting with light, her elbow a competing set of fireworks, the rain soaking her jeans and hair.

A pair of young women hurried over and crouched beside her, one on each side. "Are you all right? Can you stand up? Do we need to call an ambulance?"

She wanted to shake them off, but their expressions were earnest, and she could see Jenna doing this, helping an "old" woman to her feet, but she was appalled. Her ears burned with embarrassment. "Thank you."

It was hard to get her balance with one girl on each side, hauling her up, and that increased her humiliation approximately one hundredfold. They probably saw her as really old, when she wasn't, not at all, and still fit. Anyone could fall.

Finally, she was righted and brushed her coat off, and her butt. "Thank you," she managed. "I'm good."

The first girl, wearing a miniskirt and dark tights, kept her fingers lightly on Veronica's arm. "Sure?"

Veronica nodded. "Thank you for your kindness."

They waved and let her be. Veronica picked up the umbrella, but it was wet on the inside now, and she'd broken one of the stretchers. She shook it out as well as she could and folded it, tucking it under her arm, then limped toward home.

Everything stung. Her tailbone, the jarring impact to her head, her elbow, which really hurt quite a lot. Tears welled up in her eyes, and her hair, wet from the rain, started to drip onto her shirt.

What the hell was she doing? Why was she even in England, when she could be at home with her kids? Even if they were doing something on Christmas that didn't include her, she could have come up with a celebration of some kind, to maybe start making new memories or start to heal the family wounds. Something.

Instead, she'd deserted all of them.

This was such a bad idea. She thought of her kids, swarming into the apartment to talk her out of the trip. Why hadn't she listened?

She was too old to start over, start a new life. She wanted the old one back. Her beautiful home and flowers, the reliable cadence of the year, holidays and birthdays and family traditions. The granite solidity of Spence's family, which had been such a lure. They took family seriously, with traditions and a culture all their own, and seemingly eternal, bits and pieces dating back to great-grandparents who'd escaped the stuffy society of the east to build a new life in Colorado. Where they'd promptly re-created their family legacies in a Western font.

She had loved that family grounding so much. It felt like magic, like a net that could hold you no matter what.

Now all of it was gone. Running away to Europe with a highly unstable young woman, and trying to resurrect her old thesis wasn't going to get it back.

The recognition pierced her. Under cover of the rain, she let tears flow, holding her arm close to her body so she didn't have to move her elbow.

Two blocks on, she realized she was passing the welcoming windows of a bookstore. She didn't even think about it—she was inside before she knew it, greeted by the heady scent of coffee, and books, and the low murmur of voices layered with classical music. Everything in her body let go.

She dropped the umbrella in a stand by the door and wandered in, just looking curiously until she got the hang of it, then climbed a set of stairs and wandered that level, too, then headed back down to history and local history, which of course showcased titles from the Bloomsbury group. Despite her study of Elsie, she hadn't read much by the rest of the group, so she browsed several books—poetry and criticism and novels and gardening. She picked up a slender copy of Virginia Woolf's *A Room of One's Own*, which she probably should already have read, but hadn't, and a travel book by Vita Sackville-West, *Passenger to Tehran*, which seemed appropriate.

Her body settled as she wandered. Her breath slowed, her joints loosened.

In the coffee shop, she bought a flat white and took it to a table by the window, where she leafed through *Country Living*, pages and pages and pages of genteel rustic beauty—gardens and farmhouse tables set with linens and old plates and fat candles. Such a relief!

Magazines had been a lifeline for her as a teen. In those pages, she spied a different kind of life, one with healthy food and kindly light and flowers snipped from the garden. Of course she'd fallen hard for Spence's family home! Drinking her coffee, she thought about the home she'd created there, the garden beds she'd planted. They'd been worthy renditions, and she could take some pride in that. She considered Elsie, who'd been forced to leave a home she loved in India, then another she loved in England, and finally was forced into a role she didn't want in a country that never felt like home.

But she'd made the best of it. Only a handful of her paintings survived, but they were widely acknowledged to be masterful. She'd done her best with what she had.

Veronica sat back in her seat, sipping milky coffee as she watched people hurry by in the rain. The life she had loved so much was gone. Really and truly gone. She would never have it back.

So what now? She didn't have some wild artistic talent to pour her loss into. She might be able to write the thesis, finally, but was that what she really wanted?

She had no idea. What in the world was she going to do with the next thirty or forty years?

A sense of someone nearby made her look up, thinking she would have to share the table. She pulled her bag closer to her side, and looked up with a distracted smile, remembering that maybe Americans smiled too much and she should do that less.

Except that she was American, and maybe that was okay.

It was Henry. Surprised and more pleased than she would have admitted, she offered a genuine smile. "Hello!"

"May I join you?" Henry said in his distinctive voice. "Or is this a rare moment of peace?"

Milky light spilled over his lean form, the worn-thin chambray shirt with its rolled sleeves showing tanned arms, his craggy face with wide mouth and aggressive nose. He carried a worn leather jacket over one arm. It crossed her mind that she found him attractive, that the scent of him rustled her skin.

"Please," she said, gesturing toward the open chair.

He carried a solid stack of books he settled on the table. "What did you find?" he asked, pointing to the books at her elbow.

She showed him. "I've been walking around the neighborhood of some of the Bloomsbury set, and I realized that I'd never read *A Room of One's Own*."

"I haven't, either. You'll have to let me know how it is."

"I will. What did you get?"

He turned the spines toward her. "More Mughal history. I seem to be on a kick."

"That's a lot of weight to drag around on a trip."

"Yeah, but I like used history books." He opened one and flipped through the pages, showing her the notes someone had written in the margins, blue ink in a spiky hand. "I like seeing what somebody else thought about the material."

In this light, she could see silvery threads in his dark hair. "That's a good way to look at it." She closed her magazine, placed a hand on the glossy cover. "I was just contemplating the question of what the hell I'm going to do with the rest of my life."

"Pretty weighty question for a rainy day."

"I guess." She showed her palm, which had marks from the pavement. "I slipped, a couple of girls rescued me, and I felt about four hundred years old." She laughed at herself. "I mean, it brings home thoughts of mortality."

"Maybe you could ask Mariah where she got her cane."

She laughed again. "I'll do that."

"Maybe," he said calmly, "the question to ask is, What do you want?"

"I wanted the life I had," she said, aware of the bubble of grief expanding again. She cleared her throat, forcing the tears back.

He nodded. "What was that?"

"It's hard to capture in a sentence or two. And I'm afraid it will sound unbearably suburban."

"Try."

She took a breath. "Okay. I miss my garden. I planted this massive garden over twenty years, and it was one of the most beautiful things I ever made."

"I'm sorry."

His quiet manner gave her courage. "I miss my beautiful kitchen. And when my kids were little, and when I thought I'd just live in that house until I died."

"None of that is suburban."

"It is, though. The house is in a nice little leafy neighborhood in Boulder, and my ex was a professor, and we had dinner party rounds once a quarter, and—" Tears gathered in the back of her throat, and she paused to let them recede. "And it's all . . . gone. I have no idea what's next."

He nodded. "It's hard to make a transition like that. Mariah is right there, too."

"I guess she is." Veronica gave him a rueful expression. "Hers is so much worse than mine."

"It's not a competition," he said kindly. "You've lost the life you loved, and so has she."

She closed her eyes, breathing slowly. Nodded.

"Maybe you just need to look at it in a different way. You're free in a way that you probably never will be again. Maybe freer than you ever have been."

"Well, except for that pesky little money thing."

He shrugged ever so slightly. "Money isn't the same thing as your life."

"That's a very privileged point of view. Money is at the core of everything. You can't do anything without it."

"I mean, sure, to a degree, but you're a woman of some education and resources. You can make money." He gestured to the shelves. "What about a bookstore?"

A puff of possibility blew away some of her despair. She raised her eyebrows. "I might like that."

"I thought so. There might be lots of things like that. You don't have to get it all figured out in the next five minutes. There's some freedom in not knowing the next step."

"That has honestly never occurred to me," she said. "Thank you."

～

As they walked out, Henry having offered a ride, he said, "I went back to the café this morning, to see if I could get any more information." He opened the car door for her, waiting in the drizzle for her to climb in.

"And?" she asked as he came around.

"No dice. I waited to get the son alone, but he was so jumpy about getting caught, I took pity on the guy."

"Too bad."

"Did the letters have anything?"

"I haven't got them yet."

A nod. "How's Mariah?"

"Still hiding in her room. I think it might be time to make her get up."

"Agreed. She's gotta face it all, her grief and the lost dreams."

A sympathetic arrow pierced her chest, and she pressed her hand against it. "Ow."

"I know. But it's time."

"Have you ever had to make a new life?"

"Yeah," he said, but offered no embroidery.

"Oh, come on, you can't be all stoic and mysterious now."

He grinned. "Is that what I am, stoic and mysterious?"

"Don't try to get out of it."

"It's pretty dark."

"And a mother murdered in a grocery store isn't?"

"Fair." He smoothly turned onto the street alongside the hotel. "But now isn't the best time."

"All right," she said, gathering up her packages. "Thanks for cheering me up."

"Anytime."

CHAPTER NINETEEN

In her bedroom, Mariah was frozen. Physically, but mostly mentally. She couldn't seem to shake the swells of despair. She huddled under her blankets, shunning anything but tea and sandwiches. She watched Tyler Henry on her iPad and wished she could believe there might be something on the other side.

She'd found Tyler while she was still in the hospital, those first weeks when she was deeply drugged and unable to come to terms with anything that had happened, not the death of her mother or the wounds of her own body. She lay in a gray miasma of pain, day in, day out, unable to focus on anything.

One day, she discovered the streaming world of psychic mediums. So many of them! She loved the seat-belt guy, and the loud but somehow trustworthy Long Island lady, but it was Tyler Henry, a young psychic with kind eyes who helped people episode after episode, who caught her. A delicately made gay man whose mother accompanied him on many of his journeys, he had made a giant name for himself, and she loved to watch him, endlessly. She'd seen every episode a half dozen times, and sometimes liked to imagine what he would say if she could get an audience with him. "Did someone close to you die violently?" he'd ask, scribbling on the paper he always had. "Was it your mother?"

But she didn't even know if he was doing that anymore. And he was so famous she wouldn't be able to get anywhere close.

She'd been a little famous, too, once upon a time.

Her mother would be appalled that Mariah wanted to use a psychic to talk to her, but that didn't matter in the slightest. It didn't actually matter that she'd never be able to see Tyler herself. Just knowing that other people talked to the dead helped.

By the fourth day, Mariah knew she should get up, but she couldn't seem to find the will. The encounter at the café had derailed her so badly because it made plain there were things about her mother's life that she had never shared. And now, Mariah would never know about them, would never know why it was important. It brought home the truth that Rachel was *dead*, and would stay dead no matter what quest Mariah engaged in.

Aching, she searched the internet and TikTok for more psychic readers. She could always watch *Medium*, based on a woman in Arizona who really had solved crimes with her abilities, but as she scrolled through the episodes, Veronica burst into the room.

"Okay, enough," she said, and briskly pulled open the curtains. Milky sunshine poured in through the windows. Mariah blinked at the brightness.

"What are you doing?" she protested, holding up a hand.

Veronica tugged the covers off Mariah's legs. "Time to get up. It's an absolutely gorgeous day, and we need to get out in it." She tossed the duvet onto a chair. "The cleaners need to get in here and fumigate, too."

"It's not that bad."

"Mmm. If you say so." She turned and opened her bag. "What do you want to wear? Do you want me to pick something?"

"No, for God's sake. I'll do it. Get out of here and let me shower."

"I'll order some breakfast for a half hour."

The light penetrated the cave of her soul, fingering life. "Fine. Now, go."

Sitting up, she looked out the window. Thin sunshine warmed the landscape, and just the sight of it was somehow uplifting. She stood and stretched, then limped into the bathroom. Her leg was stiff, but not sore.

As she turned on the hot water, she ranked the depressive episode as a six. Sometimes they were much worse and lasted a lot longer—a week, sometimes two or three—where she fell into the pit, an unrelentingly dark warren where every thought was a monster or a harridan, making fun of her, reminding her of all the things she'd never do again—fly down a slope covered in fresh powder, lose herself in training for an event she was almost sure she couldn't accomplish, meet her mom for lunch in some ski resort or see her in the waiting area of the Denver airport when she came home for a brief stint.

The monsters told her that her life was worth nothing. Worse, that no one's lives were worth anything.

Lost in those dark halls, she wanted only to slide into the abyss completely, disappear. And yet, her body stubbornly reminded her to eat, to drink water, to go to the toilet. Her skin itched and she scratched.

Now steam filled the room and she stripped down, breathing in the softness. The mirror, some modern fancy thing, didn't get steamed up, and she leaned in to look at her pores, seeing that she'd slept away the rings below her eyes. Her shoulders were thin, and she needed to get back to lifting—

Or . . . fuck. Memory reminded her that she didn't do that anymore.

Stepping into the hot shower, she reached for the tricks her therapist taught her. One long breath in, her hands on her belly, feeling her lungs expand. She let it go, feeling her belly move. Her body. This body, in this minute, was okay. Her mind, this minute, in this shower, was okay. The water felt good on her skin, her face, her hair. The shampoo smelled of nectarines.

She remembered that Veronica had probably looked her up on Google and now knew what had happened. It caused a hiccup in assembling peace. Would she get all weird about it, be solicitous, her eyes getting all gooey with pity? Resistance zigzagged down her neck, bringing her shoulders up to her ears.

Is it true? One of the coping questions. *Is it true, or are you telling a story? Is there a better one?*

She didn't know yet. Shaking out her shoulders, she let water pour over her face, over her throat and breasts. Veronica had been pretty ordinary when she came into the room, and actually, she'd done exactly the right thing. Got her up out of her bed. Henry must have helped. Or maybe Jill.

Whatever.

As she dressed, she felt clean and hungry, and maybe even curious about what might happen today.

~

Veronica had ordered a massive breakfast, eggs and bacon and toast, fruit and yogurt with granola and berries, coffee and juice and even a glass of milk. Mariah's stomach growled, and she sat down to feast. "Jeez, this is delicious," she said. "Aren't you eating any of it?"

"It's ten o'clock. I ate hours ago."

"Yeah, what'd you have? A piece of toast? A section of orange?" She gulped the milk, which was not usually her favorite, but it tasted great, cold and refreshing. She was probably dehydrated.

Veronica raised a brow. "Toast and oatmeal, as if it's any of your business."

"True," Mariah said. "You're just so thin. A little more food wouldn't kill you."

She perked up. "Really? You think I'm thin?"

Mariah pushed a plate of bacon over. "Why do divorced women get so thin, anyway?"

"What do you know about divorced women?"

"My coach got divorced and lost about thirty pounds. You could see her bones." She grabbed her wrists in illustration.

Veronica eyed the bacon, then suddenly pulled a slice onto a plate. "Maybe we stop cooking for other people and cook for ourselves," she said, cutting the meat into small pieces.

"Maybe." Mariah devoured a mouthful of eggs. They were so good here! She realized she was feeling really excellent. Nothing hurt this morning. Maybe she'd needed that long rest. "I think for my coach, she had this idea that if she was thin enough, he'd, like, see her and want her again."

Veronica visibly flinched. "Well, I did get kind of overweight the past few years."

"So what?"

"Well, that's part of the marriage contract, that you'll watch your figure."

Mariah snorted. "'Watch your figure?' Is this 1952?"

"It's not the same for your generation," Veronica said, bristling. "Girls now are mighty; they get to be who they are. Men of my generation still want women to be a certain way."

"All of them?" Mariah didn't know why she was pushing into an arena that obviously made Veronica uncomfortable. Maybe it was just interesting. The part of her brain who liked stirring things up was awakening. "Or just your husband?"

"I don't know," Veronica said with irritation.

"Let me guess. Your husband found a younger woman and blamed it on you."

Veronica tossed the fork down. "Not exactly." She stood. "I'm going to get ready. Henry will be here soon."

"Either way, he's probably a dick."

Veronica lifted her shoulders. "Which makes me an idiot, right?"

"No—"

Veronica left the table and closed her bedroom door. Hard.

Mariah ate some more bacon, pondering. There was life in the old Gen Xer after all.

CHAPTER TWENTY

In her room, Veronica found herself so furious her hands were shaking. She ripped off the dirty blouse she'd put on this morning and turned on the shower, thinking of twenty retorts she could have made to Mariah's speculations.

She shimmied out of her jeans and underclothes, testing the temperature of the water. In the mirror, she spied her shoulders, the arc of her collarbone, and for a minute, it amazed her all over again. She turned to face the mirror. That lovely line of collarbone she was so proud of, but—now she had to admit—she could also see the faint outline of ribs on her upper chest above her breasts, which were deflated by the same weight loss.

Never in her life had she been this thin. Amber said it was the divorce diet, that you just got so unhappy you didn't eat, and that wasn't far from the truth. But Mariah had unwittingly struck a nerve, too. In some part of her, didn't she imagine that if she were thin enough, more like her younger self, that Spence would remember how much passion there had been between them? Maybe he'd finally wake up and toss Fiona out in the cold.

Veronica *had* gained weight over the pandemic, but it had been such a joyous time! The whole family together, baking bread and making elaborate meals. All of them had taken on a specialty to master— Veronica worked on pies, both sweet and savory (which was how she came to master banoffee), Spence on fresh pasta. The kids all chose a particular cuisine they liked. Tim chose Thai, and had indeed perfected a peanut sauce that flavored lunches for months. Jenna focused on macarons and other French delicacies, and Ben made bread. When she looked back, her primary memory was cooking with her family to the sound of music on the speakers, their creations filling the air with the scent of love and coziness.

They had also taken long walks, and hiked the multitudes of trails around Boulder, often walking all day, feasting on grapes and crackers and brownies when they stopped for breaks. Her thighs and calves grew strong.

All of them gained weight. Her belly got soft and round, her bottom big enough she had to buy new pants. The bonus was boobs, of course, noticeable enough that Spence bought her undergarments to show off her cleavage, and at night buried himself in the new bounty.

They'd had so much sex during those long, barely structured days, eager to get to bed at night after feasting on whatever dinner they'd enjoyed, and a bottle of wine, and the playlist they took turns making. Instead of getting tired of each other, Spence and Veronica had renewed their passions, exploring each other in ways they hadn't had time to do since before the children arrived.

Even now, the memories could make her restless. They'd been very good in bed together from the very beginning, learning each other's secrets with exuberance and intent, and although it was a surprise to learn how much more they could discover twenty-five years in, it was a delight. Veronica felt eighteen again.

So she hadn't minded the extra weight. Spence had gained a bit, too. They were getting into their middle years. It wasn't surprising, and honestly, hadn't everyone gained weight during the pandemic?

Everything had seemed *so good*.

And then a woman's name kept coming up in conversations, in stories. Fiona, a visiting poet from Ireland, with the requisite accent. She looked like a caricature of a Pre-Raphaelite model, red curls tumbling over fragile shoulders, her skin blue white and utterly poreless, her pale eyes big and round. Veronica never had a whiff of warning about her—the woman seemed as insubstantial as dandelion fluff, not much older than their oldest child. Not her husband's type.

Spence grew busier and busier and more distant that semester, rarely home for dinner. In her loneliness, Veronica walked her dog, Sophie—at least she was still around!—and had begun to realize she had to find a job.

One night in early January—she could imagine he'd told Fiona that they had to get through one last holiday together—Spence came home, sat her down, and said baldly, "I'm in love with Fiona, and I'm moving out tomorrow."

He'd matter-of-factly packed a bag and left the house where she'd been happy with him for approximately 9,200 nights. The shock was so sudden, so intense, so impossible that Veronica had admittedly lost her mind for a time.

The Veronica in the mirror today, almost as thin as Fiona herself, was not that woman at all. But what Veronica hated was that she still couldn't explain how much she and Spence had loved each other. How much time they'd spent talking together about a million things, how many times they'd made love, how many meals they shared. It wasn't the cliché. *It wasn't.*

Even now, she didn't know how he'd so suddenly fallen in love with someone else, fallen hard enough to break up their family.

Her therapist once said, simply, "It happens every day."

Meeting her eyes in the mirror, she said aloud, "Shake it off." She'd wanted a new life. She had it.

~

The trip today was to visit an address in Brick Lane. It had been listed with the cafés, just an address, with no identifying remarks or insights. Henry parked as close as he could, but it was still a bit of a walk, the streets busy.

Veronica wasn't sure what she'd expected of the storied neighborhood, long popular with Indian and Bangladeshi immigrants, but it wasn't this explosion of graffiti and street art, tourist shops selling Brick Lane junk, and tourists in tennis shoes and puffy coats taking selfies. They passed many cafés offering foods from various regions, curries and Bengali specialties and something she thought might be Middle Eastern.

"None of these are on your mom's list?"

Mariah shrugged. She wore a thin pink puffer jacket that set off her blond hair and blue eyes. She moved more easily today, her cane a more natural part of her gait than it had been. Maybe she'd needed the rest.

Veronica was glad to be out, but her texts had been filled with drama this morning. Amber couldn't find a place to live, and Jenna was still freaking out over her dad's threat to pull support.

Although, Veronica had texted to her daughter, you are twenty-five years old. I think you could pay your rent if you put your mind to it.

I mean, of course! Jenna replied. But I'm already working. If I get another job, when would I have time to study?

Veronica quelled her sense of irritation. When she was in college, she'd sometimes juggled three jobs and lived in a hovel with three other people. Not that hovels could be found in Boulder these days, but the point was the same. Maybe you didn't get to have everything exactly the way you wanted it. She was, after all, a living example of that. Maybe you can find a cheaper apartment.

And bail on my friends?

I'm sure it wouldn't be hard for them to find another roommate.

Why are you being like this? It feels like you don't even care!

I care, Veronica texted. But I don't have any way to help you.

Aren't you making money? Can't
you help?

The request caught her like a splash of ice water. Jenna, you know
I have no money after the divorce.

Not even one month's rent?

No. I have to pay my *own* rent.

Fine, Jenna texted. Enjoy your grand tour.

Although Jenna meant to bring her down, it did just the opposite.
Veronica intended to do just that. She would absorb everything that
was in front of her, gobble up every single minute of this rare, fantastic
chance to travel. *Live.*

Like now, as they walked toward a grocery store with fruit stands
outside, sheltered beneath awnings. A woman filled a bag with avocados.
Veronica stopped. "Oooh. Can we go in here?"

Mariah gave her a long silent look. "You go ahead. I saw a shop
back there." She turned before Veronica could speak.

Veronica realized that it was a *grocery store.*

"Shit," she said to Henry. "I've been trying not to act differently
because I know about what happened to her, and I just stepped right
in it, didn't I?"

Henry watched as Mariah's pink coat receded. "I think she's fine,"
he said, inclining his head. "She has some of her spark back today."

"Hmm," Veronica said.

Henry smiled. "Been a victim of that spark?"

"Yep. She can be . . ."

"Yes." He gestured. "Let's go look around."

It was a large supermarket with an Indian flavor. Veronica browsed the produce, finding fruits she'd never seen, and giant versions of others. She picked up a hand of ginger that was more like an arm, and next to it, a reddish root that turned out to be turmeric. She'd seen it in Boulder, of course, that center of all foodstuffs and cooks who loved to dazzle their guests with the new and most challenging and interesting items around. The root was a beautiful color, and smelled sharply astringent. "I wonder how to change the grated amount for the powdered. It makes me want to try it," she said. "Just to see what it's like."

Henry's hands were tucked lightly in his jeans pockets, the photographer's vest giving him a dash of adventure. In the neon lighting, his eyes were more green than light brown, like a cat. "I am not called to cook anything, but I'd be happy to eat if you want to experiment."

"Sadly, I have no place to cook right now." She eyed a pile of tidy garlic, and some red onions, her brain tossing together possible meals even if she couldn't cook. "You don't like cooking?"

"Not really. I mean, I've never really learned."

"Maybe you should take some lessons."

"Maybe," he said.

She grinned up at him. "That sounds very definite."

"Cooking seems so fussy, all the ingredients, and the temperatures and the different pans and cuisines." He lifted his camera and took shots of the scene, the piled-up ginger and turmeric, the apples and grapefruits. He held the camera lightly in big hands. They were well tended, with oval nails, neatly filed.

She brushed the noticing away, slightly embarrassed. *Celestine,* she thought, referring to the spicy sex maven in that Kristy MacColl song.

"It is complicated," she agreed.

"There are some open-air markets in Mumbai you would enjoy. We'll have a kitchen there. I'll have to look them up."

"I would totally love that."

After a long, easy circle around the store, Veronica had a few things in a basket, and pulled a card out of her phone case to pay. It was rejected.

She tried it again. Same result.

"Maybe your bank blocked it because you're in a new place," Henry suggested. "Let me."

"Oh, no, you don't have to. It's just—"

"My pleasure," he said, and met her eyes. "You can cook for me sometime."

The words were light, but his hazel eyes seemed very bright. *Stop. He's just being nice.* "Okay." She let him pay.

Her phone buzzed.

Will be about an hour, the message from Mariah read. You guys look for the address, and we can eat when I'm done.

Veronica relayed the message. "We can find lunch when she's done."

According to her phone map, the address was a few blocks south of their current location. "What are we supposed to do when we get there, though?"

Henry shrugged. "This is the next clue. We have to follow it."

"*The Case of the Mysterious Address*," Veronica said, thinking of Mariah's reference to the girl detective. "Just call me Nancy." She frowned. "I can't think of her sidekick's name."

"I'm no sidekick, lady."

Veronica laughed. "Fair. *Veronica and Henry and the Case of the Mysterious Address*." Despite the gloomy day, her spirits felt light. "Do you have any theories about what this whole mystery is about? You knew Rachel pretty well."

"She never talked about her time in India. To be honest, she was opaque at the best of times."

"It's hard to get a handle on what she had in mind, just from her notes and this scavenger hunt."

"I bet. Did you get any of the letters from Jill?"

"Not yet." They turned the corner, and on the wall in front of them was an enormous mural of a woman. Around her neck were graffiti tags, and script-covered doors all the way down the block. "The mural is gorgeous."

"And it will be gone tomorrow."

"That's sad, isn't it?"

"Not everything is meant to last forever."

"Or anything, really," she said.

"Right." He paused. "This is the address."

It was a narrow shop between two larger ones—one a fabric shop, the other a bodega offering the usual mix. The window of the bodega boasted a multicolored cat, fast asleep amid cartons of laundry soap. Handwritten specials advertised loo paper, canned beans, wine.

The shop in the middle was empty, and looked as if it had been for a long time. No signage was left behind to show what it had been. Veronica lifted her cupped hands to peer into the gloom. Just an open room with a concrete floor, a ladder on one side. "Can't tell anything about it."

"Maybe they'll know next door."

She hurried to follow him as he set off for the fabric store. He greeted the man inside in what sounded like Arabic. The man, wearing a button-down shirt and well-cut trousers with a kufi on his head, responded in kind, and then, "How may I help you?"

"We're looking for someone, and they might be connected to the shop next door. Do you know what it was?"

"Oh, sure. It only closed during COVID. It was a little bookstore with books in Urdu, Hindi, and Bengali."

"Who ran it?" Veronica asked.

"Mrs. Irani," he said. "She returned to India when her father fell ill, and I believe she stayed there."

"What was the name of the store, sir?" Veronica asked.

"The South Asia Book Emporium. It was quite wonderful."

A bookstore! Veronica imagined a shop filled with towering shelves packed with history and travel and culture. "I wish it was still there!"

He bowed ever so slightly.

"Thank you," Henry said.

Veronica wrote the name down when they got outside on the street. "Hate to see a bookstore that's closed."

"Agreed," he said. "But why did Rachel have a bookstore on the list?"

"Maybe she wanted to do some research for her recipes? Or something to do with the cafés?"

"Possibly. But why *this* little shop in this faraway neighborhood?"

"Good question." Veronica looked up at the marquee over the store, but whatever signage had been there was gone. "Rachel didn't seem to care if things were obscure."

"That's true. But she wasn't deliberately opaque, either. There must be some reason she wrote down this address. I wonder if Ms. Irani is connected to the café we visited yesterday."

"Maybe." Her phone buzzed, and she glanced down. "Mariah. She's looking for us."

"I'll text her the address of the café. We can meet there."

CHAPTER TWENTY-ONE

When Mariah left Henry and Veronica at the grocery store, she smirked a little that both of them thought she was afraid to go in. Which was ridiculous. She had been in grocery stores a million times before the one time that it went bad, and had no feelings of worry or panic going into one. Not that she actually *had* gone inside one since the thing, but she didn't worry about it.

But she'd let them think that because she'd spied a tiny shop with a sign in the window that said "Psychic Medium, Readings £50." Once Henry and Veronica had ducked into the store, she circled back two blocks to the psychic. For a moment, she stood outside wondering if she was *really* going to go in. The window was ordinary, just the sign, neatly lettered. A teapot and matching cups sat in the display area.

Inside, it was similarly unadorned. No beaded curtain, no paisley scarves draped over the sofas. Just a big orange cat on a glass case that held earrings. Bookshelves lined one wall, and there was a scent of strawberries in the air.

"Hello, there," she said to the cat, reaching out to touch his big head. He butted against her palm and leaned in to get an ear scratch. His fur was thick and soft. "You're a good kitty."

She'd always wanted a cat, but her mother said—rightly—that it would be unfair to an animal to leave it all the time. "Maybe I need a kitty in my life."

"Two are better," a woman said, coming out of the back, which seemed to lead to an apartment. At the end of the hallway, Mariah glimpsed a kitchen with a red table. The woman was short and round, wearing a very ordinary matched set, top and pants. Her hair was wild white corkscrews.

"Where's the other one?"

The woman pointed to a high shelf, where a black cat perched, the end of his tail swaying back and forth. He watched them with big yellow eyes. "Jasper. And this is Marcus."

"Pretty." Now that she was here, her heart felt squashed and terrified.

"Come in for a reading, have you?"

Mariah shrugged. "Maybe?"

"You have or you haven't," she said practically. "I can't promise to give you cheery predictions, but most people get some answers."

"Okay. Yeah. Yes."

The woman gestured, and Mariah followed her to the kitchen. It smelled of coffee and fresh baking, a reassuring scent. In the middle of the room was a gleamingly restored chrome-and-Formica red table with matching vinyl chairs. "This is spectacular," Mariah remarked, hand flat on the surface.

"Oy, I love the era. All them clean lines. I did it m'self."

"Impressive."

The woman sat down with a huff, no cards or paper or anything. "I'm Hortense," she said. "What's your name, sweet?"

"Mariah."

"I don't usually like to answer specific questions," she said, "but if you want something in particular, hold it in your mind, and let's see what comes up."

"Okay." Mariah tried to think of what she wanted to ask, but all that showed up was a great big question mark, almost comically pointed.

Hortense took Mariah's hands. The woman's hands were cool and soft. Mariah had the fleeting thought that she liked Tyler's method better, just opening up to the spirit side and getting on with it. Not this touchy—

The woman's hands were getting hot. Mariah looked at them to see if they were on fire, but it was just her fingers, her palms, looking 100 percent ordinary.

"Close your eyes, Mariah," she said. "Focus on your reason for being here."

Mariah did as she was told, feeling unexpectedly emotional. Her reason for being here was the great question, wasn't it? Why was she here still if she'd lost the one thing she'd been doing her whole life? Her mother had been a great believer in purpose, in karma and dharma and all those ideas Rachel had picked up in India. In truth, Mariah wasn't sure which was which, dharma as purpose? Karma as . . . punishment?

"I'm getting a lot of turmoil," Hortense said. "Chaos and noise, people . . . Wait." She paused. "So quiet. It's unnaturally quiet." She made a pained noise. "Fear," she said breathlessly. "So much fear. So much loss—

"Jesus, Mary, and Joseph," she cried, pulling her hands away, curling them up into fists as if to close the channel. "I can't," she said.

"You can't read for me?" Mariah echoed. "I need help!"

Hortense straightened, one palm on her diaphragm. She shook her head. "There're too many voices, and many of them are at a moment of great confusion and pain." She winced and touched her temple. "Your question isn't clear enough, so they're all clamoring." She shook her head. "I'm sorry, you have to go."

"This was stupid," she said, standing abruptly. It was hard to storm anywhere with a cane and a limp, but she did her best.

"Wait," Hortense said. "A woman with dark hair says the bookstore will give you some help."

A woman with dark hair. Gooseflesh raised the hairs on her arms. "The bookstore?" Mariah frowned.

"That's all I have."

Mariah nodded. "All right." She dug in her pocket for some pound notes.

"No," Hortense said. She took Mariah's hand. "I feel your pain, love, but you've got some work to do to shed the past."

Mariah blew air between her lips. "Yeah, I didn't need a psychic to tell me that."

~

Tangled and overheated from the thwarted encounter, she tried not to cry as she called up the map on her phone. It was stupid to believe in all this crap, anyway, so why did she keep trying to get answers this way?

She tumbled right back to the dark place she'd been after the encounter at the café, and no matter how she slapped them away, tears kept sloshing from her eyes, annoying and embarrassing.

Get your shit together, she told herself sternly. She could just imagine the hoots and hilarity she'd get from the old boarding crowd if they knew she'd done that. *Find your grit.*

Shaking herself physically, she coughed and focused on the address where Henry and Veronica waited at a café. It had an old-world vibe, with Middle Eastern music on the speakers and tables crowded together in the room. It looked like it had been here forever, in the menus and the decor. A host showed them to a four-top by the window and brought them a carafe of water.

It wasn't quite Indian and not quite Persian, but a mix of both. Mariah realized she was starving, and ordered hummus and olives for the table before the host left. "How was the grocery store?" she asked.

"Loved it," Veronica said. "What did you get up to?"

She shrugged. "Just browsing."

Henry said, "We found the address and it turned out to be an abandoned bookstore."

The bookstore is the key. "What?" A shiver ran up the back of her neck. "What bookstore?"

"We don't really know. Someone named Ms. Irani ran it and went back to India, so it closed."

"That name sounds familiar."

"It does not match the woman at the café," Veronica said, "but when we get back to the hotel, I can run it through some Google searches and see if we get hits to anything else." She'd been flicking through emails on her phone and scowled. Her cheeks went bright red.

"Everything okay?"

Veronica closed the app and stuck the phone in her back pocket. "Fine."

CHAPTER
TWENTY-TWO

Things were definitely not fine in Veronica's world. In her email was an urgent note that her bank account was overdrawn. A second notice said that her rent payment had been rejected. Under cover of the conversation between Henry and Mariah, Veronica tried to figure out what had happened. Everything was automated, and she didn't use that account for anything except essentials. No way it could be overdrawn.

And now her hands went clammy as she remembered that her credit card had not worked in the grocery store. What the hell was going on?

It was still only 5:00 a.m. back in Denver, so she wouldn't be able to reach the bank for several hours.

"Sure you're okay?" Henry asked.

She waved it off. "Minor glitch, I think." But her ears felt hot with a form of embarrassment she had not felt in decades, since she'd been a scholarship student at CU working three jobs and carrying instant coffee in her backpack to get by while all her friends had credit cards funded by their parents. She had been determined that no one would know.

She'd changed everything about herself when she moved from Taos to Boulder, Colorado, a change of climate, culture, and class she was determined to navigate properly. She observed the way the monied girls cut their hair and cut hers the same; she shopped ceaselessly at thrift stores for pieces that gave her a well-tended, if faintly shabby, look. She lied about her background, saying she was from Albuquerque—a city they still looked down on. Honestly, it was shocking how little any of them knew about New Mexico, a state directly south, not even a three-hour drive away. She said her mom had been a Realtor and her dad a car salesman, careers she thought she could fake knowledge about, positions that could make a solid middle-class living, but not like a dentist or a teacher, people who'd gone to college.

She also changed her name, from Brandi (with an *i*!) to Veronica, which sounded sleek and sophisticated, the name of the elegant girl in Archie comic books.

In those days, it had never occurred to her that her mom would have been devastated that Brandi/Veronica had lied about so much, that by changing her history, she was nullifying her mother and stepfather.

It wasn't like she'd continued to lie over time. Spence and the kids knew about her life in Taos, but she didn't talk about it a lot. She tried to avoid even thinking about New Mexico, the high desert, the red earth, the hardscrabble life they'd lived there.

But this bone-deep shame over being completely broke, without a single penny or a way to get it until Mariah paid her, was searingly familiar even after almost thirty years. She couldn't bear it if Henry and Mariah suspected that she had nothing at all.

The good thing was that Mariah would keep paying her every Friday. That sum wouldn't address the missing rent payment, but it would keep her afloat here.

The rest she'd have to figure out on the fly.

"What are we ordering?" she asked, and opened her little notebook to a new page to take notes on the samples.

~

Henry dropped them back at the hotel. Mariah crashed for a bit. While she slept, Veronica paced the sitting room, from the window overlooking Russell Square to the minikitchen, around the coffee table, back to the window. When she could open the app for her bank and see the day's new activities, she saw that what she'd feared was exactly what had happened: the alimony payment from Spence had not shown up in her account. That meant that all the autopayments were refused, with the exception of the electric bill, which had come out first.

That was the stress of living hand-to-mouth. If one thing fell out of place, it could wreck everything.

She sank down on the couch, pressing the heels of her hands into her eyes until she saw spots. What the actual hell was she going to do? If she didn't pay the rent, the apartment would be lost, and she had no way to get it cleaned out between now and the first of January.

Not to mention she didn't want to lose the apartment at all.

When the clock showed it would be 10:00 a.m. in Colorado, she called Spence in his office. He always arrived at 9:45 a.m. and spent an hour on grading or preparing lesson plans. He prided himself on his systems.

He answered the phone, a landline on his desk, on the second ring. "Hello," he said pleasantly.

"It's me, Spence."

"What can I do for you?"

"I think you know the alimony check didn't arrive."

"I am aware, but as *you* are aware, the furnace had to be replaced, and the money had to come from somewhere."

Jagged anger bolted red through her veins, feeling so hot it could split her skin. "It is not my house," she said, enunciating each word.

"And. You. Are. Not. My. Wife," he returned.

"You're breaking the law!"

"Not a very important law," he said mildly. "And you have a job now."

"I do have a job," she said, trying to calm herself. "But it will not cover my rent, and I cannot afford to lose that place."

"You don't have to live in Boulder," he said. "The kids are grown. They can visit you in Denver."

His cavalier attitude hit the back of her throat, spread downward to her gut, burning, turning back on itself. Her heart raced so hard she feared a heart attack, and the soles of her feet burned on the floor. If she walked, she'd leave behind footprints of fire.

In a whisper, she asked, "What do you expect me to do?"

"I don't expect anything. You're a grown woman."

"How can you treat the mother of your children this way, Spence? You're a better person than this."

"I'm doing what I have to do to take care of my current family, Ronny."

"Don't call me Ronny," she said tightly, but he'd backed her into a corner. A hard heel of anxiety pressed into her chest. What else could she do but give in? Taking a breath, she said as calmly as she was able, "Look. I can't do anything from England. Pay me this month's alimony, and I'll sign the bloody agreement."

"Funny how you can make it work now."

"I can't. But I can't lose the apartment when I'm halfway around the world, either. And you're doing the same to Jenna."

"I'm not going to take her money away. That was just to get her attention. She needs to earn more. So do you. You're a capable adult."

Veronica closed her eyes, breathed through her nose, repeating all the things she'd learned in group about how to manage her emotions. Tears flowed down her face, but no one could see her, and as long as he couldn't hear it, she didn't care. A second, horrible thought came to her. "Did you cut off my credit card?" It had been on their shared account, although she paid the bill.

"It's time, don't you think?"

She had a debit card, which was where the money from Mariah would go. "Spence, I can get back without the credit card, but please don't force me to lose that apartment."

"Sorry," he said. "Too late. I paid for the furnace instead of your alimony."

"Spence!"

"Not my problem." He was practically whistling with victory. "I've got to go."

And he hung up.

~

Veronica couldn't sit still. She knocked on Mariah's door. "I'm going out. Do you need anything?"

"Nope. I'm good."

"I'll have my phone."

"I'm not twelve," Mariah said, pulling open the door. "Are you okay? I heard a fight."

Veronica squared her shoulders. "Nothing I can't manage." She tugged her sweater down over her hips. "Are you planning to pay me on Fridays, still?"

"Definitely. Do you need it sooner?"

Her cheeks flamed. "No. I'll be okay." But that was a lie. "Honestly, yes. My ex and I are struggling over alimony."

Mariah reached into her back pocket for her phone and pulled it out. "I have the routing number here. You want to check it and make sure it's right?"

Relief poured through Veronica, cooling the fury, slowing her heartbeat. "Thank you."

"No problem."

Veronica said, "Right now, I'm going to take a walk. Do you want me to pick up something for dinner?"

"I think I'm going out," Mariah said. "Feeling kind of restless. You do you."

Which meant she had the night to herself. "Sounds good."

She donned her coat and ran down the stairs rather than wait for the elevator. For the first time, she saw that there were profiles of the Bloomsbury set on the walls. She paused to read them, feeling something lighten with each bio. This one a painter, that one a writer, this one a lover.

What was the appeal of this group? Why did she identify so much with them? As she headed outside and crossed the street to Russell Square where she proceeded to speed walk around the winter-yellow grass, she pondered the question. Some of it was right here, these graceful squares with agreeable homes around them, a London that no longer existed.

The air was sharp and smelled of the watermelon notes of today's rain, and it was far more appealing to think about the Bloomsbury set than about her own life, which was such a shambles right now. It still amazed her that everything was so upside down. It made her think of a Leonard Cohen quote about expectations, that everyone thought they'd go out and slay the dragon, but growing older taught you that the dragon often slayed you instead.

Her nerves settled a bit as she walked. Another round and she could take a deep breath again. The dragon of mental illness had slayed Virginia Woolf, and her sister, Vanessa, loved the adamantly gay Duncan Grant all her life. Brandi Pusset had slain the dragon of her history and emerged as Veronica, the wife of a professor, who had an enviable life.

But the dragon had turned on her, burning to ash the gilded life she'd built. She was at ground zero again, her goals abandoned for the lure of children and family and comfort, with decades stretching out ahead of her and no idea what she was going to do with them.

However, unlike Virginia, who had walked into the River Ouse, she was still alive. As long as there was life, there was hope, as somebody else had said. Probably not Leonard Cohen.

Be practical, her calmed mind offered. What could she do to address this problem? She could call her landlord, for one thing, and explain the problem. Her car was sitting in front of Mariah's house, and maybe she could get Jenna to go down there and pick it up. It would be collateral for the rent.

Feeling freer, she wandered back to the hotel, and came into their suite just in time to greet Mariah pulling on a leather jacket. Below, she wore a low-cut T-shirt and several necklaces falling in layers over her . . . *cleavage* would be the wrong word . . . chest. Her hair was shiny clean and loose over her shoulders and back, and she even had a little makeup on—some mascara, lip color, faintly rosy cheeks. "You look gorgeous," Veronica said.

"Do I? Thanks." She gestured to her body. "I haven't been out at all, really. Since . . . the"—she waved a hand—"thing. All of a sudden, I just want to be in the world. Does the cane make me look super weird?"

Veronica shook her head. "No way. You look like the eccentric daughter of a billionaire."

"I was kind of going for Eurotrash."

"Nope. You, my dear"—she pushed a lock of hair over her shoulder—"are an American even at a hundred paces."

Mariah lifted both thumbs and pinkies in shaka signs, maybe ironically, and topped her look with a knitted cap that had the Olympic logo on the front.

"How many medals have you won?" Veronica asked.

"Two silver, one bronze. Never got the gold."

"That must suck."

Mariah raised her brows. "Thanks for that. People always tell me to be grateful, but I fucking wanted the gold. It sucks that I never got it." She tucked her phone in her back pocket, then pulled it back out. "Let me drop a pin on this hotel."

"That's smart." Veronica opened her phone to see a red 17 beside her messages. Ignoring them, she dropped a pin for "home" on her maps.

"This might be kind of stupid," Mariah said, "and you can say no, but what if we have tracking on for each other? Then I can find you, and if I get lost, you can find me."

Veronica asked, "Are you afraid you'll get lost?"

She looked away. "You don't have to. I just haven't ever not had that on with my mom, and it feels kind of . . . I don't know . . . dangerous or something?"

Veronica had to swallow the emotion that swelled in her throat. As casually as she could, she said, "Sure, of course. I get that."

They found each other, and Mariah cloaked herself in swagger once more, saluting as she went out. "Don't do anything I wouldn't do," she said.

Veronica snorted. "That shouldn't be too hard."

~

It felt kind of lonely in the hotel room when Mariah left. She wished she had the guts to go out herself, to a restaurant or even one of the coffee shops she could see from the window. Across the street was an elegant hotel, with rows of windows on the lowest level showing a restaurant.

But she couldn't seem to rouse herself to do it. Instead, she read her messages, almost all of them from Jenna and the boys. Nothing from Spence, which was new, but she was so angry with him, it was impossible to imagine what he'd say.

Jenna had solved part of *her* rent problem, but Veronica didn't want to call her about the car yet. Instead, she sent an email to her landlord, explaining the situation and asking for a few days to work things out.

What else could she do from eight thousand miles away?

What she could do was some research.

The early dark was settling in. She turned on the gas fire and the lamps by the window and found a sweater, then looked through the things she'd bought at Taj, and what else she had to eat here. She sampled the dates and *molokia* leaves, a bit of sweet tamarind and star fruit. All intriguing, delicious. And it felt like a treat to enjoy whatever she wanted without checking in with someone else.

After she ate, she made a fresh cup of ginger tea, opened her Notes app on her phone, and sat down at the table where she began to see if she could track down anything at all about the bookstore. When she searched for it, it came right up—the South Asia Book Emporium, Brick Lane.

The photo had been taken on a darkish day, and lights glowed within, inviting the passerby to enter. The website no longer existed, but many people had posted photos and written reviews, many in languages Veronica could not read—Hindi and Arabic and something she didn't recognize. She copied and pasted to find out what it was, and it came up as Farsi. *Parsi, Farsi,* she thought with a smile, but it was true they were connected. The Parsis had fled Persia for India, and Farsi was the language of Persia.

The reviews of the store (those she could read) praised the quality and breadth of books available, mostly history and social commentary. Some reviews referred to the owner as helpful and interested, but none mentioned her by name. She ran another search for the owner of the bookstore, and there it was, proprietor Zoish Irani.

The owner of the café was Hufriya Mistry, so not related that she could see. But both establishments had the symbol of the man atop wings. She copied it and searched images. It was a Zoroastrian symbol, and Zoroaster turned out to be the center of the Parsi culture, a monotheistic religion.

She frowned, wondering what else to search. If the book was going to be about cafés, then Parsi cafés were the centerpiece, but that didn't explain the anger of the woman who ordered them out. And why did they have an address for the bookstore?

Not enough details, she thought, sketching out a simple outline. She could barely see a shape to the possible book, but she could see the ghostly outline. That was something.

An email alert popped up. Hoping for something from her landlord, Veronica opened it. Instead, it was from Jill. *Letters #1* said the subject.

Hi, Veronica. Sorry to take so long. Not sure if Mariah told you, but my husband is recovering from

a substantial heart attack (which is why you're there
and not me—ha!). This is the first set of letters. I took
photos with my phone, and there are only a few here,
but I'll get a better system, I promise. Jill

Her phone rang, startling her. No one ever *called* her. "Hello?"
A clipped British voice said, "Is this Veronica Barrington, please?"
"Yes?"

"I have your charge here, at the Chelsea A&E. She's not injured,
but she's a bit of a mess. She's asking for you. Can you come?"

Veronica was already on her feet. "Of course."

CHAPTER TWENTY-THREE

Veronica had no idea where the Chelsea Hospital was, but she opened the location function on her phone and found the pin for Mariah. She donned warm clothes, aware of the dithering fear of getting lost on the way and being completely marooned in London without a penny. Because she was still 100 percent broke.

She couldn't take an Uber because it was connected to her now-canceled credit card. The credit card Mariah had given her the other day was probably around here somewhere, but it felt weird to go riffling through her boss's things, even if that boss was a very lost twenty-five-year-old. She did look on the dresser and nightstand, scuffling the papers and receipts aside, but found nothing.

Damn, damn, damn. She didn't have any way to reach Henry, which seemed an oversight, but she couldn't fix it now. Could she bill a cab to the hotel? She called down to the desk. "I can't bill a taxi," the young woman said. "But I can call a car for you. Will that do?"

"Yes. Thank you. It's kind of urgent."

"I'll call you when it arrives."

When the car came, she climbed in with a gigantic sense of impostor syndrome, wishing she'd taken a little time to change her clothes to be more presentable.

But the driver was calm and professional, and the drive was not terribly long. She watched the city pass by with a sense of anxiety. What had happened?

She hurried inside the doors of the hospital. A waiting room was sparsely populated with people. It was very quiet. She went to the desk to ask about Mariah. Another woman came from the bowels of the hospital and took her down a long hallway where more people waited, looking resigned. One woman had a tear-stained face and a crumpled tissue in her hand. Veronica looked away.

They went through a set of double doors, and the quiet exploded in a swarm of noise. Banks of beds divided by walls and curtains lined both sides of the room, with a nurse's station in the middle. A wail came from somewhere near the back, a child, and everywhere people were moving here and there, calls going out.

Mariah was in a bed near the far end. She looked pale, her hair tangled. Veronica hurried over and took her hand. "Hey," she said. "How're you doing?"

She shook her head, squeezing her hand back. "So not good."

"What happened? Are you hurt?"

"They say not?"

A nurse entered, brisk and kind. "She's going to be fine, Mum. A right solid panic attack."

"I'm not her mom," Veronica said at the same time Mariah said, "She's not my mom. I told you she's dead."

"Not me, you didn't, but never mind." She checked Mariah's pulse. "Better. You can take her home."

"Wait!" Mariah cried. "I'm not ready to go! I think I might need more drugs."

"You've had plenty, and you've had a lot to drink. We wouldn't want to kill you, would we?" The nurse said evenly, pulling out the IV in Mariah's hand. "Drink plenty of water and have a good sleep, and you'll be right as rain tomorrow."

"Thanks," Veronica said. "What should we do if the panic comes back?"

"You'll need to see her doctor when you get back home."

"I have stuff," Mariah slurred, waving a hand. "Xanax and shit."

Veronica frowned, not reassured. What brought the panic on this time? "Let's get you back to the hotel, and you can get some sleep."

Mariah didn't move as the woman bustled out. "I think we should call Henry."

Veronica looked at her watch. "It's nearly one a.m. Let's take a cab."

"But I need him." Her voice was hushed. "His car is safe."

Veronica paused, considering the angles. Mariah was very high, whether by self-ingested or hospital-administered means. Her panic had been severe enough she'd been brought to the emergency room. There would be little point in reasoning with her, and, honestly, what did she know about the depth of their relationship? Maybe he'd want to be informed. "I need his number."

Mariah listlessly handed over her phone, swiped open to the contacts. Veronica typed the number into her own phone. "I need it anyway." On the other end, the phone rang several times, and she felt bad about waking him. He answered on the fifth ring. "Is this Veronica?"

"Yeah, sorry to wake you."

"You didn't. Is everything okay?"

"Not really. Mariah is physically fine, but I'm at Chelsea Hospital with her. She was brought here by paramedics with a panic attack. I was going to take her home in a taxi, but she said she would feel safer with your car."

"I'll be there in about a half hour. A&E entrance."

"Thank you."

～

Mariah was groggy but able to walk. They managed to get her loaded into the back seat without much trouble, and she fell asleep almost instantly as they drove.

"Thanks for coming," Veronica said.

"Not a problem. You can call anytime."

"I didn't actually have your number until I got to the hospital."

"Is she okay?"

"Panic attack, evidently. They brought her by ambulance."

Henry looked in the mirror at the back seat. Quietly, he said, "I worry that she's not really grappled with everything."

"How could you, though, really?"

He gave her a look. "True."

"Let's keep an eye on her."

The streets were quiet at such a late hour. Soft jazz played on the radio, interspersed with a woman's smoky, educated voice. Tension flowed out of Veronica's shoulders. Henry looked a bit rumpled, his wild hair barely finger-combed, his shirttail out. "You *were* sleeping, weren't you?"

He glanced over, lifted a shoulder. "Reading."

"In bed, all cozy," Veronica said, smiling.

"It's all good." In the small space, the resonance of his voice was particularly noticeable.

"Did you do television or radio as a reporter?"

"No, photographer only. Not even video."

"Kind of a waste of a voice," she said.

"Thank you." He adjusted the heat, glanced her way. "All the men in my family have this same voice. My dad sang bass in the church choir and for a barbershop quartet."

"No way. Like four-part harmony?"

"Exactly."

"Do you sing?"

"I sing a mean Springsteen in the shower."

Which made her think of him in the shower. She looked out the window, watching the closed shops slide by. "You sound more like Leonard Cohen."

"I'm flattered. Lennie's one of the best."

"Right? What's your favorite? And if you say 'Hallelujah,' we can't be friends."

"I don't know, that's a hell of a song. Just because it's popular doesn't mean there's something wrong with it."

"So that is your favorite?"

"No. I have more favorite albums. *Old Ideas*, and the last one, *You Want It Darker*." He glanced in the rearview and changed lanes. "Favorite song is hard. 'Suzanne,' 'Show Me the Place.'" He smiled. "'Hallelujah.'"

Veronica smiled. "Fair. It's so full of darkness and brokenness."

"What's your favorite, then?"

"'A Thousand Kisses Deep,'" she said quietly, thinking about the lyrics. "It got me through some dark nights after my divorce."

"Another one about the way life fucks with you."

She laughed. "Yeah. Now I want to listen to Leonard Cohen. I bet you have some on your phone, don't you?"

"Probably. But we're almost back to the hotel."

"I hate that you're going to have to drive back."

He pulled up beside the hotel, put the Range Rover in park. "Are you inviting me up?"

Veronica looked up at him. A bar of light from a streetlight cast half his face in shadow, cut the lines of his mouth into perfect relief. He smelled of earth and forest and sky, and the air around them thickened with recognition. Possibility. "Maybe," she whispered.

He placed an open hand on the inside of her wrist. His palm was hot.

Mariah moaned from the back seat. They jerked apart.

"I need to get her safely settled."

He nodded. "It's probably easier to unload her here rather than looking for space in the garage."

"Right." She opened the door, and stepped out, not quite willing to leave that soft cloud of possibility, knowing there was nothing to be done. She cocked her head.

He held her eye. Barely nodded.

Veronica turned toward duty. *Her charge,* she thought, like an old novel. "Come on, sweetheart," she said, opening the door to the back.

Mariah stirred, wiping her face. "Jeez, I'm so fucking high."

"Can you walk?"

"I'm not a baby," she said, and tumbled from the car, nearly wiping out on the sidewalk. Veronica caught her, grabbed the cane.

Henry hopped out and rounded the car. There was no traffic, and he left the car running as he helped Mariah to the door. Veronica pulled the girl toward her, letting her lean as they staggered up the steps. Henry stood close by, his hand at Mariah's back. The elevator opened immediately, but he waited a moment.

"You got it? At this time of day, I can park for a few minutes."

The offer lit a dozen hidden places in her body, small blue lights in her palms, her throat. Other places. She swallowed. "I think I'm okay. Thanks."

"Okay." He raised a palm. She kept her gaze on his face, a soft bar of light across his cheekbone and chin, until the door closed completely.

Mariah leaned on both cane and Veronica, and they made it without incident to the room. Veronica poured Mariah onto her bed, pulling off her shoes. "How long since you've eaten?"

"I don't know," Mariah said, shimmying out of her shirt, then her jeans, climbing into bed in her underwear. "I don't think I can eat right now. I just want to sleep."

"Wait. Sit up. Five minutes." She got her propped up and ran into the kitchen, poured a glass of milk, and looked for something to eat that would be fast and easy to chew. Yogurt. When she rushed back into the room, Mariah had tilted sideways, her hair over her face. But she wasn't sleeping. She was crying. It was the broken cry of a child, a wail.

"Oh, honey." Veronica put down the milk and yogurt and settled beside her on the bed instead, lifting her up so she could get an arm around her, then tucking her against her shoulder. "Go ahead and cry. I'm here."

She cried herself to sleep. Veronica's shirt was soaked and sweaty as she settled the girl in the pillows and covered her up, pulling her hair out of her face. For a moment, she took in Mariah's finally sleeping face, and felt something long forgotten, the relief of a sick child finally dropping off.

She was mothering Mariah. Was that appropriate? Unhealthy? Was it even what Mariah needed? She thought of her conversation with Jenna about her rent. She was shoving her own daughter out of the nest to fly, then turning around and pouring mother love on this girl.

Was that wrong?

She turned off the light and closed the door, thinking of her own mother, lying in her hospital bed at the end, all skin and bones and no hair, her bright blue eyes the only light left in her. A forgotten reservoir of grief welled in her throat.

Exhausted but wound up, she put the kettle on and searched through the little packets of tea for something soothing. Lavender chamomile would do the trick. She sat down with the tea and opened her computer to browse the letters Jill had sent. Among the other emails was a note from her landlord, basically giving her five days to come up with something. Her gut twisted.

Her phone buzzed. She very nearly didn't turn it over, expecting some rant from one of her children, but in the end, she glanced at it. The number was new to her, and she'd labeled it simply "Henry." I'm listening to Leonard Cohen. Wanna dance?

She smiled. Sure. What shall we dance to?

Her phone rang and he said in his deep voice, "'Dance Me to the End of Love.'"

"Give me a second." She found the song on her phone and then held up the phone to her ear and imagined she was dancing with him.

She had to reach up a long way to loop her arms around his neck, and his big hands rested on her hips. Eyes closed, she swayed and hummed along. He sang softly. The night was dark, but much less lonely.

When it was over, he said, "Good night, Veronica."

"Good night, Henry."

Letters #1

Rachel to Jill, 1995

Dear Jill,

Finally have a sec to write a letter. Sorry I can't call, but holy shit are the rates high! I'm barely affording this as it is.

But wowowowowowowowowowowowowowowowow!! I *love* India! It's a lot, don't get me wrong, like so many people you can't even imagine it, not in your wildest dreams, a big concert of humans all around you all the time. You have to be careful on the trains because men get grabby, but mostly it's just that you're kind of smashed up against other bodies and everyone kind of just lives with it. It's weird to feel somebody's soft belly, a baby's foot (through their mom's stomach!), a hard elbow. Like so much muchness.

So much muchness. That's it.

It's so much in every way, the colors and the smells and the decorations on everything, all over the place. Semitrucks painted with gods and hung with strings of fake flowers and little murals painted on the doors. It makes you wonder why people don't do that in the US. Like, you have to be in it all the time, so why not make it beautiful?

I started classes, and I'm really happy with them. With my roommates, and everything. A lot of Brits and a few Americans, but I kinda knew that going in. I'm having a blast shopping! It's so cheap to buy certain things—I've already bought some dresses and these soft pants. It's hot. You have to wear loose clothes, but you *really* can't be immodest. Everyone stares. My roommate, Gina, showed me how to wear a scarf and how to tie these pants. I feel like a total hippie, but, I mean, that's where all those styles came from, right? Boho = India cotton and prints and anklets with bells.

But really, the food is the thing. It's so great. So many kinds of things, and all of it is amazing. I found this café nearby that serves amazing food—*bun maska*, which is a fluffy roll with filling, and fresh lime soda, and goat biryani (Yes! Goat! It's delicious!). I go there so much that one of the daughters saw me on campus and started laughing, calling out my order to me. *Bun maska*, lime soda! She's studying accounting and literature, one for her family business, one for her own interests. Her brother is here, too, a year older, but I haven't met him.

I can't believe I made this happen. I'm so proud of myself. Give mom a kiss.

Love,

Rachel

Dear Jill,

I miss you!! As much as I love all this, it's hard to be without you and Mom.

Is this thing with Jack serious? Because it kinda sounds like it. I love him, don't get me wrong, but can you really live with being Jack and Jill for the rest of your lives? Will you name your kids Peter, Peter Pumpkin Eater and Mary, Mary Quite Contrary? HAHAHAHA!

Kidding. He's a nice guy. I get it. You make a good couple.

Yesterday, I went to the food market with Zoish. Isn't that a cool name? She's the girl I met through her family restaurant. We hang out sometimes. She's so funny and energetic and outgoing. I've never been with her when people didn't come up to chat with her. Super charismatic.

The market is this huge covered space, with all these little alleyways breaking off in a million directions. I'd be afraid to get lost by myself, but I stayed close, all the while she's shouting out to this person and that one in a mix of languages, English and Hindi and whatever it is she speaks with her family, which I think is Gujarati? Urdu? (So many languages here, and the students I meet all speak at least three, sometimes four. The language of their family, the main language of their area, which might be the same, but might not, plus Hindi or Urdu and English. I haven't sorted out the differences yet, but I'm in awe. I don't even speak my own language all that well. How is it that I don't even speak Spanish?)

Anyway. We're walking through this market, and it's really hot, but the shade helps. They sell all kinds of things there, like a mall, spices and vacuum cleaners and candy and boxes of cereal, and then we came to a big farm market, which is what Zoish was there for. She haggled and chatted up the vendors, buying carrots and fresh herbs and all kinds of things to take back to the restaurant. They also get normal deliveries by truck because I've seen them there, but her dad likes his veggies fresh.

After the vegetables, she took me to a fabric stall, where her cousin or uncle or some family member showed me all these beautiful fabrics and took my measurements for an outfit. I got the clothes today, and I felt like a princess when I tried them on. Easy clothes to wear, a loose dress and leggings. I can't wait to show you. I never wore so much pink before, but honestly, it looks really good. I also have some lime green and a soft orange, though I have to leave yellow alone, still. It just makes me look sick.

School is better. I'm getting into it. Learning a lot, but still learning more outside school, which is kind of how it always is, right?

How's Mom? How's Denver? I miss you. Give Mom a kiss.

Love,

Rachel

CHAPTER TWENTY-FOUR

In the morning, Veronica crossed the street for pastries and good coffee. Before she returned, she called Henry. "Are you up yet?"

"Long time. How's the patient?"

"Pretty hungover, but okay. I'm getting good coffee now." She stepped out of the flow of foot traffic to talk. "I got some of Rachel's letters last night, and she mentioned Zoish. I would guess it's the same Zoish Irani who is the proprietor of the South Asian bookshop."

"Ah, very good. Do you feel comfortable sending them to me?"

"Of course. I'll send the other notes, too, such as they are."

"Don't forget that we have Dishoom tonight. It would be best if we take the tube. It's a hard neighborhood to park in."

"Noted." She hung up. She carried the coffee and bag of pastries back to the room and found a shaky, if showered, Mariah in the sitting room. "Hey," Veronica said. "How are you?"

"Ugh. Desperately hungover."

"I have the cure." She handed her a coffee, then arranged the pastries on a plate.

"God, you're good." Mariah roused herself to sit at the table. Below her eyes were blue circles.

"Let's just have an easy day," Veronica said. "We have the train to Paris tomorrow." She thought about sharing the letters, but Mariah had been so heartbroken the night before that she'd decided to let Mariah bring them up. There was plenty of time.

Veronica hesitated, then picked up one of the pastries for herself. It smelled of almonds and sugar, and she inhaled deeply before she took a bite, savoring the anticipation of it. It was even better than she'd imagined in her mind, and her taste buds exploded with happiness. "This is amazing."

"Mmm."

Wiping her fingers, Veronica asked, "Do you often get panic attacks?"

She shrugged. "It was the gummies. They make me paranoid."

"Paranoid enough to make a trip in an ambulance?"

"No, not usually. But then, I'm getting used to this version of myself, aren't I?" She twisted a rope of pastry into a circle and took a nibble from the side. "I just got kind of disoriented and—" She sighed. "It wasn't just a panic attack. I had a monster flashback."

Veronica took a bite to keep herself from speaking too soon. Wordless, she raised her eyebrows: *Say more.*

"They told me it might happen, but I've only had one other one, so I didn't think I'd have to worry about it."

"Are you talking to a therapist or counselor or anyone?" Veronica asked.

She rolled her eyes. "Dude. Who can counsel me over this shit? Seriously."

Veronica thought of when she'd been ordered to take group therapy. It made her furious at first, but even during the first session, she found her guard coming down. "You might be surprised."

"Maybe." She rubbed her temple. "Can we talk about that some other time, though? I really have a fucking headache."

"Sure." Veronica picked up the phone and ordered tomato juice.

Mariah gave her a reluctant smile. "Thank you."

They spent the day reading and napping, and then took the tube to the restaurant, meeting Henry there.

From the minute they walked in, Veronica was enchanted. It was unlike anywhere she'd ever been. The walls and decorations were lusciously art deco, elegant arches and mirrors and the colors of dull orange and green. They were shown to a booth with an open view of the floor and the mezzanine. "This is so cool," Mariah said, and looked at Henry. "How come we never came here?"

"I don't know." He shrugged. "Your mom wrote to me about it just a couple of years ago." He nodded, looking around. "It captures the feeling of Parsi cafés," he said, and tapped the menu. "You should read all this. It's great background."

Veronica hardly knew where to focus her attention first—the setting itself, and the beautiful young servers, the music playing a soft jazzy something that underlined the mood, the cocktail menu classic favorites like Negronis and martinis, all with a little extra twist. "Great nonalcoholic cocktails," she commented.

"Seriously," Mariah said. "I'm even tempted."

Veronica read the story told on the menu, about Parsi cafés coming into their own in the Bombay of the 1930s. There was a graphic of what looked like the winged man but, on closer inspection, was a man and a winged circle. It was the same Zoroastrian symbol they'd seen at Café Guli. She needed to read more about the religion for context. She added a reminder to the growing list of notes on her phone.

And then, with a quiet sound, she dove into the menu. Her mouth actually watered. "I want every single thing on this list," she said, and called out possibilities. "Lamb samosas! Gunpowder potatoes! And, oh! The letters talk about goat, but I don't see any on the menu. I've never tried it."

Mariah raised her head. "You got the letters?"

Veronica had spoken impulsively. Carefully, she said, "Yes, a few. Do you want to read them?"

"Not yet."

"Understood," Veronica said.

Henry tapped the menu. "They also have *kulfi*. That's a very Indian thing."

Mariah said, "You know you want the lamb chops, Miss I Couldn't Eat Another Bite."

"I definitely wouldn't mind tasting them," Veronica said with concerted understatement, "but can we try both? The chops *and* the samosas?"

Mariah raised an eyebrow. "You're getting the hang of this. What else?"

They settled on a wide variety of dishes and drinks to sample, including a rose lassi and a cardamom lassi, which Veronica wanted to try just for the beauty of the ingredient names, *nimbu* soda, chai, of course, for the *bun maska* and two of the nonalcoholic cocktails. Henry insisted they add a salted lassi.

The server smiled as she collected the menus. "I can see you are here to indulge. I hope you enjoy it all as much as I do."

For the first time, Veronica felt like she had something of a handle on what Parsi meant. "Is this anywhere close to the Parsi cafés you've experienced in India?" she asked Henry and Mariah.

"I've never been to one," Mariah said. "We never went to India."

"Really?"

"She nixed it every time. Once we almost went, and then she canceled at the last minute. It really freaking annoyed me."

A well-tended woman in her mid-forties approached. "I'm so sorry to bother," she said to Mariah in a posh, dulcet voice, "but I am such a fan. Can we have a selfie? Is that horrible?"

"Happy to," Mariah said, leaning in to grin at the phone, flashing a shaka sign.

"I'm sorry you won't be in the games this winter. You were always my favorite."

"Thanks," Mariah said. A chilly glass fell around her. The woman took the hint, and hurried away.

"'Mean Mariah,'" Henry said.

"I was never mean to fans," she said. "I got a reputation for being a jerk, and the press loved it, but I was never mean to just"—she gestured—"people."

"Why were you mean?" Veronica asked.

"I wasn't really. I didn't see why I owed anybody any of my mental space or time. My mind was on the training and everything that goes into it." She twisted her mouth. "The boys don't get slammed for being aloof or short or whatever. They're more 'serious.'" She put the word in air quotes.

"That's brave."

Henry had a half smile on his mouth.

"What?" Mariah said.

"You were like that even when you were a kid. You never had time for any bullshit."

She grinned, and in the expression, Veronica caught a glimpse of the girl she'd been before all this happened to her, quirky and bright and brusque but also a lot of fun. Across the room, the woman who'd taken a photo with her Olympic hero kept stealing glances. Veronica grasped a little better the enormous losses Mariah had suffered.

The server brought drinks and appetizers. Veronica inhaled the mingled scents. Henry took some up-close photos, then reached for the salted lassi.

"What do you think you're going to do, going forward?" Henry asked before sipping. "Oh, wow, that's excellent." He offered it to Veronica, who used a second straw. She sipped the sharp, yogurty flavor and winced. "Maybe a little too intense for me."

"How should I know?" Mariah said. "I'm not exactly well-rounded."

"You could teach," Henry said.

"Yeah, right. Have you met me?"

"Not adults, but maybe kids."

She shrugged. "That wouldn't be so bad. But really, I just think it will be painful to be anywhere around the slopes. It'll break my heart every day."

Veronica said, "I get that."

"You'd get used to it," Henry added. "Seems a shame to give up the mountains and snow, which I know you love."

"Maybe." She shook her head. "I haven't come up with anything yet. Maybe when we get back."

"Fair enough. You have plenty of healing to do yet."

As if to deflect the attention away from her future, Mariah said, "What about you? You can't just drift around shooting arty photos."

"Well, I could, actually. It's enjoyable."

"Not very challenging, though."

He paused, picking up the *nimbu* soda. He tasted it, nodded, and continued, "Not everything has to be challenging. I've had a lot of challenge in my life. I want a little more calm now."

"Oh, you're old now, is that it?" Mariah grinned at him.

"Maybe."

Veronica tasted the rose lassi. "That's so good!" She offered it to the others, and made some notes on her phone.

Henry said, "I actually am going to do some teaching. Arapahoe Community College hired me to do some adjunct teaching on news photography."

To her surprise, Veronica felt strangely sad about that. To cover, she said, "You'll be good at that."

"Thanks."

And she could imagine him in a classroom, with adoring young men and women, teaching how to get the best shot, how to remove yourself from the scene. Why would she be disappointed in that?

Well, Spence. His profession had kind of made him a bit of an asshole. But was it the profession or the man?

"What's on your mind?" Henry asked, straightforward as ever. "Thinking about your future, too?"

"A little. It's still kind of new for me. It takes some time to let all the realities sink into your body, right?"

"Exactly." Mariah tried the Collins. "Ooh, that's excellent!" She passed it across the table. "But if you were going to do whatever you wanted, what would it be?"

The question made her feel vulnerable. "Something to do with history? Writing? Travel?" She rubbed her hands on her thighs, realized her shoulders were at her ears, and forced herself to relax. "This whole thing, researching cafés and making connections to create a story, is fantastic."

"Do it," Mariah said, and then with a droll tone, "I hear the biggest name in the arena bit the dust."

Veronica didn't know how to react at first. Was she making a joke?

"Dude! It was supposed to be funny!"

Henry shook his head. "Too soon."

"I think my mom would have laughed."

"You're probably right," Henry said, and slapped Mariah's hand on the table.

As they sampled the food, the tender cutlets, the lamb samosas, the fluffy buns, Veronica felt awash in some vague sense of nostalgia she couldn't quite capture. She'd never eaten Parsi food, so what was this place reminding her of?

They ate so much that she felt like she might explode, but there was absolutely no way she wanted to skip the dessert course. When it came, she was delighted by the strange, distinctive flavor of *kala khatta gola* ice, reveled in the combination of chili and chocolate in a pudding-and-ice-cream dish.

"Chocolate and chili is a big thing in New Mexico," she said, and suddenly she realized why she felt nostalgic—the place reminded her in some weird way of a café she'd worked in as a teenager. Her mother had worked there for twenty-five years before she got sick, and helped Veronica get hired.

The Blue Dog was situated advantageously on the plaza in Taos, and it had been in operation for more than seventy years, serving tourists and locals New Mexican food—chile rellenos, sopapillas, hot chocolate made with chile, deep bowls of Hatch green chile served with fluffy white tortillas. They made a red chile sauce with local chiles that was both hot and deeply layered, and the red chiles themselves hung on *ristras* around the room. The specials had been chalked on a blackboard by the door, and they served Mexican beers with lime and salted glasses.

It was nothing like this, and yet—it was, kind of. More like Café Guli, but even that had felt too shiny clean and new. What was she picking up here?

She looked around, letting the memories surface. She'd kept them suppressed for the most part because she'd let her mother down in her final six months by having an affair with the charming and beautiful manager of the restaurant, Tomas.

Who happened to be married, a fact Veronica (who was then Brandi) had clearly known. She knew his wife, who'd been a couple of years ahead of her at school, and who was quite thoroughly pregnant at the time.

Tomas. She didn't think about him very often anymore, but he had been one of the most beautiful men she'd ever seen, with liquid dark eyes and a ready smile, and a soulful depth of yearning she found impossible to resist. He longed for *her*. And she, devastated by her mother's diagnosis and her own fear that she'd never get out of New Mexico, fell prey to the wolf of the plaza. She was a virgin when they met. By the time she left the restaurant under a cloud of scandal and pain, she was quite thoroughly initiated into her own lusty nature.

Her mother, finding out about the affair only a couple of months before she died, slapped Brandi for the first and only time in her life. She'd apologized profusely, but Brandi knew she deserved it. A lot of people had been hurt by her actions.

And of course, her shame had been renewed over that painful public breakup when she faced the humiliating breakup with Spence. In the first instance, she'd been the mistress and vilified by her social group. She reacted with intense emotion and fury, as might be expected from a sixteen-year-old girl breaking up with her first lover.

But in the second instance, she'd been the wife who was injured. And had reacted with intense emotion and fury.

It happens every day, her therapist said in her mind.

"Earth to Veronica," Mariah said. "We lost you to New Mexico."

"You did. I was remembering a job I had when I was a teenager— these cafés are reminding me of the Blue Dog."

"The Blue Dog in Taos?" Henry said. "I've been there."

"No kidding. Do you remember when?"

He gazed into the distance. "Must have been around the late eighties. I was on a road trip with some buddies."

"You are so old," Mariah said, laughing.

"It's all perspective."

"My mom probably worked there then," Veronica said. "I got the job because she'd been there so long." Something caught high in her throat. She had taken her mother's position when she got sick.

"Small world," Henry said. His arm was draped along the back of the booth, and he touched her shoulder with one finger. "If you're tapping into something like that with the cafés, the emotion will be good for the book."

She nodded, aware that the lusty girl she'd been still lurked inside of her, and was too easily triggered outside the confines of marriage, where she'd been free to indulge it as much as she wanted.

The thought startled her. Was she afraid of her desires?

PART THREE

PARIS

I can barely conceive a type of beauty in which there is no melancholy.

—*Charles Baudelaire*

CHAPTER
TWENTY-FIVE

The next morning, they packed their bags and headed to the train for the journey to Paris. Veronica tried to veil her excitement, but inside, she was a fourteen-year-old bouncing up and down. She texted Jenna: We are going on the Chunnel train today!

It was, of course, the middle of the night in Colorado, so there was no response.

Mariah seemed much better today. Henry carried her backpack and his camera bag, leaving Veronica with only her own backpack and suitcase. It had given her pause momentarily to carry such a plain bag to the City of Light, but she didn't have anything else. She tried to make up for it with a weightless scarf in an abstract pattern to dress up her jeans and sweater and simple down jacket, because it was definitely cold and gray.

On the train, Henry sat next to her, Mariah across the table. They played cards and games while Veronica watched the landscape out the window, feeling a simple quiet unfold as the houses and businesses of the city gave way to fields, still green even in December, and the shapes of bare trees. Every so often, they stopped in a village and picked up a handful of new passengers. A woman carried a big cat in a basket, murmuring to him every so often.

Mariah curled up to sleep. Henry tugged a book out of his bag, the same one he'd picked up at the bookstore. "Any interesting commentary today?" she asked.

"I'll let you know." He held up earbuds. "Do you mind?"

"Not at all." She pulled her own out, and scrolling through her phone, pulled up a Leonard Cohen playlist. She thought about showing it to Henry, but he'd already gone under, and she felt silly anyway. After the moment in the car, things had returned to their former friendliness. Which was probably better anyway.

A second group of Rachel's letters had come in from Jill, so she spent her time reading and digesting them, collecting notes on her phone. Money had also landed in her account from Mariah, and she'd sent half to the rent, hoping it would be enough to prevent her landlord from evicting her.

She was going to have to figure out something better, but not from the train.

Instead, she focused on the letters, parsing out the time flow. What she could make out was that Rachel had gone to India to study . . . something . . . and became friends with a small group of local people, some of whom were connected to a Parsi café run by a family that seemed to have three daughters and a son.

The café was called Café Guli, like the one in England. A Google search showed it had closed in the mid-nineties, but she was able to find a few old photos of it. *Need to find a place to do some printing,* she wrote, and underlined it twice.

The café was run by proprietor Farroukh Irani, a heavily mustachioed man who stood before the café, smiling broadly. His grandfather had opened the establishment in the 1920s. One of the daughters must have been Zoish, already mentioned. Had one of the others been Hufriya, the woman from the café in London?

Mostly the letters were chatter about things she explored, places she went. She described food in quite a lot of detail.

The food is a total revelation. You think you know about Indian food, but there are so many layers and styles and kinds of cooking, it just blows my mind. Muslims cook different things than Hindus, and Parsis are in a world of their own, but even though they're all different, there are some cornerstone ingredients— mango and rice and peas and certain spices. I love the spices so much, so many different kinds. We went to a spice wallah, and there were little mountains of everything—cinnamon and mace and cloves and curry leaves and bay leaves and turmeric powder— and I wanted to buy every single thing, just to sample it. I'm learning so much about cooking, the styles of cooking that are based in one thing or another, the rules about halal, the strictures against meat, the goat and lamb and mutton, the forbidden things like cows (who really, truly do wander around all over the place, as if they're just your neighbors). It's so funny how my mind coughs up recipes and combinations to try— just like when we went to France when we were kids. I mean, I think I've always done it, but it's louder here. I write them down in my journal and can't wait to try them when I get home.

Veronica paused, excited to see an origin story in progress. The trip had shaped Rachel's delight in the food world, and it had obviously been her calling. She wanted to ask Mariah and Henry more about that, but she should also read Rachel's books, get a feel for her approach.

The young Rachel had also spent a lot of time talking about a boyfriend named Alex, who wasn't a student, but an Englishman traveling in India. Upon meeting Rachel, he'd decided to stay in Mumbai for a few weeks, and they spent a lot of time together, visiting temples and taking weekend trips to various places.

Alex and I took an overnight train up to Rajasthan. I only had a week off for the holidays, so it was a very fast tour of the main sights—we spent a day in Delhi visiting both the big mosque there and a giant Sikh temple where they feed hundreds of people every day. I loved both of them so much—the eagles that the imams feed at the mosque, the view of the city from the courtyard. I ate *jalebis* from a street vendor, even though Alex warned me not to, but I had to try. And maybe I'm getting a cast-iron stomach, or I'm just getting used to things around here, but I was fine. The Sikh gurdwara blew me away. The whole idea of feeding people as an act of service touches me. What if that was standard practice everywhere? If every church, temple, mosque in the world just . . . fed people? Can you imagine?

And ta-da! We saw the Taj Mahal. It's just so beautiful I can't even tell you. You think you know what something looks like because you've seen a million pictures, but a picture can't show you scope. It's huge. Inside, it's so quiet, their bones resting together forever. I cried, which Alex thought was silly, but I don't care.

A picture of Rachel was starting to emerge, a vivid girl with big emotions and a headstrong streak that could be a bit reckless. She'd run off to Delhi with her new boyfriend and nobody else? Veronica would kill Jenna if she did that.

She looked at Mariah, sleeping with her head nestled against the wall. This was Rachel's beloved daughter, or at least Rachel was a beloved mother. Was her daughter like her? She must look like her, or the woman at Café Guli would not have recognized her so definitely.

Casting a vision of Mariah over the young Rachel helped bring her into focus. She must have stood out, with her blond hair and very American ways.

With a frown, Veronica wondered what the Paris connection was. Why were they going there?

She referred back to the notes. The Paris list included Angelina, which had to be one of the most famous cafés in the world, but hardly Parsi or in any way related. The other place seemed more likely, Café Farroukh.

The name rang a bell. She frowned and looked back at the notes on the Mumbai cafe. Yes, the proprietor was Farroukh Irani. Another solid connection.

Maybe they were getting somewhere.

$\sim$

As they emerged from the train, gathering coats and hats and gloves, Mariah's cane and the books and notebooks they'd used on the way, Veronica received a series of texts, each buzzing as it came in. She recognized the pattern as Jenna's so didn't open it until she had a chance to read all of it.

Their hotel was nearby, and Mariah pleaded to go there first. "I don't think we can check in yet," Henry said.

"Maybe we can at least drop our bags?"

"We can ask." Veronica held out a hand. "What can I carry for you?"

"I'm good. I've only got my coat."

Henry was overloaded. He had his own bag, with at least one heavy book, his camera bag, and Mariah's bag. "Let me take hers," she said.

"Sure?"

She nodded and flung the pack over her right shoulder. "Now I'm balanced."

They stood outside the station awaiting a taxi, and Veronica took a deep breath. It was chilly but sunny. She absorbed the scene with a sense of happiness, taking in the traffic, the tourists pouring out of the station, young people in knots of three and four, families dressed up nicely, a group of children around ten or eleven years old, clearly on a school trip. They wore cranberry sweaters and plaid lowers.

"Five Guys!" Mariah exclaimed. "Let's go there first."

"Really?" Veronica said. "All these amazing places to visit, and you want a hamburger you can get in all fifty states?"

She shrugged. "I'm hungry and tired. Would it be so terrible?"

Henry touched Veronica's back. "We'll have other experiences. We can try Five Guys, too."

Veronica looked up at him, laughing. "You traitor! You want it, too."

"I'm hungry," he said. "Aren't you?"

She allowed herself to be led inside. She'd never actually been to one—so she couldn't tell if it was the same as all the others. It smelled good, of grilled onions and beef. The music overhead was some kind of pop. They scooted into a booth, Mariah by herself so she could stretch out her leg. She rubbed it absently.

"Does it hurt more in the cold?" Veronica asked.

"Yeah, I think it's the metal. But I'm all right. I can't wait to go to Angelina. That was one of my favorite places when I was a little girl."

"Is that why it's on the list?"

"I don't know. She had a thing for all kinds of cafés, and she had a couple of favorites in Paris, and New York, and Marrakech."

"And that Greek place in Colorado Springs, remember?" Henry said.

"Oh, yeah! I forgot about that one. Michelle's. The ice cream, oh my God."

"Did you know that the first café to open anywhere served ice cream?" Henry said, clearly parroting.

"And did you know that the butterfat at Michelle's is the richest in the city?"

Veronica listened to them trade memories, scanning the menu, trying to calculate the incalculable calories on a menu like this. Cheeseburgers and french fries and fried everything. And they'd be eating again a couple more times while they were here. She'd have to be careful.

Her stomach growled in protest.

"Somebody is hungrier than they admit," Mariah said, and slapped her menu down. "You need a real meal. Actual food, with no diet stuff."

Veronica flushed, ears hot over addressing food and diets in front of a man. "I'm a grown woman. I know how to feed myself."

"You know how to starve yourself, babe," Mariah said, sliding out of the booth with her cane. "I'm ordering for all of us," Mariah said. "Cool?" She looked at the other two. "Three cheeseburgers with everything, fries, and . . . what? Cokes, you guys?"

"Ugh. No Coke," Veronica protested. *"Café, s'il vous plaît."*

"Same," Henry said. *"Et eau gazeuse, aussi, s'il vous plaît."*

When Mariah went to the counter, Henry said, "I worked in a burger joint when I was a kid. My uncle owned it, out on the highway to the shore, and it was always busy."

"What did you do?" Mariah asked.

"Everything. Flipped burgers, washed dishes, waited tables, all of it. Whatever he told me to do."

"Same, at the Blue Dog," Veronica said, and she was surprised to remember it without sorrow this time.

Mariah returned, sliding in next to Henry.

"It was old-school Mexican, so cute," Veronica said. "I'm talking about the Blue Dog, the place I worked when I was a teenager. Your mom would have liked it. The walls were painted bright colors, and we wore uniforms with embroidered flowers around the neckline, and a fake flower on a barrette. It was an institution."

"No way! Did you hate it?"

She let the door swing open, visuals spilling into view. "No, I loved it. My mom was sick, and I really wanted to be busy." She paused, feeling the noise and cheer and camaraderie she'd felt spill into her memory. "It was kind of magical, you know, the things you had to learn to be good at it, the way to serve sopapillas and how to gauge the heat of the green chile and how to serve from the right side of the table, and the language of orders." A memory of Tomas flashed through her mind, his big dark hands, his smile. It arrived vividly, laced with both longing and guilt. She'd been besotted. She pushed that part of the memory out of view. "It's hard work, but it's fast paced, and if you get it right, people are happy."

"Did your mom get better?"

Veronica shook her head. "She died of breast cancer when I was sixteen."

"I'm so sorry."

"It was a long time ago."

"Still." Mariah inclined her head, measuring. "It's hard, you were really young."

Veronica nodded, shrugged. True and true, but what was there to say?

"You still like feeding people," Mariah said, spilling salt into her palm. "You offer me food all the time."

"I *do* like to feed people," she said, thinking of that big farmhouse table, her dining room filled with light. "Or I did. That might be part of my old life."

"Your mom life."

It stung in some uncharted region of her chest. The sting was a hard truth she was still grappling with. "Yeah, I guess so."

Next to her, Henry said, "Wonder what the new chapter will bring."

She peered into the future, and although she couldn't see very far, the road definitely had different features from the one she'd been walking for over twenty years.

She looked up at him. "Good question."

CHAPTER
TWENTY-SIX

The hotel was tall and narrow, Hotel Altheda, and their three rooms took up most of the top floor. In her room, Mariah flung her body across the bed and fell almost instantly asleep, her belly full, her body tired from travel.

For the first time in nearly a week, it was natural sleep, unassisted or impeded by alcohol or painkillers or antianxiety meds. Her mind flashed pictures of pleasant things at first, a dream about running when she was a child, faster than all the other kids at the track meet, her hair flying behind her. Her mom had not been there, but Jill had been, cheering and screaming when she took the blue ribbon.

And then, abruptly, she was at the ER, a small army of people around as she drifted in and out, holding her mom's hand as the team examined her leg, the wound in her side, her face, which bled buckets. All three wounds hurt so much, so loudly, and she kept telling them *It hurts! It hurts! It hurts!*

A nurse held her other hand, trying to calm her. "We can't give you anything yet, sweetheart, but it will get better soon, I promise. Hold on, Mariah, hold on. Keep talking. Squeeze my hand. We need to know you're still with us."

She looked at her mother. "What do they mean? Am I going to die?"

"No, baby. You're going to live. Keep holding on. I'm right here with you."

In her hotel room in Paris, she bolted upright, straight out of sleep, gasping for breath. Her heart raced, and she pressed both hands against it, trying to suck in a breath, *one two three*, out *two three four five six*, but her brain was racing, touching memories and strange moments all at the same time, and it didn't work.

After struggling to her feet, she grabbed her water bottle out of her backpack and took a long drink. The action eased the building panic, and she was able to take a breath.

She'd taken three bullets. The worst injury was her leg, a shattered femur, but more drastically, the femoral artery had been nicked. Not blasted, or she would have died, but she still lost a ton of blood, and at the time the nurse had urged her to keep talking, the team had been all but certain they would lose her before they could get her into surgery. The bullet in her side had miraculously not touched any of her vital organs and passed straight through her body. The bullet that skimmed the side of her face had been a horror when she first woke up, but on that, too, she'd been lucky. Only flesh was mangled, not her brain.

When she awakened days later, she cried out for her mother. Jill was there, trying to soothe her, but she wouldn't be dissuaded. "I need to talk to her," she cried. "Find her!"

Jill broke the news that Rachel had died instantly.

"No!" Mariah protested. "She was with me, the whole time!"

Jill wept at that. "I'm sure she was, honey, but her physical body was somewhere else."

Even now, Mariah could remember her mom at her side in that ER, holding her hand, looking into her eyes. "Hang on. You can do it," she'd said, her clear eyes very direct, like lasers.

But of course, she had not been there. Mariah had actually known that on some level. Hadn't she seen her mother fall?

In her current state of slight confusion and a growing sense of health—despite the setbacks—the whole thing suddenly struck her as completely bizarre. That they'd gone shopping for avocados and tomatoes and had in fact been discussing the ways to *choose* an avocado—the give of the skin, the marker of the stem end—when some random person just came into the produce aisle and shot them like they were targets in a video game. Like, for no reason. Just because he could.

In her Paris hotel room, she limped to the window, rubbing her thigh more out of habit than pain. Across the way, she could see a bank of apartments and a tricycle on the balcony. People's voices reached her, speaking not French, but some other language she didn't know.

Had her mom really been there in the ER, or had it been a hallucination? "Mom," Mariah said aloud now, "I'd like a sign. Are you out there? Or is it just a big dark space on the other side?"

That was why she kept wanting to talk to Tyler Henry, the psychic. Or the seat belt guy. They'd channel some message from Rachel, some proof that she wasn't just gone forever, but waiting in some other dimension.

"Stop it," she said, and shook her shoulders vigorously. She wasn't that person, some airy-fairy girlie girl who believed in crystals and spells and gods or heaven or past lives. She was the *opposite* of that.

Or she had been. Stripping off her clothes, she headed for the shower. It wasn't until she stepped into the tiny stall that she realized she was mulling over the words of the medium in Brick Lane: *The bookstore will give you some help.*

What did the bookstore lead to? What had her mother hidden all these years? What were all these clues adding up to? What had Rachel been trying to do?

Maybe they'd find some answers here. After a time, she fell back to sleep, and woke up to change into fresh jeans and a T-shirt from the Sochi Olympics. Today, they'd stop into Angelina. That was an easy stop, a place Rachel and Mariah had visited often when Mariah was small. She thought about the drinking chocolate and the little boxes of treats, and suddenly couldn't wait. The sun was out, she was young, and they were in Paris on a quest.

For the first time in a very long time, she felt not only alive but also glad to be. What came next? She had no idea.

But today, she would drink chocolate at Angelina.

CHAPTER
TWENTY-SEVEN

The next morning, the plan was to explore the city and visit the two cafés on their list—Angelina and Café Farroukh.

Veronica had caught up with email and messages the night before. Her landlord had sent a reminder about the rent. If she lost the apartment, what would happen to her stuff?

She finally texted Jenna. I need an urgent favor. Can you go pick up my car in Denver and bring it to my apartment?

Denver? I really can't, Mom! That will take hours!

I know. I hate to ask, but I'm desperate.

She paused, not wanting to put Spence in a bad light but also not wanting to outright lie. Then: Because of a big mess of things, I'm in danger of getting evicted. If I get the car there, it might help hold it until I get back.

Wow. Evicted? How is that even possible?

It's a long story. Can you please
help me? It doesn't have to be
today.

Mom, I really can't. Have zero hours
at the moment. Trying to get my
own rent. Ask Ben.

Veronica scowled at the phone. After all that she'd done for her daughter, she couldn't do a favor for her in return. It's pretty critical, sweet. Can you squeeze out a couple of hours?

Mom! You know it will take longer
than that, and I'm swamped! I can't!

Her fingers hovered over the keypad. Stung, she was reluctant to ask Ben or Tim—but why? They were as capable as Jenna. But they didn't have the same relationship. A little sense of discomfort ran through her heart. She didn't really trust the boys to do the same job her daughter would do.

As she debated on how to respond, she suddenly thought of her friend Amber. She needed an apartment and had been having a hard time finding one in Boulder country.

Good grief! Why hadn't she thought of her?

And why hadn't Veronica offered *before*? She'd lose the little office she loved, but Amber needed something soon.

For a moment, she felt enormous disgust at herself for not considering this offer sooner, which led to feeling more disgust over the meal she'd scarfed down like a teenager, eating the entire burger and the fries, so much food that she felt unexpectedly bloated. Probably all the salt. What an idiot—

The mental noise started to build higher and higher, like a toddler having a temper tantrum and dragging out toys from every corner of the house. She saw the chartreuse shame of the affair with Tomas, and the size of her ass at the end of the pandemic, and—

Stop.

She caught sight of her face in a mirror and was quite stricken by the twist on her lips. Holding her phone, she approached the mirror and really looked at her face. She relaxed her mouth, shook her head, looked again. Her cheekbones were almost too gaunt. The collarbones she'd taken such pride in just looked bony. No wonder Mariah had urged her to eat!

Stop!

One of the things she'd learned in the group counseling she'd been forced by the courts to take was that she was really bad at boundaries. The result was that she swallowed her own feelings over and over, which led to anger and turning it on herself, but also led to erupting like a volcano, as she had the day she'd been arrested.

What boundary did she need to set right now? She closed her eyes. Took a breath. She was in charge of her own eating. She didn't need to starve to please Spence, or eat like a teenager to please Mariah, the ex-athlete.

She did want to enjoy the experience of eating abroad, to sample things here that she wouldn't taste at home. Like the lamb kebab in London, which she'd eaten with great relish, and the snacks from Waitrose.

But before she got completely lost in her own appetite, she texted Amber: Have you found an apartment? I might have an idea.

An answer came back instantly: i'm all ears.

be my roommate.

what? what about the kids?

Of course. Amber had three kids under seven, who visited her every other weekend. Veronica had been imagining Amber would be in the room she was currently using as an office, but the kids needed a place to sleep sometimes. She typed, You'll take my bedroom and I can move into the office room. A bunk bed should do the trick, right?

Three dots.

Three dots.

Three dots.

i'm crying r u sure

> yes but there's a problem I need to
> solve. Can I call you?

Veronica started dialing, and Amber answered on the first ring. "We need to talk about the rent, girlfriend," she said. "I don't have a ton of money."

"We can split it," Veronica said, and named the figure. "Is that okay?"

"Yes! Better than okay. Oh my God, I can't believe it! That's such a nice place."

"There's a small catch, Amber."

"Oh."

"I need you to get my car from Denver to the apartment as collateral for my rent. Is that even possible?" She explained the situation with Spence, the money, the car. "I'll be evicted if I can't get this worked out."

"Ugh, I can't leave the county, remember? But I got something better. I have deposit money saved, so I can cover the whole rent."

A wild swell of relief rose through her. It almost seemed too good to be true. Veronica hesitated. "Are you sure?"

"Do I have to wait for you to get back?"

"No way. You can move in today if you want. You can pick up the key from my daughter."

Amber made a soft sound. "This is saving my life, babes."

"It's also saving mine, so we're even."

They discussed the logistics of getting the key, making sure Veronica could have a roommate, and how to move things in. "I don't have a lot, you know. My kids can sleep on air mattresses at first. I won't get into your room until you get back."

"Amber, thank you."

~

As they set out the next morning, Paris was dripping with Christmas decorations. Veronica had seen some around London, but here, there were trees and wreaths and garlands everywhere, all of them hung with ornaments and sparkling lights. It pricked some underlayer of her internal body, sticking pins in at random points. A wreath made her think of one her mother had loved, made of pine cones and red velveteen ribbon. A shop window was hung with a set of old-fashioned glass ornaments from the fifties, which were very much the same as the ones Veronica had collected over the years. She had not unboxed them last year because Spence and the kids had gone to Breckenridge and she'd only just managed to move into the apartment. Obviously, she wouldn't unbox them this year, either.

What would Christmas be going forward? This? Traveling to faraway places without any of her beloveds just to avoid the pain she felt? Avoiding the beautiful Christmas traditions she loved because the center had fallen out of her world?

Emotion swelled her throat. She didn't know. She didn't know anything. Her entire future was as murky as muddy water, where before she had not liked everything she was looking at as an empty nester (the words gave her a vision of a mother bird perched on a tree branch, peering into the distance), but she'd had a general idea of how her life would look.

Now she had absolutely no idea. It seemed particularly brutal that she wouldn't use her Christmas ornaments again; wouldn't bake cookies with her kids and decorate the tree, then have brandy with Spence after the kids went to bed.

At least the carols were all in French, making them different enough that they didn't pierce her like everything else did.

So she was already feeling off-kilter when they went into Angelina. There were two lines—one for the counter, one for the dining room—and they took their place in the one for the dining room. In contrast to the cheeriness of Christmas shoppers and the shining lights, the sky overhead was dark enough that yellow light spilled out of the upper stories of buildings across the street. It was cold. She wished for a different coat, something fluffier and more stylish, rather than her very warm but boring performance fleece. She'd draped a scarf around her neck and pulled a blue cap over her ears, but she still felt like she stuck out as a gauche tourist.

Henry constantly took photos, unobtrusively and obviously, of shop fronts and streets lined with trees and lights, the backs of two women in red coats holding hands, a little boy chewing on his mitten as if he were a dog. He took photos of Mariah, who mugged for the camera, and Veronica, who only looked at him. He smiled. "That's a good shot. You have expressive eyes."

Inside, the air smelled of a heady mix of coffee and yeast and sugar. The baroque interior had not changed a bit, and still felt ever so faintly seedy, but crystal chandeliers glittered and the tables were set for a busy day. As they sat down, Veronica looked toward the mirrored wall and remembered exactly where she'd sat with Spence on a long-ago day, twenty-eight years ago. She could see him quite clearly, as if he were a ghost: his thick white fisherman's sweater sitting so cleanly on his broad shoulders; his long, blond hair curling around his neck, falling over his forehead. He was always deeply tan in those days from being on the slopes or outside hiking; he'd been the most vigorous man she'd ever met, and had pulled her along with him, teaching her how to hydrate, how to tie her boots. She'd tried skiing and snowboarding both, but they terrified her. The hiking, however, she loved.

It had been a wild, deep bonding from the first. They were from different worlds and yet shared a view of how life should be, filled with books and knowledge and the things that went into making a good life. She loved his passion for philosophy, for ideas, and his boyish exuberance. He loved her drive toward making a comfortable home, loved that she wanted to write about intellectuals and artists in history.

They had been so entwined on that honeymoon trip! Newly married, three years into their remarkable love story. Everyone admired them, wanted to be them. They had a rare accord, a meeting of bodies and minds. He was known to kiss her passionately at parties, dance in a very sexy way when the music lent itself to that.

An all-too-familiar hollow feeling filled her chest. How had that all just disappeared? Had she been mistaken about what it really was?

No. She remembered a night during the pandemic, the children gone somewhere, just the two of them over a meal they'd cooked together, dancing to a playlist, making love on the floor by the fire. So happy.

So happy.

As if the memories had turned to arrowheads in her chest, Veronica's lungs suddenly ached. It was hard to take a deep breath, and she looked around wildly to distract herself with anything so that she wouldn't burst into tears.

"Where is the loo, do you think?" she asked Mariah.

"Um—you have to go upstairs."

Swamped with emotion, desperate to hide it, she managed, "I'll be right back. Sorry."

CHAPTER TWENTY-EIGHT

Mariah watched Veronica bolt for the ladies' room. "She seems pretty upset."

"She does. And I'm glad to see you noticed."

"She hasn't been divorced very long. Something you should remember," she said with a cocked eyebrow, "Mr. Your Eyes Are So Expressive."

To her surprise, he looked slightly abashed. "Mind your own business, kid."

"I'm not a kid, buddy."

He grinned. "No, you're not. You also seem a little better today."

She nodded, looking around. "I wonder what she reacted to in here? Nothing about this place says Colorado at all, does it?"

He shook his head, glanced toward the stairway where Veronica had disappeared.

Mariah thought of her and her mom sitting here. "How long did it take you to feel like yourself again after—"

"The bomb? A year, for the physical." His fingers moved over the top of his camera, touching the buttons, the sides, caressing it. "But you don't go back to being the person you were before. You become somebody new."

She felt the truth of that, a knowing that she could never go back to being the Mariah who could snowboard at literally a hundred miles per hour through fresh powder. "I get that. So sad, though. Do you miss it? Your old life?"

"Yeah, I guess. But unlike you, I'm not young, and it was getting pretty brutal."

Mariah took that in, thinking about the people she'd known who'd stayed too long in the competition arena, hoping for one more minute of glory. Almost worse than getting an injury that ended it all abruptly.

She spied Veronica coming back down the stairs. "Damn, she looks like she's been crying. Don't look! Let's try to cheer her up."

He covered her hand. "I'm in."

CHAPTER
TWENTY-NINE

As she returned to the table, hoping her intense crying fit didn't show, Veronica said, "That is the most beautiful bathroom I've ever seen."

"Should I go see it?" Mariah asked.

"You definitely should."

"First, let's figure out what to order. We have to have drinking chocolate and the *Mont-Blanc*," Mariah said.

"I'm going to waddle home, I swear," Veronica said.

"No, we won't! Remember, my mom's method is to order a bunch of things and take bites of all of it." She pointed to the bag Veronica looped over her shoulder. "You need to take notes. This will be a good chapter."

"Right."

Henry, perusing the menu, said, "Add the onion soup and eggs Benedict with avocado. And coffee." His leg was close to hers under the table, and he nudged her knee with his. "What will you try, V?"

The arrowheads still jabbed her lungs, but she forced herself to look at the menu. What would she like to try? What would *she* like to try? "Okay, I'll play. I want to taste the chocolate again, of course, but I'd also like to try the mille-feuille and, naturally, quiche Lorraine."

"And what else?" Mariah said. "I'm adding the apple thing."

"Not much else will fit on the table," Veronica pointed out.

"We can ask to have them bring it out in rounds."

Veronica wondered how it would feel to be so completely comfortable everywhere, all the time. Nothing put Mariah off. She believed she deserved to be wherever she was and didn't question her choices once she made them.

It must be heaven to move through the world like that.

Henry probably felt that way, too, but he was a man, and he'd traveled all over the world. Was travel part of the secret?

What made a person comfortable in their own skin? She knew a lot of her discomfort upon going to college in Boulder had been that it seemed all the students were in a much higher social class than she.

But since then, she'd lived for years as the wife of a professor, by any measure a genteel world. That should have given her some cred, if only with herself.

The trouble was that she'd been hauled off to jail for criminal mischief and domestic violence (that second bit totally unfair, in her opinion), a scenario that had reinforced the image of herself as a working-class woman wearing the sheep's clothing of a professor's wife.

Piercing her drifting thoughts, Henry said, "Why don't we take a look at the pastry case?"

"I'm going to stay," Mariah said. "My leg gets tired standing in line. If you see anything else you think I might like, order it for me."

The entire restaurant was decorated for Christmas, with garlands around doorways and along the railings. On the pastry case were trees shaped from macarons, and lights winked in surprising colors—peach and lime green and gentle blues. She hadn't anticipated the layering of Christmas melancholy with the memory of her happy honeymoon. As she stood with Henry, looking at pastries, she wished she could share the experience with Jenna, and took a handful of photos, something she would never have done if Henry had not been standing there with his very visible enormous camera. A few people gave him the side-eye, but he didn't pay any attention, and she supposed that a photographer would have to get used to people staring or not wanting him to shoot them.

"I'd love to see these shots," she said.

"Sure. Anything you want me to get?"

She pointed to the Yule log, frosted in red, and the macaron trees. He took shots of them, and then more of her; she felt the lens focus on her face as she leaned in to read the little cards before the pastries. Her tongue swept over her teeth in anticipatory glee.

They returned to the table to order, and when the server hurried away, Mariah said, "My mom and I came here the first time when I was very little, maybe only four or five. She loved it here. We had hot chocolate and the pistachio *Mont-Blanc* every time, and took macarons back to the hotel." She looked wistful. "I feel like I can see her here."

"I came here on my honeymoon," Veronica said, and the startling blue of Spence's eyes that day rose in memory. "We sat right over there." The arrowheads rustled, and she rubbed her breastbone. "I always hoped we'd come back eventually."

"Why didn't you?" Mariah asked, direct as ever.

Veronica shrugged. "Who knows? Life just . . . takes you where it takes you."

"True that. How about you, Henry?" Mariah asked. "Any memories of Angelina's?"

"No," he said, looking around, then back to them, "but I am making some now."

A glimmer of a narrative flitted over Veronica's mind. Places as points of time, or memory. She leaned forward. "So, cafés are places people visit, and return to. They can be touchstones, carry memories. Families, lives."

"That's good," Henry said.

"I'm thinking of myself at twenty-two," Veronica said, "and you're thinking of yourself at four, and we're all here together at the ages we are now, having a different experience than the ones we've had before—" She frowned. "I'm not saying that very well, but I'm feeling it." She touched her belly. "Did your mom come here before she brought you?"

"I don't know. Maybe Jill would know."

"I'll ask her. But not now." She pulled out her notebook and sketched the scene loosely, then made some notes about their orders. Twice she looked over to the table she had shared with Spence, but redirected quickly.

"I'm starting to see a kind of shape for this book," she said as they sipped chocolate and coffee and sampled pastries, a napoleon that was the flakiest thing she'd ever tasted, the quiche creamy and salty with the layers of cheese and bacon. "I'll draft an outline, and you can take a look."

"I trust you," Mariah said.

Veronica hesitated a moment, then decided to ask for what she needed, clearly and directly. "But I need to know you're going to pay me properly for my time. We need to hammer that out."

"Oh, snap. I forgot." She wiped cream from her chin and fingers. "Why don't you come up with what you think it should be, and draft out some kind of agreement, and we'll go from there."

Veronica straightened, feeling a sense of . . . soft power. "I can do that."

CHAPTER THIRTY

Mariah stretched mightily out on the street, feeling an easy happiness over the memories of her mother and herself drinking chocolate and gorging on pastries. It was a good memory, one she wanted to carry with her forever. Maybe noticing that was a good sign.

"After that feast, maybe we should walk to Café Farroukh," Henry said, consulting the maps on his phone.

"Feast!" Veronica echoed. "More like gluttony. I will not be able to eat a single bite at a new café, I don't care how far we walk."

"We don't have to eat there," Henry said. "This one isn't about the café so much as the connection to India."

"You read the notes!" Veronica exclaimed. "Thank you."

"Of course. This café is a good lead," he said, directing them toward a busy intersection. "Looks like it's too far to walk all the way, but let's head down the Seine and get the metro from a bit farther down."

"I love the name," Mariah said. "I can eat for all of us if you guys are wimps."

Veronica laughed. "You eat more than anyone I've ever met."

"Good metabolism, thank God."

"Are you up for the walk?" Veronica asked Mariah.

Her leg was fine this morning, and so was her heart. "I'm good! Great, actually."

They made decent progress until Veronica and Henry were snared by the booksellers along the river, the stalls ready to cover the books at the first drops of rain. Veronica and Henry both picked up book after book after book, but Mariah didn't read French well, so she stuck to the English titles. It was cold, but not horrifically so, and her long coat helped cover the metal in her leg. A collection of stories about women athletes caught her eye, and she stopped to flip through it, then felt that swelling sadness about the loss of her career, and put it down again. No point in torturing herself.

Another one called her name, *The Fireside Book of Deadly Diseases*. The pandemic had revived a childhood passion for viruses, triggered by a documentary on the Black Death she'd seen at the age of eight. This one chronicled smallpox and leprosy and AIDS along with many others. She tucked it under her arm.

She'd aways been somewhat interested in the processes of the body and healing, because a person didn't participate daily in such a physically challenging sport without the odd injury. Knowing why and how the body mended itself was something she'd studied. In truth, she'd always known an injury could eventually end her career. She just hadn't seen this angle.

In the hospital after the shooting, it had taken many weeks to get to a place where she could even *think* about her own healing. Thanks to Jill, who showed up every single day, and then some, she had never despaired, exactly, but she hadn't taken much interest in her own healing until she saw the X-rays of her original injury. The damage delivered by the bullet that struck her thigh was tremendous, leaving shards of bone and shredded muscles. The surgeons had pieced what they could back together, using cadaver bone and plates and screws and metal rods to reconstruct her leg. "Holy shit," she'd breathed upon seeing it. "I can't believe I can actually use this leg."

The surgeon, a woman in her fifties, said, "We worked our asses off. Nobody was sure you would even live."

"I thought I died," she confessed. "In the grocery store, on the floor, I saw my leg and how much it was bleeding and just—" She shook her head.

"Lucky for you that somebody knew how to tie a tourniquet."

She frowned. "Who?"

"You don't remember?"

"No."

"You said it was an angel when they brought you in."

Mariah winced. "An angel? That doesn't sound like me."

The doctor shrugged, looked at the chart. "That's what the ER nurse wrote down. She said you were holding your mother's hand."

She looked away. "Since my mother was dead at the time, I'm pretty sure she didn't rise up and tie a tourniquet."

"Well, count your blessings. Without that angel, you wouldn't be here right now."

That made her stomach twist. But the memory of someone tying up her leg to stop the bleed never returned.

Browsing the titles on the table on a booth by the Seine, she wondered why that person hadn't come forward. Why hadn't they stayed until the ambulance came? Maybe she or he had just gone through the store saving the lives of injured people?

Another book caught her eye, *Epidemics of the World.* She picked that up, too. Would she like being a doctor? It seemed like a hard course of study, and she hadn't had the best grades in the world. She cast her mind forward and tried to imagine herself in a white coat, in a hospital, looking into somebody's mouth.

Ew. No. She still wanted to read the book about plagues, but being a doctor—no.

But she did have to start thinking about what was next. For a while, she'd been invested in the idea that she could make a comeback. People did, even after terrible accidents. But since she still couldn't really walk without limping, the chances she could even get on a board were looking slim. At this rate, she'd be thirty before she could compete, and that was getting pretty old for an Olympic run. Lindsey Jacobellis had been in her thirties, but she hadn't suffered a shattered femur.

A hole opened in her chest. To never stand at the top of a mountain again, pausing to take in the high-altitude sky, the slope dropping away beneath her, the swoosh of boards and skis and nylon clothing brushing against itself—how could she bear it?

And yet, it seemed she had no choice.

She paid for the books and looked for Henry and Veronica, who stood side by side at a table, Henry holding a book in his hand, Veronica with her head tilted up. He was *reading* to her! He finished and handed the book over. She shrugged with a smile, apparently convinced it was a good book.

Again Mariah realized that V had begun to look a little different. The makeup she always wore like a mask was washed away from the crying she pretended she hadn't done in the bathroom, leaving her fresh faced and younger looking. In the damp, her tidy bob was demolished, curling around her face, her bangs getting long now. She wore a flowered scarf she'd picked up somewhere in London. Her thighs were still skinny twigs, but that wouldn't last long the way Mariah was feeding her.

She looked back to Henry. He was more relaxed and chatty than she'd seen him in a decade. Maybe a lot of that had to do with leaving the harsh job behind, but Mariah thought it might also be that he liked Veronica. It gave her an odd feeling, not quite jealousy, but not *not* jealousy.

Weird. She wasn't jealous in a romantic way (*ew*) but maybe she didn't want to share his attention. He was the closest thing she'd ever had to a dad. Of all Rachel's boyfriends, he'd been around the longest, almost five years, and he'd been a good influence on Rachel, but also on Mariah.

Despite the fact that it had been years since he'd been with her mother, he'd shown up a month after the shooting, and moved to Denver to be with her. What if she lost him to a girlfriend?

A red cover caught her eye as she passed a stall, and she paused. *Mediumship for the Masses*. She hesitated, telling herself she didn't believe in all that stuff. Since she didn't believe in it, then it wouldn't matter if she indulged her interest, right? Looking over her shoulder to make sure she wasn't observed, she flipped through a few pages, and before Henry and Veronica could come back, she purchased it and tucked it into her carrier bag, feeling both foolish and excited.

CHAPTER
THIRTY-ONE

Veronica found twenty books she wanted to buy at the English portion of the bookstalls, from fiction to history to garden design. She allowed herself two, an English edition of the Arabian Nights, in honor of their journey to Marrakech, and the one that Henry insisted she read, *A Moveable Feast*, the Ernest Hemingway classic.

She'd protested at first. "I'm not a fan. He was such a . . . scion of the patriarchy," she said.

Henry laughed. "You're not wrong. He was also a great writer. This is my favorite of his books, aside from *The Old Man and the Sea*."

"Of course you like him," she said, narrowing her eyes. "You're a manly kind of guy, aren't you, with a dangerous career and eyes that have seen too much?"

He grinned, undaunted. "You're not wrong there, either." He lifted a finger. "How about you let me read a passage and then you decide?"

"Okay."

He flipped through the pages, and found what he was looking for, then read two paragraphs in his deep voice about regret that pierced her. Before she could openly weep, she snatched the book from his hands. "You win."

"Of course. If you hate it, I'll double the purchase price. But you won't."

A sliver of sun broke through the cloud cover, gilding her hands and the book as if it were some sacred text, and who knew, maybe it was. But as she paid for the worn leather volume, standing with Henry on the banks of the Seine with the smell of chestnuts in the air and a belly full of sweet foods, she felt entirely happy. It moved in her body like a song.

Mariah hobbled up to them, displaying her find. "Epidemics," she said.

"Are you interested in diseases?" Veronica asked, accepting her change. *"Merci."*

"No, but it looks kind of cool. Plague and smallpox and leprosy. I guess future editions will include COVID. Which was very interesting, you have to admit."

"In a way," Veronica agreed. Tugging a lock of windblown hair from her mouth, she asked, "Where did you spend it?"

"The pandemic?"

"Yes."

"It was boring for me," Mariah said. "No competitions for a couple of years, although it was cool to have such empty slopes."

"How about you, Henry?"

He shook his head slightly. "I was headed home from Egypt when everything was grounded. I ended up spending a year in Greece."

"That doesn't sound terrible," Veronica said.

"It was, though. I lost an uncle and my grandfather, and I couldn't go to their funerals."

She remembered that his family was near New York City. "I'm sorry," she said.

He gave his usual shrug. "That's how life rolls."

~

She was glad of the chance to take the metro again, so she could study people without notice. This train was filled with a diverse crowd, their languages and accents flowing like music around her, Brits and

Americans and Africans and Asians; students of all backgrounds, and tourists speaking a dozen languages to each other. She lingered on one tall, very thin man dressed in a robe made of printed orange cotton, wondering what his apartment looked like and who lived with him and what he did for work. He got off the train a few stops in, and Veronica switched her attention to a young woman, round and blond, her feet in Dr. Martens. She texted the entire journey.

When they emerged from the metro, Henry directed them to Café Farroukh. It had vines and bougainvillea painted on the plastered exterior, and a large window lined with plants in clay pots. If it had been in her neighborhood back home, Veronica would make it a regular stop. Inside was even more appealing. The fragrance of mingled spices and roasting meat and onions filled the air—she could pick out garlic and cumin and something just out of reach.

"Wow," Mariah said. "Sure you can't manage a bite or two?"

Henry patted his stomach. "Not me."

"I don't know," Veronica said. "It smells amazing."

Mariah let go of a small whoop and held up a hand for a high five. Veronica laughed and raised her own hand, alarmed when Mariah nearly overbalanced when their palms slapped. She caught her by the upper arm. "You good?"

"Fine," she said, shaking her off.

Henry lifted an eyebrow. "Let's make this short, maybe take a taxi back. It's been a long day already."

"Back off, people. I'm good." Mariah smiled at the young man who approached them with menus. In English, she asked, "Can we have a table for three?"

The server inclined his head. Veronica had not spoken French much in decades, but she could manage this small amount. *"Une table pour trois, s'il vous plaît."*

"Oui," he said, and took them to a booth by the window.

It wasn't busy, likely due to the hour—post-lunch, predinner. Veronica pulled her little notebook out and started jotting down notes. The floor was black and white tile, and the tables had the same checkered tablecloth covered with glass as the London café. The ambiance was quite winning, and next to her, Henry shot a series of photos, his shutter a whir.

But this menu, while still Middle Eastern, was quite different from the Parsi café menus she'd been studying. "We need to taste the bread, see if it's the same as the bun in London," she said, scanning the offerings. "And the fresh lime soda. That's such a great beverage. I'm going to learn to make it at home."

"They use a spice that's pretty intense," Henry said. "Takes a little experimentation."

She grinned. "I'll remember that." He sat across from her this time, next to Mariah, and the light made his eyes the color of pears. For a moment, she was caught in them, surprised when he didn't look away.

She said, "I would gladly sample every lamb dish on this menu, but I would die of my stomach splitting open."

Henry stood. "I'm going to find out if the owner is here. This would be a good time of day to talk to someone."

"Did you see the story on the back side of the menu?" Mariah asked. "I can't read it, but maybe you can."

Veronica flipped it over and started reading. It was slow at first as her brain tried to arrange the French into a form she could digest. As the story cleared, she said, "Oh, wow. This is really good." She put the menu down and took a photo of the entire story so she could come back to it later.

"What does it say?"

"Paraphrasing: Café Farroukh was established in 1997 when Chamani Irani emigrated from Bombay to Paris and brought many of her family traditions with her. When she married a dashing Egyptian, the two combined their cultural food traditions to come up with a unique and popular cuisine that has been a Paris favorite for over two decades. Chamani returned to India when her husband died, and the restaurant continued in the capable hands of her daughter, Nav."

Henry approached the table, a woman beside him. "Our hostess," he said, gesturing toward a strikingly beautiful woman in her twenties with enormous dark eyes and thick, black hair caught in a barrette. She wore an apron over a T-shirt and jeans. "This is Navaz Osman."

"Hello," she said in English. "How may I help you? You're searching for information on my family?"

"We are," Veronica said. "Can you sit with us?"

"Yes, thank you." She slid in next to Mariah, who looked like a sturdy sunflower next to a rose.

To Veronica's surprise, Mariah said, "We think my mother might have been friends with someone in your family back in India."

"I don't know if I will be much help. I was born in Paris."

"Is the café named for someone, do you know?" Veronica asked.

"My grandfather. He had a Parsi café in Mumbai years ago, Café Guli." She pointed to the menu with the story. "I know he moved to Delhi."

Café Guli matched the name of the London café. "Did your mother have siblings?" Veronica asked.

"There were four of them. Three girls and a boy. Something happened to the brother, but my mother would never speak of it."

A shiver of excitement ran up Veronica's arms. "Was it linked to the family leaving Mumbai, do you think?"

"Yes, I think so." She glanced toward the window to the kitchen, twirling rings on her fingers. "She would not like me talking about this."

"Is she here now?"

"No, no. When my father died, she wanted to return to India. She lives in Delhi now."

Henry said, "Would she talk to us, if we went there?"

She shrugged, made a noise. "Who knows? She does what she wishes, my mother."

"Can you give us her phone number or email or something?"

Navaz pressed her lips together, looking from Veronica to Henry, who sat beside her, then over to Mariah. She touched Mariah's hand. "My mother would not be pleased if I did that."

Disappointed, Veronica nonetheless understood. "Thanks for taking the time to talk to us."

"I should return to my duties," she said. "Allow me to send out our favorites."

Veronica and Mariah exchanged a glance. "Please do."

CHAPTER THIRTY-TWO

All at once, between one bite of a roll and the next, Mariah crashed. It was as if someone had pulled a plug in her toe, and all the buoyancy and energy that had held her up through the day drained instantly from her body. She dropped the bun on her plate and fell back against the seat, almost dizzy with exhaustion.

"Even *you* can't take another bite?" Veronica teased.

"I guess." She touched her forehead where sweat had broken out. "I need to go back to the hotel. Like five minutes ago."

"Oh! Okay." Veronica was on her feet in two seconds. "Let me just pay the check, and we're out of here."

Henry helped Mariah out to the curb. She leaned on him, feeling as if she couldn't breathe properly, pressing a hand to her diaphragm. A sense of danger wound through her brain, *alert alert alert*. "Am I having a panic attack? I don't know what happened."

Henry raised a hand for a taxi. "Maybe the backfires. They were pretty loud."

"I don't know what you're talking about."

"The motorcycle that backfired about six times outside the window? The yelling?"

She looked at him blankly, feeling a ripple of warning, a rustling she pushed away. "Maybe I was in the ladies' room."

"Hmm. Maybe so." He opened the taxi door and stood outside waiting for Veronica. She bustled out, the scarf flying, and Mariah, still gripping her chest, was suddenly grateful for her. For both of them, coming on this trip with her.

When they started driving, the panic started to ebb, and by the time they got back to the hotel, her only lingering symptom was exhaustion. Veronica helped Mariah settle in, making sure that she had water and small snacks—"not that any of us can eat another bite for three days"— and Mariah waited until she was gone to strip to her underwear and T-shirt, throwing her bra in the corner. From her bag, she took out the book on mediumship, and pulled the curtains as if someone might see her reading it.

But she couldn't focus. Every time she thought she was calming down, her heart skittered anew, or her nerves jumped all at once for no reason.

She got on TikTok and scrolled until she found one of the mediums she followed doing a live reading. She was a Black woman in her fifties, wearing a white hairband, her braids flowing backward over her plump shoulders. Candles flickered beside her, and her voice was calm and quiet. "I'm seeing an older gentleman . . ."

Mariah's heart, which had been alternating intense pounding with fluttering, fell into a steady, even beat. Her limbs, exhausted by the day and her own rigidness, softened. Within moments, she was asleep.

Away.

CHAPTER
THIRTY-THREE

After she settled Mariah, Veronica went to her room, opened a bottle of water, and took a small sip. Her stomach was so full from the piles of food she'd consumed today that she looked about six months pregnant, but for once she decided to forget about it and do something more interesting than obsess that she was not the right size or the right person or the right whatever. Today she could forget it.

Her mind buzzed with the information they'd picked up at Café Farroukh. She opened the file on her tablet with the notes about the cafés, and reread the handful of letters Jill had managed to get to her. The actual facts were fairly thin. Rachel talked about Zoish, her university friend in Bombay, and Café Guli, which she loved. The family owned and operated it, obviously, if Zoish had gone shopping for vegetables.

Three girls and a boy, Navaz said, and something happened to the boy. What Veronica could piece together was that Rachel made friends with the family in Mumbai. That café closed sometime later. The family scattered—the father to Delhi, two girls to London. The third sister had opened the Paris café, Café Farroukh.

Which sister was the one Rachel befriended? She looked through the letters. Zoish. The sister who opened the London café was named Hufriya. The sister in Paris was Chamani. That left Zoish, who had opened the bookstore.

Two sisters had returned to India—one when her father fell ill, the other because she'd become a widow. Did they perhaps live together now? If she found one, would she find the other?

One question she should have asked Navaz was the brother's name. With that name, she might have been able to track down more information.

She didn't have a great connection to the internet, but she ran a quick search for Café Guli in Mumbai. Nothing. She frowned, tried again. The London café came up, listing the proprietor as Hufriya Mistry.

What was their maiden name? She searched back through her notes and found the father's name again as proprietor of the Bombay Café Guli, Farroukh Irani. Not only proprietor, but patriarch, and all three daughters had shown their devotion. Zoish had returned to nurse him when he became ill. Hufriya had honored the family by naming her café after the one they'd left behind. And . . . she checked her notes, the third sister Chamani had given her café her father's name.

Why had they left India entirely instead of leaving with their father to Delhi? Where was their mother? And what happened to the brother?

The cursor blinked as she tried to peer through time to find answers. Her brain offered possibilities, ideas—

She was so focused that she jumped a foot when a knock sounded at her door.

It was Henry, wearing his leather jacket, as if auditioning for a movie role as a dashing war photographer. His hair, like hers, responded to the damp air by curling more wildly, and for a single second, she considered simply flinging the door open and inviting him into her bed.

There might be women brave enough to do that, but she wasn't one of them. Instead, she raised a hand, like a middle-school girl. "Hi. What's up?"

"Want to go walk some of those meals off?"

"Man! Do I ever. Let me grab my coat."

"Layer a sweater under if you have it. It's cold."

She found her threadbare cashmere and yanked it on, then her blue hat, her ultra-warm fleece, gloves, and the flowered scarf. "Ready!"

He smiled. "Good."

Outside, he said, "I know you haven't read it yet, but I thought I would give you a little Hemingway tour, if you're open. You seem to like history."

"A little," she said with understatement. "It'll give me context when I do read it."

"That's what I thought." He pulled a woolen cap down over his head, wrapped a thick scarf around his neck, and pulled gloves from his pockets. "It's a pretty substantial walk, maybe a couple of miles to get to the first group of landmarks. Do you want to take the metro?"

"I'm happy to walk as far as we can. Besides, walking is a good way to see a place, don't you think?"

"Always."

Night provided a proper backdrop for twinkling Christmas lights. Shop windows gave glimpses of the goods within. They walked a while without speaking, and for once, Veronica didn't feel the need to fill every silence. She liked his company, and he made her feel safe, both physically and, she realized with some surprise, emotionally.

"You seem to know Paris quite well," she said after he directed their turns, this way, then that. "Have you lived here?"

"I did, just a year when I was young. I had a job as an international stringer, and it was a good place to jump off into various hot spots."

"Like where?"

"A lot. Bosnia, a lot of the Yugoslav conflicts. Afghanistan, always. Algeria."

"Algeria!" she echoed. "That's like the setting of a black-and-white movie, the dashing French Foreign Legion soldier in love with the daughter of a noble family."

He smiled. "Maybe you should write a screenplay."

"Maybe," she said without commitment. "Are you still doing that work?"

"No." His voice was gruff. "Not for a while now."

She waited.

"Caught in the flood of departures from Afghanistan when the US pulled out. A bomb."

"Oh, wow. I'm sorry."

He shrugged. "It was kind of amazing it hadn't happened before, frankly." He pointed to their slight left, where a bridge came into view, the black river glinting below. They walked toward the bridge, and she left the question alone, allowing him to embroider or not.

Eventually he said, "It was mostly a mangled shoulder and a concussion, and some burns, but when I healed, I never recovered the stamina I needed for fieldwork." He gave her a sad smile. "It's a young man's game, honestly."

"What do you do now? I mean, I know you're doing this project with Mariah, but what do you generally do?"

"Some commercial work, but most of it is fairly straightforward travel stuff. I have a handful of clients who pay quite well." He paused, hands tucked in his pockets. "I don't strictly need to work—I never spent any money for thirty years. I was always on assignment."

A twinge of envy ran through her. She wanted that for herself, the comfort of savings to create a bulwark against the world. "Nice to have that freedom."

"I didn't really set out to do it," he said. "But I'm glad for the privilege." He glanced at her. "I gather the divorce has been difficult on that level?"

"Yes." She sighed. "My own fault, though. I should have prepared. Virginia Woolf warned women that they need some money and a room of their own."

"Well, she had a lot of privilege, right? I'm guessing you saw marriage as a way of helping nail down some security."

The observation lessened her creeping sense of shame. "That's true. I still knew better, and now I'm trying to figure out how to create a life I love and will support me when I'm a bit too long in the tooth."

"Pish," he said, more sound than word. "You're not that old."

"Well, thanks."

In the middle of the bridge, they stopped to look toward the Cathédrale Notre-Dame de Paris, still cloaked in scaffolding. The water shimmered and danced, catching orbs of orange from the streetlights, and, magnificently, the lights shining from the enormously imposing cathedral. Veronica caught her breath. "Imagine you're a peasant bringing your produce or your goats or whatever to market, and *this* rises up in front of you."

"I have never once thought of that," he said, his arms propped on the balustrade.

"I'm so fascinated with history." She looked into the river, following the line of the church in the water.

"You have a unique view of the world."

"Do I?" She shifted her view, following the scaffolding up and up until it almost made her feel dizzy. "I always feel like I'm so boring." It surprised her, that it just popped out like that.

"From where I sit, you're always thinking about what you see, how it connects to other things."

"Thanks."

"You'll do a great job with the book, I think. Rachel would be pleased."

A gust of wind slammed into them, forcing her to close her eyes until it passed.

"Time to go," Henry said.

She nodded, looking back to the cathedral, wanting a selfie with him in this magical moment. But was that too weird?

He'd taken three steps away when she said, "Wait!"

He turned.

"Would you hate it if we took a selfie?"

"Not at all." He loped back, hands in his pocket, and leaned down to position his face near hers. She smelled something sun washed and clean, and shampoo, and felt his shoulder pressed into hers. Veronica smiled without showing her teeth, but he grinned and leaned close. Before he could move away, she said, "A couple more." She dared herself to smile broadly, all teeth, and felt his hair curling into the side of her face.

"Thanks." She tucked the phone back in her pocket and slid her glove back on.

"Send me a copy, will you?"

"Of course," she said on a swell of delight.

A couple of blocks on, he pointed out a few landmarks. A bar, a house, a little café, all once frequented by the famous writer. "Can we stop in that bar?" Veronica asked.

"There's a better one."

"Okay. I trust you."

He grinned. "Glad to hear it."

She knew when they came upon it, a building on the corner, light both above and below. Crowds of people smoked at the tables along the sidewalk, their voices making a musical weaving of their enjoyment. Someone laughed, a boisterous sound, and Veronica felt herself smiling in response. "This is it, right?"

"Yes."

"It makes me think of a van Gogh painting."

"I know which one you mean." He took off his glove and offered his bare hand. "Shall we?"

Pleasure ran through her body as she took her glove off. His hand was warm, enormous, enfolding hers completely. She liked the way he led them through the crowd, and wondered if they'd even be able to sit down.

But inside, it was much less crowded. A young man asked if they wanted a table, and Henry said to Veronica, "Good?"

"Great."

The table was small, tucked against a wall, but offered a good view of the dining room and a bank of windows. "Ah," Henry said, "do you see the plaque on the wall above the banquette?"

Above a booth occupied by two men having a fierce conversation, their heads close together, was a brass rectangle. "Yes."

"That's one of the places he wrote. Hemingway."

Veronica allowed herself to imagine the young writer bent over his paper, scribbling away. She wondered if he'd preferred pencils or pens—which led to wondering when portable pens were even invented—and whether he liked lined or unlined paper. It gave her a sense of excitement, that this person, so long now gone from the earth, had started his journey here. "It's unexpectedly thrilling," she said. "I mean, some of his molecules might still be hanging around in here."

"Could be."

A waiter came by asking if they wanted drinks, but Veronica said they needed a minute, realizing that she'd responded in French without thinking about it. It was coming back. "I don't really want a martini or anything like that," she said, "but you have whatever you want."

He scanned the menu. "I'm not much of a hard-liquor guy."

"Not even in Algiers?" she said.

He laughed as she'd hoped, and his eyes twinkled when he said, "Not even in Algiers."

"You're completely ruining my imaginary vision of a hardened war correspondent." She scanned the menu, too. "What do you think, then?"

"How about kir?"

"Yes! Perfect."

"And a profiterole. We'll split it, have a couple of bites, just to say we have."

"I'm going to waddle home, I swear," she said, and allowed the menu to fall. "But yes."

After they ordered, Henry said, "People turn to booze in war zones to shut things off. I tried the gin answer as a young photographer, but for me, it doesn't work. I just can't find the switch to forget, and instead I ruminate and replay endlessly."

"I get that." She admired the shape of his cheekbone against the soft light, thinking of him as a young man. "It just doesn't seem to give me the big thrill other people get from it. Now, give me some pizza rolls, and I'm there."

"Pizza rolls?"

"Yes," she said. "The pepperoni ones." The waiter returned. "Merci." She sipped the drink. "I grew up in a house with a working mom and not a ton of money—a little MTV, some pizza rolls or maybe some ramen noodles, and a can of root beer, and life was seriously great."

He laughed. "Youngster. I was overseas when MTV got big."

"Oof, so you are *really* old."

He measured her across the table, his eyes bright. "Am I?"

To her amazement, she blushed ever so slightly. To cover, she said, "By the time you were overseas you were eating oysters on the half shell, right?"

"Hardly. You've not seen junk food addiction until you've seen a college guy two hundred miles from home."

"Like what?"

"The usuals—chips and candy bars and pizza." He leaned forward, dropping his forearms on the table, which put them much closer together. "But when I was a kid I didn't want anyone to know what we were eating at home. Working-class Italian family, and although everybody likes spaghetti and lasagna, they don't think *trippa* is so great."

"There's a lot of judgment around food. Classism, really, if you think about it."

"Such as?"

"Well, like your tripe, and my pizza rolls. I learned to cook using Hamburger Helper because hamburger was a dollar a pound, and my mom could make it quickly when she got off work—as a waitress, by the way, working with food all day to come home and make more food for the family."

He looked over his shoulder with mock furtiveness and turned back with a glitter in his eye. "What's the worst thing you still eat as an adult?"

Veronica laughed, loud enough to draw a mini scowl from the men across the way. "So many," she said, sotto voce. "My kids are so humiliated that I like sweet-potato casserole."

"The kind with the little marshmallows on top?"

"Yeah."

He let go of a soft moan. "Man, I love that stuff. My aunt Rita used to make it every Thanksgiving."

"Yes. But I have to admit . . ." She glanced to her left and peered around Henry's shoulder. "My worst failure as a foodie is that I love"— she dropped her voice to a whisper—"Miracle Whip."

"Not Miracle Whip!" He shook his head. "I'm sorry, I can no longer be seen in your company."

For one second, she thought she'd revealed too much, and then he laughed. "I hate it, but I have something I bet you don't like." He leaned in. "Bologna. With pork rinds. On white bread."

"Ooh, that's pretty disgusting."

He grinned. "It's a gift. I also love cheap hotdogs. The cheaper the better."

She nodded in perfect agreement. "How about those little casseroles with beans and wienies?"

"God, yes! And boxed macaroni and cheese with the packets."

"SpaghettiOs!" she cried.

"White Castle," he said, and kissed his fingers.

She laughed. "We didn't have those, but, baby, I ate my share of Taco Bell tacos."

"Now that's not a bad food, really. It's basically meat and lettuce and corn tortillas. Not so junky."

She raised her brows.

The waiter brought their profiterole at that moment, as if to underline the horrors of the conversation. Veronica looked at the exquisite creation and started laughing. Henry grinned. "Don't tell anyone."

"Not a word."

Outside the bar, they paused. "Ready to head back?" Henry asked.

She looked at her watch. "It's only seven thirty."

"That is the answer I was hoping for." He took her gloved hand in his, and they walked toward the shine of the cathedral in the dark. The whole city sparkled, living up to its moniker of the City of Light. "We can head for a metro station farther down and take the train back. Good?"

"Great."

"How long were you in Paris before?"

"Three days was all we could afford. Enough to hit the highlights, but that was about it."

"The Louvre, the Eiffel Tower, that kind of thing?"

"Oh, no. No way Spence wanted any museums. I was dying to visit the Musée d'Orsay, but he didn't want to spend our honeymoon in museums."

He frowned. "I had the impression he was a professor."

"Yeah, philosophy," she said. "But really, he's a ski bum at heart."

His brows rose. "Really. What does he think about your traveling with Mariah?"

"Uh . . . wow," she said, and laughed. "I haven't told him, I guess." She pressed her lips together. "I've been pretty pissed off at him, and I didn't want him to stand in my way. But I wonder if—" She broke off.

"If?"

"He would be nicer if he knew. He's done some money things while I've been traveling that are—" She shook her head. "Mean."

"Sorry to hear that."

"That's probably too personal. Sorry."

"Not at all. Too bad we don't have time to get to the d'Orsay tomorrow."

"Another time. This is a pretty packed trip."

"You'll have to come back."

She nodded noncommittally.

"You don't think you will?"

First I have to pay my rent, she thought. "We'll see. There's a lot going on back home."

"Do you want to talk about it?"

"No," she said firmly. "Where do you live now?"

"In Denver."

"What?" She stopped dead. "I thought you were based in Europe or something. You met us at the airport!"

"Has this not come up before? I was in Europe, but when Mariah was so badly hurt, I came to Denver to help out. I ended up really liking the city." He paused. "Ironic, because it was a sticking point between Rachel and me. She didn't want to leave her sister, and I didn't want to live in a sprawling Midwestern city."

"It's not the Midwest!" she cried. "It's the mountains."

"That's what she said." He gave her a regretful smile. "In my world, there are no other cities in the US besides New York, and maybe LA."

"Oh, so a place snob, huh?"

"Guilty. The sad thing is, that stubbornness probably cost me a good relationship."

"You loved her?"

"I did. I think you would have liked her, too. She was funny and bohemian and, well, she raised Mariah. You can see a lot of how she was right there."

"Mariah's pretty mighty. I can imagine how she was before the injuries." She looked up. "I'm sorry, though, that you lost a good relationship over stubbornness."

"I'm probably romanticizing. It's easy to look back and think, *coulda, shoulda, woulda.*"

"Yeah." The idea rolled around in her mind. Had she romanticized her marriage? She honestly didn't think she had, but what, then, had gone wrong? What had turned him into this caricature of a bad ex? "I feel like I made a lot up about my marriage, but maybe I didn't. It's just so hard to know."

"Maybe all of it is true," he said.

A sense of spaciousness blew through her at that. Maybe he really had been a good husband, and now he was a really bad ex. She didn't have to decide right now.

They walked in the beautiful glittery dark, followed by the ghosts of their past.

In a flash she realized it didn't have to be that way. That this moment, right now with Henry, who was smart and interesting and made her feel alive, could just be about her. And him.

She halted, taking in the pinpoints of light, the river, even the sharp cold. "The past is the past," she said. "Tonight, though, you and me are in Paris. We are alive." She looked up at him. "We are attracted to each other. Or at least, I'm attracted to you."

A very small smile played around the edges of his mouth. "It is definitely mutual. What should we do about that?"

"Maybe you could start by kissing me."

"I would like that." He bent down and gathered her face in his hands, and when she lifted her chin, he kissed her. She wanted to keep her eyes open, looking at the expanse of his eyebrows, the ruggedness of his cheek, but his mouth was lusher than she'd expected, and he was very skilled at kissing, and in the end all she wanted to do was sink into him, all the way, giving herself up to the place their bodies joined. He tilted his head, and she opened to him fully, and they kissed deeply, kissed a little wildly, making soft noises. His arms dropped and pulled her closer, and she ran her hands under his coat, wishing she had taken off her gloves. He pressed her lightly against the lamppost, and without breaking the kiss, she pulled off the gloves and let them fall on the ground, worth it when she found the hot skin of his back, the knobs of his spine. Her own coat fell below her hips, but he cupped her bottom, pulled her into his thigh. In the dark of a Paris night, with the damp smell of the river running behind them, they fell into each other, drunk on the moment, on each other. Every cell in her body danced.

"Look at the old people making out!" a boy catcalled in English.

It made Veronica laugh. Henry called out over his shoulder, "You only wish you had this woman, fools." As one body, they turned toward the subway. Without breaking stride, Henry captured her gloves from the sidewalk and handed them to her.

CHAPTER THIRTY-FOUR

The metro ride back to the hotel was short, considering how long they'd been gone. The car was crowded, and they had to stand most of the way, holding on for balance. Veronica looked around at the other riders, mostly young and chatting. One party of Americans, maybe in their early twenties, were talking too loudly, but were so full of themselves and life and the fact that they were on the metro together that it was impossible not to love them. One boy had shiny blond hair like Spence once owned, and his girlfriend leaned into him, a little tipsy maybe, her own hair long and shining, healthy with the vibrance of life. It made her melancholy in a way. She'd flung away that magical time by marrying Spence, having babies so young.

Not that she'd trade the kids. But maybe she wanted a do-over where she had them maybe ten years later, so she could have been free to wander the world like these young adults.

She shook her head. She wouldn't have had the resources at this age. She didn't actually have them now. That was the thing that social media conveniently overlooked—it took money to be a vagabond.

#LotsOfItActually

What brought her back to the moment was the scent of Henry, sunny and sharp. Every time she caught a whiff, it sent little erotic messages to various bits of her. *Touch me touch me touch me.*

She looked up, and he was looking down, and the collision of gazes scattered thoughts of nostalgic speculation right out the window. She didn't look away this time, and to her deep delight and surprise, he bent down to kiss her lightly. A promise. An acknowledgment.

As they came out of the station, her phone started to ding. And ding, and ding. She ignored it for a while, wanting to keep the world out, but finally she had to pause on the platform. "I'm sorry. I have kids. I probably need to see what's going on."

"No worries. Let's sit over there on that bench."

She nodded. The wind was sharpening now, the knives of it finding a bit of her neck, her thighs where they were only covered by her pants. Henry sat between her and the wind, and she said, "You don't have to do that."

"I know."

She opened the message app. Seventeen new messages. As expected, most of them were from Amber, and the news wasn't good. It ended with Landlady has a policy against anyone with an ankle bracelet.

sorry can't help

"Shit, shit, shit," she said aloud, then tsked. "I thought I'd found a roommate, but the landlord won't let her in because she has an ankle bracelet." She scowled. "That's got to be illegal."

"I'm sure it is."

"But what am I going to do to stop her at this distance?"

"Report her?"

She took a breath, feeling the pressure of the problem press down on her breastbone. "I'm afraid she'll evict me." She stood. "Never mind. This is not your problem. Sorry."

"We can talk it out if you want."

"No, I'll make some calls when we get back to the hotel." She gave him a regretful look.

He stood. "It's all good."

She felt resentful that her old life, with all the messy loose parts, was interfering with a holiday romp, but she couldn't let Amber down. Or herself, honestly.

At the hotel, they rode up the elevator silently. Veronica cast around for ways to break the hush but couldn't come up with anything, and he didn't, either. They just looked at the light over the doors like strangers, side by side.

In the foyer between the rooms, she said, "Thanks for such a great adventure."

"You're welcome," he said, and the sound of his low voice rumbled against the back of her neck. "Hope you get things worked out."

She nodded and let herself into her room, where she leaned on the door, thinking about what she was giving up in the form of Henry's skin. Henry's mouth. She gave herself a solid twenty seconds to feel the vast disappointment, then kicked off her shoes and picked up the phone.

There were other texts, from Jenna and from Tim, but nothing from Spence and nothing from her landlady. Those were voice messages.

She called Amber first, but she didn't answer, which gave her a pang. She was probably angry, and understandably so. Next she called Spence. "You rang?" she asked. "Gonna send my money after all?"

"You're a grown woman and can take care of yourself. No, that's not why I was calling. Ben broke his leg in a bike accident and won't be able to go skiing. I was wondering when you'll be home."

"What? Wait! Is he okay?"

"It's a straightforward tibia-fibula break, and he should heal fine. He just doesn't want to go to Breck with everyone skiing."

"Poor guy. I can't believe he didn't call me."

"He didn't want to bother you."

That was sweet. "I need to call him. Was there anything else?"

"He can't be alone, Ronny."

"Well, there's nothing I can do from here."

"You can't come home early?"

"No. I'm five thousand miles away." She felt a sizzle burn up the back of her skull, snap across her nose. "I'm *working*."

"Yeah, poor thing, traveling all over, ghostwriting or whatever."

"It's actually exactly that. I'm doing research for a ghostwriting project." The distance gave her a view of her life she'd never seen. "I'm not coming back to babysit my twenty-year-old son when a) he's perfectly capable, and b) his father is right there and can manage the situation just fine."

"We leave for Breck tomorrow. It's a family tradition."

That stung. She took a breath. "Boy, I do know that much. You need to hammer this out with him. He can stay on his own or he can go with you, or you can stay home and celebrate Christmas with him."

"Leaving him alone is pretty harsh. It's Christmas."

"I get that. But again, you two have to work out how to solve the problem."

"There's a lot going on here, Ronny. I can't go into it right now, but the furnace problem revealed a bunch of other stuff, and Fiona has not been well through this pregnancy, and the kids are on my ass about a million things. I need this break."

She couldn't help it—she laughed. "Figure it out. I can't help you."

"Ronny!"

She knocked on her desk. "Sorry, gotta go."

She hung up. And wanted to tell somebody on the planet that she'd just stood up for herself with her absurd ex.

The first thing she had to do was call Ben. He answered on the first ring. "Hey, Mom."

"Hey, babe. You broke your leg? How are you?"

"It's not too bad," he said. "They gave me some good painkillers for a few days anyway."

"Be careful with them."

"No, I thought I'd get addicted and then get a heroin habit." He scoffed. "Of course I'm careful. You know me. I don't like to get high, unlike a certain sibling of mine."

"It's nice to hear your voice. I'm so surprised you didn't call when you did it."

"I know you're trying to figure things out. I didn't want to get you all worried. I was pretty sure it was a straightforward break, and I could let you know later. But I guess Dad got there first."

"He did. You don't want to go to Breck?"

"No, Mom. Even before the break. There's all kinds of drama going on. Fiona barfs every five minutes, and she's kind of a drama queen, and there's something wrong with the house, so Dad's all freaked out, and—I dunno. It would just be better to hang with my friends who aren't going home for the holidays. We'll have turkey TV dinners and drink a shit ton of beer."

She laughed. "Great. Sounds fabulous. I'll call you on Christmas Day, for sure."

"Dope."

"Anything I can do for you from here?"

"Bring me a British movie star. Love that accent."

Veronica laughed. "I'll do my best." She paused, remembering that she hadn't told her ski-crazy children that she was traveling with Mariah. "By the way, the person I'm traveling with is Mariah Ellsworth, the snowboarder."

"What? The Olympian? I thought she was killed in the supermarket shooting."

"No, that was her mom. Mariah was pretty badly injured, which is why I'm helping her."

"Awesome, Mom. Seriously. Is she nice?"

"Um." She smiled to herself. "*Nice* is the wrong word, but I like her. You would, too."

"All right, I gotta go. Have fun, Mama."

"I will. I love you, son."

"Love you, too."

She sent a text to Amber, who still hadn't returned her call. Amber, this sucks so much, but I'm trying to figure out things on my end. THE

OFFER STILL STANDS, but it's hard to get things done from this far away. Call me. I'm worried.

Last, she called her landlady, who answered on the third ring. "Nancy speaking," she said, like the administrative assistant she'd once been. She'd saved every spare penny and bought the building in the early nineties, turning it into five apartments at a moment that turned out to be prime. She'd always been slightly judgmental and nervous.

"Nancy, it's Veronica Barrington. I heard from my friend that you wouldn't allow her to share the apartment because she has an ankle bracelet."

"Well, no, that's a lie," she said defensively. "She was not very clean, and she drove a ramshackle wreck of a car. I can't trust a person like that in my building. This is a nice place."

"She's not a criminal," Veronica said as calmly as she could. More flies with honey, as her mother always said. "She's just in a hard place right now. She had a bad marriage and is trying to get to a better place."

"Not my problem. How do you think everybody in the house will feel when they see that house arrest thing on her ankle?"

"It's illegal for you to refuse her on that condition."

"Well, it's not illegal for me to evict you when you haven't paid the rent."

"She was going to pay the rent for me until I can get back into the country. I told you this. My husband pulled my alimony, and I'm in Europe on a job. I've been a good tenant for a year."

"I heard through the grapevine that you had a domestic-violence arrest, too. So, two peas in a pod. No, thanks."

Veronica's cheeks flamed, and the heat spread to her ears, her scalp, before she could speak. "I didn't hurt anyone," she said. "I lost my temper on a very bad day." She clenched her jaw. "That's stupid, but hardly criminal, and Amber did even less." She'd fought back against a husband determined to kill her, but that was none of Nancy's business.

"I don't care. You're out, and if you're not here to collect your things by the first, I'll leave them on the lawn."

"Nancy!" she cried, but the phone was dead.

With a sense of panic, she called Jenna. "Mom, I'm on the way to a meeting. Can this wait?"

"No. My landlady is evicting me, and I need to get my things out of there. I need your help."

"Mom, I am so swamped right now!"

She felt as if she'd been slapped. "Jenna! I never ask you for anything, and I'm in trouble. I need you to make some calls, find somebody to help get my things out without spending money. Ask Tim to help you. I'll have to put it all in storage."

"Maybe this is a sign, Mom. This trip has never been a good idea. Maybe you just need to come home and deal with it."

"I'm working!"

"So am I! Ben broke his leg, you know."

"I just heard." The flames burned around her ears again, touched her eyes. She couldn't believe her daughter was refusing to help. "But I'm not coming home. I am *working*."

"Whatever." She tsked. "I'll make some calls. But you have a lot of shit."

"Not really, but thank you. Let me know. I love you."

"I love you, too. I'm sorry, this is all just a lot."

"Yeah, it is. I know." For once, she didn't say she was sorry.

She didn't think it was legal for her landlady to evict her on such thin cause. Thinking of the roomy kitchen, the old walls, it felt like losing the family house all over again. She chewed her thumbnail thoughtfully, stopping when she bit too hard and realized that she hadn't shed the habit after all.

To solve all these issues, she just needed to set Mariah down and talk out the contract for the book. Ghostwriting, as Spence said so accurately. Some kind of payment plan, maybe an advance, even a small one, would see her through until she got home.

Was she being greedy? It wasn't like she knew what she was doing, and she was in Paris, for heaven's sake, had flown first class, was eating more than luxuriously. To ask for more seemed very cheeky.

Except, a small voice argued back, the arrangement had been for companionship to start with. Taking notes was one thing and she would have been happy to do that part. Doing the groundwork to write Rachel's planned book was quite another thing entirely.

Rubbing her eyes, she suddenly realized it was nearly midnight and they had a plane to catch in the morning. She'd revisit the thought when she had a fresh brain.

CHAPTER
THIRTY-FIVE

At some point in the middle of the night, Mariah awakened. She limped to the bathroom, feeling the not-unpleasant sense of having worked her leg a bit. In the mirror, she thought she looked better than she had for a while. Maybe Paris agreed with her.

Maybe it was fresh air and moving her body.

Back in her room, she rummaged through her bag to find snacks, nuts, and pretzels and a bottle of Ribena from London. She carried them to bed and curled up with her iPad. It was 2:00 a.m., so she probably needed to get back to sleep eventually, but she'd slept hard since five, so she wasn't really lacking.

But, wow, it was so quiet! The world felt as empty as an apocalypse. It was the thing she hated the most about life right now. She'd never really been alone much, like, ever. She'd either been with her mom or her coaches or traveling in a pack with other athletes in a dozen variations, training or in dorms for an event or in a house with slopes somewhere nearby. Often there was a man in her bed, or she was asleep but somebody else had a lover in a bed nearby.

In short, her former life had been communal. Now it was solitary. Sleeping alone, awake in the middle of the night alone. She knew Henry and Veronica were close by, but she didn't feel like she could wander into one of their rooms and curl up next to them or jump on the bed to wake them up, both of which she would do if her mom was still here.

Here. As if she was in another room and could come back.

Loneliness left a hollow in her lungs, making it hard to settle. She scrolled through the offerings on all her streaming services, and couldn't find anything interesting. She wasn't a big reader, but she'd downloaded some books recommended on BookTok, and went through them, reading a few pages here, then another, but she was too restless for that, too.

She got up and went to the window. The silence in the room was deafening, and even outside, very little moved. A taxi drove by. A traffic light flashed in the distance. A lone person crossed the street and disappeared. The whole world was asleep.

Or not. Across the alleyway, she saw a kitchen with a light on, hands taking a kettle from the stove. Higher up was a living room with a TV flickering. She scanned the buildings for other signs of life, and found them. Lights on. Movement against curtains. She wished there was some magic way to contact anyone who was awake and lonely. *Look out your window,* she'd say. *Wave!*

She laughed at herself. That probably already existed; it was called the internet. But had anyone ever written a program where you could contact people nearby?

That would probably be weird.

With a sigh, she headed back to her seat on the bed and scrolled TikTok for live reels. "Hello, Mariah," said a woman with enormous arms chopping onions.

Not her speed. She clicked another and another, and finally found a woman in a turquoise blouse reading oracle cards. "Loneliness is rampant," she said in her heavily accented English. Mariah halted. "But it does not need to be. The Mother tells us to lean on each other." She turned over another card, held it up to the camera. "This is for Mariah. The Wise Woman wants you to reach out, baby. Reach out."

Electrified, Mariah typed in, "I miss my mother so much."

The woman nodded sagely. She closed her eyes, shuffled the cards in her hands, her red nails glistening in her ring lights. "Mmm. Mmm," she said. "She misses you, too. She wants you to know you're on the right track." She showed the card she'd drawn, a stylized drawing of a physician. "She wants you to go to medical school. Is that right?"

Stung, Mariah just stared. She'd never wanted to go to medical school, or at least not since she was six and playing doctor like every other kid on the planet.

She was so disappointed that she closed the app and then her tablet, aching with the desire to believe in people who just wanted to take her money.

Medical school.

As if.

In the morning, she felt aggravated. Henry snapped at her when she got up late, but she'd been up in the middle of the night! What did he expect?

They headed to the airport at midmorning for the trip to Marrakech. At the airport, waiting at their gate, both Henry and Veronica were distracted, typing into their phones. Veronica had some issue going on at home, and Henry was deep into his book. He'd always been like that, able to switch off with a book at the drop of a hat. She wished she liked reading fiction. She had been leafing through the plague book, which was fascinating, but it was hard to read for more than an hour or so. She started feeling dizzy and tired. The doctors had told her that it was a side effect of her brain injury. It would heal in time, almost certainly. In the meantime, she needed a transportable hobby.

She was bored. Restless. She peered over at Veronica's phone and saw that she wasn't texting—duh, it was the middle of the night in Colorado—but playing a game. "What are you playing?"

"Hue," she said. "It's really aggravating, but it's also really fun."

"It's pretty. You just move the squares?" She watched as Veronica shifted a block that looked blue to a section of other blues, and it was quite green in comparison.

"*Just* makes it sound easy, but it will occupy my brain for ages."
Mariah looked it up and downloaded it to her phone.

"You'll like it better on your tablet," Veronica said, and swore. "I'm actually pretty terrible at it, but it's weirdly relaxing anyway."

Mariah opened the app and started a game, moving squares. "What's happening with the book and my mom's letters and all that stuff?"

"Well, it's still a bit of a question mark. We've tracked down some people, but I don't have any more of your mom's letters, which is where the real help will be, I think." She swore as she dropped a square and had to pick it up again. "Do you remember anything she talked about with the book, what she wanted to do with it?"

"No. I wish I had paid attention," she said, slumping into the chair. "I mean, she didn't really talk all that much about it, but she was excited about café culture."

"Do you know if she was under contract for this book?"

"No. She wasn't. Jill checked into all that with her agent, so that the royalty checks can all come to my bank account now."

Veronica nodded. She glanced up, and her eyes were the color of a turquoise bracelet Mariah had bought in Spain a long time ago. Purple shadows slung below them. "That's good." She sighed as the screen lit up with soft music and rewarded her for placing the last square. "I sent you an email about an agreement for the book. It might not make any money if it's ghostwritten. Have you thought of that?"

"Not really, but it's kind of about finishing the project for her, you know?"

"That's fine, and it's a good idea for you."

"Dope. I'll have Jill hammer something out. She's a lawyer. We don't need anything super detailed at the moment, right?"

"Right. Honestly, I just need to get paid."

"I get it."

Veronica closed her tablet and looked at Mariah. "This is delicate, but I worry about you a little. Are you going to have enough money, going forward?"

"Oh!" Mariah gave a hooting laugh. "I'm super good."

Henry chuckled. "Understatement. Rachel and Jill's father was Alexander Ellsworth, of Ellsworth Manufacturing. He had something like two hundred and forty-two patents."

"Seriously?" Veronica shook her head. "How do I keep finding this stuff out?"

"Well, we really haven't known each other that long. And probably not that many people know who he is."

"Okay, I guess I don't have to worry about you financially anymore."

"Just financially?" Mariah echoed, almost flirtatiously. It felt good to have somebody actually worry. Jill did, of course, but her hands were full right now.

"No, I worry about your future, but I'm trying to mind my own business." Veronica raised a finger. "Back to the book, ghostwriting, all of that. You should know that I've done a lot of writing, but I haven't written a book. You might want someone more experienced when it comes time. Or the publisher will."

Mariah cocked her head. "I already know you're a good writer. You've written me a ton of emails." She leaned on her knees. "Nobody needs to know what you've done before—you just do this, and then we'll get some money for both of us. Henry's photos will be a big part, too, so naturally we have to pay him. Worth it, though. Wait until you see the pics."

She looked at Henry, and Mariah saw that he looked back, something loud moving between them. "I believe it," Veronica said. She drew in a breath. "Okay. Would you ask Jill to take care of the contract when she can?"

"'Course. Do you need an advance now?"

Veronica blushed a cherry shade, all the way down her neck. "No, I'm good. But it would be nice to get this going." She picked up her paper cup, realized it was empty. "Actually, that's a lie. I do need some money."

"Cool. We can work it out."

"Great." As if she needed something to do, she popped up. "Want a cup of tea?"

"The plane will board in just a few minutes," Henry said.

"I'm okay." Mariah sat up straight, then sank back to the chair, rubbing her temple as if to make the dizziness disappear.

Veronica said, "Have you given much thought to what you might do now?"

"What do you think?" she snapped, and then straightened. "Sorry. I think about it all the time, and I'm just blank. I've been an athlete my whole life, and I thought I'd be doing it for a lot longer." She snorted. "A psychic told me I should go to medical school. What a joke. I don't even like to read."

"Does it interest you? Medicine? I saw the book on diseases."

"Well, it's one thing to *think* about diseases, epidemics and all that. Who hasn't thought about that, after the pandemic? It was super interesting when they talked about why it was so bad, and how come people died, and then the big race to find a way to keep it from killing us, and then the virus started like, fighting back, mutating like a video-game monster."

"Yeah, it was interesting."

Warming to the subject, Mariah looked at her leg, touched the scars beneath her jeans. "And then, you know, all the stuff that happened with my body after"—a rippling twist of memory, quickly shoved aside—"everything. There was a lot of damage. I was really fucked up. This whole piece of bone was pulverized, and they managed to put enough of it back together that I can walk. That's crazy, right?"

"It is." Veronica eyed the leg, but, of course, it looked normal in clothes. "Reading isn't the most important thing for studying medicine. Especially now, I'm sure, with so much available in audio and all that. Have you ever been tested for eye issues or maybe dyslexia?"

"Why would you ask me that?" She suddenly felt stupid, like she'd given something away.

Veronica waved a hand, dismissing the irritation in almost the same way her mom used to do. "Don't get in your head about it. I'm just asking because you do like thinking and you're interested in everything. My oldest son is dyslexic, and he has such bad astigmatism that it took two years to figure out it wasn't the glasses, it was his brain."

"Yeah?" Something moved in her heart, a flutter like a wing. "So I don't have to be a big reader to go to medical school?"

"Well, you'll have to figure out how to study, but there are a lot of things around to help all kinds of learning differences."

"Huh." She narrowed her eyes, peering into a possible future. "I don't think I want to be a doctor, exactly. Kind of . . . too many fluids, you know?"

Veronica laughed. "Yes. Medicine is a big field, and you don't have to decide anything. Now or ever. But if you want help with the practicalities eventually, I'm your woman."

Mariah nodded. "Thanks."

The man behind the desk announced their flight. As they got in line, Henry and Veronica pretended to ignore each other, and Mariah rolled her eyes. "I want to sit by myself this time," she said, knowing they'd want to sit together but would pretend they didn't.

"Fine," Veronica said. She didn't look at Henry, but he looked at her. And smiled.

PART FOUR

MARRAKECH

Traveling—it gives you home in thousand strange places,
then leaves you a stranger in your own land.

—*Ibn Batuta*

CHAPTER THIRTY-SIX

Marrakech was sunny, and warm enough to get away with a sweater—a very welcome change. As the passengers wandered out of the airport, they visibly relaxed, shedding heavy coats and thick mufflers, speaking in happier tones. Veronica tipped her face up to the cascade of warmth as they waited for a taxi, smiling at the negative sun that stained her eyelids. "I thought I loved rain. But this is heaven."

"We've hardly had a single sunny day since we left," Mariah said, stepping back as the taxi driver loaded her bag into the trunk. "That never happens in Colorado. You've lived there all your life, right?"

"I moved there from northern New Mexico," she said. "Same difference. Sunny, almost always, even in the depth of winter."

As they drove to the medina, the view reminded her of New Mexico. A line of blue mountains pinned the horizon at the end of a flat, open span of desert. Instead of walking stick cacti, there were small groups of palm trees. People obviously lived among them, dressed in draped bright fabrics, heads covered against that very sunlight, and probably by religious observance. The earth was reddish, and big homes were built of adobelike materials, walls keeping out the desert. Within were likely courtyards, just as there were back home.

Home. She hadn't really thought of New Mexico as home for a very long time. And yet, it was impossible not to see it here, the enormous impossibly turquoise sky, the reddish earth, the brown faces. The streets were busy with foreign tourists and women carrying cloth or net bags, their feet in sandals beneath flowing skirts. Two young men traded conversation on a corner, tapping each other as they told stories.

The taxi driver stopped outside a big square and said, "I can go no farther. Can you make your way?"

Henry said, handing over a fistful of bills, *"Shukran."*

"I'm starving," Mariah said as they got out. "Can we eat soon?"

"Let's get to the *riad* first," Henry said, shouldering her backpack along with his own. "Do you have a protein bar or something?"

"Dude, they're packed with sugar."

He gave her an unconcerned shrug. "Your choice."

With a disgruntled sigh, she reached into her cross-body bag and pulled out a wrapped bar, making a show of peeling it and taking a big bite.

Veronica grinned at Henry. He lifted an eyebrow in return.

They made their way through a labyrinth of alleyways, shaded and cool. They passed shops offering all sorts of things—spices and chess sets and leather bags meant to appeal to tourists, but also a store with small appliances and another with beans, all a jumble of narrow stalls, some brightly lit, like the jewelry shop where an orange cat lounged on the step, his tail flicking up and down, some darker, some illuminated by skylights cut into the roof, covered by grids and clear roofing.

It was the oldest place she had ever been, Veronica thought with some wonder.

She thought of Rachel's letters, the endless warrens of the market in Mumbai. It was probably very like this, an ancient form of marketplace.

And here, too, it opened to a central plaza where vendors sold foodstuff and household goods. Cats were everywhere. Slumped in the shade, perched on steps, peering through a shop window. "Why so many cats?" she asked.

"They're good mousers," Mariah said, reaching out to scratch the ears of a tortoiseshell sprawled over a display of toilet paper. He lifted his head against her fingers as if it was his due.

"Cats are considered ritually clean," Henry said. "The Prophet had several."

"I love that," Veronica said. "I miss having cats."

"Did your kids have pets growing up?" Mariah asked. "My mom said we were never home enough, and she was probably right."

"My ex doesn't like cats, so we had dogs." A perfect visual of Sophie's gray-and-white face rose in her mind, eyes blue as morning. It choked her unexpectedly, and she had to hold her breath for a second. "*I* had a dog," she said, thinking of Sophie following her room to room, patiently sleeping at her feet wherever she was, kitchen, living room, bedroom by the side of the bed. "She died suddenly when I was getting divorced."

"Terrible timing," Henry said.

She saw herself taking a walk of shame down the sidewalk between her perfectly planted perennials, each one set in place with her own hands. "It was pretty awful."

Surprising how much pain the memory still caused. Veronica felt it in her chest, pressing against her heart, filling her lungs with congested loss; in her gut, the shame of it. And there, like lava running along the edge of a black rock, hatred.

It startled her. The emotion was quite, quite clear. Not the anger she had believed it was, not frustration—hatred, clear and burning.

She took a breath, focusing on the beauty of the patterns of sunlight cast by screens overhead, patterns of ornate grids, flowers, concentric circles. It made her think of the stained-glass windows at Notre-Dame. "I read somewhere that these kinds of shapes express the same sacred geometry as the medieval windows in cathedrals."

"I can see that," Mariah said. "Did you guys go to Notre-Dame?"

"No," Veronica said. "We did a Hemingway tour."

"I figured you went out when I was sleeping."

Henry looped an arm around Mariah's neck. "And you were right."
She laughed.

They made more turns, left, right, then into a tiny clear alley and
up to a doorway, carved and elegant, where the space opened into
reception. When they were escorted to their rooms, the journey echoed
the medina, another winding trip, up some stairs and down and around,
walking along areas open to the floors below, and light coming in from
above. Little areas were set with chairs or settees in bright colors, pink
and blue and patterned, in velvet and stripes and motifs she didn't know
how to name.

And everywhere were tiles, on the floors and walls and posts and
tables. Intricately laid in patterns of rectangles and diamonds and
flowers and color. The opulence lit something in her deepest heart, and
she thought of Rachel expressing the "so muchness" of India and how
much she'd loved it. The extravagance thrilled Veronica, made her feel
more and more alive with every step.

She stopped in an alcove to admire a chair with a yellow cushion.
Sunlight fell in angular blocks across it, the very picture of serenity. *Sit
here*, it said. *Breathe.*

"I feel kind of drunk in here," she said.

Henry touched her hand, the back of his knuckles to the
back of hers.

"We're all close together," Mariah said, opening a door that led to a
lavishly appointed bedroom that overlooked a patio with bougainvillea
growing in pots, and greenery tumbling from overhead. Again the roof
was covered with grid-work and glass, which probably helped shield
the area from the heat.

Two other doors opened to the same space. "You can pick,"
Mariah said.

"Oh, that's okay. You choose."

"I've been here about twenty times," she said, a soft smile making
her look younger. "You haven't."

She thought of Sophie's beautiful old face, and the walk of shame, and the ridiculous surprise of this entire trip. Maybe she could just accept the gift. "Okay," she said. "Thank you."

All three rooms were beautiful, of course, appointed with brass and gold and tile and velvet. The bathrooms were a delight, tiled with flower patterns meeting stars meeting the soothing stretch of flat rectangles. She chose the room with *all* the details and colors and a deep tub tiled in turquoise and dark blue.

Who would she be in this room? How would it change her?

"How long are we here?"

"Three days," Mariah said. "Then to India."

She would be sad, Veronica knew, but she wouldn't think about that yet. Today, she would be here, in this place, with these people and see what happened. Out of her bag, she took the copy of *One Thousand and One Nights* she'd picked up in Paris and laid it on the nightstand. It looked just right.

~

They agreed to take some downtime, closing their doors to the patio. Despite her delight, Veronica was tired, and crawled between the crisp linens to nap. When she woke up in the red room with its stars and moons and brass lamps and red chandelier, she felt like Scheherazade. What story would she tell to stay?

She washed her face and neck with a cool cloth, looking at her face in the mirror. In the soft light, she looked younger, happier. The circles beneath her eyes were gone, and even her mouth looked fuller, as if she'd relaxed.

An intrusive thought about the apartment and Spence and Jenna refusing to help her knocked into her consciousness, and she physically shook her head. *Not now.* It would be Christmas in two days and she wanted to forget all the trouble and drama back home. When would she ever be back in this magical place?

She sent a quick text to Ben, asking him how he was feeling, and one to Jenna, telling her not to forget to get her things out of the apartment.

Quietly, she opened the doors to the patio and let in a breeze. Soon they would go find some dinner, but she had some time to simply enjoy this space. She settled on the wide settee and propped an embroidered pillow in her lap, gazing out at the tumble of scarlet flowers, listening to the soothing sound of the fountain. It was easier to look at her life from this distance. All the things that had been causing her so much pain seemed suddenly so small and strange and far away. Although she'd been afraid she'd be bereft without the close company of her children, she found she was doing all right on her own. She'd survived them growing up and landed in this new chapter of her life. And while she was angry at both Spence and her landlord, those seemed small and far away, too.

Sitting here was what mattered.

A gray cat sat beside the table, cleaning its paw, completely at home. Where did they come from, these cats? She had no idea, but it delighted her. *Cats killed scorpions,* she thought, remembering something from childhood. Mice and rodents and big bugs. Useful creatures.

And beautiful. The sleek fur and curl of paw, the thorough way it cleaned every single molecule of the space between its claws. A cat seemed just right in this world.

She thought of Rachel's letters home from India. It was fortuitous that Veronica could come to these places naively, as Rachel had. If she had come to all these locations with impressions already formed, it would be hard to treat them with a fresh eye. The idea of trying to get those observations on the page gave her a sense of excitement, a stirring somewhere deep in her DNA.

Henry appeared at the door with a tray in his hands. "Are you busy?"

"Not at all. Just daydreaming."

He'd traded heavy boots for leather sandals, and the sight of his naked arches gave her a jolt. "I ordered some tea and snacks to see us through to dinner. Mariah is still sleeping, but we can order her more when she wakes."

The carved silver tray held a selection of apricots, dates, olives, almonds, and bread. Her stomach growled, right on time, and she laughed. "I guess I can't protest that I'm not hungry."

"Good."

She delicately filled a saucer with three dates, two apricots and four almonds. "I love dates," she said.

"I remembered."

She'd bought some in London, at the grocery store, but these dates were moist and enormous and filled her mouth with a recognition that she'd never eat dates with the same understanding again. She closed her eyes, focusing. "Oh my God," she whispered, "this is one of the best things I've ever tasted."

He watched her eat. When she swallowed, he picked up another date and offered it to her. "They're fresh."

She held out her hand, but he shook his head slowly, his eyes going golden, and held the fruit between his fingers. A shimmer lit her body, and she leaned forward and opened her mouth. His thumb grazed her lip. She blinked, chewing, and reached for an apricot, holding it out for him.

He leaned in to take it, deliberately closing his mouth over her fingers. "Mariah will be here any minute," she said.

"She will," he agreed, and picked up another date. She slurped at his finger and laughed, then bit it lightly. He glanced over his shoulder. "I'd kiss you, but for all that she's being laid-back, I'm not sure Mariah would be all that happy about something between us."

"I agree," she said, leaning forward decisively, the action making her shirt gape at the top. She wished for her pandemic cleavage, but maybe a glimpse of breast would be good enough.

He seemed to enjoy it.

Their knees brushed. Veronica covered his almost naked foot with her entirely naked one, and electricity shot between them, almost shocking.

And then, of course, Mariah's door opened, and the girl came rolling out, all muscular energy—and her limp, quite pronounced today. Her expression was sad, or maybe it was only the angle of the light against that scar cutting through her cheek. Veronica wondered that it hadn't been more carefully repaired by plastic surgery—or was this the best they could do?

Maybe not everything was fixable.

The phrase settled in her body. Maybe not everything was fixable. She thought of her life, the divorce, the fact of children not stepping up the way she hoped, the mess of Christmas for everyone back home, her own struggle to keep her appetites under control.

Under control. She wanted everything to be in her control, and maybe it just wasn't. The thought brought release, a sense of . . . possibility. If everything was not in her control, maybe she could spend more time enjoying whatever was right in front of her.

She blinked. What would that even feel like?

CHAPTER
THIRTY-SEVEN

Mariah felt beautiful tonight. As she settled a napkin on her lap, she felt eyes on her. Her hair was freshly washed, her dress of Moroccan origin, made of light airy cotton with long sleeves and a modest neckline, the hem falling just below her knees. She'd cinched the waist with a long braided-leather belt of her mother's and worn long, delicate earrings that caught the light of the candles. People noticed her, the women and the men, and she beamed a little, knowing it was random, not unique to her, like being a flower in bloom. Once her mother told her to enjoy it—it didn't last forever.

Veronica received a text. "It's from Jill," she said. "First of all, your uncle is home."

"Yay!" Mariah said.

"She also sent more of the letters from your mom to my email, which is good. I got a lot out of the first few." Veronica, too, looked especially good tonight, Mariah thought. Her hair was loose on her shoulders, waving softly, and she'd lightened up on the makeup, just a little shine on her mouth, some mascara. There was a glow in her eyes, and Mariah thought it was Marrakech. It affected some people that way.

But those clothes! She wore a plain white shirt that buttoned up the front, and jeans. She needed something new. "Let's go shopping tomorrow. Find some clothes. Yeah?"

Veronica hesitated. "I'm happy to go with you, but I'm not a big shopper for myself."

"We'll see," Mariah said. "Tonight"—she raised her mint tea in a glass decorated with blue and gold around the top—"let's enjoy Marrakech."

"Is there another city with more of a sense of mystery?" Veronica asked, raising her glass.

"So many," Henry said in his rich voice. "You'd like a lot of them, I think."

"To exploration."

They toasted.

"Are we ordering like your mom would have?" Veronica asked, scanning the menu.

"Let's just have a normal meal," Henry suggested.

"I'm down with that," Mariah agreed. The night was cooler than she'd imagined, and she pulled a shawl around her shoulders. "I definitely want some finger foods, the olives and apricots and bread," she said, "although I know you guys already had some."

They debated the qualities of tagines, and *pastilla*. "Pigeon?" Veronica echoed. "Hmm. It's new, but . . . that's hard to think about, for me."

"Some women here don't eat pigeon or dove to honor a woman named Lalla Zohra, who took the shape of a dove at night to fly around the city and do miracles," Henry said. "You can just claim to be one of her acolytes."

"That's a great story," Mariah said. "I've never heard it before."

Veronica beamed at him. "Thank you for letting me off the hook."

Henry smiled back, lingering, and Mariah saw something shining from him. A light she hadn't seen in him before.

Oh, shit. It was *Veronica*. Who sat there all dewy and pretty, all for Henry.

That raised a lot of tangled feelings in her gut, things she didn't have any right to feel, and she didn't want to deal with them anyway. She focused back on the menu.

After they ordered, she realized she was still too cold. "I need to get a sweater," she said. "Veronica, do you want me to grab something for you?"

Veronica scooted back her chair. "I'll go."

"I've got it. The exercise is good for me, right?" She waved Veronica back down. "Where is it?"

"Mine is on the back of the couch, I think. I had it there earlier."

"I'll be back."

She wove her way through the network of hallways and stairs, remembering the tricks she'd learned over time, and let herself into the small complex. A lamp glittered in the courtyard between their rooms, casting star-shaped light on the walls and the fountain. She picked up Veronica's sweater and turned back toward her room, noticing a cat lounging by the fountain. She reached over to stroke its ears.

The cat growled at something behind her, and Mariah jolted in fear, worried it might be a snake or something, but when she turned, there was nothing. Only the lamp, shimmering, and then—

Oh, cold. Such cold. Despairing, icy cold. A hundred times worse than whatever was in the basement at home. She froze in it, arms locked around her chest.

And then it was gone.

For a long minute, she stood still, waiting. Was she just out of her mind? Were all the psychic shows she'd been watching making her imagine things?

The cat wound around her ankles, and she bent down to pet it. "What do you think, baby?"

It blinked, gave a little meow, then headed off through some hidden door and disappeared. The lamp shimmered, steady and bright.

She shook her head and went back downstairs.

CHAPTER THIRTY-EIGHT

In Mariah's absence, Henry slipped his big foot out of his sandal, and covered Veronica's arch with his own. In the candlelight, he looked rakish, his thick hair curling against his neck, that full lower lip inviting.

She felt awash in a mingling of things she'd forgotten existed. Anticipation, for sure, but also simply pleasure. Pleasure in looking at him, in feeling his skin against hers, in imagining how it would be to kiss him again.

What would it feel like to simply enjoy the moment at hand?

Her phone buzzed on the table, and he covered her hand. "Don't look. It will only make you upset."

She laughed and turned the phone face down. "You're right. Imagine what it was like to travel before the ubiquitousness of phones."

"Oh, I did. Internet cafés. Phone calls from obscure places at weird times to try to connect. You didn't travel as a student?"

"God, no. I was about as broke as it is possible to be. I had a scholarship that paid tuition and books, but I had to work for everything else—rent, food, beer."

He inclined his head slightly. "That's not the background I imagined for you when we first met."

"Really?" She tried not to care, but she did. "What did you think?"

"I don't know." He frowned. "More upper middle class, I guess."

"That's two decades of life in a university town. I'm a good mimic," she said, and for the first time, it made her laugh. She *was* a good mimic. It wasn't a flaw; it was a survival skill. "I lived in a trailer. Not even a double-wide."

He held up his hands in mock horror. "Not single wide! The horror." He picked up a piece of melon with his fingers. "Do you still have family back there?"

"Two brothers, but they're a lot younger. We don't really talk. Christmas cards, the odd email."

"Sounds lonely."

The word landed. She looked at the candle, recognizing that aside from her kids, she didn't really have a life or a community at all these days. "You know, once my mom died, it felt like the world was an empty place, that there would never again be someone in my corner the way she was." She looked in the direction where Mariah had disappeared. "And it's really true. No one loves you like your mother does."

He touched his chest with an open palm. "My mom died a few years ago, but it wasn't really the same as losing one young."

"And I didn't lose mine violently, like Mariah."

"Still," he said, touching her hand lightly. "You lost her. And then your family lost its center."

"Yeah." Memories of the early winter dark came back, the trailer somehow a hundred times emptier than when her mother had just been at work, her struggle to keep making dinners of Hamburger Helper and spaghetti while her brothers played Nintendo and her stepdad checked out in his tool shed. "And I got out."

"Good for you." He moved his hand away, lifting his chin toward Mariah, who limped through the tables toward them. Veronica realized that she hadn't been using her cane as much.

She sat down breathlessly. "I think we might have a ghost on our patio," she said, handing Veronica her sweater.

"A ghost?"

"I know, I know, everyone thinks it's stupid, but I swear I *always* feel them. I feel them in my mom's house all the time, and it's fucking creepy, man."

Veronica weighed her response. She knew that some people who were grieving wanted to believe in the afterlife. Should she take it at face value? Reassure her that it was nothing?

She opted for a question. "What do they feel like?"

Mariah pulled her sweater around her. "It's like a cold spot, really cold, like black-hole cold. And"—she picked up some bread and took a big tear out of it—"there's an emotion to it."

Despite her disbelief, Veronica felt a sweep of goose bumps up the back of her arms. "What kind of emotion?"

"It's always different," she said, relaxing enough now to lean forward and fill her plate with apricots and dates and nuts. "Every time, it feels like something else. The one in the downstairs bathroom at my mom's house is a little sad, but it's okay. There's something in the basement that feels way worse." She ate an apricot, staring at the flickering candle. "The one in our rooms is sad—no, like, *inconsolable*." She looked up at Veronica, her pale eyes vulnerable. "You think I'm crazy, don't you? I don't blame you."

"I don't know if there are ghosts or not, but you're definitely giving me some feels," she said, laughing and rubbing her arms. "Haven't you stayed in these rooms before?"

"Yeah, but I never ran into this ghost before."

Across the table, Henry had been silent. "Are you watching mediums on TikTok again?"

Mariah lifted a shoulder. "Maybe once in a while. And—*ImighthaveseenapsychicinLondon.*"

Veronica looked between them, very sure that it was none of her business this time.

Henry folded his hands, thumbs meeting. "Did it help?"

Mariah lowered her eyes. Shook her head. "No. She didn't even want to deal with me because there was too much around me." She put the last phrase in quotation marks. "I mean, that's probably all the people who were suddenly murdered, right?"

"Maybe," he said, and the rolling depth of his voice rumbled right through Veronica's body. Why did a deep voice sound so wise? "But the point is that it upsets you in the long term. And it doesn't help you heal."

Mariah leaned forward earnestly, gesturing with an almond. "I think maybe that I just might need the *right* psychic. I mean it probably costs a fortune to get one of the celebrity people, but—"

"No," Henry said.

"You're not my dad, dude. You can't tell me no."

His gaze was as solid as granite. "True."

She ducked her head. "Sorry."

As if called, the server arrived with food. Veronica covered Mariah's hand with her own, offering comfort without having to make a judgment. Mariah allowed it.

They talked about other things over dinner, swimming back to the more polite versions of themselves—memory and depth and raw bits covered over with discussions of food and plans for the following day. The lamb tagine was tender and sweet, and so delicious that Veronica found herself eating every single bite, down to the last grain of rice. "So good!" she pronounced. "I will never understand why people don't like lamb."

"It's a principle," Mariah began, but Veronica held up her hand. "No lectures tonight."

"I'd gamble most animals here are not raised on factory farms," Henry said.

"I'll drink to that," Mariah said, holding up her third glass of wine. She glittered as brightly as one of the lamps throwing stars on the walls.

The courtyard reminded her again of New Mexico, the water and the glow of lamps, the reddish color of the walls. An unexpected longing for the plaza in Taos struck her, a place she had not returned to for over twenty years.

When Henry got up to shoot some photos of the swimming pool and courtyard, Mariah leaned over. "Can I sleep with you in your room?"

Veronica, startled, said the first thing that came to her mind. "There's only one bed."

"I know, but it's big. We can both fit. Or I can call for a cot."

The luxurious imaginings she'd been entertaining about Henry's skin popped like a cartoon balloon. It was almost Christmas, Mariah was spooked, and what was her job here? To be a companion.

To a young woman, not her hot ex-almost stepdad. "Of course. I vote for the cot, however, nothing personal."

"Sure, no, I get it. Thank you."

"Can you forgo the TikTok psychics for a night?"

She grinned. "Yes. Netflix psychics only." At Veronica's expression, she said, "Just kidding."

Veronica studied Mariah's face for a long moment, and for a little while, the young woman met her gaze with an amiable mask.

Then she looked away, the mask dropped, and the depth of grief washed her face with gray loss.

She was lost, this one, a motherless child. Veronica touched her arm. "Whatever gets you through the night."

CHAPTER THIRTY-NINE

To: VeronicaBarrington@timelink.com
From: Jill@comech.com
Subject: More letters

Hope you're finding some help in these letters. I have tried to read through them before I send them out and I just can't bear it, not yet. She was such a vivid human, and I will miss her until the day I die.

Which is probably too much for an email between people who don't know each other, but I feel like you're in the middle of it whether you knew you would be or not.

Let Mariah know that her uncle Jack is healing well now. He's out of the woods at last.

Jill

Dear Jill,

Hope you're having fun. I got a great score on my latest paper and feel very proud of myself. I feel like I'm living a dream and hate the idea of coming home, ever, honestly. I've learned so much about food and cooking and how to feed people. Zoish has been teaching me how to cook so many things, and it's weird how much I love it. We don't cook at the restaurant, of course, because I kind of get the impression that it's not really done, that men are the ones in charge there.

But she cooks at home. Her mom died two years ago, and the whole family has been pretty sad about it. Zoish is the oldest daughter, so she cooks for her siblings. Her brother is the oldest, but he's not really around that much when I'm there. He's studying architecture and studies or works all the time. He's polite when he's around. We had a good conversation about how art deco was a response to the Victorian model of excess, and it didn't really change my mind, because I love the Victorian thing in Denver so much, but he made some good points. He said that Bombay is known for its art deco designs, that Zoish should take me and show me.

So we might do that.

In the meantime, she lets me cook with her. Spicing is so important in Parsi cooking, like other forms of Indian cooking, which varies a lot according to where you are. I'm learning how to use goat and lamb, which are in everything, like hamburger at home.

Gotta go study.

Love you,

Rachel

Postcard: Chowpatty Beach

Jill,

Doing some great exploring with some of the Brits in classes. Spent a day here, eating food from all these different places. *So good!* They have a festival where they carry Ganesha (the elephant/man god) to the ocean. It's so dazzling my eyes hurt. Letter coming. xoxox

Dear Jill,

I got your letter and I am not brave at all—I'm a big messy noob, wading out into the world and getting dirty.

Of course I make a fool of myself! *All the time!* But it's worth it. If somebody gets mad at me, I just figure I can make it right by learning more. Apologize later!

Anyway, this is the letter I promised in my postcard. I had such a great day. I'm so sunburned I look like a lobster, but it was such an interesting time. Zoish, Darshan (her big brother, the architect student), and I did a tour yesterday of some art deco sites in Mumbai. There's a whole block of apartment buildings along a beach that are built in that style, and it's impressive to see them.

I loved seeing all the architecture, but I just liked being in Bombay with people who know it, who could point things out like the art deco apartments, and the best chai wallahs, these little bakeries, and certain kinds of food. I'm learning to eat so many new things—*dosas*, which are a very thin crispy bread or like a crisp crepe, a tiny bit sour and just so interesting. There are so many kinds of chutneys, some with the familiar things like tomato and onion and coriander (cilantro, which was so confusing at first! The whole plant is called coriander here, not just the seeds like in the US), but also a million other kinds (mint! mango! carrot! beetroot!). The multitudes of chutneys remind of me of the trucks all painted and decorated with flowers and altars—why not add more?

I have been thinking lately I don't want to study liberal arts anymore. I'm still in love with Indian history and poetry (I'm sending you a book of poems by Kamala Surayya that I think you'll like.) but maybe that's not where my work is. Maybe that's something I love but don't have to center my life around. Remember when you went crazy for Marco Polo? (Or maybe that was me. Haha. The explorers and the silk road and people who were writing gorgeous things thousands of years before Cleopatra). I definitely don't want to teach—I'd have to kill people—and I don't think I have the right personality for university life anyway.

What I might want is to do something with food. Not cook, exactly. I like it, but that's a really hard road. But maybe when I come back, I'll go to culinary school and try a bunch of things on. Do you think mom will be super mad?

I'm glad you're so happy with Jack, Jill (ha!). I wish I could meet somebody more like some of the guys I know here. They're respectful, and not so . . . I can't put my finger on it. Like, they're nicer. It doesn't feel like they're trying to figure out how to put the moves on you all the time. (Because they aren't, probably!) Families still arrange marriages for kids, and they laugh if you start getting freaked out about it. Zoish said, "it's not like we're married off to some evil duke who will beat us forever. We get to meet the boys and get to say which ones we like." Not like Western people have the marriage record to be proud of.

Love,

Rachel

Dear Jill,

That party sounds like a blast. You're so good at hosting! I can't wait to try a booty cocktail. (Haha!!)

It's getting hotter by the minute, and I have to admit it's kind of hard sometimes. On days with some wind, it's bearable, but then you'll get a day where there isn't a single breath, and the air feels like a solid block, like something you could cut. I'm so tempted to cut my hair off, but then I'll be cold when the snows come next winter, so I've just been twisting it off my neck. So much hair. Too much. I never appreciated how much it weighs before.

School is good. I got an A+ on a paper exploring the Victorian gingerbread and how it reflected society vs. the art deco movement, which freed people up in a strange but undeniable way. Darshan helped me track down the right research, and we're getting a lot closer. He is so handsome, Jill! The most soulful eyes, dark dark dark, but not black, because you can see his pupils, and the longest lashes I've ever seen on a guy. And he always smells so good. I don't know if it's soap or cologne or what, but it just kind of gets under my skin. When he leaves a room, I can smell it lingering, like his body leaves an aura.

It's really not done here, but we hid behind some trees at this park and kissed. I wanted to faint! It was so powerful, like our souls have been waiting for us to meet again at last. I said that, kind of, and he pressed his forehead to mine and said, "Yes, I remember." So romantic!

We talk and talk and talk, about everything, home and time and history and books and lots of architecture and colonialism and everything. We talk and walk and eat. I feel like he gets me, like he knows what I'm going to say before I say it.

I don't think I've ever really been in love before, but I just live for the moments when we are together—not very often! Never enough! It's strange to want somebody so much and know we can't do anything about it. It's weirdly sexy, I don't know why.

I'd better get back to my studies. Send cool air! I'm down to my bra, and my roommate will be scandalized if she comes back.

Love,
Rachel

Dear Jill,

Only 19 days left here! I'm so so so sad. This has been the most magical time in my whole life. I don't even feel like the same person! I look back to who I was the day before I left, and it's like I was a different girl, so naive and full of so many things that were wrong. It's kind of hard to remember what I thought India would be before I got here—I thought of paisleys and elephants and the music I didn't know was called a raga before. My head, my heart, my soul, my body are all packed full of new things. New ideas.

Last week, I went to Delhi with Darshan. It was sneaky, and I felt kind of bad about keeping a secret from Zoish but nobody could know we were together. He said he had a school trip, and I pretended I was going to see my old boyfriend Alex, and then we met at the train station and went to Delhi. I was both happy and sad that it might be the last time, but it was beautiful, too. Watching the scenery fly by, falling asleep to the sound of the wheels on the tracks, waking up a little bit to hear voices.

We visited the big Sikh temple there. I covered my head, and we sat and listened to *ragi jathas* playing in a room covered in gold, and then we ate a meal called *langar* with everyone else, lentils and bread. It's a thing all Sikhs do, offer a meal at the temple every day for whoever wants to eat. I don't know why, but I cried sitting there, eating. Like how is this not a thing everywhere, all the time, in every city in every place of religion? I love them for this meal. It made me want to be a better person, to somehow bring this back with me.

But I don't know, it feels so big, and who do I think I am?

The last day, we walked through this big park, and the sun was slanting down at that evening angle, you know what I mean? Everything was golden and hazy, like the sun was dancing with the air. A pair of ladies in saris walked ahead of me, chattering, and some girls in Western clothes were acting like they were the best of the best, like fourteen-year-old girls always do. Darshan and I were having a deep talk about history and time and how little we matter—how ancient humanity is, and history. We visited the palace of the Mughals who first settled there, and I kept thinking about how small we are, in time and place and our little bodies.

I know. I know. Kind of depressing, but kind of . . . I don't know, uplifting? Like we matter, but we also really *don't.*

A giant eagle swooped down and landed right in front of us and just stared for a minute, then dismissed us, boom, and flew away. It felt like it meant something, a symbol or a message. In the US, I'd be all about the Native American symbolism, but does an eagle mean the same thing here? Darshan laughed and laughed. He said everything is a symbol, and nothing is. That's how he talks.

I am sad to leave here. I am going to miss Darshan so much! I hope he can get a visa to come visit.

But I'm also looking forward to being home. I want twelve cheeseburgers when I get there. Miss you.

Love,

Rachel

CHAPTER FORTY

Instead of a night of juicy sex, Veronica slept like the dead in the cool room, dark and insulated. It was, in fact, one of the best sleeps she'd had on the entire trip.

In the between time before she fully awakened, images from Rachel's letters wafted over her imagination. The boy with dark eyes, the eagle, the sense of being so in love all wound around her mind, giving her a fuller picture of Rachel as a young woman, just becoming herself.

Mariah was still buried in the covers when Veronica got up, so she pulled on yoga pants and a sweatshirt to slip out to the courtyard. Henry was already there, dressed and ready, reading on his tablet while he drank coffee. A cat, not the same one from yesterday, sat on the back of the chair, tenderly sniffing his earlobe. He looked as graceful and at ease as a cat himself. His feet were bare.

"Good morning," she said, combing her fingers through her hair self-consciously. "Is there enough for me?"

"Yes. I can call for more fruit and bread if you like."

It was so weirdly luxurious and not like her real life at all to be waited on all the time, but a person could get used to it. Sitting on the velvet love seat with her own tablet, she nodded. "Yes, please."

She'd left her phone in the other room, but that didn't save her from a barrage of texts. They popped up in a long green line on her tablet, and she sighed, scrolling through them with as much indifference as she could summon. It struck her that it was Christmas Eve today, here, so middle of the night there, but still, by now the family had gathered in Breckenridge to ski.

It seemed very far away, a diorama of a time she'd read about. In texts, Ben complained that his dad had made him go, even though he couldn't ski. Jenna complained that Fiona was too precious and picky. She also apologized for the fight they'd had, but notably didn't offer a time to clear the apartment. Spence complained that the kids were being awful and spoiling Christmas.

She looked up, tossing the tablet aside with a noise of annoyance. So much complaining!

Instead of engaging with any of them, she poured a cup of coffee from a silver pot, stirred in chunks of amber sugar and cream, and took a sip. A bird sang somewhere, the fountain tumbled musically, and everything else was completely quiet. She let go of a breath. "This place is magical," she said.

"It is. I've been coming here for a long time," Henry said. He passed a small plate of pastries and orange sections to her, and she took it gratefully.

"How did you find it?"

He looked up, admiring the bright falls of bougainvillea. "On a holiday from a pretty bad stretch of reporting. I stayed for three weeks, and by the time I left, I was knitted back together." He paused. "For a time."

She wondered what that would have been like, to face the worst of humanity, rest from all the seeing, then go back. "Such a hard job."

He nodded. "In some ways."

"Important, too."

"I hope it was."

Nibbling the edge of a slice of grapefruit, she said, "I read the new crop of Rachel's letters. She clearly fell in love while she was in India. Did she ever talk about that?"

"No. She didn't really talk about her past."

For a moment, Veronica measured him. "Maybe I'm naive but that seems like something you eventually share with your lover, right?"

"It does."

"Was she hiding something, maybe?"

He tipped his head in consideration. The cat's tail swung around his neck, and he reached up to give her a scratch. "Maybe."

"Maybe you should read the letters. Maybe you'll see something I haven't."

He looked away for a moment. Frowned. Then a nod. "All right."

"You don't have to."

"Do I strike you as someone who says yes when he means no?"

She raised her brows. "No. Give me your address." She opened her email, tucked a bite of date into her mouth, and nodded, hands ready. She typed in his email, clicked on the first set of letters, forwarded, then the second and third. "Done."

Mariah stumbled out of Veronica's room, her hair a tangle. "I'm going to my room," she said. "I think I have food poisoning."

"Oh no!" Veronica leaped to her feet. "What can we do for you?"

Mariah's face was the soft green of a snake's belly. She waved them off. "Nothing. Nothing. Leave me alone. Urk. I can't talk." She ran into her room and slammed the door.

Veronica looked after her, worried. "Should we do something?"

"She told you what she wants."

"But—" Veronica thought of one of her kids and how she would react.

She would hover. She always hovered.

Maybe she could learn something new. "I guess she did."

"I'll check on her in an hour or so, but she's been through this before." He looked at her. "Why don't you get dressed? I'll make sure she has what she needs, and we can go explore."

"Okay."

He stood, loose limbed and easy in his body. She liked the silver bracelet he wore around one strong wrist, his big hands. When he saw her watching, he raised an eyebrow. "Something on your mind?"

"So many things," she said.

An arrow of sunlight warmed the air between them, the silence full of possibility.

"I'll get ready."

CHAPTER
FORTY-ONE

It was a cool, cloudy day. Henry and Veronica wandered, turning into this alleyway and that, admiring jewelry and fine leather and home goods. They talked to many cats and once, got caught in a minor traffic jam when a wagon with a wide load of wooden furniture had to navigate a congested turn. More than once, they had to squeeze against a wall to allow a motorcycle to whizz by.

Every shop owner wanted to talk, and were delighted to speak with Henry in Arabic, and to a lesser degree, Veronica in her rusty French, laughing and negotiating in a blizzard of words that fell like copper coins around her.

At last, they sought the address that Rachel had included in her list, one without much information attached. It was not easy to find. They had to stop and ask directions three times, circling closer and closer until at last they came to a small street with only two doors. One was painted blue, and the other had a hand symbol in the middle, a symbol that was everywhere in the medina. Veronica said, "A hand like that shows up in New Mexico, too."

"Well, New Mexico was settled by the Spanish, and Spain was heavily settled by North Africans, so it's probably the same thing."

She gave him a look of admiration. "So it is."

He grinned, brushed the back of her hand with the back of his own. "Stick with me, kid." He knocked on the door, and for a while it didn't seem anyone would come. As they were about to turn away, the door opened abruptly, and a Western man with a grizzled beard and sandals barked in French, "What do you want?"

Henry waved Veronica to the fore. "Sorry to bother you," Veronica said in the same language. "I'm a writer doing some research, and I wonder if you knew a woman named Rachel Ellsworth."

"Rachel?" He shook his head and switched to British-inflected English. "You must have the wrong person."

On a hunch, Veronica said, "Did you spend time in India in the mid-nineties?"

He straightened. "I did. Do you mean American Rachel, from somewhere in the Midwest, maybe? Chicago, someplace like that?"

"Denver. You knew her?"

"Barely. We traveled around some is all. Bit of fun."

Veronica remembered the first boyfriend from Rachel's letters, the guy she'd traveled to Delhi with the first time. "Are you Alex, by any chance?"

"I am." He stepped back. "You'd best come in, then."

They followed him into a courtyard overgrown with plants. A gray dog, quite old, sat panting by a set of stairs. The man sat and gestured for them to join him around a table inlaid with tile. Without asking, he poured them all water from a glass pitcher. "What's this about? Is Rachel dead, then?"

It was such a bald question, but she supposed that was quicker. "Yes. She was killed just over a year ago in a shooting."

"Jesus," Alex exclaimed, his bright-blue eyes peering hard into her. "Bloody American shootings—they're like a virus. I'm so sorry to hear that."

Veronica nodded. "She was a food writer, and left notes for a book on Parsi cafés, and to a lesser degree, cafés in general."

He stroked his grizzled chin. "That tracks. She was never going to be a professor. Can I read her books?"

"Yes. I'll leave you a list." Veronica opened her notebook and scribbled Rachel's name and *The Wonders of Spice*, the book she was most known for. "We don't know why she wrote your address down. Do you have any idea?"

"She quit drinking or something, have to go through her amends?"

"I don't know. Henry?"

"Not that I know of, but maybe it was along those lines if that's what occurred to you. Did she owe you an amends?"

He looked down, and the angle made him look quite a lot older. "I used to think so. We were in love, traveled all over India together. And then she met this girl and dropped me like a hot potato."

That was an angle Veronica hadn't considered, that Zoish might have been the love interest. But in the interest of keeping an open mind, she asked, "Were they lovers?"

"Nah. I mean, people weren't out then the same way, but I don't think so. They were friends, tight friends, but something happened, and they fell out in a big way. I saw Rachel just before she went home, and she wouldn't even talk about it, said it was all too horrible. She was wrecked about it."

"Something to do with the family of her friend?"

"Maybe. The girl wasn't speaking to her."

Veronica looked at Henry. "Do you remember the family name?"

"Nah. But they ran a café we all loved, Café Guli. It had been in the family for eighty years or something like that." He paused, staring into the past. "They had this sandwich, a *bun maska*, that we all loved so much. Rachel wasn't all that careful with food—she'd eat street food and take a drink of water if someone offered it, saying you couldn't be rude, but we all liked Café Guli. You could count on it."

Henry laughed. "Never changed, either. And her daughter is back at the *riad* right now, nursing a case of food poisoning."

"Well, to my knowledge, Rachel never got sick. She had a cast-iron stomach."

They sat for a moment. "Anything else?" Alex asked.

Veronica hesitated then asked, "Do you know if she fell in love with someone?"

He shrugged in a lazy way. "Maybe. That would account for her ghosting me. I think she wanted to try to stay in India, but it fell through."

"Really." That was new information.

"Yeah, but it was a challenge, you know. Where to live, what to do for work. She didn't really have the chops."

Veronica imagined a young Rachel wheeling and dealing to try to extend her visa. Was there more in the rest of the letters? But there couldn't be many more if the last one was a few weeks before she left. What had happened in those last days?

Maybe Jill knew what happened with Zoish.

"Well," she said, standing, "thanks for your time. If you give me an email address, I can send you a copy of Rachel's book list."

"Ah," he said, waving a curmudgeonly hand. "I don't do email. I don't even have a computer."

Veronica smiled. "Here, then." She ripped out the piece of paper from her notebook. "This is her name and her most well-known book."

He accepted it. "I might have to go find an internet café or something."

"Or," Henry said, "find it on your phone." He pointed to a late-model Apple phone on the table.

Alex nodded. "Cool."

~

Back at the *riad*, Veronica checked on Mariah and found her deeply asleep. In the courtyard, Henry settled with a blanket on the settee and a tray of tea he'd had sent up when they arrived. She wrapped herself in a blanket and sat nearby, her shoes discarded, her knees tucked under her. The evening was overcast, quiet, but the lamps were lit, throwing their magical stars, and the fountain trickled, and far away was the sound of someone shouting happily. She accepted a glass of tea and settled back.

"It doesn't feel like Christmas Eve at all," she said.

"No." He stretched out, his big feet on the heavy table, his head back on the cushions. She admired his craggy profile, the rather too-large nose, his square chin. "I have to admit it's been a long time since I celebrated in any kind of traditional way. I was always on the road."

"Does your family have a lot of traditions?"

"I'm Italian, of course we have traditions—for everything. But yeah, a lot for Christmas, the seven fishes, midnight mass." He pursed his lips. "Other things I'm sure I've forgotten. How about you?"

"I thought I'd be miserable missing my kids, and I'm not." She tucked her hair behind her ears. "I mean, I do miss them and all the things we would do leading up to the day, but mainly, Christmas week was about reading for me. They all love to ski, and I'm just not into it, so I stayed behind in the lodge and read."

"That sounds all right."

"Yeah, it was."

"What was it like when you were a kid?"

She hadn't thought about that in a long time. "First, it was tamales on Christmas Eve. Somebody's grandma was always selling them by the dozen, so we'd pig out on tamales and Christmas cookies and string popcorn for the tree, make construction-paper stars with glitter." She grew quiet, remembering. "I realized when I was older that we didn't have any money, but it never felt like that, you know? I always had some toy I'd been wanting, and she'd make a turkey or a roast chicken, and we'd sing carols and all that stuff. All the things. It was just my mom and me then. My dad was never really around. She married my stepdad when I was ten, and we were more of a traditional kind of family after that."

"Did you like him, your stepdad?"

"I loved him. He was a good guy. And it helped to have more money coming in."

"That's nice."

Henry drained his tea and set the glass on the table. He looked at her for a long moment. Veronica looked back, and a soft cloud of yearning enveloped them. She thought of his kiss, his big hands. He took her glass, too, and set it aside, then moved gracefully, smooth as a cat, across the space separating them. "I don't think Mariah is going to wake up, do you?"

"No," she said quietly. Stars of yellow light danced over his craggy jaw, touched his eyebrow. He brushed hair from her forehead, followed the line around her ear, down her neck. Veronica flowed into her body, occupying her limbs entirely, and let their longings lead her. She raised her hands to his face, cheekbones under the pads of her palms, eyebrows at her fingertips, jaw at her wrists. His eyes shone with flecks of reflected light. She stroked the length of his nose, his full lower lip. "I haven't had sex with anyone but my ex in about three decades," she said quietly.

"Are you okay?"

"Very," she said.

He waited, letting her lead, and it gave her permission to take her time. Languor and heat ran just below her skin as she bent closer to kiss him, find again that shock of surprise at the ripeness of his mouth. They opened to each other, kissing like adults who knew exactly what they wanted. After a time, he pulled her into his lap, and she straddled him, unbuttoning his shirt so she could touch his skin, and he skimmed her sweater off over her head, then her T-shirt, and gave a slight audible sigh as the skin of his palm touched the bareness of her skin. He ran his palms down her sides, up her back, down her arms, finding her hands and tangling his fingers with hers, all the while kissing and kissing, their pelvises moving slowly against each other.

"Let's go to my room," she murmured.

"I thought you'd never ask. Wrap your legs around me."

"You can't carry me!" she protested quietly.

But she wrapped herself around him, legs and arms tight, their chests sweating ever so slightly, his hands clutching her rear end hard. It made her dizzy with heat, and when he tumbled her down in the red room, she shimmied out of her jeans, casting them off the side of the bed. He skimmed out of his clothes too, and when he was naked, she held up her hand, breathless. "Wait. Let me look at you."

He touched his belly, lazily, his thigh, giving her full view of him, his leanness, his scars, the burn marks over one arm and his left side, his penis alert and ready. "Okay," she whispered, and he fell down with her, wrapping her up, kissing her hard, and then they were all in, blending, blurring, his big mouth and his big hands and his long legs, and her arms and breasts and hands and mouth. So much, so much, so much. Veronica gave herself to it entirely, wanting never to forget this particular Christmas Eve in Marrakech.

CHAPTER
FORTY-TWO

Mariah stirred at some point in the dark, dehydrated and exhausted, but the intense food poisoning had passed through her. Moving like a very old woman, she made her way into the splendiferous bathroom, turned on the tap to the bathtub. It was deep, shaped by a copper tub surrounded by tile work in shades of blue, dark to light. The fixtures were brass. On the sink was a bottle of rose water, and she added a generous amount, then stripped her sweaty clothes off and sunk into the luxuriousness with a bottle of water at her side.

Thank God.

She could imagine her mother sitting on the edge of the tub, pouring in more rose water. *A good bath cures everything,* she always said. A good bath, a solid walk, good food, always. The right spice, the right tea, a proper meal. Those were the cornerstones of Rachel's life.

"I miss you so much," she said aloud.

No one answered. A wave of hard grief slammed into her, unrelentingly present, as if it was a monster that could chew her up and swallow her whole. For a long moment, she contemplated sinking lower and lower and lower in the water until she disappeared. In a way, it would be so much easier.

But, oh my God, her mother would be pissed!

She sat up slightly and forced herself to drink a few more big gulps of water, waiting to see if they stayed down.

It's just the food poisoning, a voice said in her mind. A voice that, yes, did sound like Rachel. *It's depressing to feel that sick, like you're going to die, but you just want to die and don't.*

"But when am I going to start feeling better?" she asked the empty room. "How long can I live like this?"

Until it's better.

She sunk to her nose and blew out bubbles of frustration. In the water, her body looked lean and unharmed, and she had a sudden memory of what it felt like to move around the world in a healthy body. She'd taken so much for granted!

And really, she was lucky. But lucky didn't really help with what was next. How did a person fill a life when the main things she lived for were gone? It wasn't like she had some plan B. It had always been skiing, her mom and Aunt Jill, and the things that would come out of her Olympic performances—sponsorships, pro skiing, maybe even her own product line of some sort. Her mom was always thinking up ideas.

What would her mom tell her now?

The question sent a breath of soft green peace through her angsty wanderings. What *would* her mother suggest?

CHAPTER FORTY-THREE

In Veronica's room, much later, Henry spied the copy of *One Thousand and One Nights* and picked it up. "Have you started reading this?"

"Not yet."

He sat, leaning back against the headboard, and opened it. "Shall I read to you?"

She curled into his side. "Yes, please."

The room was dark save for the pool of yellow lamplight on the night table. His body was warm, and when he opened the book and began to read, his voice rumbled from inside his chest to her cheek. Drowsy and sated, she listened to the story of Scheherazade cleverly spinning tales to a betrayed sheikh. "I didn't know she was telling stories to save all the other women in the realm," she said. "Heroic."

"Mmm." He finished the first story, and on the cliff-hanger of what would happen, he closed the book and set it aside.

"You're stopping there?"

"It wouldn't be very respectful to the tale if I just kept going, now would it?"

She chuckled. "I suppose not."

He turned off the light and slid down next to her. "Do you like being held when you sleep?"

She did, but it seemed needy to say so. "Do you like it?"

"I do," he said, his velvety voice rolling over her in the dark. "Get comfortable."

Veronica curled up on her side, and he fitted himself around her, his arm draped over the curve of her waist, his chest against her back. His skin was hot. "Good?"

"Very." Veronica drew his hand up to her cheek and kissed his knuckles. He kissed her shoulder. With the sensation of his body behind her, his skin against hers, she felt safe and sexy, and deeply, deliciously satisfied. As she closed her eyes, her last thought was simply, *Henry.*

~

When she awakened, Veronica found herself alone in the bed. She sat up, looking around. "Henry?" she called. But there was no answer. Maybe he'd gone to call for some breakfast. It would be like him, and they didn't really want to reveal anything to Mariah at the moment.

Given the little space of solitude, she piled up the pillows and tugged the covers over her naked breasts, a smile curling her mouth. The moments of the night came back to her in flashes—his calf sliding over her leg; the feeling of his hands on her waist, her breasts; his kisses. Had she ever known anyone who kissed so well?

She sighed, the luxury of good sex easing all the molecules in her body. This morning she was enfolded in the cloud of satisfaction, of having given and received pleasure, admiration, release, and it was easier to forgive the woman who gave in to emotionally unhealthy sex to give herself some relief. A person could manage the physics on her own, but it was hardly the same thing as sex with another body.

Henry, though. Not just a body. His warm voice, those big hands, his delicious lips—

Good God, a voice said in her mind. *Don't get all wrapped up in a holiday fling! How many women do you think he's had sex with? Hundreds?*

At that moment, he opened the door a crack. "Can I come in?" he said quietly, which made her think Mariah was still asleep.

"Of course." When he entered, carrying a tray of coffee and pastries and yogurt, the mean voice in her head dropped away. "I haven't gotten up," she said, laughing. "And here is my breakfast! Which is only fitting for a room where royalty dwells."

He smiled, carrying the tray to the bed. Veronica felt delightfully wicked pulling the covers over her naked breasts, aware of the small, precious injuries on her body from sex, the slightly sore muscles, the little bruises. He kissed her, and that was somehow arousing all by itself, that she was naked and he was dressed. "How are you?" he asked.

"So good." Veronica laughed. "Also ravenous. How about you?"

He kicked off his shoes and settled on the other side of the tray, reaching for a cube of melon. "Same."

"It seems rather imbalanced that you're dressed and I'm not."

"If I get undressed, we will not eat our breakfast." He offered her a small plate.

"Sensible," she said, gobbling a handful of almonds, then a date and a glass of water. "And hot."

He, too, ate eagerly. "This might not be enough, actually. I'm starving."

"We've stretched out our stomachs with all the pigging out!"

"Or we've just expended a lot of calories."

"Or that." She buttered a slice of bread. "Should we rouse Mariah and go down for a bigger meal?"

"She's awake. She just didn't want to get up yet." He lifted a shoulder. "It's Christmas."

"Oh my God, I forgot!" She chortled. "I can't believe I've been dreading this so much and now I forgot." She slapped her forehead in the classic gesture, and the sheet fell to her waist. She grabbed it, embarrassed. "Sorry."

"Don't be sorry on my account." He reached over and tugged with one finger. "Maybe I'm not that hungry for food."

"But what about Mariah?"

"She's hiding away for a little longer."

The sultry expression in his eye ignited everything all over again. Carefully, unconcerned with the sheet falling way, she picked up the tray and set it aside. She opened her arms.

~

An hour later, they emerged from her room one at a time. Henry went first to his room, and Veronica showered, dressed, and carried two small gifts out with her.

Mariah had emerged, hair wet from a shower. Her color was better, but she still had circles under her eyes. She wore yoga pants and a T-shirt for the Beijing Olympics Veronica had seen her wear several times. They all needed to do laundry. "Good morning," she said.

"Good morning." Veronica set down a gold-wrapped package on the table. "And Merry Christmas."

"Aw. You didn't have to." But she picked it up with excitement. "When did you have time?"

"I've been shopping at least three times when you were ill or indisposed in some way. How are you feeling, by the way?"

"Okay." She plucked the wrapping carefully, completely opposite to what Veronica would have expected. "I'm weak, but the poison is finished with me. I ordered some oatmeal and bananas for breakfast."

"I'm glad you're better."

"You never get used to that kind of slam. It's awful. I don't know what I ate that you guys didn't, but I guess it doesn't matter."

"No." Still starving, Veronica filled her small plate to the brim. "Did you ask for a big pot of coffee?"

"I did." An eyebrow rose. "Although I see both of you have had some coffee already."

Veronica met her eyes. It would be undignified to lie to an adult. "Yeah, about that—"

She waved a hand. "I'm not blind. You've been all thirsty for each other since the first day." She looked at the package, removed one more small piece of tape. "I'd rather you keep it off-screen, for, you know, reasons." When she looked up, a welter of tears hung in her eyes. "It makes me think of my mom."

Impulsively, Veronica moved to sit beside her, wrapping her arms around her. "I know," she said, feeling tears in her own eyes. "It's a lot. Everything that you're going through is a lot. I'm so sorry."

Mariah leaned into her, heavily, as if she'd just been waiting for arms. "I miss her so much. I hate that it's Christmas and she's not here, that I'll never spend Christmas with her ever again."

Veronica let her weep, rocking her ever so slightly. "Of course you miss her." She felt weepy herself, a thousand new emotions crowding her heart, her throat. She was lonely without her kids and the family traditions, but it was also good without them, to not have to be responsible for everyone else, and to be able to do something she liked instead of sitting in a ski lodge by herself all day. "I used to say I was glad of the time alone on Christmas while my family skied," she said, "but I kind of hated that they always wanted to do that, when I didn't like to ski at all. I'm glad to be here today."

"They sound like jerks," Mariah said, straightening.

"Not really. I just didn't stand up for myself that well."

"Are you getting better?"

"Maybe. A little."

Mariah opened the box and pulled out an antique locket Veronica found the day she wandered around London. It was tarnished, carved, and had been inexpensive, but she'd gone to a print shop and got a photo of Mariah and a photo of Rachel to put in it. "They're just photocopies, but you get the idea."

"This is so thoughtful!" Mariah hugged her. "Thank you. I feel like a shit now because I didn't get anything for you guys."

"Don't. I just happened to see it."

Henry emerged, carrying a bag of laundry. "They're coming to collect my laundry. Anyone else?"

"Definitely." Both women dashed into their rooms. Veronica shoved everything into a plastic bag she'd carried for dirty clothes, and Mariah had one for hers, too. A young man came to pick them up and promised they'd be back by evening.

"We have a plane to catch tonight," Mariah said.

"No problem, mademoiselle."

Another man arrived on his heels, carrying a tray heavy with food and drink. There was a pitcher of red juice, bowls of melon and dates, oatmeal and a pot of tea, breads and pastries and nuts. "Merry Christmas," he said. "I hope you will enjoy."

"Henry!" Mariah said, admiring the table. "This is beautiful! Thank you."

They gathered around the small table near the fountain. The weather was cool but not unpleasant, and as they feasted, they chatted about what to do for the day. Veronica gave Henry a package, which contained a properly aged–looking memento mori coin, and she could tell he was pleased. He had gifts for each of them, too, a book on Ayurvedic medicine for Mariah, and a small brass rendering of a cat for Veronica.

"I'm so touched," Veronica said, smiling.

Mariah held up her book. "Ayurvedic medicine?"

He shrugged. "You like alternative medicine. This is at least rooted in ancient current practice."

"Huh. Well done. Thank you. What should we do today?" Mariah asked. "We should get out in Marrakech before we have to leave."

"Agreed. Let's go to the gardens," Veronica said. "I can't face any more eating."

They both laughed. "Great idea. Henry, would you give us lessons in photography?"

"Can do," he said. "I'll bring a macro lens."

"We can forget about Christmas entirely," Veronica said.

"That was the whole point of being in Marrakech at Christmas," Mariah said, and raised an eyebrow.

"Great plan," Veronica said, and high-fived her. "Let's go play tourist."

CHAPTER
FORTY-FOUR

Mariah had been dreading Christmas for months. As they toured the Jardin Majorelle gardens, she felt something inside let go, and her entire body felt more at ease.

"I'm surprised it's so busy," she said as they made their way around the paths thick with tourists.

"The weather is good, and Muslims don't celebrate Christmas, so it's just a normal day here."

"True." The crowd did seem to be mainly made of up non-Europeans in many different modes of dress, jeans and Western dresses, hijabs and tunics and loose trousers. A young blond woman sashayed through the crowds in a sundress that was almost nothing, her hair braided in cornrows, a big African necklace around her throat. Mariah raised a brow toward Henry. "Can you spell *clueless?*"

He shrugged. "People do their thing."

Veronica swooned over one plant and then another, naming them by their Latin names, cacti and palms and the odd trailing vine. She was lost in it, her fingers brushing over the leaves of a flowering tree, raising her head to look at the weavings of plants overhead, and bending over to examine some in pots. She exclaimed over the lily pond and the pools with fountains.

"You *really* like plants, don't you?" Mariah said.

"I really do," she said. "When I was a girl, plants were something my mom used to beautify our world. Petunias and geraniums brightened things up inside, and all the potted plants made our trailer seem like a place where happy people lived."

Mariah almost said *A trailer?* but stopped herself in time. Rude, even for her. "Did you have a garden in the house your kids grew up in?"

"Yeah." She took a breath. "It was the worst part of leaving, honestly. It was beautiful, and my ex is never going to take care of it." She shook her head, then physically shook her shoulders. "Not a thing I can control, but yeah—I look forward to planting a new one someday."

It was probably right then that Mariah started hatching her plan, but she said, "Maybe that's your job going forward, plants or something."

Veronica looked up, her fingers lightly cupping a tender pink flower. Henry clicked his shutter, and she smiled. "Maybe it is. Thanks for the idea."

"Sure."

"Show me how to take a picture of a flower, Henry."

"Of course." He looped the camera strap over her neck, and said, "Look through the viewfinder."

She did. Unlike looking through her phone camera, the world narrowed to a square of color. Peering through the viewfinder was like seeing everything through a magic door, all distractions chopped away. The vivid orange flower with a long red tongue, the curve of its petal downward, the blur of the background.

"Turn the focus to see how it works," he said, placing her finger on the right spot. "Now shoot some pictures, just to see what you have."

She did, feeling something tilt a bit with each snatched moment. Just this one, only that. Here, then gone. Again.

"Good. Keep moving the focus and your body, and shoot experimentally."

Mariah became aware of a sense of . . . quiet . . . in her body as she followed instructions. She shot several photos, raised her head, focused in the distance on a blue wall, a yellow pot, the alternating pattern of checkerboard tiles. Quiet, quiet, quiet.

Testing it, she raised her head and looked at the scene, just holding the camera. She still liked looking at the vividly blue wall, the pots placed just so against it, but the sense of quiet bled away. She ducked back into the camera, and there it was.

"Wow," she said aloud, shaking her head. "I didn't know it would feel so different to use a real camera."

Henry smiled. "Now I want you to see how the depth of field works. Turn this and look at the difference in the background. It goes from being totally in focus to blurring out."

"That is cool," Mariah said, and shot several photos at different depths, then moved to a cactus against a tiled wall. She shot it in clear focus, the spines crisp, the background of the garden bed behind it blurring out. She turned the dial, made the background clear, changed it back to soft. Raised her head at different levels, and then found herself focusing on the square wall with the round edge of the pots.

"Good one," Henry said.

She raised the camera to his face, his long chin, his thick eyebrows. He waited for her to click the shutter a few times, and then nudged her gently to focus on Veronica, who was kneeling with a tiger-striped cat beside a trio of giant cacti. She hadn't bothered to do anything with her hair, and it was wavy, loose, shining. She held her hand out to the cat, who arched against her palm. Mariah took the photo.

And suddenly, she had a sense of herself now, shooting the photo, and sometime in the future, looking at the photo she'd just taken. She had a sense of time weaving over itself, both of those moments standing side by side, connected only by Mariah's part in both. It made her a little dizzy, and she straightened.

If all of time folded over itself, the past and the future and the present touching at certain places, that meant her mother still existed somewhere, and in some places, Mariah wasn't even born, and in some threads, the unhappy boy who'd marched into the store that day was also somewhere before he did that terrible thing, and—

Suddenly, she couldn't breathe. Hand to her throat, she found herself suspended in a flashback of that moment, that singular moment when she knew but didn't know what was happening, what that noise was. Hanging there, that moment, seeing her mom, standing beside her with an avocado in her hand, then not standing there and Mariah was eye level with her on the floor, the cool tile floor and there was so much blood—

"Ugh." She reached for Henry, and he caught her arm.

"You're okay," he said. "Take a breath. In, out."

She gripped his arm hard, but the scene didn't leave her, and it was so loud, so present, that she squeezed her eyes closed, smelling oranges and something disgusting, coppery, so awful. Blood, which was under her face and there was something wrong with—

She slammed her hands over her ears, trying to get away from the roar in her head, curled her body protectively, feeling her shoulder bang against something hard. Time stopped, got lost, became something else, not minutes lining up in a row, but circling, folding, flashing memories, a blue box of macaroni and cheese on the floor, changing color as the cardboard soaked up blood, a visual of her foot at an impossible angle, the sudden recognition that her leg was exploding with pain, the hands of a person—what person?—tying a tourniquet made of a belt around her thigh.

Twisting, flashing, noise.

She came back to herself twisted up against the wall, the camera caught between her legs and belly, Mariah and Henry creating a human curtain to guard her from prying eyes.

"I'm okay," she said.

They turned, each reaching out a hand to help her, but neither hand belonged to her mother, who had been holding an avocado, round and green. A blistering sense of anger rose through her. She slapped their hands away and stood, yanking Henry's camera off her neck.

"Leave me alone," she growled, and stalked away. The blond woman with her braids had a selfie stick and was filming herself against the blue wall. "You're a fucking idiot," she said. "Put some clothes on, brush your hair."

The woman lowered her phone and smirked. "Jealous much?"

Mariah started toward her, filled with a kind of violent lust that wanted to knock the woman down, break her phone, end her fatuousness spilling out into the world, distracting from all the things that were genuinely wrong, like—

A body caught her from behind, hard, and brought her up short. "Leave her," Henry said. "Let's go." She tried to shake out of his grip, but he held her unmercifully hard, and he was a big man, a strong man.

"She's a fucking idiot!" Mariah repeated.

Of course the woman turned the camera and filmed it, the tempest in the courtyard of the Jardin Majorelle, and Mariah roared with impotent rage. An official in a uniform approached them and spoke in quiet French, "Please come with me, mademoiselle."

She would have broken free of Henry, gone back for the girl, since she was in trouble, anyway, but he didn't ease up at all until they were outside the gates. "Sit down," he said. "I'll get a cab."

The fight went out of her, and she sank down on a bench, trembling with the aftermath of her blinding rage. She bent her head into her hands. "Oh my God, what's wrong with me?"

Veronica sat down beside her and offered a bottle of water. She said nothing. Mariah grabbed the bottle and chugged it, and the water cooled her throat, then her belly, and it radiated outward. After a minute, she raised her eyes. Veronica simply waited, her expression calm. "What's wrong with me?" she asked again.

"You're angry. With good reason."

Mariah collapsed backward against the wall, a sense of helplessness welling in her eyes, her throat.

Veronica said, "I once had such a bout of rage that I ended up getting arrested."

"You? Were you a teenager?"

"Nope." She laughed a little. "It was less than two years ago."

"Tell me."

"When I was in the middle of my divorce, I was trying to find a place to rent that would let me bring my dog, Sophie. She wasn't that big, but she was a husky mixed with chow, and apartments don't like those dogs, so I was having a hard time. She was very old, and I felt anxious about leaving her at the house—I just wasn't sure anyone would give her the love I did."

Something about the tone of her voice settled Mariah a little.

"She had a cold or something, coughing, and I took her to the vet, and they gave her some antibiotics, which had to be administered every four hours. She didn't really like pills. Dogs don't." She shook her hair out of her face, her eyes hidden behind her sunglasses. "A slice of cheese always did it, so I bought some American slices and gave my ex instructions. I called him regularly. I went over there every afternoon when Fiona—the girlfriend—wasn't around." She sucked her upper lip into her mouth. "And then I had training for a job in a call center, which—don't laugh—I was desperate to land, and I had to work two days in a row, past the afternoon hour I was 'allowed' to visit my own dog."

Mariah felt where it was going, this story, and she wanted to tell her to stop, but she wanted to hear, too.

"Well, I'm sure you've guessed. They didn't give her the antibiotics regularly, and they weren't paying attention well enough, and Sophie . . ." Her voice cracked. "Died. Of something that shouldn't have been fatal. They just neglected her and she died.

"So I went over there, and Fiona said it wasn't the right time of day, so I took a brick out of *my* garden, and I started breaking windows."

"What?" Mariah gasped.

"Yep." She shook her head. "They were really great windows, too, leaded glass, some of them." She brushed a tear away, turned her hand over and took Mariah's. "I managed to shatter most of the windows along the front porch and around one side before the police arrived."

Henry sat beside Veronica on the other side. "And they arrested you?"

"Domestic violence. And I had to pay damages, too," she said, a laugh escaping and turning into a painful sob she caught and swallowed, as if she wasn't allowed even that moment of grief. "I had to take classes, and I'm still not allowed to come within a hundred feet of the house."

"He deserved it," Mariah said fiercely. "What a dick."

"Yes." She was quiet, looking into the distance. "The thing is, it didn't bring Sophie back. And I'm still suffering the consequences of losing my temper. I know a dog is not the same as a mother, but I don't think there's a lot of difference in the violence you were feeling just now and the violence I felt that day."

Mariah imagined Veronica, so proper and hungry for approval, in handcuffs. She still felt restless, the noise popping in her head every so often, but something about Veronica's tone of voice centered her. Maybe the violence stemmed from helplessness.

Which made her think of the boy with the gun, the one she wanted to punish, and his violence. Had that come from helplessness, too?

She thought of Veronica, breaking windows methodically, being dragged away by the police. She raised her head. "I hate that that happened to you."

"Thanks. The point is, I don't want you to give yourself more trouble. You've had plenty, right?"

"Yeah," she said. "Yeah. Thank you."

On the way back to the *riad*, Mariah asked, "Did it feel good to break things?"

"It was very satisfying."

Henry chuckled. The low, warm sound made all of them smile.

CHAPTER
FORTY-FIVE

Their clothes were in tidy stacks when they returned, freshly laundered and pressed. They all went to their rooms to repack and get things ready for the flight that evening. Veronica marveled at the delight of someone else doing her laundry, pressing and folding her blouses. Had anyone else done her washing since her mother died? She tried to remember a time and couldn't.

Another moment of wonder. She smiled to herself.

Veronica went to Henry's room. "Can I talk to you for a minute?"

"Of course."

His room was no less gorgeous than hers, the tiles here blue, the accents in pink velvet and yellow. Admiring the inlays on a lamp, she said, "Don't you kind of wonder how beige and white became so popular? I keep looking at all this tile work, and it makes everything beautiful. Why are we in a season in America of painting everything white?"

He made a *psssh* noise, shrugged. "I'm not the design guy, but I hear you. Why not have some color?"

"In her letters, Rachel talks about semitrucks in India being painted and covered with flowers and wonders why that's not done in the west."

"Did she? That makes sense. She was definitely not a minimalist. You've been to the house, right?"

"Yeah. Do you miss her?"

"Rachel? No. Not as a lover. We were friends, and I miss that part."

Veronica nodded, wondering if that had seemed a needy question. She was out of practice being cool and hard to get.

But was that who she wanted to be? Hadn't she been pretending to be a particular person, some imaginary version of herself, long enough? Maybe at some point she could just be herself, warts and all.

What would that feel like?

"What's up?" Henry asked. He had sorted his clothes into piles on the bed, socks, underwear, pants.

She sank into the pink velvet chair, running her fingers over gold fringes. "Do you think maybe Mariah needs to go home, rather than pushing on to India?"

He took a breath. "I've been thinking about that, too." He tucked the neatly rolled socks into his duffel. "She's getting worse."

"Yeah. I'm no expert on PTSD, but I'd say she needs at least some more counseling and maybe some meds. She hasn't really dealt with everything yet."

"Well, how could you? How could anyone?" He sank down on the bed, and rubbed his face hard. "I've been around a lot of PTSD, and she's a classic, top to bottom."

"It would be more surprising if she didn't have some. Such a trauma."

He nodded, expression sober. Light fell on his face from the open door, showing one side in the light, the other in shadow, and she wanted to take *his* picture. A wave of protest and longing moved through her—*I don't want to end this adventure yet!*—and the visions of India, visions that were like things torn from a magazine, not real and yet calling her, saris and sacred cows and color, and maybe now semitrucks decorated with plastic marigolds, dispersed like sand paintings in the wind. Mariah's well-being came first.

"We should talk to her about it."

"About what?" Mariah said, striding into the room. She'd changed into a blue peasant blouse that left the graceful line of her collarbone exposed. Her blond hair was swept up into a messy bun, and she carried an airy scarf. "My little freak-out today?"

"It was an episode of PTSD," Henry said, folding his hands. "And it's not the first one."

"I'm fine," she said. "I haven't been doing my breathing exercises, and I ran out of Xanax. I wasn't sure how to fill a prescription in London."

"You didn't think you should ask about that?" Veronica asked.

She shrugged. "You guys are taking this way too seriously. Honestly, I appreciate your concern, but I'm not your kid. You're both *working* for me, and I want to follow it through."

They exchanged a glance. "Mariah," Veronica said, "I think maybe you should give it some more thought."

"Yeah, kid," Henry said. "Take a beat."

"Look," Mariah said, exasperated, "I'm fine. I'll get the prescription filled, and if I feel panic attacks coming on, I'll tell you. When I get home, I promise I'll do some more counseling." She pressed her hands over her heart. "Promise, okay?"

Both Veronica and Henry were silent.

"With or without you, I'm going," Mariah said. She looked from one to the other. "Who's in?"

Veronica sighed. "Better you're not alone. I'm in."

"Right, and we have the mystery to solve!"

"We're making a lot of progress," Veronica said. "The letters are helping piece things together."

"Yeah?" Mariah tucked hair behind her ear. "I don't think I can read them yet."

"That's okay. I'm doing it for you."

Henry hadn't spoken. "You need to get the meds. And some real help in the lineup. We're here for you on this trip, but you have to do something when you get back."

"Still not my dad."

"Still your friend, and somebody who worries about you, and I am the photographer, so if you want me, you have to agree to my terms."

Mariah rolled her eyes. Crossing her arms, she said, "Fine."

"And," Henry added, "you need to get the contract between you and Veronica together. By tomorrow."

"It's Christmas. No one will be reading email."

Veronica leaped to her feet. "Shit! I haven't even texted my family!"

"You have time. Do it now."

She ran back to her room, her heart pounding in guilt. It was only noon in Denver, she realized, and maybe that was okay. She called Ben first, since he'd been trapped in the lodge. His voicemail picked up. "You know I won't listen, but you can leave a v-m if you want."

"This is your mom, I'm leaving a voice message just in case you want to hear my voice on Christmas. Sorry I haven't called sooner, but we were out in Marrakech today. Hope your leg feels okay and that you're not too bummed out that you can't ski. I love you so much!"

Then she texted most of it to him, too, but he didn't reply to that, either. Maybe he was lost in a video game.

She followed suit with both Tim and Jenna, first a voice message, then a text. Neither of them replied, but she was quite sure *they* were on the slopes.

Duty finished, she sat for a moment in the beautiful room, realizing that she had not one iota of longing to be at the lodge. Of course she would have loved to hug her kids, but honestly, Jenna still had not replied to Veronica's request to rescue her stuff before January first, and that made her mad. Tim had barely texted since she'd left.

And actually, not one of them had called *her*. The phone system did go both ways.

The guilt of forgetting to call slid away, and she used the phone another way, to take pictures of this room where she'd been so happy, where she'd taken a lover for the first time in decades. She'd wondered who she'd be in such a space when she first entered the room.

Maybe it was just herself.

Her phone buzzed with a text. Reluctantly, she turned it over. It was Amber. Merry christmas! where r u?

MERRY CHRISTMAS! I'm so happy
to hear from you! I was so worried
about you. Are you still mad at me?

never mad at u, silly

but dragon lady is a bitch

i hope you're ok w/her

Veronica took a breath. Whatever happened, Amber didn't need to worry about Veronica. I'm good. In Marrakech!

She sent a picture of the *riad*.

whoa where is that? Egypt?

Close. North Africa. Did you find a
place?

yeah the duplexes on Connor. u
know?

Veronica did vaguely. Rent assisted, big rooms. Congrats.

ty talk soon, k?

xo xo

She sighed and put the phone aside. At least one of them had a home.

PART FIVE

INDIA

The land of dreams and romance, of fabulous wealth and fabulous poverty, of splendour and rags, of palaces and hovels, of famine and pestilence, of genie and giants and Aladdin lamps, of tigers and elephants, the cobra and the jungle, the country of a hundred nations and a hundred tongues, of a thousand religions and two million gods, the cradle of the human race, the birthplace of human speech, mother of history, grandmother of legend, great-grandmother of traditions.

—*Mark Twain*

CHAPTER
FORTY-SIX

The flight was surprisingly long, almost twelve hours, putting them on the ground at eight in the morning. The three of them had been scattered around first class, so Veronica hadn't been able to keep an eye on Mariah. Henry ambled by three or four times, until Mariah, irritated, said, "I'm not drinking, okay? Promise."

Veronica surprised herself by sleeping almost all the way. Now, as they taxied to the gate, her heart was in her throat. India! She was actually physically here. She peered out the window eagerly, hoping to see . . . something.

But it was only a big airport, the same as any other. As the plane taxied, she opened her phone and saw a long string of messages from her kids, largely Jenna, and a couple from Ben, one from Tim, wishing her Merry Christmas.

Jenna texted: I'm sorry I missed you.

Great day on the slopes. Perfect powder.

are you really traveling with Mariah Ellsworth? If you'd told us that, we wouldn't have been so

worried about you. Not like she's
going to strand you somewhere,
right? Is she good now? Healthy?
Seems like it would be hard to
recover.

and omg, I'm going to call you.

Veronica clicked on the voice message. "I'm sad I can't talk to you today. It's been super, super weird with Fiona and Grandma. They do not like each other at all, and it's been like a tug-of-war all day. Fiona gets all fainty and swoony, like some Victorian heroine, and it's extremely annoying. She didn't ski at all, of course, and then she whined about it, and I'm pretty sure Dad is down at the bar drinking whiskey to get away." A pause. "It's really not the same without you. I hope you're having a good day in Morocco. We'll be here through the New Year, as always, but home in the evenings. Love you, bye."

Veronica closed her eyes. Through the New Year. So she wouldn't be back in time to save Veronica's things. How could she solve this problem from so far away? Could she get a storage facility and maybe hire someone to move the most important things?

Except that would cost almost as much as the rent, most likely. Not that Nancy was going to let her stay anyway. If she was home, occupying the apartment, she might be able to fight the eviction, but it was impossible from here.

Was she crazy for not going home right away? She would return to no home, no job, and with only a little money. Where would she even stay?

A wave of terror filled her heart, making her sweat. Was this the stupidest thing she'd ever done?

Around her, people were standing up, gathering their things. A businessman, well tended and smelling of some alluring aftershave, gave her a nod. She got her things together. Henry was at the end of the aisle, and she followed them out.

It wasn't home. It wasn't England. The voices rising and falling around her as they headed for the customs line held cadences new to her, and her heart lifted a little. She saw a young woman, no more than twenty, with a long black braid and dozens of red bracelets on her arm, striding along in a blue sari.

India.

Her heart whispered it. She was here.

Today, she was here. She might go home to nothing, but she couldn't really do anything about that right now, so she might as well drink up whatever she could before she had to don the tatters of that old life.

Then they emerged into the airport, and Veronica looked around, seeing Hindi words and packaged snacks that were nothing like she'd ever seen, and when she stopped in the ladies' room, there was a woman working, clearly for tips, and Veronica was annoyed with herself that she didn't have any rupees, though a kinder voice asked how she would have known to prepare for that. Instead, she found a pound coin in the outside pocket of her purse, and gave the woman that. She dipped her head in thanks.

A sense of calm filled her, even as they crept through customs. She presented her visa and was delighted to receive a stamp, and she eagerly took in the details of the people making their way outside.

A taxi waited, driven by a short man with dark hair combed back from his face and deep-black sunglasses. He loaded their suitcases and they got in the taxi. Tiny fake flowers lined the inner edges of the vehicle, and the ceiling was painted in pink and red stencils. Veronica smiled, thinking of Rachel's letters.

"No beige," Henry said, smiling. He took her hand, lifting a brow for permission. They were smashed close in the small car, with Mariah and her bad leg in front. Veronica curled her fingers around his in answer.

The driver took off, and they plunged into the city, down a highway lined with tall buildings, some offices, others clearly apartments, and then along a shining river connected to the sea in the distance. Couples parked along the center concrete wall, kissing, and Veronica wondered why they'd choose such a dangerous spot.

She admired the stretch of water sparkling into the distance, the shape of the bridge. She peered at the faces in the cars and taxis, wondering what that woman did for work, and how that man spent his weekends and what that little girl had eaten for breakfast. And yes! She spied a semitruck decorated exuberantly, Kapani and Sons trucking. "Trucks like that charmed your mother, Mariah."

"Really? Is that in her letters?"

"Yes. You might really enjoy them, honestly."

"Yeah, maybe I should read them." She turned. "Forward them, will you?"

"Of course."

It was not a very long trip, and the driver pulled up before what was clearly an apartment building across the street from a park. Henry paid him and Mariah headed to the door with instructions in her hand. Veronica paused, listening. The street was fairly quiet, only distant sounds of traffic and a pair of people talking somewhere, and alternating bird calls. She could pick out a woodpecker, and almost certainly some kind of crow, but others, too, sweeter, songbirds. She hadn't even thought about the bird sounds she might hear.

Amid the noisy chirping of something small and repetitive, Veronica unmistakably heard the sound of a rooster.

The front door opened to the code, and the flat was on the top floor, with two bedrooms and a sofa bed, and a wide terrace overlooking the street below. "This is so great!" Veronica exclaimed. "I'll take the sofa bed."

"Or," Mariah said slyly, "you and Henry could share. You are anyway, right?"

"Not your business," Henry said, and Veronica felt her cheeks getting hot. "Let's just drop our stuff and get out of here, shall we? It will get hot at midday."

"Right now?" Mariah said. "I'm starving. We need to buy groceries."

"We can do that on the way back," Henry said. "Today we should have breakfast at Britannia and Company. It's one of the most famous Parsi cafés, and it's not far from the location of Café Guli, where your mom used to go. Maybe somebody around there will have answers to what happened to the family."

"You've been here?" Veronica asked.

"No. I read the letters, and did some research." He glanced at Mariah. "Making hay while the sun shines."

Veronica nodded. Her heart ached in a million ways—that Mariah was growing more unstable, that the trip was proving hard on her, that her own life was a mess back home, and if she was honest—mostly she never wanted the trip to end at all. She wanted to explore everything outside that door, and then the rest of India, and then the world.

But all she had was now. "Let's do it."

CHAPTER
FORTY-SEVEN

Once they landed, Mariah tried to be on her best behavior. Henry and Veronica had almost called an end to the trip after Mariah's rage-fest at the garden, and now she needed to show everything was cool, no matter how she felt inside. A couple of times, she found herself making barbed comments or a snide aside, but she kept it to a minimum.

And honestly, India was a lot, all at once. So many people! She'd never seen so many people in the streets, on walls, on roofs, and . . . everywhere. The apartment was a pool of quiet, with a garden on the roof and a cute little kitchen, not that she wanted to cook. She was jet-lagged and irritable, and when Henry said they should go to the café, she wanted to balk.

But she saw the look they exchanged. Henry wanted to take the trains to the neighborhood they were going to, but Mariah protested. "Let's just pay the money for a taxi."

So they did. This time, Mariah slid into the back with Veronica, leaving Henry to sit in the front. As always, he chatted with the driver, asking questions to get him going about life in Mumbai, about his kids, about the signs advertising housing and the economy.

The window was open, and the air was warm. Almost hot, honestly, which was a relief after all the cool weather they'd been experiencing. Veronica said, "It feels good."

"Yeah," Mariah said. "Probably wouldn't be great in August."

"August is monsoon season, madam," the driver said. "Hot, but rainy, too. A lot of rain."

Veronica smiled. "I have this idea that I'd like the monsoons. I grew up in the desert, and we had monsoons, but maybe not exactly the same. It would rain really hard in the afternoon, giant thunderstorms, and then cool everything off for the evening."

"Not so different," the man said, nodding.

The taxi stopped at a light, and it was a busy intersection, so they sat a long way back. Gazing out the window, Mariah saw a blond woman in a green blouse that was exactly like one Rachel had owned, with little white dots all over it. She sat up, peering hard to see the woman's face as she turned to talk to her friend, and they waited at the light. The woman brushed her hair out of her face, and Mariah was electrified. "Henry!" she cried, and swallowed the rest, *It's my mom,* when the woman turned fully, and Mariah saw she was no more than twenty, and, yes, she looked like her, but not really.

The mediumship instructions came back to her. That those who'd crossed over showed all kinds of manifestations and signs. The green blouse was a sign. Maybe that person was a vision of Rachel when she was here in the city when she was young.

"What is it?" Henry asked.

"Do you see that lady? In the green blouse?"

Obediently, he looked around. "Where?"

"Right there on the curb. In the polka-dot blouse." If he couldn't see her, maybe it was a manifestation of Rachel.

"Yeah. I see her. Do you know her?"

Disappointment plunged her mood into dark gray. "No. I just thought the blouse was like my mom's."

Veronica took a protein bar out of her purse. "Want one?"

"I'm not seeing things," she snapped.

"I didn't think you were. I just thought you might be hungry."

"I'll wait," she said darkly, leaning on the arm rest. "Don't want to spoil my appetite."

Veronica laughed. "Is that even possible?"

She knew it was a joke, but it irritated her. "Athletes need a lot of fuel."

Veronica took the hint and tucked the bar back in her purse. She was quiet for a long time, and that was aggravating, too.

But Mariah didn't want to go home until she finished this quest, so she swallowed her annoyance and said, "Sorry. I'm a little jet-lagged."

Veronica nodded, but her attention was really on the sights beyond their windows. Mariah had faded to nothing.

CHAPTER FORTY-EIGHT

The Parsi café was on a quiet street. It crouched on the block like an old man, shirt pressed but thin. The signs were bright and clean, but the walls were grimy with the density of time and city dirt.

Veronica felt a little thrill as they walked through the doors, seeing the roots of the places they'd visited in London and Paris, the original checkerboard tablecloths, the chalkboard with specials for the day. The windows were covered with grillwork, and a mezzanine looked over the dining room.

It was busy. Students and businessmen, tourists with backpacks in one corner, a mother and father and child in another. "Good morning!" said the host, a tidy man in his late sixties. "Three of you?"

"Yes," Henry said.

Veronica drifted behind them, devouring details—the peeling paint on the walls, the exposed wires, the kitchen with cooks visible behind a pass-through window. The specials of the day were prawns berry *pulao*, and mutton biryani. *Mutton,* she thought. She'd eaten lots of lamb but couldn't remember if she'd ever tried mutton.

But probably not today, either. It was early, and she wanted the classic breakfast, the *bun maska* and chai, as she'd read about. As she sat, still gathering details, she said, "This is *great*. I feel like I'm seeing through Rachel's eyes for real."

Mariah looked a bit sour at that, and Veronica tried to tamp down her effusiveness. But this was the real thing, the cafés they'd been tracking, and she hoped she could tap into whatever it was that Rachel had been meaning to express.

She could see that the other cafés had been much too shiny, but of course you couldn't import this level of time. Taking out her phone, she started tapping in her notes, and noticed a sign that had the rules of the place, including at the bottom, "No Photography."

"No photography," she said aloud.

"We probably have to pay a licensing fee," Henry said. "I'll find out once we order."

"What do you think you're going to get?" Veronica asked Mariah. "What's the game plan?"

"I don't know. You can decide today. I'm going to find the toilet."

She flung her menu on the table and strode to the host, who pointed her to the back. Veronica stared after her. "She is not doing well."

"Agreed."

"I don't know how to proceed," she confessed. "I'm not her mother, but if I were, I'd want to get her back home ASAP and get some help."

"We can just try to wrap it up as fast as we can. Maybe skip Delhi."

"I think that's where the sisters are, though. They're the ones who can tell us what happened."

"Is there still a mystery, though?" Henry asked.

"I think there is. I mean, why did the sisters leave Bombay? Why open the restaurants in London and Paris?" Veronica covered her heart with both hands. "Not solve the mystery! How can you just walk away?"

He smiled, slow and easy, and she loved that he looked completely at home even here, a place he'd never been. "I see you do not agree."

The server came to their table, a friendly man in his fifties. "Americans?" he guessed.

"Yes. Have you worked here a long time?" Veronica asked. "It's wonderful."

"I started here as a dishwasher when I was fourteen," he said, straightening his tie. "In those days, there were many more cafés of this kind, but they're all closing now. This one and a few others are the only ones left."

On impulse, Veronica asked, "Did you ever know a place called Café Guli?"

"Sure! Not too far away." He pointed with his pencil, over his shoulder. "Farroukh Irani; my father knew him. It closed long ago, twenty, thirty years."

"We have visited some cafés his daughters created in London and Paris," she said. "Did you know them, too?"

"I did," he cooled ever so slightly as Mariah returned. "I didn't know they'd gone to Europe. We all thought it was America."

"Did you know their brother, too?"

His expression closed. "It was a long time ago." He readied his pencil. "What would you like to order?"

Interesting. Veronica took the hint, and ordered a simple breakfast. Mariah also ordered a bun and egg and chai. Only Henry, a big man with a big appetite, ordered a full meal. "And bring three fresh lime sodas, please," he added.

"Oh, yes," Veronica said. "I forgot. Thank you."

Mariah looked as if she'd washed her face with cold water. The edge of her hairline was wet, her skin faintly pink. "In other news, you might be happy to know that I've been texting with Jill about a contract for the book, and she thinks the best answer is to pitch to my mom's publisher."

"Really."

"It won't be as much as they paid my mom, obviously, but she thinks they'll be really happy to publish this 'posthumously.'"

Veronica glanced at Henry, slightly alarmed. It was one thing to make a deal with Mariah, quite another to make one with a publisher. "What would they need in order to go ahead?"

"I'm not sure. I think she said—" She pulled her phone out and punched up the message string. "Yeah. You'll need to send a sample chapter and an outline of what you think the book will be like."

In the kitchen, a dark man made a joke to another man in a language Veronica couldn't understand. A server swung by with a tray full of drinks and placed three tall glasses of a pale-green liquid on their table.

A publishing deal! Her heart skittered. What did that even entail? What did she know about any of this?

Except, maybe she did know. She'd been intimately involved in Spence's pop philosophy book. She'd helped with the structure, the outline, and read every single chapter before he turned it in. "Okay," she said. "Thank you. I'll see what I can pull together."

"You're welcome," Mariah said, and drank from her glass of soda. "Oh, man! That's really good. Maybe I'm dehydrated." She reached for the glass of water, and Henry halted her.

"I'll get bottled."

"Yeah. I keep forgetting." She shook her head. "It just seems weird that everyone who lives here can drink the water, but we can't."

"I know what you mean," Veronica said. "I knew a professor who never drank anything but bottled water wherever she went, even the next state over, because she said the gut gets mixed up when it gets different bugs in the water."

She nodded. "So do you know how you'll set up the book?"

Veronica pursed her lips. "Maybe. I think your mom was enchanted with the original Parsi cafés, so we can start there. How much of your mom's story do you want in there?"

"I don't know," Mariah said. "I guess I haven't thought about that. Maybe we need to get to the end of the story before I decide. And I'll read the letters. Thanks for forwarding them."

"Sure. Whatever you decide is fine. If we don't include her story of coming to India, I'll focus more on café culture through history, and connect to each of the places we've explored."

"That sounds good," Henry said. "I can send you a sampling of photos, too. Maybe they'll inspire you."

"Good." A wild sense of possibility buoyed her. What if she could pull this off? What if?

~

After they ate, Veronica wanted to find where Café Guli had been, and see if they could find anyone in the neighborhood who'd known the Irani family. As the server had suggested, it turned out to be within walking distance. It gave them a chance to see the area, too: dogs cheerfully running the streets, cats on motorcycle seats, trees offering shade. And, all at once—

"A monkey!" Mariah cried, pointing. "Three of them!"

The trio sat along a high roofline, and the small brown creatures looked at them curiously. One munched something from his palm, his tail running down the side of the building. Veronica chortled. "How amazing!"

"Don't ever feed them," Henry warned. "They're like seagulls."

"I don't really know about seagulls," Mariah said. "Why are they like them?"

"Opportunistic. They won't leave you alone once you feed them."

"Have you been around them a lot?" Veronica asked.

"Here and there." He laughed, and pointed as another one who popped over the edge of the roof grabbed something from the one who'd been eating and ran away. The first monkey squealed and gave chase. "Exhibit A."

"It's still amazing that they're just . . . out here."

"It is," Henry agreed. He flung an arm around Mariah's shoulders. "Are you feeling better?"

"Yes. I think maybe I was hungry. That food poisoning was awful."

"Good."

"Ooh, look!" Mariah said and pointed at a fabric store. A dazzling variety of fabrics hung in the window, vivid reds and saturated blues, cotton prints Veronica vaguely remembered were called chintz.

Mariah pointed to a fern-green chintz printed with white branches. "You'd look awesome in that green."

"Thanks. It's really pretty." Aware that she'd been marching toward her goal like a dog on a scent, she paused to give Mariah some focus. Maybe that was the main thing she needed, attention. "Which one would you choose for yourself?"

"Mmm. I think I look great in red," she said without smugness. "But that blue and gold is killer."

"You would look amazing," Veronica said. And she wondered if maybe Rachel had shopped on this street, if the café had been along here. She kept the thought to herself, afraid to upset the equilibrium Mariah seemed to have found.

She also suddenly wondered whether Elsie had been on this street at some point, more than a century before. She'd been born in Mumbai, then called Bombay, and spent her formative years here, but Veronica had no idea where. She probably didn't have time to track it down, but it suddenly seemed sad that she wouldn't have a chance. When would she ever be back?

But maybe she was no longer the woman whose life she wanted to document. Maybe that was an idea left over from another time in her life.

Hmm. How did she feel about that? She nudged the spot where Elsie had lived for so long, and there wasn't much left there. Elsie had fled to some other writer or scholar's brain.

Interesting. Maybe Elsie had been like a coat she'd carried from her other life, a way to keep warm until she found new clothes. The idea carried a soft kindness. *Thanks, Elsie,* she thought.

"Maybe we can wander back here," Henry suggested. "You could bring some fabric home and have something made."

"Why don't we just go in now?" Mariah asked.

"Of course," Veronica responded, but she really wanted to keep going with her quest, find the shop owner who might remember Café Guli. She quelled her impatience.

They wandered, admiring, stopping at this or that fabric. Veronica found herself forgetting the quest, she was so immersed in beauty. Such color! So many gorgeous patterns. Her mind made pillows and skirts and bedspreads and curtains and wallpaper. When she realized she was envisioning them in her old house, it was deflating. She remembered she had no money, that she didn't live there, that she actually didn't have a home at all.

Mariah wanted to buy three different fabrics, and then asked Veronica if she was going to get one. "No, not now," she said.

"Oh, let me buy you that green one. Please?"

She glanced back at the delicate print. Henry regarded her calmly, arms crossed. "Okay," she said. "Thank you."

Purchases made, they headed back out. It was definitely getting hotter now, the sun hard and high overhead. The street bustled with humans and vehicles and animals, all weaving around each other easily. Dizzying.

They walked awhile longer, and then Veronica looked up. "I think this is the block." It was a shady street with big trees. It was busy everywhere they'd walked, but this was more so, with lines of motorcycles parked, and shops offering paper products of many kinds. "Is this the stationery district?" She squelched a yearning to go inside and explore them all, one at a time. Then her attention caught on a building across the street. "Oh! It's the Faravahar!"

Directly across from them was an impressive stone building with carved decorations and two massive, beautiful silver statues of the man with wings behind him.

"It must be an *agayris*," Henry said. "A fire temple." He shot a series of photos. "That's a good sign for the café being close."

They stopped, looking around. Veronica thought of the conversation Henry had with the man in Brick Lane. "I guess we can just start asking, right?"

"Yes." He gestured for her to lead the way.

Nervous but determined to do it herself, she stepped inside a shop. She was glad when it was a woman about her age, wearing a green-and-yellow cotton sari. "Hello," Veronica said.

"Hello, madam. How may I help you?"

"I'm looking for a place that might have been on this street once. The Café Guli."

The woman pursed her lips, thinking, then bobbled her head. "I don't know that one."

Veronica nodded, then, "Who might have the oldest shop along here, do you know?"

"That will be Mr. Gupta in the print shop."

"Thank you."

"No problem, madam."

Henry touched the middle of her back on the way out. "Well done."

On the street again she looked around. People were pouring through the street, on bicycles, on motorcycles, on foot, in the street, and on the sidewalk. They talked on their phones, or not, marched with purpose and ambled along with a shopping bag dangling, eating fruit or chips. The day was heating up, and Veronica wiped sweat from her forehead. She looked at the shops carefully, trying not to be distracted by Hindi lettering, little signs advertising everything, and the obscuring nature of soot. "There," she said.

This time, they were in luck. A man stood outside a print shop, watching the world. "Hello," Veronica said. He looked past her to Mariah, who stood out like a lime in the midst of oranges.

He gave her a nod, and Veronica took this to mean she should continue.

"I'm looking for someone who might have known the family who ran Café Guli," she said. "Did you know them? Was it around here?"

He looked at Veronica, then back to Mariah. "I did. The Irani family."

"Do you know where they went?"

"They left."

"Do you know why? We know they left, and the daughters ended up in Europe, but we don't know about the brother."

For a long minute, he measured her, his dark eyes unreadable. "Darshan," he said, shaking his head. "He died."

Veronica felt a shimmer of warning. Getting closer now. "Oh, I'm sorry," she said. "Do you know what happened?"

He shook his head. "It doesn't bear speaking of," he said. "Now if you do not wish to have something printed, please go."

Mariah stepped forward, all luminous youth and earnestness, her hand on her cane. "Please," she said. "I'm looking for something my mother wanted me to know. The sisters might be the only ones who know what it was."

He stared at her without pity for a long moment. "The café was there," he said, pointing across the narrow street, and from here, the old letters were visible. Café Guli in faded blue paint behind a more recent sign declaring it to be a Chinese takeaway. "The sisters live in Delhi, but I don't know where."

"And the brother?" Veronica pressed.

"I told you. He died." With a firm gesture, he picked up a package. "Now you will allow me to return to my work."

Darshan dead, Veronica thought, and a scandal that forced the restaurant to close, the family to scatter. A hollowness lodged in her belly. *Rachel, what did you do?*

CHAPTER
FORTY-NINE

Mariah agreed to take the train back to their apartment. It was busy and crowded, but Henry used his body to block the women from the press, and they had a view through the windows. Veronica thought about Rachel's letters and how she'd spoken of being squished together on trains, of the magic she found in the city.

But she also gave herself up to the sights and sounds along the way, the splendor of office buildings and coffee shops and bridges, and shantytown settlements made with cardboard and plywood. Like homeless camps, she thought with a start, and it was such a surprising thought, with so many levels of meaning, that she had to put it aside for later.

When they emerged and walked the three blocks to the apartment, it was like entering another world. Leafy trees and balconies filled with plants, and less foot traffic, most everyone wearing western dress. "This must be rich-people land," Mariah said. "So many designer bags."

"How can you tell?" Veronica asked.

Mariah twisted her lips. "What planet do you live on?"

Veronica shrugged.

They retreated to separate corners when they arrived in the apartment. Henry insisted Veronica take the bedroom, and she gratefully closed herself into the cool. She stripped off her blouse and jeans, resolving to dig out her skirt before they left again, and stretched out on the bed.

But of course she couldn't sleep. A thousand images and snippets of interest and sounds and impressions crowded into her mind. Fabric melded with the walls of the café, which melded with a rickshaw rushing by mixed with an old woman begging, her face implacable.

So much, she thought. *So much.* Her phone was silent, because the time difference was twelve hours, and no one in her world would be awake at three in the morning.

What a relief!

On that relief, she dozed, and when she reemerged, she found a pair of shorts and a T-shirt and went to find Henry. He was stretched out on the couch, which was a little too short for him, so his ankles hit the armrest. "Hey," she said. "Why don't you come where it's more comfortable?"

"Did you nap?" He sat up, shaking his shoulders.

"A little." She found herself eyeing the tanned skin at the open neckline of his shirt, and the buttons. "It's hard to let go of all the"—she gestured around her head—"everything in my head."

"Anything I can do?"

She looked over her shoulder at the other closed door. "Maybe."

He stood gracefully and held out his hand. "Happy to help."

～

Two hours later, she awakened to sweaty nakedness. Henry was still asleep, sprawled out on the bed like a starfish, a sight that gave her a soft buzz of pleasure. Long limbs and not too much hair, his skin a warm olive she liked very much. Everything about him was appealing, honestly, the way it was when anyone was in the first rush of infatuation. In time, he wouldn't be so perfect. In time, the sight of his wrists wouldn't send sex vibes to all the parts of her. In time, seeing him wholly naked would lose its force.

But for now, right now, it was as potent as an elixir from a genie's bottle, and she leaned in to touch the round of his biceps, the edge of his chest, his side. They'd made love only an hour ago, and she wanted to do it again, and that shamed her in some distant place. Until she realized he was watching her, and judging by the evidence, he wouldn't mind another round. She straddled him boldly and bent to kiss him, fiercely glad to be right here, in this room, right now. He captured her head and kissed her back, and she thought he was glad, too.

~

When they emerged later to find something to eat and drink, Mariah was still in her room. Veronica frowned and knocked quietly.

"Come in!"

"We're going to sample the cookies and snacks. You want to check them out?"

Mariah hurriedly gathered a bunch of papers. "Yes! I'll be right there."

Veronica paused. Was she hiding something?

But Mariah gave her the big blue eyes, and Veronica shut the door and came back into the dining area. They'd picked up some bananas and oatmeal on the way back to the hotel, but then had hit gold with a small market close by—the snack shelves had been overflowing with possibilities, cookies (biscuits) she knew, many she didn't, the usual chips in odd flavors she'd seen in the UK, and many kinds of salty snacks she'd never heard of. They'd purchased a selection.

Mariah emerged, and again her color was looking better and better. Maybe the rage had just been a leftover from her bout of food poisoning.

Veronica brought all the packages to the table. "Should we start with sweet or salty?"

"All of them!" She grabbed a bag of bhel mix. "I'm so curious about this."

On her side of the table, Veronica grabbed Happy Happy biscuits. "I can't resist the name." She tasted it, a kind of chocolate chip cookie. "Ooh, really sweet." She pointed. "How about you, Henry? Don't you want some junk food?"

"I was enjoying the show."

"Do I have crumbs on my face?" Mariah asked.

Veronica brushed her own face. "No fun if you don't get involved."

So Henry dived in, too.

As they sampled, Mariah said, "I read the letters."

Veronica halted with a banana chip halfway to her mouth. "And?"

"I mean, obviously something terrible happened, but we don't know if it had anything to do with my mom, right?"

"Right," Veronica said. "But if she had nothing to do with it, why was she working on the book?"

"Maybe she didn't realize anything happened after she left. Or somebody wrote to her about it, or . . ." Mariah shrugged, chewing thoughtfully and looking into the bag of mixed snacks. "This is really good."

"I hear you," Veronica said slowly, "but why the big outline? It seemed like your mom was on a quest."

"Or she just wanted to visit everybody."

"Maybe."

"The only people who will really know are the sisters," Mariah said. "I think we have to go to Delhi and find them."

"A big task," Henry said, "since no one wants to talk about it."

"Well," Veronica said, "we know that Darshan died, and I'm guessing that's what caused the big . . . whatever. Maybe we can find an obituary for him."

"Yeah," Henry said, "but that's not getting us any closer to the sisters."

"I think we should look on Facebook and Instagram," Veronica said.

"Whoa, brilliant," Mariah said. "We can run their names."

"Or we can find the Paris Café Farroukh and see if either of the sisters follows it."

"Huh," Mariah said. "You're kind of good at this, aren't you?"

Pleased, Veronica shrugged one shoulder. "Research is research. The tools are different now, but it's still the same process."

"Maybe Jill knows something, too," Mariah offered. "Ever since we started, it felt like she wasn't telling me everything." She plucked one more cookie from a bag of Hobnobs. "Did she send all the letters?"

"I don't know. Maybe you should ask her."

"I can do that." She sighed and put the bag down, brushing her fingers together. "I hereby pronounce Indian snacks the top of the junk food chain. But I'm going to explode if I eat any more. We should take a walk."

"Wait. Isn't that my line?"

She grinned. "I know. We switched. *Somebody* worked up an appetite."

Veronica refused the bait. "Maybe we could look up where the Chowpatty beach is. Your mom went there with her friends, and it sounds kind of interesting. A lot of art deco buildings."

"I'm down."

Henry said, "I'll find out where it is."

In the meantime, Veronica opened Facebook and found Café Farroukh. "Bingo."

"That was easy."

She nodded, pulling up her notes and the names of the sisters. The sister who'd opened the Paris café, Chamani, and Zoish, who'd opened the bookstore on Brick Lane.

Both had responded to many posts for Café Farroukh. Some responses she could read in French; others, written in Hindi, she could not. Her heart sped up a little as she clicked on their pages. Hufriya was there, too—which of course she would have been. Why hadn't Veronica *started* with Café Guli in London? Oh well.

Both Hufriya and Chamani's pages were private, but Zoish's had the banner of a bookstore and a business address.

"Here it is," she said, and turned the computer around for them to see it. "She came back to Delhi and opened another bookstore."

Mariah looked pale. "A bookstore?"

"What's wrong?"

"Um, nothing." But she looked unsettled.

"Chowpatty is barely a mile," Henry said. "Let's do it."

"Wait," Veronica said. "Let me see what Google has to say about Darshan Irani." She ran the name. "Oh. That's not helpful." She turned the screen to show it to the others. A long line of results with the same name showed up.

"We don't know when he died," Mariah said.

"Let me try another way." She ran the name and the name of the café together and got three hits, all showing the same dry paragraph. "Darshan Irani, son of Farroukh Irani, owner of the Café Guli, died tragically on June 1, 1996."

The end of Rachel's time in India.

No one said anything. Finally, Mariah said, "I wonder what happened. And I wonder why my mother never talked about this, ever."

"Sure you want to keep going?"

"Can't stop now, can we?"

Henry stood. "Let's go check out the beach. We're here. We might as well catch a sunset."

~

They arrived as the sun was lowering over the Arabian Sea, and people were collecting rocks or shells on the beach in the long red-gold light. They walked in the sand, Henry taking pictures with a kind of glee—photos of the people, of the signs and buildings, of the water and the curve of buildings framing it.

Using her phone as a source, Mariah narrated their journey. "'Chowpatty Beach is known for a Ganesha celebration every autumn,'" she read. "That would be cool to see."

"It would be. A lot of things would be great to explore," Veronica said, again feeling that pinch of yearning. "It's a big world."

"I like thinking of my mom here," Mariah said. "Hanging out with her friends." She paused. "I feel close to her here." She pointed to a bank of buildings. "Those must be some of the apartments she talked about, right?"

"Probably," Veronica agreed.

"It seems weird that the buildings are still here and she's not." She looked at her feet on the sand. "Like maybe she walked right here. How strange is that?"

"It is. The restaurant my mom worked in is still there on Taos Plaza." Veronica snorted. "And Tomas is probably still making moves on unsuspecting young women."

"Did he make moves on you?"

Veronica gave her a rueful grin. "Oh, yeah. I fell hook, line, and sinker." For the first time, she realized she'd been sixteen and her boss nearly thirty, and the person in charge was the bad guy, not her.

Not her.

Henry walked backward as he took shots of their conversation. Veronica felt the moment acutely—Henry looking so dashing that women cast looks his way under their lashes, the sense of a moment in time she'd never forget, and again that feeling of being here now and remembering it later, the sweetness of being here, the fleeting sense of it already flying away.

"I think we all knew somebody like that," Mariah said. "I had a really shitty boyfriend when I was sixteen. He was so jealous of my ability, and he was honestly just a dick, but I couldn't think of anything except him."

"I remember that guy," Henry said. "What was his name, Georgio or Davido or something?"

Mariah laughed. "Sergio."

"How about you, Henry?" Veronica tossed out. "Any bad girlfriends at sixteen?"

"God, no." He turned the camera vertical and took a series of shots. "I was the worst geek in my neighborhood. Big camera, big glasses, feet like a Great Dane. Girls ran the other way."

Both women laughed. Veronica then said, "You've grown into your feet now."

"Thanks."

"I think we might have to have one more thing," Mariah said, pointing to a food stall with a line of customers. "Isn't kulfi a thing here?"

Veronica laughed, clutching her belly. "I am so stuffed."

"I agree with Mariah," Henry said, taking photos of the stall. "How can we resist? We can just take a couple of bites."

So they stood in line. It felt easy, an evening out on the beach, a place where people could come and let go of the day. Children ran around in circles, chasing each other while adults licked ice-cream cones and laughed at the stories they told. "I'm so glad I'm here right now," she said.

"Me, too," Mariah said, bumping her in a friendly way.

"Me, too," Henry said, taking their photo.

They took their pastel-colored dish to a clear spot on the beach and sat down. The sun was just touching the horizon, and the sky around was softly gray, the edges of the beach picking up orange. Veronica sat between the other two.

"This reminds me of my childhood," Henry said. "My grandparents had a shack in a little Jersey Shore town, and we'd spend as many weekends and summer days there as we could. Sunset was always the best." He leaned into Veronica, touching arms.

She pressed back subtly. "Do they still have it?"

"Somebody does. I'm not sure who actually owns it, but the family shares it, and once a year, as many people as possible go, renting all the shacks along the shore—which are not really shacks anymore—and have a big end-of-summer blowout."

"I would love to have that kind of family." Veronica sighed. "Cousins and aunts and siblings and all of it."

"Me, too," Mariah said.

"It has its upsides," he admitted.

"How long since you went?" Mariah asked. "God, I'm going to be sick from eating, but this is delicious."

"Long time," Henry said.

"You should go."

He nodded, looking at the families around them, all watching the sun perform its nightly ritual. "I should." He brushed his hands off. "I have a suggestion."

"Okay." Despite her protests, Mariah finished the dish for all of them.

"There's nothing else in Mumbai, so maybe we should just grab a night train to Delhi, get there tomorrow."

Veronica felt a quickening. "How long does it take?"

"I looked it up. About fifteen hours."

"Can't we just fly?"

"We could," he said. "But when will we pass this way again?"

Veronica heard a song in her head, and deeply wanted the train.

Mariah eyed the sun, a tiny sliver that was then swallowed by the horizon. "Okay," she said. "Let's do it."

CHAPTER FIFTY

Mariah found the train station overwhelming, but Henry seemed to know his way around, and they were settled without much trouble. They had seats in an open compartment with little beds that pulled down for comfort, but they didn't do it right away. A family sat down the next section up: two little kids excited by the adventure, a tired mom, a dad who pretended to read a newspaper and played a game of peekaboo with the baby.

Veronica was bent over her phone, typing vigorously to someone.

"It always seems like it's bad news when you're getting texts," Mariah commented.

Veronica laughed. "You know what? It always is. I don't know why I'm still responding."

"Do you want to talk it out?"

"No, thanks. It's all stupid divorce stuff. Never any fun for other people." She bent her head over the phone, her hair tumbling forward. It seemed more alive somehow, falling freer. "I can't really ignore my daughter, even if she's annoying me."

Mariah nodded. It reminded her that she hadn't texted Jill, so she did that quickly before they got moving. Henry had already told them not to expect Wi-Fi, but it was fine now.

Hey! I'm on a train on the way to Delhi. How was Christmas and everything?

A text came back immediately. Hey, stranger. Christmas was quiet. Jack is doing very well, so we'll take that as the best Christmas gift ever. SO good to hear from you. Are you enjoying yourself? Did you read your mom's letters?

Yeah. Just today. It's a good trip.

How's Henry? And Veronica? Did she turn out to be a good companion?

She's really good, honestly. Better than I expected. I think she'll do a good job on the book.

Glad to hear it.

Hey, wondering if my mom talked about what happened after her last letter? Did you send *all* the letters?

...

...

...

Mariah narrowed her eyes. Why was it taking so long? Can I call you tomorrow? Jill asked.

I'd rather do it now?

She waited. The phone was in her hand. No dots. Some new passengers settled across the aisle, two young women with hennaed hands. They giggled together, sharing something on one's phone.

Impatient, worried that the train would start moving, Mariah dialed her aunt. "What is *up*, Jill?"

"It's complicated," Jill said. "And I'm tired, and you're so far away, and I just would rather wait to talk about it."

"You're freaking me out."

She was quiet for a long minute. The train started moving very slowly. "Hurry," Mariah said. "I'm going to lose you."

"I'll send the last letter to Veronica. There are—"

The call dropped. Mariah dialed again, but she didn't pick up, or it wasn't going through. Holding the phone, she asked Veronica, "Is your phone still working?"

"Yes. Unfortunately." She held it close to her belly, as if to muffle the buzzes Mariah could still hear.

"Can you get online and see if Jill sent another letter?"

"Sure." She opened the app. They started moving faster, out of the station and into the city. Lights sparkled all around. Mariah saw into rooms, saw laundry on a line, and a woman cooking. They passed a tall apartment building, most with lights on, and kept moving. She called Jill again. Still didn't pick up.

"Nothing," Veronica said. "But I think I lost service. What's going on?"

"I don't know. I'm kind of worried about what happened to my mom back then. She didn't want to tell me."

Veronica held her phone in her lap, looking at her. Henry sat next to her, reading his fat history book again. His glasses made him look less like the wild photographer and more like an ordinary guy. *Getting old, too,* she thought. Wrinkles around his eyes and on his neck. He sat next to Veronica, and she thought, with a start of surprise, that they looked like they belonged together. Not like a new couple, but one that had been together for ages and ages. As if they were supposed to be—

Ugh. A snap of irritation crossed her sinuses, the back of her neck. Restlessly, she moved her shoulders. "Whatever. She wants you to read the letter first."

"Okay."

Henry lowered his book. "Are you sure you want to know all this, kid? Maybe sometimes it's better to let things go."

"You've already said that." She wiggled her leg. "I didn't come all this way to just drop it. It couldn't be anything that bad, because she was living a perfectly normal life." Beyond the window, the city shimmered, lights upon lights upon lights. So many people in one city. More people in this one city than lived in the whole of some US states. "And I know it's not some mystery about my bio dad, because I wasn't born until two years later and I already ran those DNA tests."

Henry raised his eyebrows. "Did your mom know you did that?"

"Yeah, I told her. I just wanted to make sure I didn't have some weird genetic disease or something, but he's an ordinary white guy in California she had a one-night stand with on vacation."

Veronica gave her a quizzical look. "Does it bother you, that you don't know him?"

"No," she said, shrugging, and meant it. She nudged Henry's shin. "This guy is the only person who ever felt like a father type."

"Thanks, kid," he said. "Ditto."

"Anyway," Mariah continued, "I think my mom wanted me to get to the bottom of this. It's a big story in her life, right?"

"Yes," Veronica said. "So how do you want me to handle the letter? You want to read it, or not?"

Suddenly, Mariah felt afraid, and she leaned back, curled into the corner. "I don't know." She reached into her pocket for an Ativan and popped it with a drink of water. "Who has the snacks?"

Veronica passed the bag over. "You are a bottomless pit."

"Boredom eating," she said, and pulled her earphones up over her ears, then tuned the world out with a playlist, watching the lights that never ended, until they suddenly did. She nibbled salty snacks and let the music carry her away until the Ativan did its job and knocked her out.

CHAPTER
FIFTY-ONE

Veronica asked if she could sit by the window, and Henry traded with her. After tucking his backpack behind him, he pulled his coat over his shoulder and was asleep in minutes. Nice trick.

Mariah, too, was deeply, slobberingly asleep, stretched out in the seat, her head on a sweater. The whole car seemed to be snoring lightly, various notes coming from different corners, robust, deep snores and slight ladylike whistles, a punctuation here and there from someone who probably thought they didn't snore at all. The vulnerable humanity of the chorus touched her. Next to her, Henry joined in, a very quiet rumble.

A three-quarter moon moved with them, lighting small villages and fields and the odd river or lake. It was lonely to be awake, to be on this train, to be worrying about her family back home, but it was also weirdly touching to be on this train with so many others, in the middle of the night in a country far, far away.

As soon as they'd left the beach, her phone started buzzing with texts from Jenna, who dramatically detailed the horrors of the family ski trip. Fiona and Spence's mother, a patrician pillar of the Boulder inner circle, had engaged in a serious fight. Veronica found herself thinking more kindly of Fiona, pregnant and far from her Irish family, stuck with a WASPy crew in the mountains. She'd probably wondered what the hell she'd gotten herself into.

Veronica read all of it, fiercely glad she was far away, and responded mildly. It will blow over. You know your grandmother likes things to be civil. It's hard to imagine her in a fight.

It was mainly Fiona. Dad was miserable.

He made his bed. But she typed, Sorry it wasn't much fun. How's Ben?

he hitched a ride with a friend back to Boulder, the traitor.

good for him. Hey, are you going to get my stuff?

will she hold on to it until the second? We aren't coming back before then

A wave of fury moved in her chest, but then she realized she was asking everything of Jenna and nothing of the boys. I'll ask Ben.

he has a broken leg!

well, you won't do it, so . . .

And she did. I need help, son. Urgent. No response, which wasn't that strange. When are you coming home? Jenna asked.

not sure. I'll let you know.

it's weird to have you so far away.
I hate it.

I miss you, too, but I love this trip

you've changed

Veronica gripped the phone, feeling the truth of that in her gut. She didn't need to please her children, or her ex, or really anyone. That gave her space to breathe in a way she didn't think she ever had.

I have. It's healthy. I've gotta get
some sleep. Let me know if you
change your mind on my stuff. I'm
trying not to think about it being
thrown on the lawn

Nancy is too prissy to do that

I think she'll do what she has to do
to get me out

she can probably raise the rent

maybe. anyway, goodnight

gn

The fact that she'd changed and felt better about her life didn't solve the problems of where she would live when she got back or what she would do about her things and the very real money pressures that could wreck her life. She could cover the payment to the state for damages with her money from this trip, but it wouldn't be enough to find another apartment, especially not in Boulder.

Where would she be a year from now? It was almost impossible to see even a month in the future, much less a year.

Henry sat up, shaking out a shoulder. "Want me to read to you?"

She looked at him. Where would this even go? Would she remember him fondly, a faraway lover? Or would—

He patted his lap, and Veronica gave in, lying down on his legs and closing her eyes as he began to very quietly read the next installment of *One Thousand and One Nights*. His voice enveloped her like a blanket, and she relaxed into him, feeling him stroke her hair as if she were a cat. And like a cat, she purred, comfortable and warm.

~

Delhi was a slam to the senses. They emerged from the train station into a world of horns and shouting and the smell of gasoline and dung and urine and spices and sunbaked fabric and perfume. A whirl of humans moving in a dozen directions, and stray dogs, and vendors selling chai and bottled water and sweets and maps. Henry used his size to push through the crowds and found them a rickshaw, giving the driver an address.

The rickshaw was a thrill itself. Veronica hung on as they whizzed through breaks and the driver leaned on his horn. She saw a white cow by a gate, shaded by a tree with thousands of small leaves; and a tall bus with passengers peering back at her out the window; and motorcycles with one person or three; and trucks piled with six, plus two hanging on the back; and skinny youths in sandals with dusty feet; and another cow. *So much,* she thought. So much muchness, as Rachel had said.

The hotel was modest on the outside and on the inside, but the rooms were pleasant enough, lit with soft purple track lighting. Mariah said, "You guys don't have to act like you're not sleeping together. I mean, really. I'm not stupid."

So they both took their things to the same room. Mariah was grouchy again. They all wanted showers and a nap. Henry suggested they have a light meal first, which they ate in their rooms, parathas and chai and a dish with rice and peas and spice that was quite hot.

Weary from all their travel, still jet-lagged beyond expression, Veronica lay down on the bed, covered with a light quilt, and slept hard. They all did, no one stirring until morning.

Veronica dressed quietly, trying to avoid disturbing Henry, and went to the rooftop café to see if she could get coffee. A youth with a thatch of black hair falling on his forehead offered her a chai. She accepted gratefully, carrying it to the wall. The street was just waking up. Birds sang cheerfully, songs she didn't recognize, and a big raptor of some kind crouched on a wall, scanning the ground below for breakfast. A woman swept the street with a broom, and a man pulling a wagon piled with vegetables moved into view. Several people came out to buy his produce, and when they'd finished, he moved along. Across the narrow street, a man on his rooftop brushed his teeth, looking at the world, and she was caught by a wild, deep happiness to be here, witnessing the ordinary scene of people greeting their day.

Whatever happened when she had to go back, no one could take this moment away from her.

She thought of Elsie, the artist whose work had been heavily influenced by her girlhood in India. Veronica sipped her milky spiced tea and narrowed her eyes, seeing in the hazy golden light something of the mood in her paintings, something in the shape of the shadows.

Again, she nudged the place where she'd so long nursed the idea of writing that thesis, and found nothing. In a way, she thought she was feeling Elsie's journey, understanding some of what had influenced her, but writing some dull thesis was no longer appealing. She didn't want to go back to school.

Maybe she just wanted to write.

The thought was both exhilarating and terrifying. What did she know about writing anything? Not much. But she'd somehow stumbled into an opportunity to learn, a chance to make a leap if she had the courage to try.

Into the soft air, she thought of her mother, who had worked far too hard and died younger than Veronica was now, and asked quietly, "What do you think, Mom?" She let herself imagine her mother standing beside her. *Beautiful, baby,* she would say. *Would you look at that!*

In her pocket, her phone dinged. For a moment, Veronica wondered if she should ignore it and not allow the world in at all. What day was it, anyway? December 27? 28? She was losing the thread with all the time-zone changes.

She gave in to her curiosity, but it was only one, and it was from Jill. Tell Mariah I can't find the last letter.

Ok. Is that true?

> No. But it's honestly a letter of
> despair, and I don't think it will do
> her any good.

Veronica paused, thumb hovering. If it's all right with you, I'd like to read it myself. To understand what happened.

Three dots.

Three dots.

Ok.

> Thank you.

How is Mariah doing?

Not great, honestly. Most of the
time, she seems about six seconds
from a panic attack. We have some
business here in Delhi, connected
to the people Rachel knew here,
and then I think we're cutting our
losses and coming back. So, the
next couple of days.

Good. Let me know. You've been
really good to her, thank you.

Glad to help.

She lowered the phone and drank the last dregs of her tea. What
could be so bad in that letter? What would they find out today?

CHAPTER
FIFTY-TWO

The trio met for breakfast on the rooftop, eating omelets and little bananas. Mariah was grouchy after sleeping in fits and starts, growing more and more irritable as the night passed. The window of her room looked out to a wall, and she wasn't confident enough in her knowledge of this world to go out exploring on her own.

And honestly, if a person could sense ghosts, there were a lot in this hotel, and everywhere they'd been since arriving on the train. If you could see them walking around, Mariah thought they'd be all through the crowds, walking right along with everybody else. Hundreds, all woven into the fabric of the human flow here. Right now, sitting at the little table with a view of tumbles of old buildings, she thought she could feel ghosts sitting right here with them, one right by Veronica, a friendly spirit, so nothing to worry about, but not all of them were.

But where was her mother? If Mariah was so good at sensing ghosts, why couldn't she sense her own mom? Surely Rachel would be here now, while they explored her past.

Or maybe, she thought, peeling another banana, it was just her imagination, and it was all bullshit. Way more likely.

"What's the plan today? And did Jill send the last letter?"

"No, I didn't hear from her."

"I'm going to text her again."

Henry put a hand over hers as she started to pick up her phone. "Maybe just let it go for today. Let's find the bookstore, see what we find out."

Veronica said, "I'd like to be at the Sikh temple in time for the midday meal. It made a big impression on Rachel, and I think it guided her work to a degree. That sense of service."

"Let's get going, then."

~

Mariah prepared by wearing a hat and a loose blouse and harem pants that covered her limbs. She braided her hair in a single tail down her back, and carried the cane in case she needed it. Henry led them to the metro, but he wanted photos constantly—the boy selling peanuts, a pair of monkeys climbing a drainpipe, a trio of women crouched in the shade of an overhang selling bracelets. Veronica was delighted by everything, touching Henry's arm, gesturing discreetly for Mariah to look. They both stopped to admire the door to a library.

A library? She shook her head. "You two are strange."

It made her feel alone that they had formed such a deep connection. Alone and lonely. Which was just the way life was going to be from now on, wasn't it? For the first time, she realized that she'd not only lost her career, she'd lost everyone connected to it. Her friends had been really nice about calling at first, but they were all engrossed in training, and who had time to keep up with a washed-up ex-Olympian?

The train was crowded, of course. So crowded she could feel the breath of someone on the side of her neck. A little girl with her hair in a tight braid stared at Mariah the entire way, and so did her mother. She smiled at the girl, and the girl giggled, falling into her mother's side.

It was as they were getting off the train that she saw her mother. Clearly. She stood on the platform, wearing that green shirt with the dots. She'd been fooled the day before, so Mariah looked away, but when she looked back, Rachel was still there. She lifted a hand and waved. "Mom!" she said emphatically, and tried to move through the crush of exiting passengers to get across the platform. "Wait!" she cried, and then she was swallowed by people taller than she, and they all surged toward the exits, and she couldn't see where she was going.

She halted by a pillar, and waited for the crowd to leave her behind, keeping her head down. "Are you all right, miss?" A young woman asked.

"I'm fine, thank you." Mariah looked around for her mother, but, of course, she was gone. A cry went up from the center of her heart. *No!*

Veronica showed up instead. "I thought we lost you," she said, shaking her head. "Are you all right?"

She shook off her hand. She had to keep it together or they'd hustle her back home in three seconds flat. "Fine. Just got a little distracted." She looked back to the spot where her mom had been. *Come back!*

CHAPTER
FIFTY-THREE

The temple covered a vast area, boasting a beautiful gurdwara, outbuildings, and a pool. Veronica was glad of the scarf she wore, pulling it over her head as they entered the complex. Mariah, too, had a thin cashmere scarf she pulled out of her backpack. The delicate color, a soft blue, and light fabric gave her another layer of beauty, emphasizing her eyes, making her look not like an Olympic athlete but a Madonna. "You look so beautiful," Veronica said.

Henry took Mariah's picture. A man handed him an orange strip of cloth to tie around his head. He looked older without his hair, but his eyes were large and clear, the color of a pond. He raised an eyebrow. She nodded.

He raised his camera and took her photo, too. She only looked into the camera, solemn, which felt right on holy ground.

They took off their shoes and left them in an anteroom, then filed into the main part of the gurdwara, a vast space covered with gold. A group of musicians played and sang a *kirtan*.

As they sat in the area set aside for that purpose, Veronica felt a sense of quiet move through her. Was this what holiness felt like? The music smoothed her nerves, and the splendor of the room dazzled.

She had not been raised with any kind of religion. The people around her were largely Catholic or practiced Native religions, sometimes both. The area around Taos was layered with saints and legends, with rituals and holy dirt, but she'd never keyed in. All she'd ever wanted was to escape.

What had she missed? Did Catholic churches feel like this? Mormon?

"Are you Catholic?" she asked Henry.

In answer, he pulled a medal from beneath his shirt. She'd seen it before, but only now did she realize what it was. "Who is that?"

"Saint Veronica," he said, and smiled. "Patron saint of photographers."

She flushed, feeling her middle warm. "I guess I chose a good name," she said.

He inclined his head. "Chose?"

"Long story," she said. "I'll tell you another time."

"Can we move on to the next part?" Mariah said. "I'm hot in here."

"Sure." They moved with another group out of the temple toward the food hall. As they sat down in rows with hundreds of other people, Veronica said, "This is what struck your mom, that they feed so many people here every day."

"It was the best letter, don't you think?"

"I liked all of them, but yes." On one of the flights, she'd looked up the practice and said now, "Every Sikh temple in the world does this. Everyone takes a turn at service, and they feed whoever shows up."

"Anyone?"

"That's my understanding."

A woman on Mariah's other side said, "Yes, anyone." Her accent was British. "I belong to a community in London. At our langar, we feed two hundred and fifty people most days, sometimes more."

"Thank you." Veronica thought of Rachel posing the question to Jill: What if every temple and church and mosque did that?

A middle-aged woman in a simple tunic gave each of them bread, and a man with a luxurious beard followed behind giving scoops of lentils and vegetable curry. A sense of possibility and peace filled her, and she imagined America's thousands and thousands of churches opened for lunch every single day in every single city and town in the country. *How could that change the world?*

"Did Rachel have food charities or support something in particular?" she asked.

Mariah said, "Maybe? I think she did a lot around supporting free breakfasts and lunches for kids in all schools."

"That's been very successful, at least in Colorado."

"She was involved in several charities," Henry said. "Someone did an article on it when she died. I can't remember who, but *The Washington Post* or one of those papers. They made note of the fact that she died in a grocery store. In a good way. I'm sure you could find it." He scooped lentils with his bread. "This is really good."

"I guess they have lots of practice."

He chuckled.

To Veronica's surprise, Mariah engaged in a deep conversation with the woman from London, asking questions and listening carefully to the answers. Dressed in the boho outfit with the scarf around her head, she looked younger, like a girl traveling to a yoga retreat. Was this how Rachel looked in those days?

Veronica frowned. Mariah also looked exhausted, with bluish circles under her eyes and the scar showing very white against her cheek. She felt a thread of worry.

Help her, she thought, maybe a prayer. If there were any gods around, surely they would listen in a place like this.

CHAPTER
FIFTY-FOUR

The bookstore was in some neighborhood far from the temple, and Mariah wondered why they were even bothering. It was *hot*. Even in her loose clothes, she felt sweat trickling down her back and between her breasts, making the cloth stick to her legs and arms. How did people stand it in the summertime?

They didn't always, she thought. "Didn't a bunch of people die of the heat here last summer?" she complained as they waited for a train.

Henry said, "It was a hundred and ten degrees." He showed her his phone with the temperature. "It's eighty-six today."

"Hot," she said with a scowl. "How long do you think it will take to get to the bookstore?"

"Not that long. Here's the train now."

The train was slightly less awful, with air conditioning diluted by many bodies, but at least she could breathe a little. She smelled something herby and a deeper note of something spicy that made her think of Marrakech. Which made her think of her mother the last time they'd gone together, buying so much soap that they'd had to stuff bars in every corner of their bags and luggage. Her backpack had smelled of the medina for months afterward.

The lunch had made her think of her mom. Mariah had grown up on lentils. They were a cornerstone of their lunches; the way someone else might eat a peanut butter sandwich or a salad, Rachel cooked lentils—red, yellow, green, French, whatever. And the lentils at the temple had been flavored the same way, ginger and cumin and almost too much chili. The meal had warmed her belly in a way she'd forgotten.

Oh, Mom, something in her cried. *I miss you!*

Henry leaned over to speak into Veronica's ear, probably close only so that she could hear him over the noise of the train, but he pressed his free hand into her neck, and Mariah saw his thumb stroke her neck. Veronica listened, smiling, then looked up and grinned at him.

Why was everyone else having a better time on this trip than she was? And while she was on the subject, what had she ever done to deserve such a terrible thing falling into her life? Not everybody in the grocery store died or even got shot (and she could imagine how that must have been, going home after all the questions, shaky and scared and still no milk in the house, and now somebody else would have to buy it, because no way they were going into another grocery store today). Why did Mariah? Why did her mom? Why didn't Mariah die? It would have been so much easier.

Her heart double thumped, extra hard, at that. Did she want to die?

No. Honestly, not at all. She just wanted to stop feeling this pain, this agony of missing her mom and her other life, all the time, every second of every day. She felt swamped by it, as if she wore pain like a cloak she couldn't put down. It interfered with her breathing, with her ability to see the world or other people or the future. How could she function like this?

How long would it last?

She closed her eyes, pressing her forehead against her hand where it gripped a pole. A burning ache rose in her throat, burned in her eyes. *Don't cry don't cry don't cry.*

"This is our stop," Henry said, his hand on her back to make sure she exited ahead of him. Veronica looked back to make sure Mariah was okay, holding a hand out as if she were five and might trip. "I'm fine," she said, and then really did trip on something, careening forward until she caught herself with her cane. The motion wrenched her ankle and the sore place that still showed up in her leg, and it infuriated her. Both of them reached for her in alarm, and she shook them off, draping her scarf over her head and shoulders again, then heading for the exit.

Henry caught the back of her shirt. "This way," he said, pointing.

She shifted direction, trying to keep her head up, but was she ever going to be good at anything ever again? Not that she really thought she should know how to navigate a metro station she didn't know, but it just felt lately like there was nothing. Maybe it had been a mistake to spend her entire youth focused on the slopes.

They emerged from the station, and it was quieter here, with a lot of trees. There were fewer people on the street, and the buildings were more modern, with generous balconies filled with plants and trees. The shopping was of the type to support a residential area, a food market, restaurants, even a mall. She felt herself take a breath of relief. The crowds and heat had been tangling her nerves.

"I'm not sure we're in the right spot," Veronica said, checking her phone. "Maybe a few more blocks"—she pointed to the right— "that way?"

"Turn the phone around," Henry said. "Other way."

"Oh, yeah. Got it."

The mall entry was just ahead, and Mariah was curious about it. "Let's check out the mall?"

"Can we do it on the way back?" Henry asked. "I'd like to get this bit done."

"Okay." Just then, a woman walked toward them wearing big dark sunglasses, her hair tied back in a low ponytail, a straw hat shading her face. A jolt of electricity knocked through Mariah's center, and she halted, forcing herself to look closer. The green blouse, with little dots, simple white pants.

Rachel.

She didn't look their way, just opened the door to the mall and went in. Mariah bolted after her, dragging her back leg, and pushed through the doors into a hallway. "Mom!" she cried, but the woman kept walking.

Mariah couldn't run. It was a physical impossibility, but she hobble-walked as fast as she could, trying to keep the green blouse in sight. A sense of terrible, terrible dread rose in her chest, filled her throat. "Mom!" she cried. "Be careful!"

A shower of bullets destroyed the ordinary scene. People didn't scream, they just ran as fast as they could, ducking, holding their hands over their heads. Mariah dropped to her knees amid the avocados rolling on the floor, and saw the green blouse shredding, disappearing.

She howled.

CHAPTER
FIFTY-FIVE

Veronica ran after Mariah when she dived through the mall doors. Mariah disappeared into a tangle of shoppers, and Veronica heard her heartbreaking cry, "Mom!"

Henry was with her, and they were close to catching up when Mariah fell to her knees, letting go of a moan of such deep, guttural sorrow that people around her recoiled. Not everyone. A woman dropped down beside her, touching her arms, her shoulders, murmuring comforting words.

Veronica got to her first. "Mariah. You're safe."

She was shuddering and crying and screaming, clearly terrified, and Henry bent down, scooped her up and carried her outside where he set her down in a shady place. She bent over, covering her head, her face, her head again.

"What do we do?" Veronica whispered.

He squatted with Mariah. "I'm here, baby," he said. "I'm here. We're in Delhi, not Colorado."

She bent over, hyperventilating. "I can't breathe. My heart is going to explode. Help me!"

In his calm, warm voice, he said, "You're not dying. It's okay. Breathe for me. In—"

"I can't," she gasped. "I can't. I can't."

"You can."

Veronica took her scarf off and soaked it with water from her bottle, offering it to Henry, who used it to wash Mariah's overheated face.

"I saw her," Mariah cried. "I saw her go into the mall, and I followed her." She broke off with a keening sound. "She's not here!"

Henry looked up at Veronica. "I'll take her back to the hotel. You find the bookstore and talk to Zoish."

"No, I really think I need to come with you. I'm worried about her. Let's just forget the rest of it."

Henry tucked Mariah close to his chest. "Shh. It's okay, kiddo. You're safe. I've got you." Over her head, he said, "You have to finish. I've got Mariah. You go."

Veronica looked over her shoulder, courage leaking away like gasoline from a tank. "No. I feel like she needs me."

"She also needs this story about her mother finished, and you're the one who can do that. I'll keep you posted."

Veronica touched her belly. "I'm scared."

"It'll be easy. You were already leading the way."

Veronica looked toward the street, at Mariah, so overwrought. "Maybe we should forget this. Maybe it's a sign that we shouldn't find out what happened."

"It'll be fine. Follow the directions, and then call for a rickshaw or a taxi to take you back to the hotel."

"I don't think I—"

His clear eyes steadied her. "Of course you can."

This is your life, something said inside her. She pulled out her phone. "Let me drop a pin for the hotel. What's the name of it?"

"Hotel Bonne," he said.

She looked up. "Really?"

"It'll be a substantial ride, but tell him you'll tip very well."

She dropped the pin, and tucked her water bottle in the pocket of her backpack. Every single cell in her body wanted to go back with them. This seemed like a scary trip to take on her own.

But honestly, she had a phone. She had a plan. The book needed this interview, and she was the one who could do it.

She thought of her children on Thanksgiving day, aghast that she'd travel to India, and then their "intervention" to get her to stay home. She thought of the joy she'd found this last month, doing what she wanted.

Mariah keened, her face in her hands.

"Get her to the hotel. I'll be fine. See you in a couple of hours." She helped Mariah to her feet, and on impulse, hugged her. "You're gonna be okay, honey, I promise."

Mariah clung to her. "I'm so scared."

"I know. But you're going to be okay. I promise, all right?"

Tears wet her neck, and Mariah's fingers were tight on her shoulders. "I'm sorry."

"Oh, honey," Veronica said, lifting her head. "You have nothing to be sorry for." She brushed hair out of her face, pulling strands away from her wet cheeks. "Henry's got you, all right, and I'll go get the rest of the story from Zoish."

"Okay. Okay." She swung back toward Henry. He raised a hand and flagged a rickshaw. Veronica took a breath, looked at her phone, and set out to find the bookstore.

CHAPTER
FIFTY-SIX

It really was quite hot, Veronica thought as she followed the directions on her phone. Her back was sweating against her backpack, even though she'd taken almost everything out. The trek led into a busy stretch of businesses, and all at once, she was in the middle of the city again, with a donkey pulling a wagon and a BMW with darkened windows driving by, and, not what she expected in this landscape. A motorcycle whizzed by, startling her, and she stepped back and—

A hand came out of nowhere, grabbing her arm so hard that Veronica was knocked sideways. Before she could gain her footing, she was on the ground. Two people—three?—tore her backpack off her shoulders. Her elbow smashed into the ground, and she felt her blouse rip along the seam of the shoulder.

She fought to hold on to the bag. Someone shoved her, and she banged her head on the corner of a building. She saw stars for a minute, and smelled something rank, not just trash, but rot and urine and some unidentifiable miasma she couldn't identify. She tried to hold on to the strap, but they flipped her over, yanked it off, and by the time she swung back to her rear end, they were gone, disappeared in the crowd.

Shaken, she felt wet on her face and wiped it off, finding it bloody, from her lip maybe. She didn't dare lick it. Her hands were black from the grime on the street, and her stomach gave warning. A monkey skittered down a drainpipe to stare at her, his hand out.

Before she barfed, an old woman in a blue sari knelt beside her, offering a dry cloth. She mimed wiping her face.

"*Shukran,*" she whispered, and winced at the Arabic. She should have spoken in the Urdu she'd practiced, but couldn't remember the difference in her distress.

But the woman just waited as Veronica wiped her mouth, her face, and it came away disgusting and bloody. Her hands shook. She didn't know whether to offer the cloth back or just hold it.

The woman had red powder in the part of her hair and a bindi between her eyes. Her hands were gnarled, her wrists lined with bangles. She patted her chest and pointed to Veronica, who looked down to see that she'd lost a button in the fall and her bra was showing. She pulled the edges together and buttoned the one above, and it held together. The woman gave a little shake of her head, satisfied; then, before Veronica could get to her feet, she was gone.

She stood there a moment, trying to get her bearings. People passed by; some gave her a curious look, but many did not. Maybe they thought she was drunk. Or maybe they just couldn't spare much energy for every person in distress they saw in a given day. The monkey sat on a wall, staring at her with his strangely serious-looking face. "You couldn't have bitten their ears or something?" she asked.

He only cocked his head.

The backpack hadn't held a lot of value. A jacket, her fancy water bottle, some cash, and her driver's license. The passport was back at the hotel. She wasn't really hurt, just shaken. With a sigh, she reached into her back pocket for her phone.

And that, too, was gone.

She wanted to cry. She wanted to bury her face and howl in embarrassment and shame and fear. How would she get home? She had some cash in her front pocket, maybe enough to get a taxi, but she realized she quite fiercely didn't want to give up. The monkey chattered, as if agreeing. She smoothed her hair and her blouse and looked around.

Where had she been going? Arabian Sea Books. It didn't seem like it had been that far. Maybe from the bookstore, she could call Henry.

Except she didn't know his number, did she? Or Mariah's, or anyone else's. Who memorized numbers? Standing in the shade, frozen, she tried to figure out how to proceed.

The faces of her children, doubting her ability to make the trip, rose in her imagination. She squared her shoulders and headed in the direction she'd been going. You always remembered more than you thought you did, as she'd always told her children. Trust your instincts.

So she bore left and walked a couple of blocks, but then walked back down, thinking she'd missed it. Heart beating threadily, as if waiting to fail, she looked around carefully. No bookstore that she could see.

A market stall stood on the corner, and a woman waved flies away from her produce. Veronica approached. "Do you speak English?"

The woman bobbled her head. No? Yes? Not an answer. She kept moving, trying two more stores without success. In a radio store, a man typed on a computer, and he did speak English. "Do you know where a bookshop is, called the Arabian Sea?" Veronica asked.

"Ah. Yes. People miss it because it is upstairs." He took her to the doorway and pointed down the block a little. "The red door. It will take you there." He eyed her kindly. "Would you like a bottle of water, madam?"

"I don't have any money."

"No charge."

"Yes," she said, "very much."

He fetched her a small bottle from a cooler near his feet. She thanked him in English, then asked, "What is *thank you* in your language?"

"*Shukria,*" he said, and made a gesture of prayer hands.

Veronica returned it. "*Shukria.*" So close to the Arabic. When she had time, she would look up where the languages coalesced.

Buoyed by his kindness, she crossed the street, hoping she didn't look too disheveled.

On the door was a sign in Hindi she assumed must be for the shop. She opened it to find a dark, narrow set of stairs. A little intimidating, but she made her way to the top. The stairs opened into a light-drenched room filled with books. Music played from somewhere, and a handful of customers were browsing. No one looked up as she crossed to the main counter, where a young woman with long, glistening hair cross-referenced two charts. She caught sight of Veronica, and she looked concerned for a moment, then covered her lapse with a poised expression. "Hello," she said. "May I be of assistance?"

Veronica touched her mouth, tasted the blood still welling slightly. "Sorry, I had a little fall. I'm looking for Zoish Irani. Is she here?"

The young woman measured her for a long moment. "Who may I say is here?"

"My name is Veronica Barrington," she said. "But she won't know me. I'm here about Café Guli in Mumbai."

One exquisite brow arched. "I will speak to her. Wait here."

Veronica turned to take in the room. Shelves of golden wood held books both used and new, from what she could see, and in several scripts. The room smelled of scholarship and possibility.

"Good afternoon," said a voice behind her.

Veronica turned to find a woman in her fifties with enormous dark eyes and a deep bust. Her hair was swept into a chignon. She very much resembled her niece in Paris. "Hello," Veronica said. "I would offer my hand, but I had a fall, and they are not very clean."

"I see. Come with me."

Veronica followed her into a small hallway, and she showed her a lavatory. "I'll be waiting in the back, over there," she said.

In the mirror, Veronica saw that she wasn't particularly fit for a conversation. Blood had smeared along her cheek, and she had a fat lip and a bump on her forehead. Using water from the tap and her hands, she rinsed her face off and patted it dry, then finger combed her hair into place. For a moment, she was struck with how different she looked from the Veronica she'd left behind. She had little makeup on, but it was fine to see her face just as her face. It maybe made her eyes bluer. Her hair, freed of being straightened every day, waved and curled randomly, and her bangs were far too long, swept to the side.

She looked like her mother.

She also looked like herself.

"Hello," she said. "Nice to see you."

Then she headed out into the other room to see if she could finally get the story of Rachel.

Zoish sat at a round wooden table in a small area next to a counter with a hot plate. "Would you care for chai?" she asked.

"How kind," she said. "But you might want to wait. I've come to talk to you about someone you might not want to talk about."

"Oh?"

"I'm traveling with a young woman who is tracing her mother's steps in India, Mumbai, really. She knew you."

Zoish sighed. "The only American woman I've known well is Rachel Ellsworth."

Nervously, Veronica nodded. "Yes."

"And her daughter is also . . . American? Not a child she brought home with her?"

Was that hope in her eyes? "No. Mariah was born a few years later."

"I see." She shrugged. "What do you want?"

Veronica folded her hands. "Rachel was a food writer. She was killed in a mass shooting about a year ago, a shooting in which her daughter was also badly injured. She left behind notes for a new book, rooted in Parsi cafés, largely because she loved the one your family ran."

Zoish looked away, blinking. "I'm sorry to hear she met such a brutal death." After a moment she added, "I quite loved her, you know. We met first, long before she and Darshan."

"I have read some of her letters. She loved you, too."

"Not enough," she said. "I warned her, but she wouldn't listen to me, and I knew my brother would—"

Veronica held up a hand. "I don't really know the story. She never told anyone. I only know that she met you and loved Café Guli, and that something terrible happened to your family that caused you to scatter."

A tsk. Zoish looked at her hands, pressed together. Her nails were bright red, freshly manicured. "My brother fell in love with her, so madly, madly in love." She shook her head. "She loved him, too, but it wasn't the same. She didn't realize that he'd have to give up everything if they married, that she would be all he had.

"And then she *did* realize. And she broke it off." She took a breath. "And my foolish brother hanged himself."

Veronica sucked in a breath, her heart squeezing in pain. "Oh, dear. I am so sorry. What a terrible story."

"It was a vivid scandal in our world, which is a small world, close. My father came to Delhi. My sister Hufriya went to London, and I went with her. Our other sister moved to Paris." Composed, even-tempered, she said, "It was devastating to be exiled."

Exiled. Veronica understood that very well. "Your sister took one look at Mariah, Rachel's daughter, at the London Café Guli, and immediately ordered her out of the restaurant."

"Do you have a picture?"

"I do!" Veronica reached for her phone. "Or I did. My phone was stolen." She pointed to her face.

"What a calamity!" She stood up. "You must have a cup of chai before you leave."

"Thank you."

As she prepared a pot and measured tea, water, and milk, Zoish said, "Hufriya adored Darshan. She's terribly bitter. It was easier for me to forgive her." She shook her head. "We were all so young, so full of heat."

Veronica nodded, thinking of her own moments of fury, smashing windows out of a need to somehow express her pain.

Zoish asked, "Are you married, madam?"

"Divorced, I'm sorry to say." But she thought of the woman she'd been then, lashing out in despair, and the woman she had started to become. She revised. "No, I'm not sorry. It was hard, but I'm in a better place without him."

"Same," she said. "Now tell me what you will do with this book. I am intrigued that Rachel wanted to write about Parsi cafés. It's such a rare world, and fading away, I'm afraid. Perhaps I might be of help?"

"Oh my gosh, yes! That would be amazing."

~

Veronica returned to the hotel, thoughtful after the long discussion with Zoish. They had exchanged email addresses, and Veronica knew the book would be better with her input.

Since she was, after all, the start of the whole thing.

When Henry opened the door to her, he stood still for a long moment. "Rough journey, huh?"

"I got mugged. I need to pay the taxi." She gestured. "Can you do it?"

"Yes. Wait here." He dashed out to the taxi in bare feet and settled the bill, then came back. "What happened?"

"Two guys stole my backpack and my phone."

He opened his arms, and she stepped into the circle. "Are you okay?"

"I'm good." His chest was solid and warm, such a relief after the hard afternoon. "I have to admit I panicked when I realized they'd taken the phone, too. I was only a few blocks from the bookstore, but it was kind of hard to find, so I just started asking people."

He made no move to stop her, just held her, stroking her back.

"How is Mariah?" she asked.

"She's sleeping. She took something to help calm her down, and I brought her back and poured her into bed."

"Poor baby."

"Tell me more about what happened to you."

"A woman helped me when it first happened, and then a really nice man at a radio shop told me how to find the bookstore, and then—" She lifted her head. "Zoish was . . . amazing."

"Why don't you change your shirt, and we'll go upstairs to the roof and have some dinner and a drink?"

"Yes. First, I have to kill my phone and credit cards."

Using her tablet, she marked the phone locked and erased it remotely. She reported the two cards stolen. Not that it would matter—they were maxed out—then looked to see if her social media accounts had been accessed. She changed the passwords, and changed her email password. "There are probably other things I should do, but honestly, I can't think of them right now."

"It'll be fine. Go get washed up, and let's get you some food."

She ignored the texts waiting for her and took a quick shower, found a clean shirt, and brushed out her hair. Her forehead was bruised, and it might be a pretty solid black eye by morning, but she was in one piece. The passport was here, safe, so she could get home.

They sat at a table in the open air, eating *matar kulcha* and sticky, hot cauliflower. Each of them ordered a cocktail flavored with mango. Veronica was bone tired, and she had a mild headache, but she also felt a stirring of possibility in the ideas she'd gathered for the book, the cafés, but also the foods themselves, the reasons people loved their local things. "What a wild day," she said.

"Tell me about Zoish."

Veronica condensed it, the background and the sad story of Darshan, whose rash act had destroyed his family. "I can see why Jill didn't want to send the last letter to Mariah. It must have been about this."

"Did you get it?"

"Not yet." She savored a bite of very spicy cauliflower. Her eyes watered. "Sometimes, the heat level is a lot for me."

"You have to work up to it. I spent a couple of years in Thailand and never could eat the hottest hot."

"Such a glamorous life," she commented, and sat back, finished. Then, "We have to take her home."

He nodded. "She wasn't well enough for this trip, and I feel like I let her down by not realizing that."

"You were giving her autonomy. That's everything."

He barely shrugged, then reached for her hand on the table. "Is it all right to say I wish *our* journey wasn't ending?"

She nodded, turning her palm upward to grasp his hand back.

"I know you're still in the middle of a divorce and all that entails, but do you think you'd be open to seeing if this feels so—good—when we get back?"

She brushed his fingernail with her thumb. "I have a lot to figure out, and honestly, Henry, I'm kind of a mess. I'm worried that I'm looking for the romantic solution to my problems rather than trying to sort them out."

He lifted her hand and kissed the palm. "Fair."

Every cell in her body shimmered. "All that said, I'm not opposed to seeing you back in Colorado."

"Thank God." He bent close. "I'm not going to kiss you in public here, but I plan to do a lot of it after dinner."

"I will look forward to that." She touched her swollen lip. "But maybe easy kisses?"

He laughed. "Of course."

THE LAST LETTER

Dear Jill,

I've been crying so hard I can barely see. This has been the worst day of my life. Darshan, my friend here, hung himself in his family's restaurant today, the café I've been telling you about. And it's all my fault.

Oh my God, I can't believe this. I can't believe I was so stupid, that I didn't understand.

We went to Delhi together. It was so romantic, at least I thought it was, and we made love at last, and had the most beautiful two days ever. So in love! On the way back to Bombay, he asked if he needed to talk to my parents, and said his parents would be angry, but he thought he could bring them around, and it turned out he wanted to get married. Married!

I thought he was kidding at first, but he was very upset when I said no, that I would be going back to the US in a few weeks, and we could write letters. He begged me, made his case, and almost convinced me, but Jill, I can't live here, and I'm too young to get married. How would I completely change who I am to live here as his wife?

He kept trying, but I got upset and said he had to stop talking about it, and he did, but then when we got back, he made this big plan, and I just said he had to stop calling me, that I wouldn't marry him.

And Jill, oh my God, I can't even see, he killed himself. Why would he do that? And how can he do that? I am the worst person in the world. I don't know what to do. How will I live with this for the rest of my life?

I don't even know if you'll get this before I get home, but I wanted you to know.

Rachel

PART SIX

DENVER

Travel makes one modest: one sees what a tiny place one occupies in the world.

—*Gustave Flaubert*

CHAPTER FIFTY-SEVEN

The trip back to Denver was uneventful. They all sat together so Mariah wouldn't be alone, and she mostly slept all the way. Veronica shared Rachel's last letter with Henry, but they agreed it wasn't to be shared with Mariah. At least not yet.

Cutting the trip short meant that Veronica would get back in time to move her things out of the apartment, although it wouldn't leave her much time to find a new place. She'd just have to hit the ground running when she got back.

It was snowing as they emerged from the airport, adding to the inches already on the ground. "It's startling, isn't it?" Veronica said.

Mariah looked up, let the flakes fall on her face, and closed her eyes. "I love snow so much. I'm going to have to figure out a way to be in it even if I can't do what I have in the past."

Looking at her upturned face, Veronica felt pierced. "You will," she said. "You're such a badass."

Mariah gave a hoarse laugh. "Look who's talking!"

"My kids are going to flip out," Veronica said, touching her cheek gingerly. The bruises had worsened over the last twenty-four hours, as bruises would do, and she looked bad enough that people stared. It didn't really hurt much after the first day, so it was all surface stuff.

Henry had driven to the airport, so he brought them all to Mariah's house. "I have to just get back to Boulder," Veronica said. "I have two days to get out of my apartment."

"What?" Mariah asked. "What are you talking about?"

Veronica took a breath. "It's a long story, but I'm getting evicted as of January 1. I was hoping my kids would deal with some of it, but they've all had excuses, some better than others."

"Jeez. What're you going to do?"

Veronica shrugged. "Find a new place."

"Nope." Mariah flung her arm around Veronica's shoulders. "Nope, nope, nope. We'll help you."

"*I'll* help you," Henry said, lifting her suitcase into the back of her Subaru. So familiar. So strange. The car was a relic from another life. Another her. "What are you going to do with your things while you look? Do you want me to hunt down a storage unit?"

"Um." She looked up at him, so calmly offering help. She felt comfortable with him, with his sense of integrity that felt reliable and real. Emotion welled up in her eyes. It was so strange to have help. "Yes. That would help a lot."

He squeezed her hand. "Done."

Mariah crossed her arms. Snow fell on her puffy jacket and slipped away, but it stuck to her hair and eyelashes. "You can say no, but I have lots of room. You can stay with me until you find a place."

Veronica looked at her, hope rising.

"I mean, like as my roommate, of course, not as a 'companion.'" She put the words in air quotes, giving away her nervousness. "Not that I'm a bargain, as you know. Kind of nutty in the head and all, but there's so much space and—"

"Yes!" Veronica said, tears stinging her eyes. Gratitude made her impulsively pull Mariah into a hug. "I would really love that. I won't mother you, I promise."

Mariah gripped her back, hard. "Well, you can a little, if you want."

Veronica closed her eyes, throat tight, realizing she could hardly have borne it if she'd had to leave this delicate, tough, challenging, complex being here alone in Denver. Mariah had changed her life. "I'm so glad I met you."

"Me, too."

"It'll just be temporary, until I can find a place here."

"That's fine." Mariah stepped back, clearing her throat. "I really don't want to be alone yet."

Henry said, "Aw hell," and gathered everybody into a hug. "Come on in."

The three of them stood on the sidewalk in the falling snow, wrapped up together in the unit they'd become.

CHAPTER FIFTY-EIGHT

Six Months Later

The day was the very best of Colorado weather—cloudless azure sky, thin breeze, temps in the low eighties predicted, though it was still cool this morning. Veronica inhaled the fresh, dry air and stretched happily.

Her new apartment, on the ground floor of an old Victorian not far from Mariah's house, came with an old-fashioned cutting garden. Veronica had had to sign an agreement that she would take care of the flowers, a sweet little gift from the universe that she accepted happily. Just now, the irises were blooming extravagantly, late because of several spring snows. The blossoms were purple and yellow, peach, the classic blue, and even one gorgeous red one. She didn't even know irises came in red.

This morning, she collected blooms for a party to celebrate Mariah's twenty-sixth birthday. The guest of honor was already here, slicing strawberries in the kitchen as Veronica came back in. She'd cut her hair to her shoulders, a simple change that made her look more adult, and she wore a red sundress, the fabric laced with gold that emphasized her tanned arms. "These strawberries are so amazing." She offered one, and Veronica snapped it up with her lips.

"Ew," Mariah laughed. "Slobber."

"You look great," Veronica said, filling a vase with water.

"You, too! I'm so glad you didn't use the fabric from Delhi to make pillows."

Veronica let Mariah talk her into having a sundress made from the dazzling fabric. The vivid colors made her complexion sing in ways that were startling and thrilling. "You were right."

Henry came in from the farmer's market down the street, carrying a net bag of fresh lettuces, celery, and fruit. He, too, had cut his hair, preserving some curls but bringing his look into the twenty-first century. He'd taken a studio in an arty district, where he was experimenting with altered photos and montages that expressed a single idea—light in dark places was one of them; another was hands reaching for something, her favorite. On her wall hung a trio of framed images from their trip, all Henry's elegant, moody character work. One was of Mariah in India, the day at the Sikh temple, her hair slipping out beneath her scarf, her eyes uplifted and filled with wonder. Another was of herself in Morocco, staring simply at the camera, troubled but strong. The final was of her and Mariah together, laughing over something at the table at Café Farroukh. She had her own photo of Henry in her bedroom, tousled and sexy in her bed in Marrakech, shirtless and wry.

"Do you want me to make a salad?" he asked.

"Sure."

Veronica had invited her children to visit her new apartment for the first time. Their relationship upon her return had been deeply strained, but Veronica realized they'd been grappling with the big shift in their lives, too. It turned out Spence's money panic was real. He'd lost the house that had been in his family for a hundred years, and his situation was so terrible the kids were all scrambling for ways to pay for the rest of their college educations. She was devastated for Ben, the only one who hadn't finished his undergrad, but he seemed to embrace it all with happiness. He'd dropped out of college entirely and was traveling, inspired, he said, by his mother.

When she first returned from India, Veronica had stayed with Mariah. She hadn't spoken to Spence at all. It wasn't worth the angst, and she'd given him way too much power in her life. He'd been unworthy of that trust. The idyll of family, tradition, stability had proved to be an illusion. Family wasn't a bloodline. It was a unit, built piece by piece.

Now, someone else lived in the house she had so loved. She hoped they'd discover some of the flowers she'd planted, but she didn't have any control. Life switched and turned upside down all the time. It was sad, and she would always miss that beautiful place, but it was time for a new life.

Staying with Mariah had worked out well for both of them for a few months. Mariah had enrolled in an intensive outpatient treatment program for sufferers of PTSD, and it had given her an armory of tools. When Veronica saw that she was stable, she'd looked for a place on her own. This place had been perfect, and in the same neighborhood. Mariah thought she might sell her mom's house, but it was a decision both Jill and Veronica urged her to wait on. Time enough.

The publishing company had been happy to look at Veronica's proposal, but in the current cutthroat market, they were unwilling to give her an advance to write it, even with the promise of Henry's photos. They asked her to write it, then resubmit when she was finished. It was a little disappointing, but honestly, she would have been panicked about accepting an advance when she wasn't sure what she was doing. This gave her time to develop the ideas and write them without pressure.

In the meantime, she was working on the possibility that Rachel's tragic love affair could make a novel, which she had discussed deeply with Mariah for her approval. Mariah was very enthusiastic, so Veronica was exploring the idea. It was wildly satisfying.

To actually support herself, she had found work at a greenhouse, and while it wasn't a ton of money, she had some savings from the travel payments. It was enough to make it work.

"Veronica, can you help me?" Henry asked from the doorway.

She smiled. They'd plotted this bit together for Mariah's birthday. In her bedroom was a very large photo collage/montage that Henry had worked on for several months, not at all a scrapbook, but done in his thoughtful, new arty voice. "You like it?"

"It's amazing," she said, and stepped close to stand on her toes and kiss him. "*You're* amazing."

"I have another for you, too."

"It's not my birthday."

"Yeah, I just like you."

This was smaller, wrapped simply in plain paper. It was a photo of Veronica that last night in India, her lip swollen, her hair untamed, her eye starting to blacken. Hazy light surrounded her as she gazed into the camera, at Henry, her eyes shining with calm and the kindling of lust.

"What a shot," she said quietly, feeling everything she'd felt that moment, the whole power of the journey tipping over to change her, irrevocably.

"It's my favorite," he said in his rumbling voice, shifting her hair over her shoulder. It was growing out, long and not quite curly but never straight. "I have it in my room, too."

The relationship continued to be the easiest thing in her life. He was a kind, honest, clear-sighted person with integrity and good sense, which meant she could trust him completely. He'd given her plenty of space to explore her new life, and never pressured her.

She clasped it to her chest. "Thank you, Henry."

He kissed her, and she never failed to be surprised at the lusciousness of his mouth. "You are the best kisser in the world."

"Am I?" He kissed her again.

"Nope, nope, nope," she said. "We're going to have guests any second."

"I'm looking forward to meeting your kids."

"Me, too. But I'm afraid you'll be overshadowed by the great Mariah Ellsworth."

"That's right. They'll be dazzled by the Olympian."

re all the same age," she said. "That seems weird. I feel like
better relationship with Mariah."

"You were probably more yourself with her."

"Hmm. Maybe so." She touched his craggy cheek. "I love you,
you know."

He softened, touching her cheek in return. "I love you."

"We got lucky, didn't we?"

"Was it luck? Or are we just grown-ups who know what we want?"

"That too," she said. "Either way, I am so glad I met you."

"Ditto," he said with a wink, and took her hand.

"Let's show Mariah the—what should we call this kind of work? It's
not a photo, and it's not a painting. Artwork?"

"Sure," he said, and carried it out into the other room.

CHAPTER
FIFTY-NINE

Mariah loved Veronica's kitchen. It sat in a corner of the apartment, facing the garden, and it was filled with light. The counters and cabinets were all freshly rendered versions of the originals, with dark-green cupboards and white pulls, and a cute, rounded fridge. Maybe she'd like to live in a place like this eventually.

She was beginning to see who she might be after . . . everything.

No. Be specific. Who she'd be after the shooting and losing her mother, and her career. The program had taught her that there was power in claiming things, in naming them, even if it made others uncomfortable. She had been through a brutally violent trauma, and being able to claim that helped.

She'd also learned that she wasn't alone, not by any means. Her group was small, but there were members who'd suffered a number of different kinds of violence, crime to war to car accidents. All of them had things to overcome.

Henry and Mariah came into the kitchen with one of his new works of art. "Happy birthday," he said, and propped it up against the wall.

Mariah pressed her hands to her mouth. It showed Mariah and Rachel, a large portrait of the two of them when Mariah was about ten, sitting next to her mother on a train, her head on her shoulder. Rachel was smiling softly. The photo was shaped out of hundreds of other photos, different sizes, all of the two of them, or each of them separately, commemorating the years they'd spent together. "Henry," she said through her tears, "this is the most beautiful thing I've ever seen."

He hugged her. "I'm so proud of you, kiddo."

"I love you. You're my only dad, you know."

He kissed her cheek. "And you're my only daughter."

Mariah acknowledged a swirl of emotions then, loss and joy, regret and hope, and most of all gratitude for the people who'd stood so solidly in her corner at her darkest moment. Family came in all kinds of guises.

She propped the artwork against the wall in the living room, and people started coming in. Jill and her husband, Jack, arrived, and he was looking quite recovered. Veronica's children arrived together, and she didn't know what she'd been expecting, maybe mini versions of Veronica, but they were all tall, sculpted country-club kids, blond and athletic. "You guys got a great mom," she said when she met them.

"We agree," Jenna said, and in the glance she shot at her mother, Mariah saw that she missed her. A good sign.

Another guest was a slim dark woman bearing a plate full of cupcakes. Three children trailed behind her, spit shined for the day. "Amber!" Veronica cried and wrapped her in a tight, rocking hug. "I'm so glad you came! Come in, come in!"

Mariah stepped forward. "You're the famous Amber! I've heard so much about you."

"Ditto," Amber said with a grin. "You've done her a world of good."

"It goes both ways," Mariah said.

The party spilled out to the little garden, where they ate cucumber sandwiches and strawberry shortcake. The children tossed a ball with Jenna, and played with a cat who slinked over the fence.

When Mariah blew out the candles, Henry said, "Speech! Speech."

She rolled her eyes, but she stood up anyway. "I'm glad to see the end of twenty-five. Twenty-four was worse, but I don't remember a lot about that transition. I'm starting to feel like a real human again. I've been offered a job with Diane Foundation, as a spokesperson to help change gun laws, and I'm happy to tell you that I've taken it." Everyone clapped, and she continued. "I am so grateful to the people here. Jill, you've been my rock and I love you. Henry, you're my one and only. And, Veronica—" To her amazement, she felt choked up enough that she had to pause. "You fell into my life like a fairy godmother, and I love you so much. Thank you."

Veronica's tears flowed, too. "Ditto," she said, and hugged her.

Mariah looked over her shoulder and there, in the garden, was Rachel. She wore an old housedress she'd loved, and her hair was loose on her shoulders. She looked happy as she kissed her fingers and waved the kisses toward her.

Then she was gone, and Mariah knew that she was well and truly gone.

But Mariah was here now, and that was everything.

ACKNOWLEDGMENTS

So many, many people were in my thoughts as I wrote this book that I will almost certainly forget someone, so please forgive me. First are some of my fellows on my first trip to India in 2019. I was determined to make the trip despite quite a number of things that nearly stood in the way, and the fact that no one in my circle wanted to go with me. But I joined a group and happily made friends with Jane Clarke, Michelle Brown, and Amy Darnell on a trip led by the knowledgeable and funny Ripudaman Singh Pansal. It was a memorable—and clearly inspiring—trip.

Another journey that contributed to this book was an artist's trip to Marrakech, where I met a knot of kindred spirits: Dana Nash, Krissy Uehling, Patty Marcus, and Patricia Hunter McGrath. Morocco enchanted me, but nothing more so than those hot days under the tent painting. I learned so much from all of you and am so very glad to know you.

Finally, I have to give a shout to my mother, Rosalie Hair, and my husband, Neal Barlow, who shared with me those beautiful rooms in the Morton Hotel on Russell Square in London, days which were magical and memorable despite our various cases of COVID and assorted falls and all the things that can go wrong on a trip. Love you both.

I owe a great debt of gratitude to Sonali Dev, who read for cultural missteps on my part and found some before they arrived in the world. Anything remaining is entirely my lapse.

And always, always, thank you to my readers. You are everything, and I'm grateful to each and every one of you. This journey of my books wouldn't be possible without you.

ABOUT THE AUTHOR

Photo © 2009 Blue Fox Photography

Barbara O'Neal is the *Washington Post, Wall Street Journal, USA Today,* and Amazon Charts bestselling author of nearly twenty novels of women's fiction, including the #1 Amazon Charts bestseller *When We Believed in Mermaids,* as well as *Memories of the Lost, This Place of Wonder,* and *The Starfish Sisters.* Her award-winning books have been published in over two dozen countries. She lives on the wild Oregon Coast with her husband, a British endurance athlete who vows he'll never lose his accent. For more information, visit her online at www.barbaraoneal.com.